PENGUIN BOOKS

BEL-AMI

GUY DE MAUPASSANT was born in Normandy in 1850. After his parents' separation he lived with his mother, who was a friend of Flaubert. As a young man he was lively and athletic, but the first symptoms of syphilis appeared in the late 1870s. On the publication of the first short story to which he put his name, 'Boule de Suif', he left his job in the civil service and devoted his energy to professional writing. In the next eleven years he published dozens of articles, nearly three hundred stories and six novels, the best known of which are *A Woman's Life*, *Bel-Ami* and *Pierre and Jean*. He also travelled around the world, led a hectic social life, lived up to his reputation for womanizing and fought his disease. By 1889 his friends saw that his mind was in danger, and in 1891 he attempted suicide and was committed to an asylum in Paris, where he died two years later.

DOUGLAS PARMÉE studied at Trinity College, Cambridge, the University of Bonn, and the Sorbonne. During the war, he served in RAF Intelligence and in the Government Code and Cypher School at Bletchley Park. Following a postwar stint in Berlin, he joined the French department at Cambridge and became a Fellow at Queens College, a position he held for sixty years. He died in 2008.

GUY DE MAUPASSANT
Bel-Ami

Translated by DOUGLAS PARMÉE

PENGUIN BOOKS

PENGUIN BOOKS

Published by the Penguin Group
Penguin Group (USA) Inc., 375 Hudson Street, New York, New York 10014, U.S.A.
Penguin Group (Canada), 90 Eglinton Avenue East, Suite 700, Toronto,
Ontario, Canada M4P 2Y3 (a division of Pearson Penguin Canada Inc.)
Penguin Books Ltd, 80 Strand, London WC2R 0RL, England
Penguin Ireland, 25 St Stephen's Green, Dublin 2, Ireland (a division of Penguin Books Ltd)
Penguin Group (Australia), 250 Camberwell Road, Camberwell,
Victoria 3124, Australia (a division of Pearson Australia Group Pty Ltd)
Penguin Books India Pvt Ltd, 11 Community Centre, Panchsheel Park, New Delhi – 110 017, India
Penguin Group (NZ), 67 Apollo Drive, Rosedale, Auckland 0632,
New Zealand (a division of Pearson New Zealand Ltd)
Penguin Books (South Africa) (Pty) Ltd, 24 Sturdee Avenue, Rosebank,
Johannesburg 2196, South Africa

Penguin Books Ltd, Registered Offices:
80 Strand, London WC2R 0RL, England

This translation was first published in Penguin Books (UK) 1975
Published in Penguin Books (USA) 1975
This edition published 2012

1   3   5   7   9   10   8   6   4   2

Translation copyright © Douglas Parmée, 1975
All rights reserved

LIBRARY OF CONGRESS CATALOGING IN PUBLICATION DATA
Maupassant, Guy de, 1850–1893.
[Bel-Ami. English]
Bel-Ami / Guy de Maupassant ; translated by Douglas Parmée.
p.   cm.
ISBN 978-0-14-311910-4
I. Parmée, Douglas.   II. Title.
PQ2349.B3E5 2012
843'.8—dc23   2012010152

Printed in the United States of America

Except in the United States of America, this book is sold subject to the condition that it shall not,
by way of trade or otherwise, be lent, resold, hired out, or otherwise circulated without the publisher's
prior consent in any form of binding or cover other than that in which it is published and without
a similar condition including this condition being imposed on the subsequent purchaser.

The scanning, uploading, and distribution of this book via the Internet or via any other means
without the permission of the publisher is illegal and punishable by law. Please purchase only
authorized electronic editions, and do not participate in or encourage electronic piracy
of copyrighted materials. Your support of the author's rights is appreciated.

ALWAYS LEARNING   PEARSON

BEL-AMI

PART I

TAKING the change for his five-franc piece from the woman behind the till, Duroy left the restaurant. A well set-up man, with all the swagger of an ex-cavalry N.C.O., he drew himself up, twirled his moustache with a familiar soldierly gesture and swiftly cast his eye round the room over the belated diners like a handsome young man looking for fish to catch.

The women had looked up and were watching him: three little working-class girls; a slovenly, unkempt middle-aged music mistress with a permanently dusty hat and a dress which never fitted properly; and a couple of middle-class housewives with their husbands, regular customers of this cheap little restaurant.

He remained standing on the pavement for a moment, debating what to do. It was 28 June and he had exactly three francs and forty centimes left to see him through to the end of the month. This meant either two dinners and no lunch or two lunches and no dinner, whichever he preferred. He remembered that the midday meal cost twenty-two sous as against thirty sous for dinner, so that by restricting himself to lunch he would earn a bonus of one franc twenty. That would be enough for a couple of sausage sandwiches plus two glasses of beer at some café on the boulevard: these were his main expense and the great pleasure of his evenings. So he set off down the Rue Notre-Dame-de-Lorette.

He strutted along as if he were still in uniform, with his chest stuck out and legs slightly straddled as if he had just got off his horse, and, shouldering his way through the crowd, he strode down the street with complete disregard for everyone else. His top hat, which had seen better days, was cocked at an angle over one ear and his heels made a smart click as they struck the pavement. He seemed to be offering a permanent challenge to someone, the passers-by, the houses, the whole of the town, with all the cockiness of a good-looking soldier now reduced to civilian life again.

Although his suit had cost a mere sixty francs, there was a certain flashy elegance about him, a trifle common, but undeniable. Tall, well-built and fresh-complexioned, with his light-brown hair touched with auburn, his crisply curling moustache brushed back over his upper lip, his piercing blue eyes with their tiny pupils and his naturally curly hair with its centre parting gave him a strong resemblance to the sort of young scamp favoured by popular novelists.

It was one of those summer evenings when Paris is completely airless, and in the steamy night the city was sweltering like an oven. A stink of sewage was wafting from the granite outlets of the drains, and through the low windows of basement kitchens the effluvia of stale sauces and dishwater were overflowing into the street.

Under the archways of their carriage entrances, shirt-sleeved concierges were sitting astride their cane-bottomed chairs smoking their pipes and the passers-by were creeping along exhausted, hat in hand to cool their brows.

When he had reached the boulevard he stopped once again, undecided what to do. He now felt tempted to walk on up to the Champs-Élysées and the Avenue du Bois de Boulogne and find a breath of fresh air under the trees, but he was tormented by another desire, an urge to meet a woman.

What would she be like? He had no idea but he had been waiting for her day and night for the last three months. And sometimes, thanks to his good looks and raffish air, he had managed to steal a few moments of love here and

4

there. But he was still hoping for something more than that, something better.

He could feel his heart beating faster with lust as the street-walkers sidled up to him whispering: 'Coming upstairs, handsome?'; but his pockets were empty and without money he dared not follow them; and he was waiting, too, for something different, less vulgar, a different kind of kiss.

Yet he was fond of places where whores congregated, he liked their dance-halls, their cafés and their streets; he liked rubbing shoulders with them, talking and chatting familiarly with them, inhaling their cheap pungent perfumes, feeling them all around him. For they were women, women for loving. He did not feel for them any of the instinctive contempt of the family man. He turned his steps towards the Madeleine and followed the crowd as it drifted along, prostrate with heat. The large cafés were crammed to overflowing with their customers spread out all over the pavement, drinking under the harsh light of their brilliantly illuminated terraces. On the little round or square tables, there were glasses of liquids of every hue, brown and red, yellow and green, while the limpid cylinders of ice sparkled invitingly in their decanters of ice-cold water.

Duroy had slowed down now and his throat was parched with thirst. It was a burning thirst such as you feel at the end of a hot summer's day and he could imagine the delicious sensation of a cool drink slipping down his throat. But if he were to drink even two small beers that evening, it would be goodbye to his meagre meal tomorrow night and he knew all too well the feeling of ravenous hunger at the end of the month.

He said to himself: 'I must hang on until ten o'clock and then I'll have my glass of beer at the Café Américain. But my God I'm thirsty.' And he looked at the men sitting drinking at the tables, all of them able to quench their thirst as and when they pleased. He walked briskly on past the cafés with a jaunty air, summing up at a glance, by their appearance or their dress, the amount of money each of them was likely to have in his pockets. And he was seized by a feeling of anger against all those people sitting there so contentedly. If you went through their pockets, you'd find gold coins, and silver, and copper there. On an average, each of them must have at least forty francs, and there were a good hundred or so in the café; a hundred times forty francs is two hundred louis! 'The swine!' he muttered to himself as he strutted elegantly by. If only he could have caught one of them in a quiet corner, he'd have wrung his neck without a second thought, my God, he would, just as he used to wring the necks of the peasants' chickens when he was out on manoeuvres in the army.

And he thought of his two years in Africa and of the way he used to intimidate the Arabs in the little outposts in the south. His mouth twisted into a cruel grin as he remembered one escapade which had resulted in the death of three Ouled-Alane tribesmen and had provided him and his comrades with a score of hens, two sheep and some money, as well as something to joke about for the next six months.

They had never found out who was responsible and, indeed, they had never really tried, because an Arab was considered more or less fair game for the military.

But Paris was different. You couldn't just set out on a nice little looting expedition with a pistol in your hand and a sword at your side, just as you pleased, with no danger from the law. He had all the instincts of an N.C.O. let loose in a conquered country. How he would have liked his two years in the desert again! What a pity he hadn't stayed on! But there it was, he'd hoped to better himself by coming home. And now ... well, what a mess he was in!

His tongue made a little dry click as he ran it round his mouth as though to discover how parched his palate was.

The exhausted crowd drifted slowly by as he kept thinking to himself: 'The swine! All those stupid idiots have got money in their pockets.' He knocked against them with his shoulder, whistling a cheerful little tune under his breath. Some of the men he jostled turned round with a scowl, while the women muttered 'What a horrible man!'

He went past the Vaudeville and stopped in front of the Café Américain, wondering whether to drink his beer now because his thirst had become almost unendurable. Before making up his mind, he looked at the time on the illuminated clocks in the middle of the street. It was a quarter past nine. He knew himself only too well; as soon as he had a glass of beer in front of him, he would drink it up. And then what would he do until eleven o'clock?

He walked on. 'I'll go as far as the Madeleine,' he said to himself, 'and then come slowly back.'

As he was approaching the corner of the Place de l'Opéra he passed a stout young man going in the other direction whose face seemed vaguely familiar. He turned and followed him, trying to remember who it was, muttering to himself: 'Where on earth have I met that chap before?'

He searched about in his mind, without success, until suddenly, in the strange way memory works, he saw him in his mind's eye, less stout, younger and wearing the uniform of the hussars. He exclaimed out loud: 'Well I never, it's Forestier!' and, lengthening his stride, he caught up with the man and tapped him on the shoulder. The walker turned round, looked at him and said: 'What can I do for you?'

Duroy started laughing.

'Don't you recognize me, old man?'

'No, I'm afraid I don't.'

'Georges Duroy, of the 6th Hussars.'

Forestier held out both his hands.

'Well I'll be damned! And how are you?'

'Very well. And how about you?'

'Oh, not so well. My chest is troubling me at the moment. I've been coughing for six months in the year ever since I caught bronchitis in Bougival, the year I came back to Paris. That must be four years ago now.'

'Good Lord! But you look fit enough though.'

So Forestier took hold of his old comrade's arm and started talking about his illness, his consultations, the opinions and advice of his doctors and the difficulty of doing what they advised because of his job. They said he ought to spend the winter on the Riviera but how could he? He was married and a journalist, with a very good position.

'I'm editor of the political section of *La Vie française*. I cover the Senate for *Le Salut* and occasionally provide the literary column for *La Planète*. As you can see, I've come a long way.'

Duroy looked at him with surprise. He had changed a great deal and become much more mature. Now he had the look and manner and clothes of a successful and self-confident man, with the paunch of someone who lived well. In the old days he had been lean, slight, athletic, boisterous, scatterbrained, rowdy and always in high spirits. Three years in Paris had turned him into someone quite different, plump and serious with a few grey hairs already on his temples, even although he could only have been twenty-seven at the most.

'Where are you going?' Forestier asked.

'Nowhere in particular. I was just taking a stroll before going home,' Duroy replied.

'Well look, would you like to come along to *La Vie française* with me, I've got some proofs to read. Then we'll go and have a beer together.'

8

'I'm with you.'

And they set off together, holding each other's arms with that easy camaraderie that exists between old school and regimental friends.

'What are you doing in Paris?' enquired Forestier.

Duroy shrugged:

'More or less down and out, that's what. When I'd served my time, I wanted to come here to ... to make my fortune or, in fact, just to live in Paris; and now, for the last six months, I've been working as a railway clerk at 1,500 francs a year, not a sou more.'

Forestier whistled:

'Good Lord, that's not much.'

'You're right. But what else can I do? I'm alone, I don't know anyone, there's no one whom I can go to for help. It's not the will that's lacking, I just haven't got the means.'

His friend looked him up and down, like a practical man sizing someone up, and then stated confidently:

'Look, old boy, here everything depends on how pushing you are. Anyone who's a bit smart can become a Minister more easily than a chief clerk. You've got to assert yourself and not go around begging. But how on earth did you land up with only a job as a railway clerk?'

'I looked around and I couldn't find anything else. But at the moment, I do have another possibility; I've been offered a job as riding-master in the Pellerin riding-school. There I'll be getting 3,000 francs at the very least.'

Forestier stopped in his tracks.

'Don't do that. It's idiotic when you ought to be earning 10,000. It'll completely ruin any future prospects. In your clerk's job at least you're out of sight, no one knows who you are, you can get out of it if you're determined enough and still make your mark. But once you're a riding-instruc-tor, that's the end. It's like being a head waiter in a Paris restaurant where all the smart people go. If you give riding lessons to important people or their sons, they'll never be able to get used to the idea of seeing you as an equal.'

He stopped talking, thought for a moment, and then asked:

'Did you get your baccalauréat at school?'

'No, I failed it twice.'

'Not to worry, as long as you stayed on at school long enough to sit for it. If someone mentioned the name of Cicero or Tiberius, would you know what they're talking about, roughly?'

'Roughly, yes.'

'Good, that's all anybody knows, except for a couple of dozen silly idiots who are quite incapable of doing anything about it. It's not difficult to appear bright, don't worry. The main thing is never to show obvious ignorance of anything. You prevaricate, avoid the difficulty, steer clear of the problem and then catch other people out by using a dictionary. All men are stupid oafs and ignorant nincompoops.'

He spoke with the vigorous self-confidence of a man who knows what life is about, with a smile on his face as he watched the crowd go by. But suddenly he was seized by a fit of coughing and had to stand still until it was over. Then, in a disconsolate tone of voice, he added:

'Isn't it a bore not to be able to get rid of this bronchitis? And here we are in the middle of summer. Ah, this winter I'll go off to Menton and get well. I really shall have to do it, there's nothing more important than one's health.'

They reached the Boulevard Poissonnière, in front of a large glass door with an open newspaper stuck on both panels. Three people had stopped to read it.

Over the doorway huge gas-flares were spelling out the words *La Vie française* in letters of fire like a signal. And as the strollers suddenly emerged into the blaze of light cast by these three words, for one brief moment they stood out with absolute clarity, as plainly visible as if in broad daylight, before disappearing just as suddenly into the gloom.

Forestier pushed open the door. 'Come in,' he said. Duroy followed and went up a luxurious, but dirty, staircase which was visible from the entire street. They came to an entrance hall, where the two messengers greeted his friend, and finally ended up in a sort of dusty, run-down waiting-room with dingy green imitation velvet curtains, spotty and moth-eaten, which looked as if the mice had been at them.

'Take a pew,' said Forestier, 'I'll be back in a sec.'

And he disappeared through one of the three exits which led out of the room.

The place was pervaded by a peculiar, indescribable smell, the smell of a newsroom. Duroy sat quietly, a trifle intimidated but, above all, surprised. Men were scurrying to and fro through the various doors, disappearing before he had time to look at them properly.

Some of them were young, even very young, busy-looking, holding sheets of paper which fluttered in their hands as they ran; others were type-setters whose ink-stained canvas overalls revealed snow-white collars underneath and cloth trousers as smart as any man about town; they were carrying lengths of printed paper, damp proofs straight from the press. Sometimes a little man would come in dressed with ostentatious elegance, wearing an extremely close-fitting coat, trousers which were too tight over the calves and with his feet pinched into exaggeratedly pointed shoes – a fashionable gossip writer bringing in his evening copy.

And others were coming in, with a dignified, self-important air, wearing flat-brimmed top hats as though their shape set them apart from the rest of humanity.

Forestier came back holding the arm of a tall thin man of

between thirty and forty, dressed in tails and white tie, very dark, with a pointed moustache and a look of complacent arrogance.

Forestier took his leave of him deferentially. The other man shook his hand: ''Bye, my dear fellow,' and went downstairs quietly whistling to himself, with his stick tucked under his arm.

'Who was that?' Duroy asked.

'Jacques Rival, you know, the well-known gossip columnist and duellist, too. He's just been in to read his proofs. He, Garin and Montet are the three wittiest topical columnists in Paris. He earns 30,000 francs a year here for two articles a week.'

And as they were leaving, they met a fat little man, long-haired and scruffy, who was coming puffing upstairs.

Forestier said good evening even more deferentially:

'That's the poet Norbert de Varenne,' he said, 'the author of *Dead Suns*; he earns vast sums too. Every short story he gives us costs us 300 francs and the longest is less than 200 lines. But let's go to the Napolitain. I'm dying for a drink.'

As soon as they had found a table Forestier called out: 'Two small beers', and downed his in a gulp, while Duroy sat sipping his, rolling it round his mouth and savouring it like something rare and precious.

His companion was silent and seemed to be lost in thought; then, abruptly:

'Why not try journalism?'

The other man looked at him rather taken aback, and then replied:

'But ... the truth is, I've never written anything.'

'What the deuce. You must have a go. I could use you to get information for me, approach people, go and see them. You'd have 250 francs a month to start with, and all your travelling expenses. Would you like me to mention it to the boss?'

'I would indeed.'

'All right, then. But there's something you must do. Come and have dinner at my home tomorrow evening. There'll only be five or six people, the boss Monsieur Walter and his wife, Jacques Rival and Norbert de Varenne, whom you've just seen, and a woman friend of my wife's. Agreed?'

Duroy went red in the face as he hesitated, a trifle confused. Then he mumbled:

'The trouble is ... I haven't got the proper clothes.'

Forestier nearly fell off his chair.

'You really mean to say you've no evening clothes? But that's something you simply can't do without. In Paris, you realize it's better to be without a bed than not to have evening clothes.'

Then, abruptly, he fumbled with his finger and thumb in his waistcoat pocket, pulled out a few gold coins, took a couple of twenty-franc pieces and put them on the table in front of his old comrade, saying in a bluff, friendly voice:

'You can let me have them back when you're able to. Go and hire the clothes you need or put it down as a deposit to buy them by instalments. Anyway, get fixed up and come round to dinner at my home tomorrow at 7.30. It's 17, Rue Fontaine.'

Duroy was touched and picking up the money, he stammered:

'It's terribly kind of you, I really am grateful. I promise you I shan't forget...'

His friend cut him short: 'Good, that's that. Another drink, don't you think?' And he called out to the waiter: 'Two beers!'

Then when they had been drunk, he said:

'How about a little stroll for an hour?'

13

'Yes, indeed.'

And they set off again in the direction of the Madeleine. 'What do you think we might do?' Forestier asked. 'People say that there's always something to do in Paris when you go for a stroll. But it's not true. Whenever I go for a stroll in the evening, I never know where to go. It's no fun to go round the Bois de Boulogne unless you're with a woman and you can't always have one handy. The cafés where they have music may be all very well for my chemist and his wife but they're not for me. So what is there to do? Nothing. There ought to be a summer amusement park, like the Parc Monceau, open at night so that you could hear some really good music while you sip a nice cool drink under the trees. It wouldn't be a real amusement park but just somewhere to loaf and stroll about. The entrance fee would have to be high so as to attract the pretty ladies. You'd be able to walk along proper gravel paths with electric light and sit down when you felt so inclined and listen to some music in the distance, or close to. We did have something roughly like it at Musard's but with too much dance music and it was rather common, not spacious and shady enough, not enough gentle lighting. You'd need a really lovely garden, absolutely enormous. It would be most attractive. Where do you want to go?'

Duroy was at a loss and could think of nothing to suggest. In the end, he said:

'I've never been to the Folies-Bergère. I wouldn't mind going to have a look at it.'

His companion exclaimed:

'Good Lord! The Folies-Bergère? We'll be absolutely roasted. Anyway, all right, it's always quite fun.'

So they swung round and went up the Rue du Faubourg-Montmartre.

The front of the theatre was blazing with lights which

14

illuminated all the four streets which meet there. A row of cabs was waiting for the performance to end.

As Forestier was going in, Duroy stopped him. 'We've forgotten to get tickets.'

Forestier answered smugly:

'You don't need to pay when you're with me.'

As they approached the entrance to the main hall, the three men at the door touched their hats. The middle one held out his hand.

'Is there a decent box free?'

'Of course, Monsieur Forestier.'

He took the slip of paper which was handed to him, pushed open the heavily padded leather-covered door and they went into the auditorium.

The remoter parts of the theatre, the stage and the other side of the hall were partly hidden by a bluish haze of tobacco smoke which whirled up from the cigars and cigarettes that everybody was smoking and finally collected under the ceiling and round the chandeliers, forming a cloud of smoke over the top gallery, crammed with spectators. In the vast corridor leading to the circular promenade, where a painted tribe of prostitutes were on the prowl, mingling with the sombrely dressed crowd of men, a group of women was waiting for any newcomers in front of one of the three bars, presided over by three heavily made-up, raddled dispensers of drink and love.

In the tall mirrors behind them you could see their backs and the faces of the passers-by.

Forestier forced his way through the throng like someone with a right to receive proper respect.

He went up to an attendant.

'Box 17?' he asked her.

'This way, sir.'

They found themselves enclosed in a little red-carpeted

open wooden box containing four chairs of identical colour jammed so close together that you could hardly slip between them. The two friends sat down. To the left and right of them was a long curve of identical little boxes sweeping round to each end of the stage; in them, there were other people sitting with only their heads and shoulders showing.

On the stage three young men dressed in tights, one tall, one of medium height and one small, were taking it in turns to perform on the trapeze.

First the tall one took a few quick steps forward, and with a smile waved to the audience as though blowing a kiss.

Beneath his tights you could see the bulging muscles of his arms and legs as he stuck his chest out to disguise the size of his paunch; he looked like a barber because his hair was divided into two equal halves by a parting which ran exactly down the middle of his head. He jumped gracefully up to catch the trapeze and, hanging from his hands, spun round like a gyrating wheel; or else, straightening his arms, he remained suspended in the air holding his body up by the sheer strength of his wrists.

Then he jumped down, smiled as he once again waved to acknowledge the applause from the stalls and ran to the side of the stage, his muscles rippling with each step.

Then the second one, shorter and thicker-set, came forward and went through the same performance, followed by the last one who was even more heartily applauded.

But Duroy had lost interest in the show and kept turning his head all the time to look at the place where the men and the prostitutes were circulating all together.

'Look at the stalls,' said Forestier. 'Nothing but the great middle-classes with their wives and children and amiable silly faces who've come to see the show. In the boxes, you've got the men about town, a few actors and dancers, a few medium-priced tarts; and then, behind us, the most peculiar mixture of males in Paris. Who are they? Take a good look at them. You've got every sort and kind, from every class, but most of them randy and dissolute. You've got the clerks – bank clerks, salesmen, minor officials, reporters, pimps, officers in mufti, would-be dandies in evening dress who've had dinner in a smart little restaurant and have just come from the Opéra before going on to the Italian opera; and in addition, a whole lot of shady characters who completely baffle description. As for the women, there's no mystery about them: the women who take a late snack at the Café Américain, the twenty- or forty-franc whore who's on the look-out for a rich foreigner who can afford a hundred and tips off her regulars when she's free. In six years you get to know the lot: you've seen them in the same places every night, all the year round, except when they're undertaking a little health treatment in the police hospital at Saint Lazare or at Lourcine.'

Duroy had stopped listening. One of the women was resting her elbows on the back of their box and watching him. She was a plump brunette, plastered with thick white make-up, her long black eyes framed in eye-liner and enormous false lashes. Her vast bosom was bursting the seams of her dark silk dress and her lips, like a gaping red wound, gave her an extravagantly passionate appearance, animal-like but exciting.

With a nod of her head she drew the attention of one of her friends who was going by, a fair red-head, also fat, and said to her loudly enough to be overheard:

'I say, there's a nice-looking boy. If he'd like to have me for a couple of hundred francs I wouldn't say no.'

Forestier turned round with a smile and tapped Duroy on the thigh:

'That's you she means. You've made a hit, old boy. Congratulations.'

The former N.C.O. had blushed as he mechanically fingered the two gold coins in his waistcoat pocket.

The curtain had gone down; the orchestra was now playing a waltz.

Duroy said: 'How about a stroll round the gallery.'

'If you like.'

They went out and were immediately caught up in the throng of promenaders. Pushed and pulled and squeezed and jostled they moved along surrounded by a forest of hats. The whores were moving round in couples through this throng of men, gliding through them and sliding past their elbows and chests and backs, looking very much at home and at their ease like fish in their element in the midst of this stream of males.

Duroy was in raptures of delight as he let himself be carried along, drinking in the air vitiated by the smell of tobacco, human bodies and the scent worn by the trollops. But Forestier was puffing and sweating and coughing.

'Let's go into the garden,' he said. And turning left, they made their way into a sort of covered garden that was kept cool by two large and hideous fountains. Men and women were sitting drinking at zinc-topped tables scattered amongst the yews and thuyas.

'Another beer?' asked Forestier.

'I'd love one.'

They sat down to watch.

Now and again one of the female prowlers would stop and, putting on a smile, ask: 'How about a drink, dearie?' And when Forestier answered: 'A nice glass of water from the fountain' they would move on, muttering: 'Miserable lout!'

However, the large brunette who had been leaning on the back of their box reappeared, marching arrogantly along arm-in-arm with the big blonde. They made a very well-matched couple.

She smiled when she caught sight of Duroy, as if they had already exchanged private thoughts with their eyes, and drawing up a chair, she calmly sat down opposite him, told her friend to sit down too, and then, in a loud voice called: 'Waiter, two grenadines.' Forestier, rather at a loss, said: 'You've got a cheek, haven't you?'

She answered:

'It's your friend who's taken my fancy. He really is wonderful. I think he could make me do something silly.'

Duroy felt self-conscious and tongue-tied, so he stroked his curly moustache with a vacant smile. The waiter brought the two grenadines which the two women gulped down straight away. Then they stood up and the brunette, giving Duroy a friendly little nod and a gentle tap on the arm with her fan, said: 'Thanks, dearie. Not very talkative, are you?'

And they went off swaying their hips.

Forestier burst out laughing:

'Well, well, old boy, I hope you realize that you really do hit it off with the ladies? You must cultivate that. It could take you far.'

He stopped for a moment and then went on in the thoughtful voice of someone thinking out loud:

'They're still the quickest way to succeed.'

And as Duroy continued to smile without saying anything, he enquired:

'Are you going to stay? I'm going home. I've had enough.'

The other man muttered:

'Yes, I'll stay a little longer. It's not very late.'

Forestier stood up.

'All right, then. Goodnight, see you tomorrow. Don't forget, 17, Rue Fontaine, seven-thirty.'

'Right. See you tomorrow. And thanks.'

They shook hands and the journalist went off.

As soon as he was out of sight, Duroy felt free, and cheerfully fingering once more the two gold coins in his pocket, he stood up and set off through the crowd, peering around him as he went.

He soon caught sight of the two women again, the blonde and the brunette, still sailing along like proud beggars through the crush of men.

He made straight for them and when he reached them, his courage evaporated.

'Have you found your tongue?' the brunette said to him.

He stammered: 'Yes, of course,' and then found himself unable to add another syllable.

They all three remained standing there, blocking the movement of the walkers who swirled around them.

Then suddenly she said:

'Do you want to come back to my place?'

And, trembling with desire, he said abruptly:

'Yes, but I've only got twenty francs on me.'

She smiled unconcernedly:

'That doesn't matter.'

And she took his arm to show that she was taking possession of him.

As they left, he was thinking that with the other twenty francs, he could easily hire evening clothes for the dinner next day.

CHAPTER 2

'MONSIEUR Forestier please.'

'Third floor, on the left.'

The porter had answered his query in a friendly voice that bespoke respect for his tenant. Georges Duroy went upstairs.

He felt somewhat embarrassed, self-conscious and ill-at-ease. He was wearing evening clothes for the first time in his life and he was worried by their general effect. He felt that there was something wrong with the whole outfit, from his boots which, although quite smart (he was proud of his feet), were not made of patent leather, to his shirt, for which he had paid four francs fifty at the Louvre that very morning and whose dicky was not stiff enough and already becoming creased. As his other shirts, the ones he wore every day, all had something wrong with them, it had proved impossible to use even the least tattered of them.

His trousers were slightly too big, fitting badly over the legs and hanging in creases round his calves; they had that crumpled look of borrowed clothes on a body that they were never intended to cover. The only thing that was more or less correct was the tail-coat which happened to be roughly the correct size.

Slowly and uneasily he went upstairs, his heart pounding. Above all, he was worried at the thought of appearing ridiculous; and then suddenly he found himself face to face with a man in full evening dress, watching him. They were so close that Duroy recoiled with a start and then stood dumbfounded: it was his own reflection in a tall wall-mirror on the first floor landing which produced the effect of a long gallery. He was overjoyed as he realized how much better he looked than he could possibly have believed.

As he possessed only a shaving mirror he had been unable to see himself full-length. And as it was very difficult for him to see the various parts of his makeshift outfit, he had been exaggerating its failings and was in a panic at the thought of seeming a figure of fun. But now that he had suddenly caught a glimpse of himself in the mirror, he had not even been able to recognize himself; he had taken himself for someone else, a man about town whom at first glance he had thought extremely smart and distinguished-looking.

And, as he peered more closely, he realized that the general effect was, in fact, satisfactory.

So he started examining himself like an actor studying his part. He smiled, held out his hand towards himself, gesticulated, expressed feelings of surprise, pleasure, approval; and he tried out different kinds of smile and expressions in his eyes for flirting with the ladies and showing admiration and desire.

Somewhere on the staircase a door opened and, startled, he began to go quickly on upstairs, fearing that one of his friend's guests might have seen him smirking at himself.

When he reached the second floor, he caught sight of another mirror and slowed down to watch himself as he went by. It seemed to him that he looked really elegant. He was moving well. And he was filled by an inordinate self-confidence. Looking as he did, surely he would succeed, taking into account his urge to make his mark, the determination that he knew he possessed, and his enterprising nature. As he climbed the last flight he felt a longing to run and jump. He stopped in front of the last mirror, brushed his moustache with his customary gesture, removed his hat to arrange his hair and murmured quietly, as he often did:

'What an excellent invention.' Then he reached for the bell and rang.

Almost immediately the door opened and he found himself facing a footman in evening dress, clean-shaven and solemn, so immaculately turned out that once again Duroy lost some of his composure without quite understanding why. Perhaps because of an involuntary comparison between the cut of their clothes. The footman, who was wearing patent leather shoes, took Duroy's overcoat, which he was carrying over his arm to hide its stains, and asked:

'What name shall I give, sir?'

And he announced him through a raised doorway leading into the drawing-room which Duroy now had to enter.

However, completely losing his composure Duroy stood rooted to the spot, almost breathless with fright. He was about to take his first steps in the world for which he had been hoping and dreaming. Nevertheless, he stepped forward. A blonde young woman was standing alone waiting for him in a large, well-lit room, full of plants, like a conservatory.

He stopped short, completely nonplussed. Who was this woman smiling at him? Then he recalled that Forestier was married and the realization that this pretty, elegant blonde must be his friend's wife completed his discomposure.

He faltered: 'My name's . . .'

She held out her hand: 'I know. Charles told me how he met you yesterday evening and I'm very glad that he had the good idea of inviting you to dinner tonight.'

He blushed to the roots of his hair, not knowing what to say, feeling himself being examined and inspected from head to foot, weighed up and judged.

He wanted to apologize, to invent some reason to explain the shortcomings of his dress; but he could find nothing to say and felt afraid of broaching such a dangerous topic.

She pointed to an armchair and, as he sank into the soft resilient velvet and relaxed into the gently caressing embrace of its thickly padded back and arms, he felt as though he was moving into a new, fascinating and delightful world, taking possession of it, that he was becoming somebody, that he had found salvation; and he looked at Madame Forestier whose eyes had not once left him.

She was wearing a dress of light blue cashmere which showed off to the best advantage her full bosom and her lithe figure. Her bare arms and bosom emerged from the frothy white lace which adorned the short sleeves and bodice of her dress, and her hair, swept up on top of her head, left the nape of her neck covered in wisps of downy curls. Under her gaze, which reminded him, for some unknown reason, of the prostitute he had met last night at the Folies-Bergère, Duroy was regaining his confidence. Her eyes were grey, a sort of blue-grey, which gave them a strange expression; her nose was delicate, her lips full, her chin somewhat fleshy, her features attractive but irregular, her expression at once friendly and mischievous. She had the sort of face whose every line has its own particular appeal and seems full of meaning, whose every movement seems to express or to hide something.

After a brief pause, she asked him:

'Have you been in Paris long?'

Gradually recovering his self-possession, he replied:

'Only a few months. I'm employed in a railway office but your husband led me to hope that he might be able to find me something in journalism.'

Her smile grew broader and more friendly as she said quietly, dropping her voice: 'I know.'

The bell rang again. The footman announced: 'Madame de Marelle.'

She was small and dark, the sort of woman people call a

little brunette. As she came briskly into the room, he saw that she was wearing a simple black dress, which fitted her like a skin from head to foot.

Her only splash of colour was a red rose stuck in her black hair which emphasized her particular type of face and added the sudden sharp note which it needed.

She was followed by a little girl in short skirts. Madame Forestier rushed to meet them:

'My dear Clotilde.'

'Madeleine darling.'

They kissed each other. Then the little girl held up her face with all the composure of a grown-up.

'Good evening, cousin Madeleine.'

Madame Forestier gave her a peck on the forehead and then made the introductions:

'Monsieur Georges Duroy, a good friend of Charles; Madame de Marelle, a friend and distant relative,' adding: 'You know we don't stand on ceremony in this house. I do hope you agree.'

The young man bowed.

And now the door opened again and a fat, dumpy little man came in giving his arm to a good-looking woman, distinguished and serious in appearance, who was taller and a good deal younger than himself. It was Monsieur Walter, a member of the Chamber of Deputies, a financier, capitalist and business man, a Jew from the Midi and editor of *La Vie française*, with his wife, née Basile-Ravalau, the daughter of the banker of that name.

Then, one after the other, in came Jacques Rival, looking extremely elegant, and Norbert de Varenne, whose coat collar was somewhat shiny and polished because of his long hair which came down to his shoulders, shedding little white specks of scurf on them.

His bow was badly tied and hardly making its first appearance in public. He came in, preening himself like an old lady-killer, and grasping Madame Forestier's hand, he planted a kiss on her wrist. As he bent forward, his long hair cascaded over the young woman's naked arm.

Finally, Forestier himself came in, apologizing for being late: he had been detained at the office by the Morel business. Monsieur Morel, a radical deputy, had raised a question with regard to a government request for funds in connection with the colonization of Algeria.

The servant announced:

'Dinner is served.'

They went into the dining-room.

Duroy found himself sitting between Madame de Marelle and her daughter. He was feeling embarrassed again and terrified of using the wrong fork, spoon or glass. There were four glasses, one slightly blue-tinted. What were you supposed to drink out of that one?

During the soup, nobody spoke; and then Norbert de Varenne asked:

'Have you been reading the Gauthier case? What a queer business!'

And they started discussing this case of adultery involving the extra complication of blackmail. They did not talk about it in the way you might comment, in a family conversation, on something published in the press, but in the way doctors talk of a disease or greengrocers talk about vegetables. There was no indignation or surprise; with professional curiosity and complete unconcern for the crime itself, they looked for its hidden, deeper causes. They tried to fathom the motives and investigate the mental reactions that had led to the tragedy as being the scientific results of a particular state of mind. The women were equally absorbed in this analysis and examination. And then other recent events were analysed and commented on, turned this way and that and weighed up exactly with the practised eye and special approach of people who deal in news, who retail every aspect of the human scene at so much per line, just as tradesmen examine and turn over and weigh up the articles they are going to supply to the public.

Then the question of a duel arose and Jacques Rival took over. That was his speciality: nobody else was competent to talk about that.

Duroy was too scared to say a word. Now and again he looked at his neighbour, attracted by the curves of her bosom. A diamond was dangling from her ear on a gold wire, like a drop of water gliding over her skin. Occasionally, she made a remark that never failed to cause smiles. She had an original, charming and amusing turn of mind, the mind of a saucy young girl who has experience of the world, who sees things in a casual, easy-going manner and judges them coolly and uncensoriously.

Duroy vainly racked his brain for a compliment but being unable to find one, he turned his attention to her daughter, pouring out her drinks, holding the dishes for her and serving her. The girl, who was more serious than her mother, kept thanking him in a solemn voice, with little nods of her head: 'It's most kind of you', while listening to the grown-ups with a thoughtful air.

It was an excellent dinner and praised by everyone. Monsieur Walter was wolfing everything, hardly uttering a word and squinting under his glasses at each dish he was offered. Norbert de Varenne kept pace with him, letting odd drops of sauce fall onto his shirt front.

Forestier, smiling, earnest and attentive, kept exchanging little understanding glances with his wife, like accomplices engaged on a tricky assignment which is going smoothly.

Faces were becoming flushed and voices grew louder.

Every so often, the servant could be heard quietly whispering to the guests:

'Corton or Château Larose?'

Duroy had taken a fancy to the Corton and he let his glass be filled each time. He was beginning to experience a delicious sensation of physical comfort, a warmth that, starting from his stomach, rose to his head and spread through every limb until his whole body was glowing. He was seized by a feeling of complete well-being, a well-being of body and mind, life and thought.

And he was beginning to feel an urge to talk, to attract attention, to be listened to and appreciated like the other men whose slightest remarks commanded respect.

But the conversation, which had never once flagged, as a word or trifling comment made it leap from one subject to the next and one idea led to another, after having been the round of all the events of the day, touching on a score of different topics, now came back to Monsieur Morel's parliamentary question on the colonization of Algeria.

Monsieur Walter, who had a coarse and sceptical turn of mind, made a joke or two between two courses, and Forestier talked about the article he had written for tomorrow's paper. Jacques Rival said that what was needed was a military government and grants of land to every officer who had served thirty years in the colonies.

'In that way,' he said, 'you'll build up a vigorous society with long experience of the country, people who like it, who know the language and are familiar with all the important local issues that are bound to prove obstacles for any newcomers.'

Norbert de Varenne interrupted him:

'Yes, indeed, they'll know about everything except agriculture. They'll be able to speak Arabic but they won't know how to plant beetroot or sow wheat. They'll even be good at fencing but very poor on fertilizers. On the contrary, a new country like that should be thrown open to everybody. The bright ones will succeed, the others will go to the wall. It's the law of the world.'

A slight pause ensued. Smiles were exchanged.

Georges Duroy opened his mouth and spoke, surprised by the sound of his own voice, as though he had never heard himself talk before:

'The main shortage there is the lack of good land. Really fertile land costs as much as in France and it's bought up by very rich Parisians, as an investment. The real settlers, who are poor, the ones who emigrate because they can't earn a living here, are forced to go out into the desert where nothing can grow because there's not enough water.'

All eyes were turned on him. He felt himself blushing. Monsieur Walter enquired: 'Do you know Algeria?'

He replied: 'Yes, I spent more than two years there and I lived in all three provinces.'

Dropping the question of Morel, Norbert de Varenne now asked him about a particular custom that he had been told about by an officer. It concerned the Mzab, a strange little Arab republic which had come into being in the very heart of the Sahara, in the driest part of that region of scorching heat.

Duroy had twice visited the Mzab and he gave an account of the customs of that peculiar country where a drop of water is worth its weight in gold, where every inhabitant is in duty bound to take part in all the public services and where commercial honesty is more highly developed than in civilized countries.

He talked animatedly, not afraid of indulging in a little embellishment, spurred on by the wine and his desire to please; he told stories about the army, talked of the Arab way of life and of the hazards of war. He even found a picturesque expression or two to describe those bare yellow lands perpetually ravaged by the pitiless, blazing sun.

The women all had their eyes fixed on him. Madame Walter said, in her quiet, slow voice: 'You could make a nice series of articles out of your experiences.' At that Walter peered at the young man over his spectacles, as he did when looking into people's faces. For eating, he looked underneath.

Forestier seized the opportunity:

'Well, sir, I was speaking to you earlier about Georges Duroy and asking if you would let me have him as my assistant to help me with my political column. Ever since Marambot left, I've not had anyone to obtain information on urgent and confidential political matters and the paper is suffering as a result.'

Old Walter looked solemn and lifted his spectacles right up to look Duroy full in the face. Then he spoke:

'Monsieur Duroy certainly has an original mind. If he cares to come and see me tomorrow at three o'clock, we'll see what we can do.'

Then, after a pause, he turned to face the young man:

'But let me have straight away an amusing little series of articles on Algeria. Tell us your experiences and tie it up with comments on the question of colonization, as you did a moment ago. It's topical, extremely topical, and I'm sure our readers will enjoy it. But don't delay. I shall want the first article by tomorrow or the day after, while the matter is still under discussion in the Chamber, so as to prepare the public.'

Madame Walter added, with a charming dignity which she always showed and which made everything she said appear an act of grace:

'And you have a very attractive title: "Memories of an African Cavalryman", has he not, Monsieur Norbert?'

The old poet, having achieved fame late in life, disliked and feared the younger generation. He replied sharply:

'Yes, an excellent title, as long as the rest strikes the right note, because that is the great difficulty. It's what they call hitting the right key in music.'

Madame Forestier was covering Duroy with a protective smile, with the eye of an expert that seemed to be saying: 'You're going to make good.' Madame de Marelle had several times turned towards him and her diamond ear-ring kept quivering as if the delicate drop of water was going to start sliding and fall off.

The solemn little girl sat quietly bent over her plate.

But the servant was going round the table pouring Johannisberger into the blue glasses and Forestier lifted his glass to Monsieur Walter and proposed a toast: 'To the long life and prosperity of *La Vie française*!'

Everybody turned and bowed to their chief and Duroy, intoxicated by his success, emptied his glass in one gulp. He felt as if he could have emptied a whole barrel in the same way; he could have devoured an ox or strangled a lion. His limbs seemed superhumanly strong and his heart full of unconquerable determination and infinite hope. He now felt at ease amongst these people; he had just established his position and won his place. He looked at the faces around him with fresh confidence and for the first time he ventured to address his neighbour: 'I've never seen such pretty ear-rings as yours, Madame de Marelle.'

She turned towards him with a smile.

'It's an idea I had to fasten a diamond like that, simply on the end of a wire. They look just like dew, don't they?'

Alarmed at his temerity and terrified of saying something silly, he murmured:

'It's charming . . . but the ear must take some of the credit, too.'

She thanked him with a glance, the sort of bright feminine glance that strikes deep to the heart.

And as he turned his head his gaze once again met Madame Forestier's eyes, friendly as ever, but he thought he could detect in them something more positive, a mischievous sparkle and an encouragement.

The men were now all talking together in loud tones and gesticulating. They were discussing the big project of the Paris underground railway. The topic was not exhausted until they had reached the dessert, because everyone had a great deal to say about the slowness of communications in the city, the disadvantages of the trams, the inconvenience of the buses and the boorishness of cab-drivers.

Then they rose from the table for coffee. Duroy jokingly offered his arm to the little girl. She solemnly thanked him and reached up on tiptoe to rest her hand on his elbow.

When he went into the drawing-room, once more he had the feeling of going into a conservatory. In each corner of the room stood palm-trees whose elegant fronds spread out as high as the ceiling, like a fountain.

On each side of the fireplace stood Indian figs with circular trunks like columns, bearing layer upon layer of long, dark-green leaves; and on the piano were two unknown plants, round in shape and covered in blossom, one pink and the other pure white, so improbable in appearance as to seem artificial, too beautiful to be true.

The air was cool and pervaded by a vaguely sweet, indefinable scent, impossible to name.

And now that the young man felt more self-possessed, he looked around the room. It was not large, the only remarkable thing in it being the plants; there were no bright colours but you felt at ease there, calm and relaxed; it wrapped itself around you pleasingly, and seemed to be almost caressing your body.

The walls were hung with a faded antique purple material speckled with little yellow silk flowers no larger than flies. The door had blue-grey curtains made from the sort of cloth used for uniforms and embroidered with a few red silk carnations; and the chairs of every shape and size were scattered haphazardly round the room; settees, armchairs vast or small, poufs and stools were all covered in Louis Seize silk or lovely Utrecht velvet, with garnet-red figures on a cream-coloured background.

'Do you take coffee, Monsieur Duroy?'

Madame Forestier was holding out a full cup of coffee, still with that friendly smile that never left her lips.

'Yes, please.'

He took the cup and, as he was anxiously leaning forward to pick up a lump of sugar with the sugar tongs from the sugar bowl proffered by the little girl, the young woman whispered to him:

'Don't neglect Madame Walter.'

Then she moved on before he had time to reply.

He drank his coffee, fearful lest he might spill it on the carpet, and then, easier in his mind, he looked for a way to approach the wife of his new employer and start a conversation.

Suddenly he noticed that she had an empty cup in her hand and was too far from a table to put it down. He quickly moved over towards her.

'Allow me.'

'Thank you.'

He took the cup away and came back:

'If you only knew what a pleasure it was for me to be able to read *La Vie française* when I was stuck out there in the desert. It's really the only paper to read outside France because it's more literary, more witty and less dull than all the others. It has something of everything in it.'

She gave him an amiable, casual smile and replied gravely:

'My husband had great difficulty in creating that sort of paper, which met a new need.'

And they began to chat. He had a fund of small talk, a pleasant voice, a caressing glance and his moustache was irresistible. Crisp and curly, it curved charmingly over his lip, fair with auburn tints, slightly paler where it bristled at the ends.

They spoke about Paris and its surroundings, the banks of the Seine, watering-places, the delights of summer, all those everyday things that you can talk about indefinitely without tiring the mind.

Then, as Norbert de Varenne came up carrying a glass of liqueur, Duroy discreetly slipped away.

Madame de Marelle, who had been chatting with Forestier, suddenly hailed him: 'Well, Monsieur Duroy, so you want to try your hand at journalism?'

And in vague terms he spoke of his plans and then started with her the same conversation that he had just had with Madame Walter, but as he now knew the subject better he was able to make a better impression, repeating things which he had just heard as if they were his own. And he never ceased to look into the eyes of his neighbour as though to give greater depth to what he was saying.

In her turn, she told him various stories in the bright, flippant manner of a woman who knows that she is witty and is always trying to be amusing; and she placed her hand familiarly on his arm and lowered her voice to impart platitudes, giving them an air of intimacy as a result. He was inwardly excited at this proximity to a young woman who was paying him so much attention. He felt he would have liked to make sacrifices for her, then and there, protect her, show his mettle; and the slowness of his replies revealed the preoccupation of his mind.

But abruptly, for no reason, Madame de Marelle called out: 'Laurine', and the little girl came up.

'Sit down there, you'll catch cold by the window.'

Duroy had a sudden strange urge to kiss the little girl, as if something of the kiss might rebound on the mother.

In a fatherly, flirtatious tone, he said:

'Tell me, little girl, may I give you a kiss?'

The child looked up at him in surprise. Madame de Marelle laughed and said:

'Say "You may today but don't think that you can always do it."'

Duroy immediately sat down, took Laurine on his knee and brushed her wavy hair with his lips.

Her mother looked surprised.

'Goodness me, she didn't run away, that's amazing. She normally only allows women to kiss her. Monsieur Duroy, you're irresistible.'

He blushed without replying and jogged the little girl up and down on his knee.

Madame Forestier came up and uttered an exclamation of surprise:

'Well, well, so Laurine has met her match. How incredible!'

Jacques Rival also approached with a cigar in his mouth and Duroy stood up to go, afraid that a clumsy word might spoil his good work and lose the advantage he had gained.

He took his leave, gently pressing the tiny hands of the ladies and firmly grasping those of the men. He noticed that Jacques Rival's was hot and dry and responded warmly to his pressure, whereas Norbert de Varenne's was damp and cold and slipped between his fingers. Old Walter's was cold and flabby, without any character or energy; Forestier's was warm and fleshy. His friend reminded him:

'Three o'clock tomorrow, don't forget.'

'Never fear, I'll be there.'

When he was once more on the stairs, he was so over-joyed that he felt the urge to run down them and started leaping down two steps at a time; but suddenly, in the large mirror on the second floor landing, he saw a man hurrying and skipping towards him and he stopped short, feeling as ashamed as if he had been caught doing something wrong.

Then he took a long look at himself, amazed at being such a really handsome young man. He smiled, well pleased with what he saw; then he took leave of his reflection with a very low, ceremonious bow, the kind of bow which you reserve for people of high degree.

Once in the street, Duroy hesitated as to what to do. He felt a desire to keep moving, to dream, to walk on and on, thinking of his future and breathing in the soft night air; but his mind kept coming back to the series of articles that old Walter had asked him to write, so he decided to go home and start work on them straightaway.

He strode quickly back towards the Boulevard de Batignolles and then went along it until he reached Rue Boursault. The six-storeyed house where he lived was occupied by some twenty small working and lower middle-class families and as he went upstairs, lighting his way with taper matches which revealed the dirty steps littered with pieces of paper, cigarette-ends and kitchen garbage, he was seized by a feeling of disgust and nausea and a desire to move out of there as quickly as possible, to go and live like the rich in clean homes with carpets on the floor. The stench of food, lavatories and humanity, a stale smell of filth and decaying walls that no fresh air would ever succeed in removing filled the whole building from top to bottom.

The young man's room on the fifth floor overlooked a sort of deep canyon, the immense railway cutting of the Western Railway Company, at the exact point where it came out of the tunnel by the Batignolles station. Duroy opened his window and rested his elbow on the rusty iron rail.

Beneath him, at the bottom of the black pit, were three red signals staring unwinkingly like the eyes of some large animal; beyond them, there were other lights and further on, still more of them. All the time, through the darkness, you could hear the long or short blasts of train whistles, sometimes near by, sometimes barely audible in the distance, over by Asnières. They modulated, like the sound of human voices calling out. One of them was approaching with a continuous wailing sound which grew louder and louder every second until a large yellow light rushed noisily by, and Duroy watched as the long string of carriages was swallowed up by the tunnel.

Then he said to himself: 'To work.' He put his lamp on the table but, just as he was getting ready to write, he realized that the only paper he had was six sheets of note-paper.

Ah well, he would open it out and write on it like that. He dipped his pen into the ink and, in his best handwriting, wrote at the top of the page: 'Memories of an African Cavalryman.'

Then he tried to find a good beginning for his first sentence.

He rested his forehead on his hand, staring at the blank square of paper spread out in front of him.

What was he going to say? He realized that he could not remember anything of what he had been saying a short while ago, not a single anecdote, not one fact, nothing at all. Suddenly, he had an idea. 'I must start by describing how I went there.' And he wrote: 'In 1874, round about 15 May, when France, exhausted by the disaster of the terrible year of 1871, was recovering . . .'

And there he stopped, not knowing how to lead into the rest of his story, going aboard the ship, the voyage, his first reactions.

He pondered for ten minutes and then decided to leave the introductory page till tomorrow and launch straight into a description of Algiers.

So he wrote: 'Algiers is a town which is all white . . .'

and then found himself incapable of continuing. In his mind's eye he could see the bright, charming city with its flat-roofed houses cascading down from the mountain into the sea but he was unable to find one word to express what he had seen and felt.

With a great effort, he added: 'It is partly inhabited by Arabs ...' Then he flung his pen on the table and stood up.

On his little iron bed, sagging from the weight of his body, he saw his everyday clothes lying where he had thrown them down, limp, empty and worn, as squalid as the tattered clothes in a mortuary. And on a straw-bottomed chair, his silk hat, the only hat he had, was lying face upwards as if begging for alms.

His wallpaper, grey with a blue floral pattern, had as many stains as flowers, ancient, dubious-looking stains that could have been squashed insects or oil, greasy finger-marks from hair cream or dirty soap suds from the wash-basin. It all reeked of poverty and degradation, the poverty of Parisian furnished lodgings. And he was filled with exasperation at his poverty-stricken existence. He told himself that he must get out of there and put an end to his impecunious life the very next day.

He suddenly felt an urge to work and sitting down at his table, once again he started trying to find the right words to express the strange, fascinating quality of Algiers, that gateway to the deep mystery of Africa, the Africa of Arab nomads and strange negroes, an Africa unexplored and alluring, whose improbable, fantastic fauna can occasionally be seen in zoos – those absurd birds called ostriches, those wonderful goats called gazelles, the grotesquely amazing giraffe, the shapeless rhinoceros and our frightening cousin, the gorilla.

He could dimly feel ideas swimming round in his mind.

He might have been able to express them in speech but he was certainly incapable of formulating them in writing. So, enraged at his incompetence, he stood up again, his hands dripping with sweat and his temples throbbing.

And, as his eye fell on his laundry bill which the porter had brought up to him that very evening, he was seized by sudden black despair. All his cheerfulness evaporated in a second, together with his self-confidence and his belief in his future. This was the end, there was nothing more to hope for, he would never achieve anything, he would never be anybody, he felt empty, inadequate, useless, a doomed man.

He went back and leant out of the window, just as a train shot suddenly and noisily out of the tunnel. It was on its way over the plains and the fields, down to the sea. And suddenly he thought of his parents.

The train would be passing near by, only a few miles from their home. He saw it in his mind's eye, a little house at the top of the hill overlooking Rouen and the immense valley of the Seine, on the outskirts of the village of Canteleu.

His father and mother kept a little tavern, a country inn called *La Belle Vue* where people would come for Sunday lunch from the middle-class suburbs of Rouen. They had wanted to make their son a gentleman and so had sent him to grammar school. When he had completed his schooling without obtaining his baccalauréat, he had gone off to do his military service intending to become an officer, a colonel or a general. But having lost his taste for army life long before completing his five years, he had dreamt of making his fortune in Paris.

After serving his time, he had come to Paris, despite the pleas of his father and mother who, now that their dreams had fallen through, wanted him to stay with them. But now it was he who was in search of a future. He was full of vague ideas of success, even though he could only dimly imagine how he would achieve it; but he felt certain he would be given an opportunity and show himself able to exploit it.

In the army, his love life had consisted of the usual facile conquests of any garrison soldier, plus one or two affairs at a slightly more elevated level, for he had seduced a tax collector's daughter who wanted to run away with him and a solicitor's wife who had tried to drown herself in despair when he deserted her.

His mates used to say: 'He's crafty and artful, he'll be smart enough to keep out of trouble.' And he had vowed that he would indeed be crafty and artful and smart. His native Norman wit, sharpened by garrison life and broadened by looting in Africa, illicit perks and dubious dealings, as well as picking up ideas of honour in the army, together with military bravado, patriotic sentiment, deeds of derring-do retailed in the sergeants' mess and the kudos of his profession, had turned him into a sort of box with several false bottoms, in which you could find bits of practically everything.

But it was the ambition to get to the top which predominated.

Without realizing it, he had started day-dreaming again, as he did every night. He used to imagine having a splendid love affair which would realize all his hopes at once. He would marry some banker's or nobleman's daughter whom he would meet in the street and sweep off her feet on the spot.

He was aroused from his dream by the shrill whistle of a locomotive which came out of the tunnel on its own, like a large rabbit bolting out of its hole, and then puffed full speed ahead towards the shunting-shed where it would be able to relax.

Then abandoning himself once more to the vague, cheerful optimism which never deserted him, he blew a kiss at random into the night, a kiss of love for the woman for whom he was waiting, a kiss of longing for the wealth which he desired. Then, shutting his window, he started to undress, muttering to himself:

'Ah well, I'll be in better form tomorrow. My mind isn't clear tonight. And perhaps I've had a little too much to drink as well. You can't do good work when you're in that state.'

He got into bed, blew out the light and went to sleep almost at once.

He awoke early, as one does when one has great hopes or worries, and jumping out of bed went and opened his window to swallow what he called a cup of good fresh air.

The houses in the Rue de Rome opposite, on the other side of the broad trough of the railway line, were shining in the light of the rising sun as though painted in dazzling white light. In the distance, on the right, you could glimpse the slopes of Argenteuil, the Sannois hills and the mills of Orgemont, seen through a gentle blue haze that seemed like a light, transparent veil left floating on the horizon.

Duroy stood looking at the distant countryside for a few minutes. 'It would be jolly nice out there on a day like this,' he muttered to himself. Then he remembered that he had work to do, quickly, and also that he would have to give his concierge's son ten sous to go and tell the office he was ill.

He sat down at his table, dipped his pen in the inkwell, rested his head on his hand and tried to think. All in vain. Nothing came.

However, he did not lose heart. He thought: 'Ah well, I'm not used to doing this. It's a trade you have to learn like any other. Someone will have to help me for my first few attempts. I'll go and find Forestier, he'll get me going on my article in no time at all.'

He dressed. When he was in the street, he realized that it was too early to call on his friend, who was probably sleeping late. So he took a gentle stroll under the trees of his boulevard.

It was not yet nine o'clock and he walked as far as the Parc Monceau, cool and fresh where it had been sprinkled.

Sitting down on a bench, he started to day-dream again. A young man was walking up and down in front of him, no doubt waiting for a woman.

She appeared, wearing a veil, her feet twinkling; they shook hands, she took his arm, and they went off together.

Duroy was seized by a passionate longing to find love, to be loved by a woman of refinement and distinction, one who wore nice perfumes. He stood up and set off again, thinking of Forestier. What a lucky chap he was!

He reached his friend's doorway just as he was coming out.

'Fancy seeing you at this time of day! What was it you wanted?'

Embarrassed at meeting him just as he was going to work, Duroy stammered:

'Well ... the fact is ... well, I don't seem to be able to do my article, you know, the one Monsieur Walter asked me for on Algeria. It's not really so surprising seeing that I've never done any writing before. You need practice for it like everything else. I'd soon get into it, I'm sure, but as I'm just a beginner, I don't know how to set about it. The ideas are there all right but I can't manage to express them.'

He stopped, a trifle uncertain. Forestier was smiling mischievously:

'I know that feeling.'

Duroy went on:

'Yes, I suppose that it happens to everyone at the beginning. Anyway, I was ... well, I was coming to ask if you would lend me a hand ... You'd be able to get it going in a jiffy, you could show me how I ought to do it. You could teach me something about style. If you don't help me, I shan't be able to get it done.'

Forestier was still smiling cheerfully. He patted his friend on the arm and said:

'Go up and find my wife, she'll fix you up as well as I could. I've trained her in that sort of work. I'm afraid I haven't got time this morning, otherwise I'd have been only too glad to help.'

Duroy hesitated, feeling suddenly shy and reluctant to do what his friend suggested:

'But it's so early, I can't call on her like that.'

'Yes, you can. She's up and about. You'll find her in my study, arranging some of my notes for me.'

Duroy was still reluctant.

'No, I can't do that.'

His friend took him by the shoulders, swung him round and pushed him towards the staircase.

'Off you go when I tell you, you silly man. You're not going to make me go up three flights of stairs again, to introduce you and explain the position.'

Duroy finally acquiesced.

'Many thanks, I'll go. I'll tell her that you forced me, literally forced me, to come up and see her.'

'That's right. She won't eat you, don't be afraid. Above all, don't forget three o'clock this afternoon.'

'No fear.'

And Forestier hurried off while Duroy started going slowly upstairs, step by step, thinking what he would say and worried about the welcome he might receive.

The servant opened the door. He was wearing a blue apron and holding a broom in his hand.

'Monsieur Forestier is out,' he said, without waiting to be asked.

Duroy stood his ground.

'Ask Madame Forestier if she can see me and tell her that her husband suggested I should call when I met him in the street a moment ago.'

He waited. The man came back, opened a door on the right and said:

'Madam will receive you.'

She was sitting in an office chair in a little room whose walls were completely lined with books, tidily arranged on black wooden shelves. The monotonous rows of volumes were made colourful and cheerful by the different types of binding, red, yellow, green, purple and blue.

She turned towards him, still smiling, wrapped in a loose, white gown, trimmed with lace, and as she held out her hand, her bare arm could be seen in the wide-open sleeve.

'So soon?' she said; and added: 'That's not a criticism, merely a question.'

He stammered: 'I didn't want to come up, but I met your husband downstairs and he insisted that I should. I'm so embarrassed that I hardly dare to tell you what brings me here.'

She pointed to a chair.

'Sit down and tell me.'

She was deftly twirling a goose-quill pen between her two fingers and in front of her there was a large sheet of paper which she had half covered in writing when interrupted by the young man's arrival.

She looked completely at her ease at the desk, just as she had in her drawing-room, carrying out her normal duties.

A subtle fragrance arose from her gown, the fragrance of a woman who had just come from her dressing-table. And Duroy tried to make out the shape of her radiant young body, plump and warm, gently caressed by the soft folds of her gown. He could almost succeed in picturing it in his mind's eye.

As he sat silent, she said again:

'Well, out with it, what do you want?'

Hesitantly, he mumbled:

'Well ... but really ... I hardly dare ... The fact is that last night I worked very late ... and this morning ... very early ... trying to write the article on Algeria that Monsieur Walter asked me to do, and I don't seem able to get it going properly ... I've torn up all my attempts ... I'm not used to that sort of work, so I came to ask your husband to help me ... for this once ...'

Pleased and flattered, she interrupted him with a gay burst of laughter:

'And so he told you to come and see me? ... That's really nice ...'

'Yes, he said that you'd get me out of my difficulty better than he could. But I didn't dare, I didn't want to. Do you see what I mean?'

She stood up.

'It's going to be wonderful to collaborate like that. I'm absolutely delighted with your idea. Look, you sit down in my seat, because they know my handwriting at the newspaper. And we'll turn out that article of yours, a really first-rate one, you'll see.'

He sat down, took up a pen, spread a piece of paper out in front of him and waited.

Madame Forestier stood watching him make his preparations; then she took a cigarette from the mantelpiece and lit it:

'I can't work unless I'm smoking,' she said. 'Well now, what's the story?'

He looked up at her in astonishment.

'But I can't tell you, that's why I came here to see you.'

She went on:

'Yes, I'll work it out for you. But if I'm to provide the sauce, you must let me have the ingredients.'

He was still embarrassed and then, hesitantly, he said:

'I wanted to tell the story of my trip from the beginning.'

She sat down at the big desk opposite him and, looking into his eyes:

'Very well then, first of all you tell me, you understand, just me and nobody else, not leaving anything out, and I'll choose what to put in. Off you go. Take it gently!'

But as he did not know where to begin, she started to interrogate him like a priest confessing someone, asking specific questions to remind him of details he had forgotten, prominent people he had met or faces which he had merely seen in passing.

When she had made him talk like that for ten minutes or so, she suddenly interrupted him: 'Now we're going to start. First of all, we'll imagine that you're writing to a friend and giving your impressions. That will allow you to talk all sorts of nonsense, make all kinds of comments and be natural and funny, if we can manage it.

'Now begin:

'Dear Henry, you were wanting to hear all about Algeria, so here goes. As I've nothing much to do in this little mud hut where I'm living, I'll write you a sort of diary of my life here, day by day and hour by hour. It'll be a trifle indelicate now and then but that can't be helped and you're not forced to show it to your lady friends . . .'

She stopped to relight her cigarette which had gone out and at once the scratching of the goose-quill stopped too:

47

'Let's go on,' she said.

'Algeria is a large French possession on the border of those vast unknown regions called the desert, the Sahara, Central Africa, etc. etc.

'The gateway to this strange continent is a charming town, all white, the city of Algiers.

'But first of all you have to get there, which is not all beer and skittles for everyone. As you know, I'm good with horses, because I break in the colonel's, but it's perfectly possible to be a good horseman and a rotten sailor. That's me.

'Do you remember the M.O., Major Simbretos, whom we used to call Doctor Ipecac? When we thought that we were due for twenty-four hours in that haven of bliss, the sick bay, we would go on sick parade.

'He used to sit in his red trousers with his big fat thighs wide apart, his hands resting on his knees, his arms akimbo and elbows in the air, rolling his big goggle-eyes and gnawing at his white moustache.

'You remember his prescription:

' "This man is suffering from a tummy upset. Give him one of my number 3s as an emetic, and then twelve hours' rest. He'll be all right."

'This emetic was a superlative remedy – superlative and infallible. So you swallowed it down, since there was nothing else to do. Then, when you'd submitted to Doctor Ipecac's magic formula, you'd enjoy twelve hours' well-earned rest. Well, old man, to get to Africa, you have to endure forty-eight hours of another sort of infallible emetic, provided by the Transatlantique shipping company.'

She was rubbing her hands together with glee at her inventiveness.

She stood up, lit another cigarette and started walking about while she dictated, pursing her lips to puff out thin trickles of smoke, which then spread out and evaporated, leaving grey trails here and there in the air, a sort of transparent vapour, a gossamerlike haze. Now and again, with her open hand, she brushed away the more persistent of these clouds and sometimes she would slice through them with a sharp movement of her forefinger and then solemnly watch the two barely perceptible sections of haze slowly vanish.

And Duroy, raising his eyes to watch her, followed her every gesture, her every attitude, every movement of her body and her face as she played this vague sort of game without ever being distracted from her thoughts.

Now she went on to invent all the happenings of the journey, portraying fellow-travellers imagined by herself and launching out on a love affair with the wife of an infantry captain who was on her way to rejoin her husband.

Then she sat down and questioned Duroy about the topography of Algeria, of which she knew absolutely nothing. After ten minutes she knew as much about it as he did and produced a short section on political and colonial geography to provide the reader with the necessary information and help him to understand the important questions that would be dealt with in later articles.

Then she continued with an excursion into the province of Oran, a fanciful excursion dealing mainly with women, Moorish women, Jewesses or Spaniards.

'That's the only thing that really interests them,' she said.

She ended with a stay in Saïda at the foot of the high plateaux, including a charming little intrigue between Sergeant Duroy and a little Spanish girl employed in the alfa factory at Ain-el-Hadjar. She described how they used to meet at night on the bare, stony mountain-side while jackals, hyenas and Arab dogs whined, barked and howled among the rocks.

And then she added gaily: 'To be continued in our next

issue.' Standing up, she added: 'That's how you write an article, my dear Monsieur Duroy. Sign please.'

He hesitated.

'Go on, sign!'

He laughed and wrote at the bottom of the page:

'Georges Duroy.'

She continued to walk about smoking, and he continued to watch, unable to find words to thank her, happy to be near her and filled with gratitude and with sensual happiness at their budding intimacy. It seemed to him as though all around him formed part of her, everything, even including the walls covered in books. The chairs, the furniture, the air full of the aroma of tobacco were something special, kind, gentle and charming which was emanating from her.

Suddenly she asked:

'What do you think of my friend Madame de Marelle?'

He was taken aback:

'Well, I think ... I think she's most attractive.'

'Yes, isn't she?'

'Indeed.'

He wanted to add: 'But not as attractive as you', but did not dare.

She went on:

'If you knew how funny, original and intelligent she is. She's a bohemian, in fact, a real bohemian. That's why her husband doesn't like her very much. He only sees her faults and doesn't appreciate her good qualities.'

Duroy was dumbfounded to hear that Madame de Marelle was married. Yet after all it was only natural.

He exclaimed: 'Goodness me, so she's married? What does her husband do?'

Madame Forestier gave a quiet shrug of her shoulders, at the same time raising her eyebrows to indicate unfathomable possibilities.

'Oh, he's an inspector in the Northern Railway Company. He spends a week in Paris every month. His wife calls it "compulsory service" or "the weekly chore" or else "Holy Week". When you get to know her better, you'll see how nice and clever she is. Go and call on her one of these days.'

Duroy now had no thought of leaving; it seemed to·him that he was going to stay on for ever, that this was his home.

But the door opened silently and, without being announced, in came a tall man.

He stopped on seeing another man there. For a second, Madame Forestier looked embarrassed and then, in her natural voice, although a slight blush had spread from her shoulders to her face, she said:

'Do come in, dear man. Let me introduce Monsieur Georges Duroy, a good friend of Charles and a future journalist.'

And then, in quite a different tone of voice:

'This is Comte de Vaudrec, our best and closest friend.'

The two men bowed, each eyeing the other, and Duroy immediately took his leave.

No attempt was made to persuade him to stay. He stammered a few words of thanks, shook the hand which Madame Forestier proffered him and bowed once more to the newcomer, whose expression continued to show the cold formality of those who move in the upper circles of society. He then left as flustered as if he had just committed a social solecism.

Once in the street, he felt depressed and unhappy, obsessed by some vague hidden sadness. He walked along wondering why this melancholy mood had suddenly overtaken him. He could not think why but the austere countenance of Comte de Vaudrec, an oldish man with grey hair and the quietly arrogant look of a person who is very rich and self-possessed, continued to haunt him.

In the course of their charming tête-à-tête, Madame Forestier had gradually cast her spell over him and it was, he realized, the interruption by this stranger which had aroused in him this black and unhappy mood that can sometimes be caused by a word, by a glimpse of someone's grief, or indeed by the merest trifle.

It seemed to him that this man had not been pleased to see him there, although he could not understand why.

He had nothing to do until three o'clock and it was not yet noon. He had six francs fifty centimes left and so he went and had lunch at Duval's. Then he sauntered along the boulevard and made his way upstairs under the sign advertising *La Vie française* just as it was striking three o'clock.

The messengers were sitting on a bench with their arms crossed, waiting, while a clerk sat behind a small high desk sorting the mail that had just come in. It was a sight calculated to impress any visitor. Everybody was dignified and smart, and full of decorum, as befitted the foyer of a big paper.

Duroy enquired:

'Monsieur Walter, please?'

The clerk replied:

'The editor is in conference. Please sit down a moment.'

He pointed to the waiting room, already full of people.

There were important, solemn-looking men wearing decorations and slovenly men whose shirts were carefully hidden and the front of whose coats, buttoned to the neck, were stained in patterns reminiscent of the coastlines of seas and continents on maps. Amongst all these men there were three women. One of them, pretty, smiling and all dressed-up, looked like a tart. Her neighbour, who had a wrinkled, tragic countenance, was also dressed-up but more austerely. She had that raddled, artificial look often found in exactresses, a sort of bogus youthfulness that has turned sour, like a stale love affair.

The third woman, in mourning, was sitting in a corner. She looked like a widow in distress and Duroy imagined that she had come to ask for charity.

Meanwhile, more than twenty minutes had gone by and nobody was being admitted.

Then Duroy had an idea and going back to the clerk, he said:

'Monsieur Walter gave me an appointment at three o'clock. In any case, please find out if my friend Monsieur Forestier is in.'

He was taken through a long corridor which led to a large room where four men were writing at a large baize-covered table.

Forestier was standing in front of the fireplace smoking a cigarette and playing cup-and-ball. It was a game he was very good at and each time he caught the enormous yellow boxwood ball on the little wooden spike, he counted: 'Twenty-two, twenty-three, twenty-four, twenty-five.'

Duroy said: 'Twenty-six.' His friend looked up while still continuing the regular movement of his arm.

'Oh hallo, it's you. Yesterday I did fifty-seven in a row. Saint-Potin is the only one here who can beat me. Did you see the boss? There's nothing so funny as seeing that old idiot Norbert play cup-and-ball. He keeps his mouth open as if he was going to swallow the thing.'

One of the sub-editors turned his head towards him:

'I say, Forestier, I know where there's one for sale, a beauty, made from West Indian hardwood. It's said to have belonged to the Queen of Spain. They're asking sixty francs. That's not dear.'

Forestier asked:

'Where is it?' And having missed his thirty-seventh shot,

53

he opened a cupboard and Duroy caught a glimpse of a score or more superb cups-and-balls, arranged in rows, and numbered like a collection of antiques. Forestier put the cup-and-ball back in its place and asked again:

'Where is this precious object?'

The journalist replied:

'A ticket seller at the Vaudeville's got it. I'll bring it along for you tomorrow if you like.'

'Yes, all right. If it's really nice, I'll take it, one can never have too many cups-and-balls.'

Then he turned to Duroy:

'Come with me, I'll take you into the presence, otherwise you'll still be hanging about here at seven o'clock.'

They went back through the waiting-room where the same people were still sitting in the same places. As soon as Forestier appeared, the young woman and the old actress both jumped up and came towards him.

He took them aside one after the other into the window recess and although they took care to keep their voices low, Duroy noticed from the way he addressed them that he was on intimate terms with both of them.

Then pushing open two padded doors, they made their way into the inner sanctum.

The conference which had been going on for an hour consisted of a game of écarté with a number of the flat-hatted gentlemen whom Duroy had noticed the day before.

Monsieur Walter was holding the cards and playing with concentrated care and cautious gestures, whereas his opponent was slapping down the thin pieces of coloured card, picking them up and handling them with all the skilled dexterity and grace of a practised cardplayer. Norbert de Varenne was sitting writing an article in the editorial armchair and Jacques Rival was lying with his eyes closed, stretched out on a divan, smoking a cigar.

The room had a fusty smell of chair leather, stale tobacco

and printers' ink; you recognized the peculiar smell of news-rooms familiar to every journalist.

On the table made of dark wood inlaid with brass there was an incredible heap of papers: letters, maps, newspapers, periodicals, tradesmen's bills, every possible kind of printed matter.

Forestier shook hands with the punters standing behind the players and, without saying a word, looked at the game. Then, as soon as old Walter had won, he made the introduction:

'My friend Duroy.'

The editor directed a quick glance over his spectacles at the young man and asked:

'Have you got my article? That would be just right for today at the same time as this debate of Morel's.'

Duroy pulled the sheaf of paper out of his pocket, folded into four.

'Here it is, sir.'

The old editor seemed delighted. He smiled:

'Excellent, excellent. You keep your promises. You'll look it over, eh, Forestier?'

But Forestier quickly said:

'There's no need, Monsieur Walter. I went over the story with him to show him how it should be done. It's very good.'

And the editor, who was now being dealt another hand by a tall man, a left-of-centre deputy, said unconcernedly: 'That's splendid, then.' Forestier did not let him begin his new game. Bending down, he whispered:

'You remember that you promised to let me h. ε Duroy to replace Marambot. Would you like me to employ him on the same terms?'

'Yes, all right.'

And taking his friend's arm, Forestier led him away while Monsieur Walter started on a new game.

Norbert de Varenne had not looked up and seemed not to have recognized Duroy. Jacques Rival, on the other hand, had given him a deliberately vigorous and demonstrative handshake, like a good friend on whom you could rely in a quarrel.

They went back through the waiting-room and as everyone looked up, Forestier said to the youngest of the women, loud enough to be heard by the other sufferers:

'The editor will see you directly. He's in conference at the moment with two members of the Budget Committee.'

Then he bustled out with an air of importance as if he was about to write out a dispatch of the gravest significance.

As soon as they were back in the newsroom, Forestier immediately took out his cup-and-ball and started to play again, interrupting himself to count as he talked to Duroy:

'Well now, you must come here every day at three and I'll tell you what errands you'll have to do and what people to call on, either during the day or the evening or in the morning – one – first of all I'm going to give you a letter of introduction to the head of Section One at Police Headquarters – two – who will put you in touch with one of his staff. And you'll make arrangements with him to get all the important news – three – from the headquarters office, official and semi-official news, of course. For the details, you must talk to Saint-Potin, who knows all the ropes – four – you'll be meeting him later on today or else tomorrow. Above all, you'll have to develop the habit of squeezing information out of the people I send you to see – five – and poke your nose in everywhere even when people slam the door in your face – six – for all this you'll draw two hundred francs a month fixed salary, plus ten sous a line for any interesting news items written by yourself – seven – plus another ten sous a line for any articles you're asked to write on various topics – eight.'

Then he devoted all his attention to his game, slowly counting: 'Nine, ten, eleven, twelve, thirteen.' He missed his fourteenth shot and swore:

'Bloody thirteen. That blasted number always brings me bad luck. I'm sure I'll die on the thirteenth.'

One of the sub-editors, who had just finished what he was doing, went to fetch his cup-and-ball from the cupboard; he was a tiny little man who looked like a child, although he was thirty-five; and a number of other journalists now came in and went to the cupboard one after the other to fetch their own cups-and-balls. Soon there were half a dozen of them lined up along the wall all steadily throwing the balls into the air, red, yellow or black according to the kind of wood they were made from. And when a competition was organized, the two sub-editors who were still working came over to act as umpires.

Forestier won by eleven points. Then the childlike little man, who had lost, called a messenger and ordered:

'Nine beers.' And they started playing again while waiting for the refreshments.

Duroy drank a glass of beer with his new colleagues and then asked his friend:

'What do I do now?'

The other man answered: 'I haven't got anything for you today. You can go off if you like.'

'And ... our ... our article ... will it be going in this evening?'

'Yes, but don't worry. I'll see to the proofs. Get the next instalment ready for tomorrow and come here at three o'clock, as you did today.'

And after shaking hands with everyone without even knowing their names, Duroy went cheerfully down the splendid staircase, with joy in his heart.

GEORGES DUROY did not sleep very well, excited by the prospect of seeing his article in print. As soon as it was light, he was up and prowling the streets long before the time when the newspaper boys would be dashing from one kiosk to the next delivering the papers.

So he went down to the Gare Saint-Lazare, knowing that *La Vie française* would arrive there first.

As it was still too early, he walked up and down on the pavement.

He saw the paper-seller arrive and open up her little glass cubby-hole and then he caught sight of a man carrying a large pile of folded papers on his head. He rushed over to see: it was *Le Figaro*, *Gil-Blas*, *La Gaulois*, *L'Événement* and two or three other morning papers, but *La Vie française* was not amongst them.

He was suddenly seized with alarm: suppose the 'Memories of an African Cavalryman' had been postponed till tomorrow or perhaps, at the last moment, old Walter hadn't liked it?

Going up to the kiosk again he realized that although he had not seen the paper come in, it was already on sale. He hurried over to the stall, flung down his three sous and unfolded it; on the front page there was nothing resembling his title. His heart began to pound: he opened the paper and with a thrill of excitement, saw at the bottom of one of the columns, in large letters: Georges Duroy. It was in! How wonderful!

He walked away, his mind a blank, clutching the paper in his hand, his hat perched on the side of his head, longing to stop people passing by and say to them: 'This is the paper you need. This one here. It's got an article by me in it.' He would have liked to shout as loudly as he could, like some paper-sellers do in the evening along the boulevards: 'Read *La Vie française*', read Georges Duroy's article "Memories of an African Cavalryman"!' And all of a sudden he felt a desire to read the article himself in public, in a café, in full view. He started to look for a place where there were some customers already. He had to walk quite a long way. Eventually he sat down in front of a sort of wine-shop, where a number of men were already drinking, and ordered a rum, as he might have ordered an absinthe, without thinking what the time was. Then he called out: 'Waiter, I'd like *La Vie française*.'

A man in a white apron hurried up:

'We haven't got it, I'm afraid, sir. We only take *Le Rappel*, *Le Siècle*, *La Lanterne* and *Le Petit Parisien*.'

Indignantly, Duroy said in an angry voice: 'What a hopeless place. Go and buy it for me, then.' The waiter hurried off and brought one back. Duroy started to read his article, saying several times, out loud: 'Excellent, excellent!' so as to attract the attention of the men sitting round him and thus make them want to know what he was reading. Then, when he went away, he left it lying on the table. The proprietor saw it and called after him: 'Excuse me, sir, you've forgotten your paper.'

Duroy replied:

'You can have it, I've read it. There's a very interesting article in it today, incidentally.'

He did not say what the article was but as he walked away he saw someone from a neighbouring table pick up *La Vie française* where he had left it lying.

He thought: 'What shall I do now?' And he decided to go to the office to draw his pay and hand in his resignation.

He glowed with pleasurable anticipation at the thought of how the chief clerk and his colleagues would take the news. His chief's startled face was particularly pleasing to imagine.

He walked slowly along, not wanting to arrive before half-past nine, because the cashier's desk did not open until ten o'clock.

His office was a large and gloomy room where the gas had to be kept on almost all day in winter. It looked out on to a narrow courtyard, facing other offices. There were eight people in the room, plus a deputy chief clerk hidden behind a screen.

First of all Duroy went to draw his 118 francs 25 centimes, kept in a yellow pay-packet in the pay clerk's drawer. He then made his way into the vast office where he had spent so many days.

As soon as he came in, the deputy chief clerk, Monsieur Potel, called out to him:

'Ah, there you are, Monsieur Duroy. The chief clerk's been asking for you several times. You know he doesn't allow anyone to be away sick for two days in succession without a doctor's certificate.'

Standing in the middle of the room to create the maximum effect, Duroy replied loudly:

'I really couldn't care less!'

The other clerks were stunned with amazement and Monsieur Potel poked a bewildered face over the screen in which he was enclosed, as in a box.

He used to shut himself up in this box for fear of draughts, because he suffered from rheumatism. He had merely made two holes in the paper in order to keep an eye on his staff.

There was a breathless hush.

Then the deputy chief clerk asked hesitantly:

'What did you say?'

'I said that I couldn't care less. The only reason I've come in today is to hand in my resignation. I've just been made sub-editor on *La Vie française* at 500 francs a month, plus so much per line. In fact, they've even published my first article this morning.'

He had been promising himself to break the news gently in order to prolong the pleasure but he was unable to resist the temptation of telling the whole story at once.

In any case, he had completely achieved the effect that he was aiming at. Nobody stirred.

Then Duroy announced:

'I'll go and tell Monsieur Perthuis and then I'll come and say goodbye.'

And he went out to find the chief clerk who as soon as he saw him, exclaimed:

'Ah, there you are! You know I don't allow ...'

His employee cut him short:

'There's no need to bawl like that ...'

Monsieur Perthuis, a burly man as red as a turkey-cock, was rendered speechless with surprise.

Duroy went on:

'I've had enough of your rotten hole. I've started as a journalist this morning and I've been offered a very good job. I wish you a very good day.'

And he went out, his revenge accomplished.

As he had said, he went and shook hands with his former colleagues who hardly ventured to speak to him for fear of being compromised, because as the door had been left open, they had heard his exchange with the head clerk.

And he went out into the street again with his pay in his pocket. He treated himself to a tasty lunch in a good, reasonably-priced restaurant which he knew; then, after he had once again bought *La Vie française* and left it behind on the table where he had lunched, he went into a number of shops and bought a few small things, with the sole object of having them delivered at his address and giving his name, Georges Duroy, adding 'sub-editor on *La Vie française*'.

Then he gave his number and street, taking care to stipulate, 'Leave it downstairs with the porter.'

As he still had time to spare he went into an engraver's who produced visiting cards on the spot, in full view of the passers-by, and had a hundred cards printed with his name and his new position underneath.

Then he went along to the paper.

Forestier welcomed him rather condescendingly, like someone dealing with an inferior.

'Ah, there you are, jolly good. I've got a number of jobs for you, as it happens. I'll be with you in ten minutes. I've got some things to finish first.'

And he went on with the letter he was writing.

At the other end of the large table sat a very pale little man, very fat and puffy, with a completely bald, white, shiny pate who was so short-sighted that he was writing with his nose glued to the paper.

Forestier spoke to him:

'I say, Saint-Potin, what time are you going to interview our chaps?'

'At four o'clock.'

'Take this young man along with you, will you? His name's Duroy. You can explain to him all our trade secrets.'

'Right you are.'

Then turning to his friend, Forestier added:

'Have you got your next article on Algeria? The first one was well received this morning.'

Duroy, taken by surprise, stammered:

'No, I thought I'd have the time this afternoon ... I had a lot of things to see to ... I wasn't able ...'

The other raised his shoulders in a gesture of annoyance:

'If you can't be more punctual than that then you're going to ruin your prospects here. Old Walter was relying on that article. I'll tell him it'll be ready tomorrow. If you think you're going to be paid for doing nothing then you're mistaken.'

Then after a pause, he added: 'You must strike while the iron is hot, damn it all!'

Saint-Potin stood up:

'I'm ready,' he said.

Then Forestier leant back in his chair, assumed an almost pompous posture and began to issue his orders. He turned towards Duroy:

'Well now. The Chinese general Le-Then-Fao and Rajah Taposahib Ramadero Pali arrived in Paris two days ago. The first is staying at the Continental, the second at the Hotel Bristol. You're going to interview them.'

Then turning to Saint-Potin:

'Don't forget the main points I mentioned to you. Ask the general and the rajah their opinion on the activities of England in the Far East, their ideas on her system of colonization and colonial domination and their hopes of European intervention, particularly French intervention, in their affairs.'

He stopped for a moment and then added, addressing the world at large:

'It will be extremely interesting for our readers to learn the views held both in China and in India on these questions which are being followed with keen interest by the public at the moment.'

He added, addressing Duroy:

'Watch Saint-Potin's technique. He's a first-rate reporter. Try to see how to pump someone in five minutes.'

Then he solemnly went back to his writing, with the

obvious intention of putting his former comrade-in-arms and present colleague in his place – at a distance.

As soon as they were outside the door, Saint-Potin started to laugh and said to Duroy:

'What a humbug! He's putting it on with us. You'd really think he takes us for his readers.'

Then they went downstairs to the boulevard and the reporter asked:

'Like a drink?'

'I'd love one. It's very hot.'

They went into a café and ordered iced drinks. Saint-Potin started to talk. He talked about everybody and about the paper with a profusion of surprising detail.

'The boss? A real Jew. And you know, you'll never change the Jews. What a race!' And he quoted amazing examples of their avarice, the peculiar avarice of the sons of Israel, the efforts they would make to save ten centimes, their haggling, their barefaced way of asking for discounts and getting them, their whole moneylending, pawnbroking attitude.

'And yet with all that, a good sort, who doesn't believe in anything and diddles everybody. His paper, which is semi-official, Catholic, liberal, republican, "Orleanist", custard pie and sixpenny ha'penny bazaar, was only founded to help him play the stock market and back up all his other ventures. He's very good at that and he earns millions by means of companies that haven't got tuppence worth of capital ...'

He went on and on, calling Duroy 'my dear chap' all the time:

'And the old skinflint talks like someone out of Balzac. Just imagine, the other day I was in his office with that aged idiot Norbert and that Don Quixote Rival when our business manager Montelin turns up with his morocco leather briefcase under his arm, a briefcase that's known all

64

over Paris. Walter peered up at him and said: "What's new?"

'Montelin innocently replies: "I've just paid the 16,000 francs we owe for newsprint."

'The old man gives a start, all surprised:

' "What did you say?"

' "I've just paid Monsieur Privas."

' "But you must be mad!"

' "Why?"

' "Why . . . why . . . why . . ."

'He took off his glasses and wiped them. Then he smiled, a funny little smile that creases his fat cheeks every time he's going to say something clever or outrageous, and in an emphatic, quizzical tone he said: "Why? Because we could have got a reduction of four or five thousand francs on it, that's why."

'Montelin, taken aback, retorted:

' "But sir, all the bills were in order, checked by me and approved by you . . ."

'Then the old boy, becoming serious again, said vigorously:

' "It's just not possible to be as innocent as that. Remember, Monsieur Montelin, that you must always accumulate debts, so as to be able to come to terms with your creditors." '

And Saint-Potin added, with an appreciative shake of the head:

'Eh? Straight out of Balzac, isn't it?'

Duroy had never read any Balzac but he replied without hesitation:

'My goodness yes.'

Then the reporter talked about Madame Walter, a dull, stupid woman, about Norbert de Varenne, an old dead-beat, about Rival, a rehash of Fervacques. Then he came to Forestier:

'As for him, he's lucky to have married his wife, that's all.'

Duroy asked:

'What's his wife like, in fact?'

Saint-Potin rubbed his hands together:

'Ah, she's a sly one, a real crafty little so-and-so. She's the mistress of an old rake called Vaudrec, who gave her a dowry and married her off . . .'

Duroy felt a sudden chill, a sort of nervous contraction, a wish to insult this gossip-monger, to slap him in the face. But he merely cut him short by asking him:

'Is Saint-Potin your real name?'

The other man answered candidly:

'No, my name's Thomas. They gave me my nickname of Saint-Potin at the paper.'

As he paid for the drinks, Duroy said:

'It seems to me that it's getting late and we have two very important people to call on.'

Saint-Potin laughed:

'I can see you're still an innocent! Do you really think that I'm going to ask that Chink and that Indian what they think of England? As if I didn't know better than they do what they're expected to think for the readers of *La Vie française*. I've already interviewed hundreds of those Chinese, Persians, Hindus, Chileans, Japanese and *tutti quanti*. According to me, they all give the same answers. All I need to do is to take my last interview and copy it out word for word. The only difference, of course, is their face, their name, their title, their age, their entourage. Now there I have to tread warily because if I tripped up there *Le Figaro* or *Le Gaulois* would come down on me like a ton of bricks. But the reception clerks at the Hotel Bristol and at the Continental will tell me all that I want to know in five minutes. We can walk there while we smoke a cigar. Total: five francs for a cab on expenses. That's how you manage it, my dear chap, when you've had some experience.'

Duroy enquired:

'It must be very profitable to be a reporter on that basis?'

The journalist replied enigmatically:

'Yes, but nothing like so profitable as doing a news or gossip column, because of the concealed advertisements.'

They were now walking along the boulevard towards the Madeleine and Saint-Potin suddenly said to his companion:

'Look, if you've got things to do, I don't need you.'

So Duroy shook hands and went off.

He was worried by the thought of the article he had to write by that evening and he started to think about it. As he was going along, he stocked up with ideas, comments, opinions and stories and he walked right up to the far end of the Champs-Élysées, where there were very few people about, because at this time of the year Paris was deserted.

After dining in a cheap restaurant near the Arc de Triomphe, he sauntered slowly back to his room along the outer boulevard and sat down at his table to work.

But as soon as he saw the large sheet of white paper in front of him all the material that he had stored up in his mind evaporated in a flash as if his brain had melted into thin air. He tried to recall odd scraps of memories and note them down, but they slipped away as soon as he thought of them or else they poured helter-skelter through his mind and he found himself unable to put them in order or into words or even to decide where to begin.

After an hour's hard labour and five pages scribbled with introductory phrases, none of them completed, he said to himself: 'I still don't know enough about the tricks of the trade. I need another lesson.' And immediately, at the prospect of another session in Madame Forestier's company and the expectation of a long, cosy, friendly, wonderful tête-à-tête, he felt a thrill of desire. He quickly went to bed, almost afraid to go back to his writing in case he suddenly succeeded.

Next morning he got up only slightly later, so as to delay the pleasure of calling on her and savour it thoroughly in advance. It was past ten o'clock when he rang his friend's doorbell.

The servant answered:

'I'm afraid Monsieur Forestier is busy working.'

Duroy had not considered the possibility that her husband might be in. However, he insisted: 'Tell him that it's me and that it's urgent.'

After waiting for five minutes, he was shown into the study where he had spent such a pleasant morning before.

Forestier was sitting writing in the seat which Duroy had occupied. He was wearing a dressing gown, slippers and a little peaked cap, while his wife, wrapped in the same loose gown as before, was leaning against the mantelpiece, dictating, with a cigarette in her mouth.

Duroy stopped in the doorway, murmuring:

'I'm so sorry. I'm disturbing you.'

His friend turned towards him with a scowl on his face and grunted:

'Well, what do you want now? Make it quick, we're in a hurry.'

Quite taken aback, Duroy stammered:

'No, it's nothing. I'm sorry.'

Forestier lost his temper:

'For God's sake, man, don't shilly-shally. You haven't barged your way in just to say hallo, I suppose.'

Now extremely nervous, Duroy decided to chance his luck:

'No ... well ... the fact is ... that I still can't quite get my article right ... and you ... you both ... were so kind ... last time ... that I hoped ... I took the liberty ...'

Forestier cut him short:

'Good God! You've got a nerve, haven't you? Do you imagine that I'm going to do your job and that all you have to do is draw your pay at the end of the month? That really is a bit thick!'

The young woman continued to smoke without uttering a word, with a vague smile on her face, that seemed to hide the irony concealed beneath her outward appearance of friendliness.

Duroy blushed and faltered:

'Forgive me. I thought . . . I believed . . .'

Then suddenly, speaking clearly and distinctly, he said:

'I do ask you to forgive me, Madame Forestier. May I thank you once again most sincerely for the wonderful article you wrote for me yesterday.'

He bowed and said to Charles:

'I'll be at the paper at three o'clock,' and left.

He strode back to his room muttering to himself: 'All right. I'm going to do it all by myself and that'll show them . . .'

As soon as he reached home, he set to work, spurred on by anger.

He went on with the account of the love affair which Madame Forestier had started, piling up one romantic detail after another, with melodramatic happenings and pompous descriptions, in a clumsy schoolboyish style and using expressions that could only have come from the pen of a sergeant. Within the hour he had knocked together an article which was nothing but a mass of confused rubbish and, brimming with confidence, he took it round to *La Vie française*.

The first person he met was Saint-Potin who shook hands energetically, like a fellow-conspirator, and said:

'Did you read my conversation with the Chink and the

Hindu? Isn't it really funny? It made the whole town laugh. And I didn't even see the tips of their noses.'

Duroy had not read any of it so he immediately picked up the paper and ran his eye over the long article entitled 'India and China' while its author pointed out the most interesting passages.

Forestier bustled in, puffing and flustered:

'Oh good, I need you both.'

And he mentioned to them certain items of political information which he wanted to have by that evening.

Duroy held out his article:

'Here's the next instalment of my series on Algiers.'

'Splendid, give it to me. I'll give it to the boss.'

Nothing further was said.

Saint-Potin took his new colleague off with him and as soon as they were in the corridor, he said:

'Have you been to see the cashier?'

'No, why?'

'Why? To pick up your pay. You ought always to draw it a month in advance. You never know what might happen.'

'Well, that would suit me very nicely.'

'I'll introduce you to the cashier. He won't raise any difficulties. They pay well here.'

So Duroy went and drew his 200 francs, plus twenty-eight francs for last night's article and this, together with what was left of his pay from the railway company, made a grand total of 340 francs.

He had never had such a large sum of money in his pocket before and he felt set up for an indefinite period to come.

Then Saint-Potin took him round for a chat to the offices of four or five rival newspapers, hoping that the information they had been asked to provide might already have been gathered by other reporters and that he would be able to worm it out of them with the help of a little blarney.

In the evening, as he no longer had anything to do, Duroy thought he would go back to the Folies-Bergère and, taking a chance, he went to the box-office:

'My name's Georges Duroy, a sub-editor at *La Vie française*. I came here the other evening with Monsieur Forestier who promised to arrange for me to have complimentary tickets. I don't know if he's remembered to do so?'

They consulted a list of names; his did not appear on it. However, the extremely affable box-office manager said:

'Please go in all the same, sir, and ask the manager yourself. I'm sure he'll be very happy to oblige.'

He went in and almost immediately met Rachel, the woman whom he had gone home with the other night.

She came up to him:

'Hallo, dearie. You well?'

'Very well, thanks. How about you?'

'Mustn't grumble. You won't believe it, but I've had two dreams about you since the other day.'

Duroy smiled, feeling flattered:

'Well, well . . . And what does that prove?'

'That proves that I like you, you big silly, and that we'll do it again whenever you feel the urge.'

'Tonight if you like.'

'Yes, all right.'

'Good but listen . . .' He hesitated a moment, a trifle embarrassed at what he was going to do: 'The fact is that this time I haven't got a penny. I've just come from the club where I lost the lot.'

Her experience of men had taught her all their tricks and their way of haggling. She looked him hard in the eye, sensing instinctively that he was lying:

'You are a humbug. That's not a very nice thing to do, you know.'

He gave an embarrassed smile:

'If you want ten francs, that's all I've got left.'

71

A prostitute who fancies a man is prepared to be generous. She whispered:

'Whatever you like, ducks. I only want you.'

And she looked fondly up at the young man's moustache, took him by the arm and, clinging to it amorously:

'Let's go and drink a grenadine first. And then we'll go for a little walk together. I'd like to go as far as the Opéra with you, just like that, to show you off. And then we'll go home early, shan't we?'

*

Duroy slept late at the woman's flat. It was already light by the time he left and his first thought was to buy *La Vie française*. He opened it eagerly. His article had not appeared and he stood on the pavement, anxiously scanning each column in the hope of finding what he was looking for.

He suddenly felt immeasurably despondent. After an exhausting night of lovemaking, a setback like this on top of his fatigue assumed the proportions of a major disaster.

He went back home and fell asleep on his bed without undressing.

When he went to the newspaper offices a few hours later, he went to see Monsieur Walter.

'I was most surprised not to see my second article on Algeria in the paper this morning, sir.'

The director looked up and said curtly:

'I gave it to your friend Forestier to read. He didn't think it satisfactory. You'll have to rewrite it.'

Furious with rage, Duroy left without a word and burst straight into his friend's room:

'Why didn't you let my article be printed this morning?'

The journalist was smoking a cigarette, lolling in his chair with his feet on the table, his dirty heels resting on an article he had just begun. In a bored, distant voice, which seemed to be coming from the bottom of a hole, he said calmly and deliberately:

'The boss didn't like it and asked me to hand it back to you to rewrite. It's over there.'

And he pointed his finger at some sheets of paper lying open under a paperweight.

Duroy was so taken aback that he was completely at a loss for words. As he was putting his article into his pocket, Forestier added:

'Today your first job is to go to police headquarters.'

And he proceeded to give him a series of errands and instructions about news to collect. Duroy went off without managing to think of the caustic comment that he was trying to find.

Next day he took his article in again and once again it was rejected. After rewriting it a third time and still having it refused, Duroy realized that he was trying to run before he could walk and that only Forestier's guiding hand could show him the way.

So he said nothing more about the 'Memories of an African Cavalryman', making the inward promise that he would be crafty and adaptable since that was what was required and that he would make himself into as good a reporter as possible while waiting for something better to turn up.

So he set about mastering the ins and outs of all that takes place in the theatre and in politics, in the corridors and ante-rooms of statesmen and deputies and learned to recognize the self-importance of minor officials and the scowls of sleepy ushers. He was in continual contact with ministers and concierges, generals and policemen, princes and ponces, high-class tarts and ambassadors, bishops and bawds, flashy imposters and men about town, Greeks and cabbies, waiters and all the rest, since for his own selfish purposes he became the impartial friend of all these people, taking all of them in his stride, measuring them by the same standards and sizing them up with a dispassionate eye, since he saw them all the time, all day and every day, going from one to the other always with the same approach and talking with all of them about the same things in the course of his professional tasks. He compared himself to a man who was drinking samples of so many different sorts of wine that he soon becomes unable to distinguish Château Margaux from red biddy.

In a short while he had become a quite outstanding reporter, reliable in his information, crafty, quick and shrewd, in old Walter's words 'a real asset to the paper', and the latter was an expert on sub-editors.

All the same, as he only earned ten centimes a line, plus his fixed salary of 200 francs, and as boulevard life, drinking in cafés and eating in restaurants, is expensive he never had a sou to bless himself with and was depressed by his continual shortage of money.

'It's an art I must discover,' he used to think to himself as he watched certain of his colleagues going about with their pockets bulging; yet he could never understand by what mysterious means they acquired their wealth. Enviously, he imagined all sorts of strange subterfuges and services rendered, every kind of accepted and acknowledged racket. He would have to penetrate the mystery, join in the tacit conspiracy and force his colleagues to let him have his share of the graft from which he was excluded.

And often as he sat at his window watching the trains go by, he would think of ways and means to set about it.

CHAPTER 5

Two months had passed.

September was drawing near and the rapid rise to fame and fortune for which Duroy had been hoping seemed very slow in coming. Above all, he was galled by his lowly position and yet he could not see the way to the top where he would acquire wealth and respect. He felt cramped in his paltry job of reporter, imprisoned in it without possibility of escape. He was appreciated but only according to his status. Even Forestier, whom he was helping in countless ways, no longer invited him to dinner and always treated him as an inferior, although he still remained on friendly terms.

It was true that now and again, when the opportunity offered, Duroy managed to place a small article, and now that he had acquired, through his experience as a reporter, a certain facility in writing and a sense of judgement which was lacking at the time he wrote his second piece on Algeria, there was now no risk that his articles on current affairs would be turned down. But the difference between that and writing on whatever subject he liked or producing authoritative political articles was as great as that between driving your own carriage in the Bois de Boulogne and doing the same thing as a cabby. What humiliated him above all was the feeling of being excluded from high society, having no connections where he would be accepted as an equal and being unable to frequent women on terms of intimacy, although sometimes a number of actresses had offered him their friendship, for the furtherance of their own ends.

Moreover, he knew from experience that all these women, whether fashionable ladies or third-rate actresses, felt a peculiar attraction and an instant sympathy towards him and he felt as impatient as a hobbled horse at the thought that he could not make the acquaintance of the women on whom his future might depend.

He had frequently thought of going to see Madame Forestier but he was restrained by the thought of their last humiliating encounter and moreover he was waiting for her husband to invite him. So his mind turned to Madame de Marelle, and remembering that she had asked him to call on her, one afternoon when he had nothing else to do he went to see her.

'I'm always at home until three o'clock,' she had said.

He rang her bell at two-thirty.

She lived in the Rue de Verneuil, on the fourth floor.

At the sound of the bell, a maid came and opened the door, a little tousle-headed girl who was still tying on her cap as she replied:

'Madame de Marelle is in but I don't know if she is up.'

And she pushed open the drawing-room door which had been left ajar.

Duroy went in. It was quite a large room with not much furniture and it had a neglected air. The armchairs, old and rather battered, were lined up all round the walls, where they must have been put by the maid, for nowhere could you feel the elegant touch of a woman interested in her surroundings. Four very poor pictures depicting a boat on a river, a mill on a plain, a ship at sea and a woodcutter in a wood were hanging in the middle of the four wall panels, each at a different height and all of them askew. You could sense that they had been hanging like that for a long time under the careless eye of a woman who never bothered to look at them.

Duroy sat down and waited. He waited a long time. Then the door opened and Madame de Marelle hurried into the room dressed in a pink silk kimono embroidered with rural scenes in gold, with blue flowers and white birds.

'Just think, I was still in bed,' she exclaimed. 'How nice of you to come and see me. I felt sure you'd forgotten me.'

She held out her two hands in a delighted gesture and Duroy, feeling very much at ease now that he had seen the shabbiness of the flat, took them both and kissed one of them in imitation of Norbert de Varenne.

She invited him to sit down and then, looking him up and down, she said:

'How you've changed! You're flourishing. Paris suits you. Now, tell me all your news.'

And immediately they started gossiping like two old acquaintances, with the growing feeling of instant sympathy and trust, intimacy and affection which make two people of similar character and background become friends within the space of minutes.

Suddenly, the young woman broke off and said in a surprised voice:

'It's funny how I feel with you. It's as if I'd known you for ten years. I'm sure we're going to become good friends. Would you like that?'

He said: 'Of course I should', with a smile that spoke volumes.

He found her extremely alluring in her bright silky kimono, less dainty than her friend in her loose white gown, less coaxing and less refined but more exciting, spicier.

When he had been with Madame Forestier with her quiet, gracious smile which encouraged you and held you back at the same time, which seemed to be saying: 'I like you' and 'Be careful', her smile which you could never properly

77

fathom, he felt above all an urge to kneel at her feet or kiss the dainty lace around her neck and slowly breathe in the warm, fragrant scent which was surely wafting from between her breasts. With Madame de Marelle, his desire was more brutal and more direct, a desire which made his hands twitch as he saw her lifting breasts beneath their flimsy covering of silk.

She talked on and on, peppering her every sentence with that facile wit that had become a second habit, just as a workman can pick up the knack required for a task which is reckoned to be difficult and then amaze other people with his skill. He sat listening to her, thinking:

'That's worth remembering. You could write a charming Parisian gossip column merely by getting her to chat about what's happened during the day.'

There was a rap, a gentle rap, at the door through which she had come. She cried out: 'You can come in, darling.' The little girl came in, went straight up to Duroy and held out her hand.

Her astonished mother murmured: 'You've made a conquest there. I can hardly recognize her.' The young man kissed the little girl, sat her down beside him and with a serious expression started asking her in a friendly way about what she had been doing since they had last seen each other. She answered him in her high-pitched little voice, her manner, as usual, sedate and grown up.

The clock struck three. The journalist stood up.

'Do come and see me often,' said Madame de Marelle, 'we'll have a nice chat like we did today. You'll always be very welcome. Incidentally, why don't we see you at the Forestiers' any longer?'

He replied:

'Oh, no reason really. I've had a lot to do. I hope very much that we'll be meeting there again one of these days.'

And he took his leave, in a much more cheerful mood, without knowing why.

He did not mention his visit to Forestier.

But during the following days he remembered her, not just in the abstract, but with the haunting impression of her physical presence in his imagination. He felt that he had taken away with him part of her, personally (and he could see her body in his mind's eye), while his heart warmed to the liveliness of her personality. He remained obsessed by this image of her, as sometimes happens when you have spent many hours in the company of a charming woman. You feel as though some strange, confused, disturbing force has taken possession of your whole being, a force that seems all the more precious because of its mystery.

After a few days he called a second time.

The maid showed him into the drawing-room and Laurine came in at once. This time she did not offer to shake hands but put up her forehead for a kiss:

'Mama told me to ask you to wait,' she said. 'She's getting dressed and she'll be here in a quarter of an hour. I'll keep you company.'

Amused by the little girl's solemn ways, Duroy replied:

'Splendid, I'll enjoy having a quarter of an hour together with you. But I must warn you that I'm not at all a serious kind of person and I like to play games all the time. So I suggest we have a game of tag.'

The little girl looked startled and then, just as a woman would have done, she smiled at the idea, which rather shocked as well as surprised her. She said quietly:

'Flats aren't made for playing in.'

He replied:

'I don't mind. I'll play anywhere. So off we go, you catch me.'

And he started moving round the table, encouraging her

to chase him while she came after him, still with a polite, rather condescending smile on her face, occasionally putting her hand out to touch him but without letting herself go to the extent of running.

He stopped, ducked and when she came up to him, still rather hesitantly, he sprang into the air like a jack-in-the-box and bounded to the other end of the room in one big jump. She thought that was funny and at last started laughing; and as she became more excited, she began to chase him properly, with shy little exclamations of pleasure each time she thought she had caught him. He shifted the chairs to block her way and made her dodge round one of them for a while before moving on and doing the same with the next. Laurine was really running now, letting herself go and thoroughly enjoying this new game. All pink in the face, she was now dashing after him like a delighted child while each time he slipped away or tricked her by pretending to be caught.

Suddenly, just as she thought she had caught him, he seized her in his arms, lifted her up to the ceiling and shouted: 'Tag off-the-ground!'

The little girl gleefully kicked her legs to escape, laughing with all her might.

Madame de Marelle came in and stood dumbfounded:

'Laurine ... Laurine actually playing a game! Monsieur Duroy, you're a magician.'

He put the little girl down, kissed her mother's hand and they sat down with the child between them. They tried to talk but Laurine was so excited that although she normally had nothing to say, she now chattered so much that she had to be sent to her room.

She obeyed without saying a word but there were tears in her eyes.

As soon as they were alone, Madame de Marelle lowered her voice:

'I haven't told you but I've got a big plan in mind and you come into it. It's this. As I go to dinner with the Forestiers once a week, I return their hospitality every so often in a restaurant. I don't like having people here, I'm not organized for that sort of thing and anyway I don't know the first thing about running a household or cooking or anything at all really. I'm a happy-go-lucky sort of person. So I invite them to a restaurant now and then but it's not very amusing when there are only three of us and the people I know don't really go with them. I'm telling you all this to explain this rather strange invitation. The point is, you see, that I'd like you to come and join us next Saturday at the Café Riche at seven-thirty. Do you know it?'

Duroy accepted gladly. She went on:

'There'll just be the four of us, two men and two women. That sort of little party is rather fun for us women who don't often have the chance.'

She was wearing an alluring and provocative dark red dress that fitted tightly round her waist and hips and over her breasts and arms; and Duroy had a strange feeling of surprise and almost embarrassment which he found it hard to explain at the discrepancy between such tasteful, well-groomed elegance and her obvious indifference towards the place where she lived.

Every article of clothing on her body, everything intimately and directly connected with her flesh, was delicate and refined, but her surroundings had ceased to have any importance for her.

He left and, as before, her presence continued to haunt his senses almost like an hallucination. He awaited the dinner with growing impatience.

Once again he hired his evening clothes, since he still did not have the wherewithal to buy them, and he was the first to arrive at the café a few minutes before the time arranged.

He was shown up to the second floor and into a small

room draped in red, whose only window looked out onto the boulevard.

On the square table laid for four, the white tablecloth had an almost polished sheen and the glasses, the silver and the chafing-dish glittered under the light of the twelve candles in two tall candelabra.

Outside, the leaves of a tree made a pale green patch which glinted in the bright lights from the private rooms.

Duroy sat down on a very low settee, red like the walls; its tired springs gave way beneath his weight, making him feel as if he were sinking into a hole. Throughout the whole area of the vast café he could hear a confused murmur; the hum of a big restaurant, consisting of the clatter of plates and the tinkle of silver, the sound of waiters scurrying along the corridors, their steps muffled by the carpet, the sound of doors being opened so that for a second or two you could hear the voices of the diners enclosed in their little rooms. Forestier came in and gave him a hearty handshake with a friendliness which he never vouchsafed in the offices of *La Vie française*.

'The two ladies are coming on together,' he said. 'I must say these dinners are rather fun!'

Then he cast an eye over the table, told the waiter to turn out a small gas-lamp that had been supplementing the candles, shut one of the casement windows to prevent a draught and chose a well-sheltered seat, announcing as he did so:

'I've got to be very careful. I felt better for a month and now it's come back a few days ago. I must have caught cold last Tuesday coming out of the theatre.'

The door opened and in came the two young women, followed by the head waiter. Hidden behind their veils they had the discreetly mysterious charm of women who frequent such places where the people around you or whom you meet all tend to be disreputable.

As Duroy shook hands with Madame Forestier, she complained that he had not been to see her again, adding with a smile directed at Clotilde:

'I see, you prefer Madame de Marelle, you find plenty of time for her.'

Then they sat down and as the head waiter handed the wine-list to Forestier, Madame de Marelle exclaimed:

'You can give those gentlemen what they want. We want some ice-cold champagne, the best you've got, sweet champagne I mean, nothing else.'

And when the man had gone out, she said with an excited laugh: 'I feel like getting tipsy tonight, let's make a night of it, really let our hair down.'

Forestier, who seemed not to have heard, said:

'Do you mind if I shut the window? My chest has been a bit troublesome this last day or two.'

'No, not at all.'

So he went and closed the other half-open casement. Then he came and sat down again, relieved and looking more relaxed.

His wife said nothing and seemed absorbed in her own thoughts; looking down at the table, she was smiling in the direction of the glasses with that same vague smile that seemed to be perpetually promising but never keeping its promise.

Succulent Ostend oysters were brought in, looking like dainty little ears enclosed in shells and melting between the tongue and the palate like salty tidbits.

After the soup came a trout as pink-fleshed as a young girl; tongues began to wag.

First they talked about a current rumour concerning a

society woman caught, by a friend of her husband's, dining in a private room with a foreign prince.

Forestier was greatly amused by the story; the two women declared that the friend had been both cowardly and caddish to tell tales out of school. Duroy agreed with them and declared loudly that every man ought to be as silent as the grave in such matters whether he had been actively involved, had only heard about it, or had been a mere onlooker.

He added:

'Wouldn't life be full of charm if we could always rely on each other's absolute discretion. Women often hold back, in fact very often, almost always, for fear their guilty secret will come out.'

And he added with a smile:

'Don't you agree?

'There are so many women who would give way to a passing whim, a sudden violent desire or an amorous fancy if they weren't afraid that their brief moment of happiness would end in a dreadful scandal and bitter tears.'

He spoke with infectious conviction as if pleading a cause, his own cause, as if saying: 'You needn't be afraid of that sort of risk with me. Try it and see.'

They were both watching him with approving eyes, impressed by the good sense of his remarks; and their friendly silence was a confession that their rigid code of morality as Parisian wives would not have survived long if they were certain not to be found out.

And Forestier, who was almost lying on the settee, with one of his legs tucked underneath him and his napkin stuffed into his waistcoat to avoid staining his suit, suddenly said vigorously with a cynical laugh:

'Good God, yes, they'd have a good time if they were sure there'd be no scandal. My God! Poor old husbands!'

And the conversation turned to love. Though he would not agree that it could ever be eternal, Duroy considered that it should nevertheless be lasting and create a bond of tenderness, friendship and trust. The union of two bodies was only the seal set on the union of two souls. But he strongly criticized the torments of jealousy, the tragedies, the scenes and the heartbreak that almost always accompany the end of an affair.

When he had finished speaking, Madame de Marelle gave a sigh:

'Yes, it's the only nice thing in life and we often spoil it by making impossible demands.'

Madame Forestier, who was playing with a knife, added:

'Yes . . . yes, it's nice to be loved.'

And she seemed to be pursuing her own train of thought, and letting her mind run on things that she did not dare to express.

And, as they were still waiting for the first entrée, they kept on taking little gulps of champagne as they nibbled pieces of crust from their rolls of bread. And slowly the idea of love permeated their thoughts and little by little filled them with intoxication, just as the pale sparkling wine trickling down their throats made their blood run faster and confused their minds.

The next course was tender, dainty lamb cutlets, lying on a thick layer of tiny asparagus tips.

'My God, that looks good!' exclaimed Forestier. And they ate them slowly, relishing the delicate meat and the rich creamy vegetable.

Duroy went on:

'When I love a woman, everything else vanishes apart from her.'

He spoke with conviction, inspired by the pleasures of the table in which he was indulging.

Madame Forestier said softly, with her usual demure look:

'There's no happiness to be compared with the first gentle

squeeze of the hands, when the woman asks: "Do you love me?" and the man replies, "Yes, darling, I do."'

Madame de Marelle, who had just emptied a fresh glass of champagne at one gulp, said gaily as she put down her glass:

'I'm not quite so platonic.'

And the eyes of the others lit up as they all sniggered approvingly.

Forestier lay flat on the settee and spreading out his arms on the cushions said solemnly:

'Such frankness does you credit and proves that you're a practical woman. But may one ask what is Monsieur de Marelle's opinion on the subject?'

With a slow shrug of her shoulders and infinite, lingering contempt, she replied emphatically:

'Monsieur de Marelle has no opinion on the matter. He is ... he's an abstainer.'

And, leaving the realm of noble theories of courtly love, the conversation descended to the primrose path of elegant smut.

They had reached the stage of witty suggestiveness, of words, veiled yet revealing, that are like a hand lifting up a skirt, the stage of clever allusions, skilfully hidden impropriety, shamelessly brazen hypocrisy, cryptic words that cover naked images and which fill the eye and the mind with a sudden vision of what dare not be said openly and enables smart society to enjoy a subtle, mysterious sort of lovemaking, a sort of marriage of impure minds, by simultaneously conjuring up, with words as sensual and disturbing as a sexual embrace, the secret, shameful desire for body to clasp body. The roast had now appeared, partridges garnished with quail and then green peas, followed by pâté de foie gras with a salad whose frizzy leaves were like froth in the large round salad bowl. They had eaten it all without

86

tasting it properly, without realizing what they were eating, entirely absorbed in what they were saying, immersed in thoughts of love.

Now the two women were both letting themselves go, Madame de Marelle in a naturally brazen way that seemed deliberately provocative, while Madame Forestier's charmingly demure and modest tone, voice, smile and general demeanor, while seeming to mitigate the boldness of the words which she was uttering, in fact emphasized it.

Sprawling on the cushions, Forestier kept on laughing, drinking and eating without a pause, now and again using an expression so outrageous or coarse that the women, rather shocked by the form as well as for form's sake, looked slightly embarrassed for a second or two. When he had delivered himself of some particularly smutty remark, he would add: 'You're doing very well, girls. If you keep on like that, you'll end up by doing something silly.'

Dessert was served, followed by coffee. The liqueurs brought an extra flush to their cheeks and befuddled their excited minds still more.

As she had promised when sitting down to table, Madame de Marelle was tipsy and this she acknowledged by chatting cheerfully on, like a hostess playing up her slight intoxication in order to amuse her guests.

Possibly for reasons of caution Madame Forestier had now stopped talking, and Duroy, realizing that he was too much the worse for drink not to compromise himself, was shrewd enough to show a certain restraint.

They lit their cigarettes and all of a sudden Forestier started coughing.

It was a dreadful spasm that racked his chest; red-faced, his forehead covered in sweat, he fought for breath as he covered his mouth with his napkin. When the attack was over, he muttered angrily: 'These parties are no good for me at all. It's idiotic.' His good humour had completely evaporated, driven out by the dreadful fear of the illness which haunted his mind.

'Let's go,' he said.

Madame de Marelle rang for the waiter and asked for the bill. It was brought almost immediately. She tried to read it, but the figures danced up and down in front of her eyes and she handed it to Duroy.

'Here you are, pay it for me. I can't read it, I'm too tipsy.' And she tossed him her purse as she spoke.

The bill was 130 francs. Duroy checked it, handed over two notes, took the change and asked in a whisper:

'How much shall I leave the waiters?'

'Whatever you like, I don't know.'

He put five francs on the plate and then gave the young woman her purse back, saying:

'Would you like me to see you home?'

'Yes, please. I couldn't find my way alone.'

They shook hands with the Forestiers and Duroy found himself alone with Madame de Marelle in a moving cab.

He could feel her beside him, so close, shut in together in this dark box briefly lit up for half a second each time they passed the gas-lights on the pavement. Through his sleeve he could feel the warmth of her shoulder and he could find nothing to say to her, not one word, so obsessed was he by the overwhelming desire to take her into his arms.

'If I were to risk it, what would she do?' he was thinking. And the memory of all the outrageous things that had been whispered over dinner encouraged him, but at the same time fear of shocking her held him back.

She was silent too, sitting back motionless in her corner. He might have thought that she had gone to sleep had he not seen her eyes shining each time a ray of light fell into the cab.

What was she thinking of? He felt sure that he must not break the silence, that one word, one single word would destroy his chances; but he did not have the necessary boldness to act swiftly and decisively.

Suddenly he felt her foot move. She had made a movement, a sudden twitch of impatience or perhaps of encouragement. This barely perceptible gesture electrified his whole body and turning swiftly, he flung himself on her seeking her lips with his, his hands groping for her bare flesh.

She uttered a cry, a little cry, and tried to sit up as she struggled to push him away; and then she stopped struggling as if her strength had deserted her and she could resist no longer.

But the cab soon stopped in front of her house and, taken by surprise, Duroy had no need to find any passionate expressions of thanks or devotion or gratitude. Meanwhile she remained seated, not moving, stunned by what had just happened. He was afraid that the driver might become suspicious and he got out first to offer the young woman his hand.

Finally she stumbled out of the cab, without saying a word. He rang the bell and as the door opened, he asked her in a trembling voice: 'When can I see you again?'

So quietly that he could hardly hear her, she whispered: 'Come and have lunch with me tomorrow.' And she disappeared into the hallway, slamming the heavy door behind her with a loud thud.

He gave the cabby five francs and set off at a brisk pace, overjoyed at his conquest.

At last he had succeeded in laying hands on a married woman, a smart society woman, a woman belonging to Parisian society. How easy and unexpected it had turned out to be!

Until now he had imagined that in order to approach and

conquer such a desirable creature, you needed to deploy infinite care and attention, be endlessly patient and skilfully lay siege with well-turned compliments, words of love, expressions of tenderness, sighs and gifts. And now suddenly, under the slightest pressure, the first one he had met had given herself to him with an alacrity that left him quite bewildered.

'She'd had too much to drink,' he thought. 'Tomorrow it'll be a different story. She'll be all tearful.' This thought troubled him and then he said: 'Ah well, that can't be helped. Now that I've got her, I'll take good care not to let her go.'

And in the tangled mirage of his hopes, hopes of achieving greatness and success, fame, wealth and love, suddenly, like a grande finale, with festoons of beautiful girls swirling through the sky, he glimpsed a whole procession of rich, elegant, powerful women who passed smiling by and disappeared one after the other in the golden haze of his dreams.

And his sleep was peopled with visions.

As he went up Madame de Marelle's staircase next day, he felt rather nervous. How would he be received? And suppose she refused to see him? Suppose she had given orders not to let him in? Suppose she told ... No, that was impossible, she couldn't say anything without running the risk of giving the whole game away. So he was in control of the situation.

The little maid opened the door. She looked the same as usual. He took heart, as if he had been expecting her to look upset.

He asked:

'Is your mistress well?'

She replied:

'Yes sir, the same as ever.'

And she showed him into the drawing-room.

He went straight up to the mantelshelf to make sure his hair and clothes were in order and just as he was adjusting his tie in the mirror, he saw in it the young woman standing in the doorway, looking at him.

He pretended not to see her and they stood eyeing each other for a few seconds in the mirror, watching each other closely before coming face to face.

He turned round. She had not moved and seemed to be waiting. He sprang towards her stammering: 'Oh, I love you, how I do love you!' She opened her arms and flung herself into his; then she raised her face and they exchanged a long, long kiss.

He was thinking: 'It's easier than I thought. It's all going very well.' And when their lips parted, he smiled without speaking, trying to express endless love in his eyes.

She too was smiling, a smile full of desire, consent and surrender.

She whispered:

'We're alone. I've sent Laurine off to lunch with a friend.'

He kissed her wrists and breathed:

'Thank you, you're adorable.'

Then she took his arm as if he were her husband and they went over to sit down side by side on the settee.

To start their conversation he needed something clever and fascinating; as he could not find it he said, hesitantly:

'So you're not too cross with me?'

She put her hand over his mouth:

'Sh!'

They sat silent, looking into each other's eyes, their burning fingers entwined.

'I wanted you so much,' he said.

'Sh!' she repeated.

Plates were clattering in the next room as the maid laid the table.

He stood up:

'I can't stay so close to you. I'll do something silly.'

The door opened:

'Lunch is served.'

He solemnly offered her his arm.

They sat face to face, looking at each other and smiling all the time, thinking only of each other, under the spell of their dawning tenderness. They ate without thinking what they were eating. He felt a foot, a little foot, groping under the table. He took it between his own and held it, squeezing as hard as he could.

The maid kept coming and going, removing the dishes with apparent unconcern, as if noticing nothing.

When they had finished eating, they went back to the drawing-room and sat down again side by side on the settee. He gradually moved closer towards her, trying to take her into his arms. But she quietly pushed him away.

'Be careful, someone might come in.'

He said in a low voice:

'When can I see you on your own so that I can tell you how much I love you?'

She leant towards him and whispered in his ear:

'I'll come and pay you a little visit in your flat one of these days.'

He felt himself blushing:

'Well ... actually ... my room isn't a very nice one.'

She smiled:

'That doesn't matter. It's you I shall be visiting, not your room.'

He urged her to tell him when she would come. She mentioned a date towards the end of the following week but in stumbling phrases he pleaded with her to change the date, clutching and squeezing her hands, his eyes shining, his face flushed and contorted with desire, the wild desire that a man feels when he has had a meal tête-à-tête with a woman.

She was amused at his frantic pleading and gradually conceded a day here and a day there. But he kept saying:

'Tomorrow . . . do say tomorrow.'

She finally consented:

'All right, then. Tomorrow at five o'clock.'

He gave a long gasp of joy and then they started chatting quietly and intimately as though they had known each other for twenty years.

The sound of the bell made them start and they sprang quickly apart.

She said in a low voice: 'That must be Laurine.'

The child came in, stopped in surprise and then clapping her hands, she ran towards Duroy, overjoyed at seeing him. She cried:

'Oh, Bel-Ami!'

Madame de Marelle laughed:

'Well now! Bel-Ami! Laurine has baptized you! That's a nice friendly nickname for you. I'm going to call you Bel-Ami too.'

He took the little girl on to his knee and she insisted on playing all the little games that he had taught her.

At twenty minutes to three he stood up to go to the office and on the stairs, through the half-open door, he whispered:

'Tomorrow. Five o'clock.'

The young woman smiled: 'Yes!' and disappeared.

As soon as he had finished his work that day, he tried to think how he might arrange his room for her visit so as to hide its seediness as much as possible. He hit on the notion of pinning tiny Japanese decorations all over the walls and he went out and bought a whole collection of pieces of coloured silk, little fans and small screens which he used to

93

hide the more obvious stains on the wallpaper. On the window-panes he stuck transparent pictures of boats on rivers, flocks of birds flying across red skies, women of all the colours of the rainbow standing on balconies and processions of little black figures on plains covered in snow.

Soon his room, barely big enough to sleep and sit down in, looked like the inside of a Chinese lantern. He was pleased with the effect and spent the evening sticking birds on the ceiling, which he cut out of the remaining sheets of coloured paper.

Then he went to bed, lulled by the whistles of the trains.

Next day he came home early with a bag of cakes, and a bottle of Madeira which he had bought at the grocer's. He had to go out again to buy two plates and glasses; and he arranged the food and drink on his dirty wooden washstand, which he concealed under a table-napkin, hiding the basin and jug underneath.

Then he waited.

She arrived at about quarter past five and, captivated by the glittering effect of the pictures, she exclaimed:

'Oh, your room's nice. But there are a lot of people on the staircase.'

He took her in his arms and was feverishly kissing her hair through her veil between her forehead and her hat.

An hour and a half later, he went with her to the cab-rank in the Rue de Rome. When she had got in, he whispered: 'Tuesday, at the same time.'

She replied: 'At the same time, Tuesday.' And as it was now dark she pulled his head towards the carriage window and kissed him on the lips. Then, as the driver cracked his whip, she cried: 'Goodbye, Bel-Ami', and the old hansom lumbered slowly off behind its white horse.

For the next three weeks, Madame de Marelle came to see Duroy every two or three days, sometimes in the morning, sometimes in the evening.

One afternoon, as he was waiting for her, he heard a loud noise on the stairs and went to his door. A child was yelling. The angry voice of a man shouted: 'What's that brat making such a hullaballoo about now?' An exasperated woman's voice screeched back: 'It's that tart what comes to see the journalist upstairs. She knocked our Nicholas over on the landing. Oughtn't to be allowed, sluts like that what don't even watch out for children on the staircase!'

Disconcerted, Duroy beat a retreat because he could hear a swift rustling of skirts and the hurried step of someone coming up from the floor below.

Very soon there came a knock at the door which he had just closed behind him. He opened it and a scared Madame de Marelle ran into the room, gasping:

'Did you hear that?'

He feigned ignorance:

'No, what was it?'

'How they insulted me?'

'Who did?'

'Those beastly people downstairs.'

'No, I didn't. What happened, tell me.'

But she was unable to speak and began sobbing.

He was obliged to take off her hat, loosen her corsets, lay her down on the bed and dab her temples with a wet cloth. She could hardly breathe. Then, when she had regained some of her composure, her indignation burst out.

She wanted him to go downstairs at once to attack them, kill them.

He kept on saying: 'But they're workers, just louts. Don't forget you'd have to sue them, that you might be recognized and arrested, ruined. There's no point in having dealings with people like that.'

She had another thought: 'What shall we do now? I can't possibly come back here.' He replied: 'That's easy. I'll move.'

She replied more quietly: 'Yes, but that'll take some time.'
Then all at once she hit upon an idea and suddenly relaxed:

'No, listen, I can arrange it, don't you worry. I'll send you an express letter tomorrow.'

What she called an express letter was a sort of telegram sent by pneumatic tube all over Paris.

She was all smiles now at the thought of her idea, which she refused to divulge; and she flung herself whole-heartedly into their love-making.

But as she went downstairs again, she was very nervous and she clung to her lover's arm to support her shaking legs.

They saw no one.

As he used to sleep late, he was still in bed when the messenger delivered the promised note at about eleven o'clock the following morning.

Duroy opened it and read:

'We'll meet at five o'clock this afternoon at 127 Rue de Constantinople. Ask for Madame Duroy's flat. Love and kisses, Clo.'

At five o'clock exactly, he went into the porter's lodge of a large block of flats and asked:

'Is this where Madame Duroy has rented an apartment?'

'Yes sir.'

'Can you show me up to it, please?'

No doubt accustomed to delicate situations where discretion is required, the man peered at him sharply and, picking out one from a long row of keys, asked:

'Are you Monsieur Duroy, sir?'

'Of course.'

And he opened a little two-roomed flat on the ground floor opposite the porter's lodge.

The drawing-room had a wallpaper with a floral pattern, in quite good condition, and mahogany furniture upholstered in a sort of green rep with a yellow design and an exiguous flower-patterned carpet which was so thin that you could feel the floorboards underneath.

The bedroom was so tiny that the bed took up three-quarters of the space. It occupied the whole end of the room and stretched from one wall to the next, the sort of bed normally found in furnished apartments, swathed in heavy blue curtains, also of rep, and hidden beneath a massive red silk eiderdown covered in dubious stains.

Duroy grumbled to himself as he reflected uneasily: 'This flat's going to cost me the earth. I'm going to have to borrow more money. She's done a stupid thing.'

The door opened, and with a great rustling of skirts, Clotilde dashed in, flinging her arms wide open. She was delighted.

'Isn't it nice, eh, isn't it nice? And no stairs to go up, it's on the ground floor, at street level. One can get in and out through the window without being seen by the porter. What a wonderful little love-nest for us!'

He kissed her coldly, not daring to ask the question which was on his lips.

She had put a big parcel down on the small table in the middle of the room. Now she opened it and took out a piece of soap, some Lubin toilet-water, a sponge, a box of hairpins, a button-hook and a pair of little curling tongs that she used for the curls on her forehead, which invariably came out every time.

And she played at moving in, finding a place for everything, enjoying herself tremendously.

She kept on chattering as she opened the drawers:

'I must bring some underwear so that I can change if necessary. It'll be very convenient. If I'm caught in a shower, perhaps, while I'm shopping, I'll come and get dry here. We'll each have a key apart from the one left in the porter's lodge in case we forget our own. I've rented it for three months in your name, of course, because I couldn't give mine.'

Then he asked:

'You'll tell me when I have to pay, won't you?'

She replied simply:

'But it's paid, darling.'

He went on:

'So I owe it to you, then?'

'But of course not, sweety, that doesn't concern you, it's a little extravagance that I want to pay for.'

He pretended to be annoyed:

'No, that won't do at all. I won't allow it.'

She came up to him and put her hands on his shoulders entreatingly:

'Georges, please, please let me do it, it'll give me so much pleasure, so much pleasure that our little love-nest belongs to me and to nobody else. You can't be cross at that? Why should you be? I want to give it to us both as a present for our love. Tell me you agree, Georgy pie, do say you agree?'

She was imploring him with her eyes, her lips, her whole being.

He resisted her persuasion, pretended to be irritated and finally gave way, thinking that, after all, it was only fair.

And when she had left, he muttered to himself, rubbing his hands and without searching his conscience too closely to discover why he had that particular thought that day:

'She's really rather nice.'

A few days later he received another express letter, saying:

'My husband is coming back this evening after a six weeks' tour of inspection. So we must put up the shutters for a week. A beastly chore, darling. Your Clo.'

Duroy was quite disconcerted. He had almost forgotten

that she was married. Now that was a man whose face he'd like to see, just once, so as to make his acquaintance.

He waited patiently for the husband to go off again. But he spent two evenings at the Folies-Bergère, going home with Rachel each time.

Then one morning a fresh telegram came, containing five words:

'This afternoon, five o'clock. Clo.'

They both arrived early. She flung herself lovingly into his arms, kissing his face passionately all over. Then she said:

'If you like, when we've made love really nicely, you can take me out to dinner somewhere. I've arranged to be free this evening.'

It was, in fact, the beginning of the month and although his salary was mortgaged for a long time ahead and he was living from hand to mouth with any odd money he was able to pick up, Duroy happened to be in funds and he was pleased to have the chance to spend something on her.

He replied:

'Would you like to go to Père Lathuille's place?'

She replied: 'Oh no, that's too smart, I'd like some odd sort of place, somewhere common, like a restaurant where shop assistants and working girls go. I adore going eating and dancing in little cafés on the outskirts of Paris. If only we'd been able to go out into the country.'

As he did not know anything of that sort in the quarter, they wandered along the boulevard and ended by going into a cheap wine-shop which served meals in a separate room. Through the window she had seen two girls sitting at a table opposite two soldiers.

At the end of the long, narrow room three cabbies were eating and there was also a man whom it was impossible to classify under any profession: he was sitting with his legs stretched out, his hands stuck in his belt, smoking a pipe, sprawled on his chair with his head lolling over the back. His coat was a collector's piece for stains and in his bulging pockets you could glimpse the neck of a bottle, a lump of bread, a parcel wrapped in a newspaper and a piece of string dangling down. His hair was thick and curly, tangled and grey with filth and his cap was on the ground under his chair.

The elegance of Clotilde's clothes caused a sensation as she went in. The two couples stopped whispering, the three cabbies stopped arguing and the individual who was smoking removed the pipe from his mouth, spat on the floor in front of him and turned his head slightly to look at them.

Madame de Marelle said in a low voice: 'It's very nice. It's just what we want. Next time, I'll dress like a working girl.' And, without any embarrassment or distaste, she sat down at a wooden table, shiny with grease from the food and wet with spilt drinks, which the waiter gave a quick dab with a cloth. Duroy, slightly ill-at-ease and sheepish, was looking round for a hook to hang his top hat on and, not finding one, he put it down on a chair.

They had mutton stew and a slice of leg of lamb with salad. Clotilde kept on saying: 'I adore this sort of place. I've got common tastes. I think this is more fun than the Café Anglais.' Then she said: 'If you really want to please me very much, take me to a dance-hall. I know a very amusing one quite close to here called La Reine Blanche.'

Surprised, Duroy asked:

'Who took you there?'

He was looking at her and saw her blush, slightly confused, as if his sudden question had revived an embarrassing memory.

After one of those feminine hesitations so short as to be barely perceptible, she answered: 'A man I knew ...', and then, after a pause, she added: 'who died.' And with a perfectly natural show of sadness, she lowered her eyes.

For the first time, Duroy thought of all that was hidden in her past and he began to speculate. Obviously she'd already had lovers, but what sort were they and what kind of society did they come from? A vague jealousy, a sort of hostility against her, stirred in him, an hostility directed against everything that he did not know about her, all that part of her feelings and life which did not belong to him. He looked at her, irritated by the secrets hidden in that pretty, silent little head, which perhaps at that very moment was thinking with regret of another man, of other men. How he would have liked to peer into her memories, explore them and learn all there was to know about them!...

She repeated:

'Will you take me to La Reine Blanche? It'll be a perfect ending to a perfect evening.'

He thought to himself: 'Ah well, what does the past matter? It's stupid of me to worry about it.' With a smile, he answered:

'Of course, darling.'

Once they were in the street, she whispered very quietly and mysteriously, in the way one confides a secret:

'I didn't dare to ask you before but you can't imagine how I enjoy this sort of bachelor outing in all these places where women don't go. For carnival I'll dress up as a schoolboy. I look awfully amusing as a schoolboy.'

When they went into the dance-hall, she held tightly to his arm, scared and pleased, casting delighted glances at the whores and the pimps and each time she caught sight of a solemn, stolid military policeman, she would say, as though to reassure herself against any possible danger: 'He's got a good solid look.' After a quarter of an hour she had had enough and he took her home.

So began a series of excursions to all the dubious haunts where the great unwashed go to amuse themselves; and Duroy discovered that his mistress had a passionate liking for prowling round the town like a student out on a spree.

She would arrive at the usual time dressed in a coarse linen dress, wearing a maid's bonnet, like a soubrette in a French farce; and despite the deliberate, elegant simplicity of her dress, she would keep on all her rings and bracelets and her diamond ear-rings. When he urged her to take them off, she said: 'Oh, they'll think they're rhinestones.'

She thought her disguise was wonderful; and although, in fact, she was merely concealed ostrich-fashion, she went into the most disreputable drinking haunts.

She wanted Duroy to dress like a workman but he insisted on wearing his fashionable clothes of the man-about-town and was not even prepared to exchange his top-hat for a soft felt one.

She consoled herself for his refusal by saying: 'They'll think I'm a skivvy who's got a rich young lover.' And she found this a delightful pretence.

So they would go into low dives and sit down at the end of the squalid smoky room on rickety chairs at decrepit wooden tables. An acrid cloud of smoke and the smell of fried fish filled the room; men in their working clothes were shouting at each other as they downed their glasses of raw spirits; and the waiter would stare at the strange couple as he put the two cherries-in-brandy down in front of them.

Scared and trembling, but blissfully happy, she would begin sipping the red fruity liquid, looking around her, bright-eyed but uneasy: each time she swallowed a cherry, she felt she was doing something wrong, every drop of the spicy, burning liquid that slipped down her throat gave her a sharp pleasure, the pleasure of forbidden fruit, of being naughty.

Then she would whisper: 'Let's go.' And so they would leave. She slipped away hastily, tripping along and holding her head down, like an actress leaving the stage, between the drinkers sitting with their elbows on the table, who looked up with a suspicious, surly air as she went by. And when she was through the door, she gave a big gasp as if she had just escaped from some terrible danger.

Sometimes, with a shudder, she asked Duroy:

'What would you do if they insulted me in a place like that?'

He said airily:

'Defend you, of course!'

And she clung happily to his arm, perhaps longing to be insulted and defended, to see men fighting for her, even those men, with her sweetheart.

But when these excursions took place two or three times a week, Duroy began to grow tired of them; moreover, for some time past he had been experiencing difficulty in finding the ten francs that he needed to pay for the cab and the drinks.

For it was now proving extremely hard to live, even harder than when he was a railway clerk, because, having spent large sums of money without thinking twice during his first few months as a journalist, always in the hope of earning vast sums the next day, he had exhausted his resources, as well as all the other ways of raising money.

One simple source, borrowing money from the cashier, had very quickly dried up and he already owed the paper four months' salary, plus six francs per line for his articles. In addition he owed Forestier 100 francs, Jacques Rival, who was open-handed, 300, and he had a horde of niggling debts that he hardly liked mentioning, ranging from twenty francs to five.

When Saint-Potin had been consulted as to the appropriate methods to employ to obtain another 100 francs he had proved unable to help, despite all his resourcefulness; and Duroy was exasperated at being so short of money, which he felt more keenly than before, because his needs were greater. He felt a simmering rage against everyone and a constant irritation which expressed itself all the time and at every turn, for the most futile reasons.

Sometimes he wondered how he had managed to spend an average of 1,000 francs a month without any excessive expenditure or extravagance; and he realized that when he added up lunch at eight francs and dinner at twelve, eaten in one of the large boulevard cafés, plus ten francs or so pocket money, which slips through your pocket without noticing, there was a total of thirty francs. And thirty francs a day was 900 a month. And that didn't include his clothing, his footwear, his linen or his laundry and so on.

So, on 14 December, he found that he had not a sou left in his pocket and had no idea in his mind how to lay his hands on one.

He did what he had frequently done in the past and missed lunch. He spent the afternoon at the paper, worried and fuming.

At about four o'clock, he received an express letter from his mistress, saying: 'Shall we have dinner together? Afterwards we can go and have fun somewhere.'

He replied at once: 'Dinner not possible.' Then he reflected that it would be stupid to deprive himself of the pleasure of her company and added: 'But will wait for you at our place at nine o'clock.'

He sent one of the messengers to deliver the note to save the price of a telegram and then started to think how he might manage to pay for his evening meal.

By seven o'clock he had still not succeeded in discovering anything. So he resorted to a stratagem of despair. He waited for all his colleagues to leave, one after the other, and when he was the only person left, he sharply tugged the bell. It was answered by the director's chief clerk, who had been left in charge of the office.

Duroy was standing nervously fumbling in his pockets and said abruptly:

'I say, Foucart, I've left my wallet at home and I've got to go to dinner at the Luxembourg. Lend me fifty sous to pay for my cab.'

The clerk pulled three francs out of his waistcoat pocket and asked:

'Will that be enough, sir?'

'Yes, that's plenty, thanks.'

And taking the three silver coins, Duroy ran down the staircase and went off to dine in the cheap restaurant where he used to end up in his days of poverty.

At nine o'clock he was waiting for his mistress, warming his feet in front of the cosy fire in the drawing-room.

She arrived full of gaiety and high spirits, invigorated by the brisk cold outside:

'If you like, we'll go for a little walk first and then we'll come back here in a couple of hours' time. It's wonderful weather for walking.'

He grunted:

'Why go out? We're very comfortable here.'

Without taking off her hat, she went on:

'If you only knew what a wonderful moon there is. It's a real pleasure out walking this evening.'

'That may be so but I'm not keen on going for a walk.'

He said this in an angry voice. She was surprised and offended and asked:

'What's wrong? Why are you behaving like that? I'd like to go for a walk, I don't see why that should annoy you.'

He sat up resentfully:

'It's not annoying me. I can't be bothered, that's all.'

She was the sort of woman who is irritated when opposed and exasperated by rudeness.

Haughtily, with anger in her voice, she said coldly:

'I'm not used to being spoken to like that. I'll go for a walk by myself. Goodbye!'

He realized that she was taking it to heart and so he quickly went over and took hold of her hands and kissed them.

'Forgive me, darling, do forgive me,' he stammered. 'I'm very nervous this evening, very touchy. The fact is that I've got lots of things on my mind, you know, troubles at the office.'

She replied, more gently but still not appeased:

'That's nothing to do with me and I'm not going to put up with the effects of your bad temper.'

He took her in his arms and drew her towards the settee:

'Listen, sweetie, I didn't want to offend you. I wasn't thinking what I was saying.'

He had forced her to sit down and was kneeling in front of her:

'Have you forgiven me? Tell me you've forgiven me.'

She said coldly: 'All right but don't do it again.' And getting up, she added: 'And now let's go for our walk.'

He had remained on his knees, with his hands round her hips. He said uncertainly:

'Please, please, let's stay here. I do beg you, darling. Do that much for me. I'd so much like to keep you all for myself this evening, here beside the fire. Do say yes, I implore you, say yes.'

She answered harshly and abruptly:

'No, I'm keen for a walk and I'm not going to give in to your whims.'

He insisted:

'I implore you, I've got a reason, a serious reason.'

She repeated:

'No. If you don't want to go out with me, I shall leave. Goodbye.'

She had shaken herself free and was making for the door. He ran after her and clutched her in his arms.

'Listen, Clo darling, do listen, do that much for me.' She shook her head without answering, struggling to free herself and go.

He said falteringly:

'Clo, Clo darling, I do have a reason.'

She stopped and looked him in the face:

'You're lying. What is it?'

He blushed, not knowing what to say. She went on irately:

'You see, you're lying ... you rotten beast.' And with tears in her eyes, she angrily tore herself out of his arms.

He seized her by the shoulders again and in desperation, ready to confess everything in order to keep her, he said despondently:

'The truth is I'm completely broke ... So now you know.'

She stopped abruptly, peering into his eyes to see if he was speaking the truth:

'What's that?'

He had blushed to the roots of his hair: 'I said that I'm completely broke. Can't you understand? I haven't got five francs, not a franc, not enough to pay for a glass of cassis if we go into a café. You're making me confess things that I'm ashamed to admit. You must agree that I couldn't possibly have gone out with you and then when we were sitting down with our drinks, calmly tell you that I couldn't pay for them ...'

She was still looking him in the face:

'So ... it's really true ... what you said?'

And there and then he turned out all his pockets, his trousers, his waistcoat, his coat, muttering:

'There you are ... now are you satisfied?'

All at once she opened her arms and flung them passionately round his neck, saying brokenly:

'Oh my poor darling ... my poor, poor darling ... If only I'd known. How did it happen?'

She sat him down and perching herself on his knees, her arms round his neck, kissing him all the time on his moustache, his eyes, his mouth, she made him tell her how such a misfortune had befallen him.

He invented a moving story. He had been obliged to help his poor old father who was in financial difficulties. Not only had he given him all his savings but he had accumulated a lot of debts.

He added:

'I'm going to have to go hungry for at least six months because I've come to the end of all my resources. It can't be helped, life has its ups and downs. Money's not worth bothering about, anyway.'

She whispered into his ear:

'I'll lend you some, may I?'

He replied with a dignified air:

'That's very kind of you, my dear Clotilde, but let's say no more about it, please. I'd be offended.'

She was silent. Then, clasping him in her arms, she murmured: 'You'll never realize how much I love you.'

Their lovemaking that evening was as wonderful as any they had ever known.

Just as she was leaving, she said, smiling:

'When someone's in your situation wouldn't it be fun to find some money in a pocket you'd forgotten, a coin that had slipped into the lining?'

He said emphatically: 'Yes, by Jove!'

She insisted on walking home because she said the moon was superb; and she went into raptures over it.

It was a still, cold night; winter was beginning. The passers-by and the horses were all moving briskly, nipped by the clear frost; and the sound of heels echoed sharply on the pavement.

As they parted, she asked:

'Shall we meet the day after tomorrow?'

'Oh yes, let's.'

'Same time?'

'Same time.'

'Goodbye, dearest.'

They exchanged a tender kiss.

Then he strode quickly home, wondering to himself what he could think up next day to keep his head above water. But as he opened the door, fumbling in his pocket to find his matches, he was amazed to feel his fingers touching a coin.

As soon as he had lit his lamp he took out the coin to examine it. It was a gold twenty-franc piece.

He thought that he must be dreaming.

He turned it over and over, wondering by what miracle the coin had found its way there. It could hardly have dropped from heaven.

Then suddenly he understood and he was filled with indignation and annoyance. Clotilde had, in fact, mentioned money slipped into a lining which you discovered in a moment of need. She must have offered him this out of charity. How humiliating!

He swore: 'All right, I'm seeing her the day after tomorrow! We'll see how she likes what I shall say to her!'

And he went to bed, furious and resentful.

He was late in waking up. He felt hungry. He tried to go

to sleep again in order not to wake up until two o'clock. Then he said: 'That's not going to help, I'll still have to find some money in the end.' Then he went out, hoping for inspiration in the street.

No inspiration came but as he walked past each restaurant, his mouth watered with hunger. By twelve o'clock, as he still could think of nothing, he suddenly made up his mind:

'All right, I'll have lunch out of Clotilde's twenty francs. That won't prevent me from paying her back tomorrow.'

So he had lunch in a brasserie for two francs fifty. When he went to the newspaper, he gave another three francs to Walter's clerk: 'Here you are, Foucart, here's the three francs you lent me yesterday for my cab.'

And he worked until seven o'clock. Then he went off to dine and took another three francs out of the same money. A couple of beers which he drank that evening brought the day's expenditure to nine francs thirty centimes.

But as he could not find any more credit or new sources of funds in the space of twenty-four hours, next day he borrowed another six francs fifty from the twenty francs which he was intending to return that same evening, so that when he turned up for their meeting he had four francs twenty in his pocket.

He felt thoroughly annoyed and was firmly determined to make the situation absolutely plain to his mistress straightaway. He would say: 'Look, I found the twenty francs which you slipped into my pocket the other day. I can't give them back to you today because my situation hasn't changed and I haven't had time to do anything about my finances. But I'm going to return them the next time we meet.'

When she arrived she was full of tenderness, eager yet apprehensive. How was he going to greet her? And for the first few moments she smothered him in kisses to stop any attempt at an explanation.

For his part, he kept saying to himself: 'There'll be plenty of time to raise the question presently. I'll try to find an opportunity.'

But he did not succeed in finding any opportunity and so he said nothing, because he could not bring himself to broach such a delicate subject.

She did not mention going out and was all sweetness and light.

They parted at midnight after arranging not to meet until Wednesday the following week, because she was dining out several evenings in succession.

The next day, while paying for lunch and feeling for the four coins which he thought still remained, he realized that he had five and that one of them was a gold one.

For a moment he thought that he had been given a twenty franc piece by mistake the day before and then he understood and he felt his heart pounding at the thought of receiving such humiliating and persistent charity.

How sorry he was at not having said anything! If he'd spoken up firmly, this wouldn't have happened.

For the next four days he explored every means he could think of to lay his hands on five louis but all to no purpose; and so he used up Clotilde's second twenty francs.

And although he said to her with an irate air: 'Look, don't try the same trick you tried the other two evenings, because you'll make me cross', she still found the way to slip another twenty francs into his trouser pocket the next time they met.

When he discovered it he swore:

'Christ Almighty!' and transferred the coin to his waistcoat pocket, because he was without a penny.

He soothed his conscience by arguing: 'I'll give it all back at one go. I'm really only borrowing from her.'

In the end, after desperate pleading, Duroy persuaded the

cashier at the paper to give him five francs a day. It was enough to eat with, but not enough to pay back the sixty francs.

And since Clotilde was once more seized by her wild urge to go round all the low night-spots of Paris, he ended by not feeling too irritated at finding the odd gold coin in one of his pockets; once, even, in his boot and another time in his watch-case, after they had been on one of their adventurous excursions. Since she felt that sort of urge which he was unable to satisfy at the moment, wasn't it quite in order for her to pay for them rather than do without them?

Moreover, he was keeping an account of everything that he received to enable him to pay her back one day.

One evening she said to him: 'You won't believe it, but I've never been to the Folies-Bergère. Will you take me?' He hesitated because of the risk of meeting Rachel. Then he thought: 'So what, it's not as if I'm married; after all, if she sees me, she'll understand the situation and won't speak to me. In any case, we'll be in a box.'

Another reason also decided him. He was delighted at the opportunity of offering Madame de Marelle a box at the theatre without having to pay anything for it. It was a sort of compensation.

He left Clotilde in the cab while he went to fetch the tickets, so that she did not see that they were free, and then came back for her. They went in, greeted by the men at the door.

The promenade was packed. They had great difficulty in making their way through the throng of men and prowling women. Finally, they reached their little box and sat down, hemmed in between the sedate orchestra stalls and the boisterous gallery.

But Madame de Marelle was hardly looking at the stage, having eyes only for the prostitutes moving around at the back of her. She kept on turning round all the time, longing to touch them, to feel their dresses, their cheeks, their hair, just to discover what such women were made of.

Suddenly she said:

'There's a large brunette who keeps on looking at us all the time. I thought she was going to speak to us a moment ago. Did you see her?'

He replied: 'No. You must be mistaken.' But he had already caught sight of her a while ago. It was Rachel who was prowling around with an irate look and muttering angry words.

Duroy had brushed by her a moment before when they were going through the throng of people and she had said softly: 'Hallo', with a wink meaning: 'I understand.' But he had not acknowledged her friendly greeting for fear of being seen by his mistress and had walked coldly on, with his chin in the air and a contemptuous curl of the lip.

Already feeling a twinge of jealousy, the woman turned round, came back and brushing past him again, repeated more loudly: 'Hallo, Georges.'

He still made no reply. By now she was absolutely determined to be recognized and greeted and so she kept on coming back behind the box, waiting for a favourable moment.

As soon as she noticed that Madame de Marelle was watching her, she poked Duroy in the shoulder with the tip of her finger:

'Hallo. You all right?'

He did not turn round.

She went on:

'Well? Have you lost the use of your ears since last Thursday?'

He made no reply and assumed a scornful air suggesting that he could not possibly have anything to do with such a trollop, even by speaking to her.

Livid with rage, she laughed and said:

'So you've lost your tongue. Perhaps your friend's bitten it off?'

He made an infuriated gesture and retorted savagely:

'Who gave you permission to speak? Be off with you or I'll call the police.'

Then with her eyes flaming and breast heaving, she could contain herself no longer:

'So that's how it is! You dirty cad! When you've been to bed with a woman at least you say hallo. Just because you're with another woman doesn't mean you can't recognize me now. If you'd given me just a nod when I went past a moment ago, I'd have left you alone. But you wanted to be snobby, so now you'll see. I'm going to tell you a thing or two. So you won't even say hallo when I meet you.'

She would have gone on shouting for a long time but Madame de Marelle had opened the door of the box and was taking to her heels through the crowd, desperately looking for the exit.

Duroy dashed after her, trying to catch her up.

Seeing them both take flight Rachel screamed triumphantly after them:

'Stop her! Stop her! She's stolen my lover!'

A laugh ran through the crowd. As a joke two men caught hold of Madame de Marelle as she was running by and made as if to bring her back, at the same time trying to give her a kiss. But Duroy, who had caught up with her, jerked her free and dragged her outside.

She leapt into an empty cab standing in front of the theatre. He jumped in after her, and when the driver asked: 'Where to, guv?' he answered: 'Anywhere.'

The cab lumbered off over the cobble-stones. Clotilde, almost in hysterics, was sitting with her face in her hands, choking for breath, and Duroy did not know what to do or say. In the end, when he heard her crying, he stammered: 'Listen, Clo ... Clo darling, let me explain. It's not my fault

... I knew that woman a long time ago, at the beginning ...'

Suddenly she dropped her hands from her face and breathlessly, with all the fury of a woman betrayed, a wild fury that suddenly released her power of speech, she let loose a disjointed flood of words: 'Oh ... you beast ... you beast ... what a cad you are! It's not possible! How humiliating! Oh, God, how humiliating!'

Then her anger rose as she began to think more clearly and marshal her thoughts: 'You've been paying her with my money, haven't you? And I was giving him money ... for that whore ... Oh, what a cad!'

For a second or two she seemed to be vainly fumbling for some stronger word and then all at once she spat it out: 'You pig ... you pig ... you pig ... you were paying her with my money ... pig ... pig ... pig.'

She could find no other word and kept repeating: 'Pig ... pig ...'

Suddenly she leaned out and catching the driver by the sleeve, cried: 'Stop', and opening the door, jumped out.

Georges tried to follow but she shouted: 'I forbid you to get out', so loudly that the passers-by gathered round and Duroy stayed where he was for fear of a scandal.

She pulled out her purse and looked for some change under a lamp; then, taking out two francs and fifty centimes she placed them in the cabby's hand saying, in ringing tones: 'Here you are ... there's your fare for an hour. I'm paying ... And take that dirty louse back to the Rue Boursault, off the Boulevard de Batignolles.'

The group of people around her were highly amused. One gentleman said: 'Well done, little woman', and a young hooligan standing by pushed his head through the open window and exclaimed in a high-pitched voice: 'Goodnight, my pet!'

Then the cab set off again, pursued by peals of laughter.

CHAPTER 6

NEXT morning Duroy awoke in a gloomy frame of mind.

He dressed slowly and then sat down in front of his window to think. His whole body felt as stiff as if he had been beaten up the day before.

In the end he was spurred into action by his need to lay hands on some money and he went to see Forestier.

His friend was sitting in his study warming his toes by the fire.

'What got you out of bed so early?'

'It's a very serious matter. I've got a debt of honour.'

'Gambling?'

He hesitated and then confessed:

'Yes, gambling.'

'A big one?'

'Five hundred francs.'

He owed only 280.

Forestier asked sceptically:

'Whom do you owe it to?'

Duroy was unable to answer immediately:

'To a . . . to a man called de Carleville.'

'Oh yes. And where does he live?'

'In the . . . in the . . .'

Forestier gave a laugh:

'In the moon, I suppose? I know that man, old boy. If you'd like twenty francs, I can let you have that much but not a penny more.'

Duroy took the louis that he was offered.

Then he went round to all his acquaintances, going from door to door, and by five o'clock he had managed to collect eighty francs.

As he still needed another 200, he made up his mind to keep the money he had collected, saying to himself: 'Damn it all, I'm not going to bother myself about a bitch like that. I'll pay her when I can.'

For a fortnight he lived parsimoniously, carefully and without women, full of good resolutions. Then he was seized by an urge to make love. It seemed ages since he had had a woman and like a sailor who goes berserk when he sets foot on land a thrill ran through him each time he saw a skirt.

So one evening he went to the Folies-Bergère in the hope of meeting Rachel. Indeed, he caught sight of her as soon as he went in, because she hardly ever went anywhere else.

He walked up to her with outstretched hand. She looked him up and down:

'What do you want?'

He gave a forced laugh:

'Oh come on, don't be silly.'

She turned on her heels saying:

'I don't mix with ponces.'

She had found the most insulting word she could. He went red in the face and made his way home alone.

Forestier, ill and run-down and still coughing, was making life difficult for him at the newspaper and seemed to be deliberately trying to find boring jobs for him to do. One day even, when Duroy had failed to obtain for him some information he wanted, in a fit of nervous irritation and puffing for breath after a long spasm of coughing, he grunted: 'God, man, you're more stupid than I'd ever have imagined.'

Georges nearly slapped his face but restrained himself and went away muttering: 'I'll get even with you for that.' A sudden idea struck him and he added: 'I'll cuckold you, old man.' And he walked off rubbing his hands with glee at the prospect.

He decided to put his idea into practice the very next day and paid an exploratory visit to Madame Forestier.

She was reading a book, stretched out at full length on a settee.

Turning her head she held out her hand without moving and said: 'Good morning, Bel-Ami.'

It was like a slap in the face: 'Why do you call me that?'

She answered, smiling:

'I saw Madame de Marelle the other week and she told me the nickname they'd found for you there.'

Realizing that no malice was intended, he felt reassured. What was there to be afraid of, anyway?

She went on:

'You're spoiling her. As for me, I get a visit whenever the fit takes you, roughly once in a blue moon.'

He had sat down beside her and was examining her with renewed interest, as if she was a collector's piece. She was charming, with fair hair of a warmth and delicacy of tint that was made to be stroked; and he thought: 'She's definitely better than her friend.' He had no doubts about succeeding; all he needed to do, it seemed to him, was to reach out his hand and pluck her like a ripe fruit.

Emphasizing his words, he said:

'I didn't come to see you because it was better like that.'

She looked at him, uncomprehending:

'What? Why?'

'Why? Can't you guess?'

'No, I certainly can't.'

'Because I'm in love with you ... oh, just a little, only a little ... and I don't want to fall head over heels in love with you ...'

She seemed neither surprised, shocked nor flattered. She continued to smile her same dispassionate smile and replied calmly:

'Oh, you can still come all the same. Nobody's ever in love with me for long.'

He was surprised, even more by her tone than by her words.

'Why?' he asked.

'Because it's pointless and I let them know it straight away. If you'd told me about your fear earlier, I'd have reassured you and on the contrary invited you to come as often as possible.'

He exclaimed, in a pathetic voice:

'As if one can control one's feelings!'

She turned towards him:

'My dear Monsieur Duroy, for me a man in love no longer exists. He becomes an idiot and a dangerous idiot at that. I stop having any close relationship with men who love me or claim to, first because they bore me and secondly because I feel as suspicious of them as I would of a mad dog that may suddenly have a fit. So I put them in quarantine until they've got over their attack. Don't forget that. I know perfectly well that for you love is merely a sort of appetite whereas for me it would be more a sort of ... of ... of communion of souls which doesn't exist in a male's religion. You understand the letter and I understand the spirit. But ... look at me please ...'

She had stopped smiling now. Her face was calm and cold and, emphasizing every word, she went on:

'I shall never be your mistress, never, do you understand? So it's completely pointless and it would even be bad for you to persist in that sort of feeling ... And now that ... the operation has been completed ... would you like us to become friends, good friends, real friends, without any ulterior motive?'

He realized that any attempt on his part would be hopeless in view of this judgement from which there was no appeal.

He accepted it unhesitatingly and, delighted at the chance of acquiring such an ally in his life, he held out both hands:

'I'm yours, Madame Forestier, to do with as you wish.'

She could detect the sincerity in his voice and she held out her hands, too.

He kissed them one after the other and then, raising his eyes, he said simply: 'Heavens, if only I'd met a woman like you, how happy I would have been to marry her!'

This time she was touched and flattered by his remark, as women are when a compliment goes to their heart, and she threw him one of those swift, grateful glances which make men their willing slaves.

As he could not find any suitable remark to resume the conversation, laying her finger on his arm, she said gently:

'And I'm going to take over my duties as a friend straight away. You're not playing your cards well ...'

She hesitated and asked:

'May I speak frankly?'

'Yes.'

'Absolutely frankly?'

'Absolutely.'

'Well then, you must go and call on Madame Walter, who thinks highly of you, and make yourself agreeable to her. You'll be able to find a home for your compliments there, although she's an honest woman, make no mistake about it, a completely honest woman. Oh, there's no hope of ... contraband there either. But you may be able to find something better by gaining her favour. I know you still occupy a rather lowly position on the paper. But don't let that worry you, they give the same friendly welcome to all their sub-editors. Believe me, you must make the effort.'

He smiled and said: 'Thank you, you're an angel ... a guardian angel.' Then they went on to talk about other, trivial matters.

He stayed for a long time, anxious to prove that he enjoyed her company, and as he left, he asked once again:

'So it's agreed, we're friends?'

'It's agreed.'

And as he had not been unaware of the effect produced by his earlier compliment, he reiterated it:

'And if you ever become a widow, I'll put my name down on the list.'

And he slipped away quickly before she had time to be cross.

Duroy was rather embarrassed at the thought of calling on Madame Walter because he had not been invited to her house and he did not want to appear pressing. But the director was well-disposed towards him, appreciated his work for the paper and liked to entrust him with the more difficult tasks. Why shouldn't he take advantage of his preference to get himself invited to the house?

So one day he got up early, went to the central market at the time when the fruit was being sold and spent about ten francs on a score of superb pears. Carefully packing them in a hamper to make it appear that they had come from a distance, he left them at Madame Walter's with his card, on which he had written:

Georges Duroy presents his compliments to Madame Walter and asks her to be so good as to accept these few pears which he received this morning from Normandy.

Next day he found in his letter-box at the newspaper an envelope containing Madame Walter's card, *To thank Monsieur Georges Duroy very much. Madame Walter is at home every Saturday.*

Next Saturday he appeared on her doorstep.

Monsieur Walter lived in the Boulevard Malesherbes in a house which he owned but part of which he let, a practice favoured by thrifty people. A single concierge, whose lodge was placed between the two doorways, acted as porter for both owner and tenant and gave each entrance the prosperous air of a gentleman's residence, with his fine uniform, like that of a verger in full regalia, his plump calves sheathed in white stockings and his official gold-buttoned coat with scarlet lapels.

The reception rooms were on the first floor, preceded by an anteroom hung with tapestries and with curtains over the doorways. Two footmen were dozing on chairs. One of them took Duroy's overcoat, the other his stick, opened a door, walked a few steps ahead of the visitor and stood aside to let him pass as he loudly announced his name to an empty room.

The embarrassed young man was casting his eyes all around him when he saw a mirror in which people could be seen sitting; they seemed a long way off. Confused by the reflection, he was first of all making off in the wrong direction, but going through two further empty reception-rooms he reached a sort of little boudoir draped with blue silk patterned with buttercups, in which four ladies were talking in an undertone, seated round a circular table on which there were cups of tea.

Despite the self-confidence which he had gained through his life in Paris and above all through his profession which brought him into constant contact with well-known people, Duroy felt somewhat intimidated by the whole setting of the entrance and the approach through deserted rooms.

He faltered: 'Madame Walter, I took the liberty ...', at the same time looking round for the lady of the house.

Holding out her hand, which he took with a bow, she said:

'It is very kind of you to call on me, Monsieur Duroy,' and she pointed to a chair into which he subsided with a bump, thinking it was much higher than it was.

Silence had fallen and then one of the women started talking again. They were discussing the weather which was turning extremely cold, although not cold enough either to put an end to the epidemic of typhoid or for skating. And each woman gave her opinion concerning the first appearance of frost in Paris; then they explained which was their favourite season, with all the obvious reasons which clutter people's heads like dust hanging about a room.

The sound of a door quietly opening made Duroy turn his head and through the two-way mirrors he saw a stout woman making her way in. As soon as she reached the boudoir, one of the other visitors stood up, shook hands and left; and with his eyes the young man followed her back glittering with black sequins.

When the stir caused by these comings and goings had subsided, the conversation abruptly turned to the Moroccan question, the war in the East and also England's difficulties in the southernmost tip of Africa.

The ladies were talking about all these things by rote, as though acting a part in a respectable society comedy, frequently rehearsed.

A new arrival now appeared, a tiny woman with curly blonde hair, and this in turn led to the departure of a tall, gaunt, middle-aged woman.

They now started talking about Monsieur Linet's chances of getting into the Academy. The newcomer was firmly convinced that he would be beaten by Monsieur Cabanon-Lebas, the author of a fine adaptation of Don Quixote for the theatre, in verse.

'You know it's going to be put on at the Odéon next winter?'

'Really? I'll certainly go to see such a very interesting literary experiment.'

Madame Walter spoke graciously, calmly and dispassionately, never hesitating as to what to say since her opinions were always ready-made in advance.

She saw that it was becoming dark and rang for lights to be brought, still listening to the conversation which was flowing on like a stream of marshmallow, while at the same time remembering that she had forgotten to go to the printers to pick up the invitation cards for her next dinner party.

She was still a handsome woman, although somewhat fat and at the dangerous age when beauty hangs by a thread. She was holding her own by dint of great vigilance, careful attention to her health and the application of face-packs. She seemed the epitome of good sense, moderation and reasonableness, one of these women whose mind runs in straight lines, like a French garden. You can walk round them without meeting any surprises and even discovering a certain charm in them. She had judgement, a discreet, well-balanced and accurate judgement that substituted for imagination, and she also had kindness, loyalty and a quiet benevolence broad enough to embrace everything and everybody.

She noticed that Duroy had not said a word, that no one had spoken to him and that he seemed a trifle stiff; and as the ladies were still on the subject of the Academy, a favourite one which always keeps them occupied for a long time, she asked:

'You must know more about this than anyone, Monsieur Duroy. Whom do you favour?'

He replied without hesitation:

'In such a matter, Madame Walter, I should never take into account the merits of the candidates, which are always questionable, but their age and the state of their health. I shouldn't look at their qualifications but at their diseases. I shouldn't try to discover if they had done a verse translation of Lope de Vega, but I should take good care to obtain information about their heart, their kidneys and their spinal cord. To my mind, a nice pathological enlargement of an organ, a nice albuminosis and above all a nice incipient loco-motor ataxia would be far more valuable than forty volumes of glosses on the conception of the fatherland in Berber poetry.'

This statement met with a stupefied silence.

Madame Walter smilingly enquired: 'Why do you say that?'

He replied: 'Because I never look further than what will give pleasure to the ladies. Well, the Academy only interests you when an academician dies. The more of them who die, the happier you'll be. But to ensure that they die quickly, they need to be elected when they're old and ill.'

As they were still rather surprised, he added:

'Incidentally, I'm like you and I very much enjoy read-ing about the death of an academician in the newspapers. I always ask myself immediately: "Who's going to succeed him?" And I draw up my list. It's a game, a very amusing little game that they play in every drawing-room in Paris whenever an "Immortal" passes on: the game of Death and the Forty Old Men.'

The ladies, although still rather disconcerted, were be-ginning to smile, because they could see the aptness of his remarks.

And as he rose to go, he concluded: 'You elect them, ladies, and you elect them only in order to see them die. So pick them old, very old, as old as possible and never worry your heads about anything else.'

He then made a very graceful exit.

As soon as he had left, one of the women said: 'What an amusing young man. Who is he?' Madame Walter replied: 'One of our sub-editors. He has only a minor post on the paper but I have no doubt that he is going to go far, very quickly.'

Duroy went down the Boulevard Malesherbes in great good humour, with a springy stride, pleased with his parting shot, saying to himself: 'A good exit.'

That night, he made it up with Rachel.

Next week a double event took place. He was appointed head of the news and gossip column and invited to dine at the Walters'. He saw at once a link between the two.

La Vie française was primarily a financial paper, the proprietor being a financier who had used the press and his parliamentary post to reach the position he had achieved. For him, simplicity and good-nature were weapons to further his career and he had always adopted the pose of being an affable, decent sort of man; but to do his work for him, whatever that work was, he employed only men whose talents he had sensed, assessed and proven, men whom he felt to be bold, wily and unprincipled. Duroy seemed to him to be a valuable man as chief editor of the news and gossip column. Until now this function had been filled by the chief sub-editor, Monsieur Boisrenard, a journalist of long experience, as punctilious, meticulous and precise as a clerk. Over the last thirty years he had been chief sub-editor of eleven different newspapers without ever changing his methods or ideas in the slightest. He went from one newspaper office to the next as someone might change restaurants, hardly noticing that the cooking had not quite the same flavour. He had no opinions on either politics or religion. He was devoted to whichever newspaper he was working for, he knew his job backwards and his experience was invaluable. In his work, he remained as blind as a bat, as deaf as a post and as silent as the grave. He had, however, great professional pride and would never have countenanced anything that he did not consider right and proper from the peculiar viewpoint of his profession.

While appreciating his qualities, Monsieur Walter had

often wanted to have someone else to put in charge of the news and gossip column, which he described as the backbone of a paper. It is this section of a paper that can start news going, launch rumours, work on public opinion and the stock exchange. Between the account of two smart parties, you have to be able to slip in the item of real importance without its being obvious, insinuating rather than stating it outright. You have to hint at what you want to say, issue a denial in terms which confirm a rumour or state something in such a way that no one believes your words. In such a column, everybody must be able to find one line at least that interests him every day, so that everyone reads it. You have to think of everything and everybody, every section of society and every profession, Paris and the provinces, the army, the arts, the clergy, the university, the law and the *demi-monde*.

The man in charge of this column and its regiment of reporters has to be always alert, always on his guard, suspicious, always looking ahead, wily, lively and resilient, up to every trick of the trade, with an infallible eye for recognizing false news at a glance, capable of judging what is to be said and what left unsaid, of anticipating what will affect public opinion. And he must be able to present it in such a way as to exaggerate its effect.

Despite his long experience, Monsieur Boisrenard lacked the master touch; he did not have the knack. Above all he lacked the sixth sense required to foresee every day the secret thoughts of his boss.

Duroy would be able to do all this perfectly and he was the ideal person to complete the editorial staff of a newspaper that in Norbert de Varenne's phrase 'steered its course through the waters of high finance and low politics'.

The men behind *La Vie française* and its real editors were half a dozen deputies who were interested in all the speculative operations launched or supported by the director. In the Chamber they were called 'Walter's lobby' and they were envied because of the money they must be earning through him or with him.

Forestier, the political editor, was merely the catspaw of these businessmen and he carried out the proposals they put forward. They would suggest subjects for his editorials and he would then go away and write them up at home, so as to be undisturbed, he used to say.

But in order to give the paper a literary, Parisian flavour, they had engaged two writers well-known in their own field, Jacques Rival, as a writer on current affairs, and Norbert de Varenne, a poet and feature-writer or short-story writer, according to the new school of thought.

Then they had engaged, on the cheap, critics of the arts, for painting, music, drama, a crime correspondent and a turf correspondent, all chosen from the large host of reporters prepared to write on anything for money. To society women, 'Domino Rose' and 'Patte Blanche' supplied the social news, discussed questions of fashion and fashionable society, etiquette, good manners and wrote indiscreetly about the goings-on of noble ladies.

And manned by this motley crew, *La Vie française* 'steered its course through the waters of high finance and low politics'.

Duroy was still in the full flush of joy at his new appointment when he received a small engraved card which read: 'Monsieur and Madame Walter have pleasure in inviting Monsieur Georges Duroy to dine with them on Thursday, 20 January.'

This new favour, coming on top of the other one, filled him with such glee that he kissed the invitation card as if it had been a love-letter. Then he went off to see the cashier to settle the big question of his stipend.

A chief editor usually has a budget out of which he pays his reporters for the news, good or indifferent, that any of them might supply, just as gardeners bring their fruit to a wholesale greengrocer.

Initially, Duroy was allotted 1,200 francs a month, a goodly part of which he was determined to keep for himself.

At his urgent plea, the cashier finally agreed to advance him 400 francs. His first thought was that he must send Madame de Marelle the 280 francs he owed her but almost at once he realized that this would leave him with only 120 francs, a sum quite inadequate to run his new section properly. So he decided to put off the repayment to a later date.

He spent two days settling in, because he now became entitled to a table of his own and a set of pigeon-holes in the immense room shared by all the sub-editors. He had one end of the room while the other end was occupied by Boisrenard whose head, covered in jet black hair despite his age, was always poring over some sheet of paper or other.

The long table in the middle belonged to the miscellaneous sub-editors. It was generally used as a bench for them to sit on, either with their legs dangling down the sides or else squatting in the middle. Sometimes there were five or six of them sitting like that on the table and looking like grotesque Chinese porcelain figures as they doggedly played cup-and-ball.

Duroy had finally grown to like this game and he was beginning to become good at it, under the tuition and advice of Saint-Potin.

Forestier, whose health was steadily deteriorating, had let him have his splendid cup-and-ball made from West Indian hardwood, his most recent acquisition, because he found it rather heavy, and Duroy would energetically fling the big ball up at the end of its string, counting under his breath: 'one-two-three-four-five-six.'

On the very same day that he was going to dinner with Madame Walter, he succeeded in scoring twenty for the first time. 'My lucky day,' he thought, 'everything's going right.' Because skill at cup-and-ball did confer a sort of prestige in the offices of *La Vie française*.

He left the office early to give himself time to dress and as he was going up the Rue de Londres, he saw a small woman scampering on ahead of him whose figure recalled Madame de Marelle's. He felt his face flush and his heart gave a flutter. He crossed the street to look at her sideways. She stopped to cross as well. He had been mistaken; he breathed freely again.

He had often wondered what he ought to do if he met her face to face. Would he acknowledge her or would he pretend not to see her?

'I wouldn't see her,' he thought.

It was cold and the gutters in the streets had a permanent layer of ice. The pavements were dry and grey under the gaslight.

When he arrived home, he said to himself:

'I must find a new place to live. This one isn't suitable for me any longer.' He felt excited and cheerful, ready to jump over the roof, and as he walked from his bed to the window, he repeated out loud: 'I've made it! I've made it! I must write to Dad.'

He wrote to him now and again; and his letter was always very gladly received in the little inn in Normandy, perched by the side of the road at the top of the big hill overlooking Rouen and the broad valley of the Seine.

Now and again he, too, would receive a blue envelope with the address written in large shaky handwriting and his father's letter would inevitably begin with the same words:

'My dear son, this is to tell you that your mother and me are well. There's nothing much happening round here. But I thought I'd let you know that . . .'

And Duroy still retained an interest in what was going on in the village, news about the neighbours and the state of the farmers and the crops.

As he stood tying his white bow tie in front of his little mirror, he repeated to himself: 'I must write to Dad tomorrow. Wouldn't the old boy be impressed if he were to see me in the house where I'm going this evening! Heavens, later on I'll be having a dinner such as he's never eaten.' And in his mind's eye he suddenly saw the dark kitchen at home at the end of the empty café room, with the row of yellow saucepans gleaming on the walls, the cat crouching in front of the fireplace like a chimera, the wooden table greasy with age and spilt drinks, a big steaming tureen of soup in the centre and a lighted candle standing between the two plates. And he also saw the man and the woman, his father and mother, two peasants, lifting their spoons slowly and deliberately to sip their soup. He even knew what they would be saying to each other every evening as they sat face to face eating their supper.

He thought again: 'I really must go and see them.' But as he had finished dressing, he blew out his light and went downstairs.

All along the outer boulevard he was accosted by street-walkers. He pulled his arm out of their grasp and snarled scornfully: 'Get off' as though insulted by their failing to recognize him. What did they take him for? Didn't the trollops know how to distinguish one man from another? The knowledge of having put on evening dress to go out to dinner with very rich, very well-known and very important people gave him the feeling of having a new personality, the realization that he had become a new man, a man of the world, a man of high society.

He walked confidently into the anteroom lit by tall bronze candelabra and with an easy gesture handed over his stick and his overcoat to the two footmen who came to meet him.

All the reception rooms were lit up. In the second one, which was the largest, Madame Walter was standing to receive her guests. She welcomed him with a charming smile and he shook hands with the two men who had arrived before him, Monsieur Firmin and Monsieur Laroche-Mathieu, both deputies and behind-the-scene editors of *La Vie française*. Monsieur Laroche-Mathieu enjoyed special importance on the paper because of his great influence in the Chamber of Deputies. He was acknowledged by all to be a future Minister.

Then the Forestiers came in, the wife dressed in pink and looking ravishing. Duroy was amazed to see on what terms of familiarity she stood with the two deputies. She held a whispered conversation with Monsieur Laroche-Mathieu for more than five minutes beside the fireplace. Charles seemed completely worn out. He had lost a great deal of weight in the last month and he coughed continually as he said: 'I ought to make up my mind to spend the rest of the winter in the South of France.'

Norbert de Varenne and Jacques Rival appeared together. Then a door opened at the end of the room and Monsieur Walter came in with two tall girls, sixteen or eighteen years old, one of them ugly, the other pretty.

Although Duroy knew that his employer was a family man, he was taken by surprise. He had never thought of the editor's daughters except in the way you think of distant lands which you will never see. And also he had imagined them as being quite young and here they were as young women. He felt the slight unease that you have at a transformation scene.

On being introduced they each held out their hand in turn and, going over to sit down at a little table which was doubtless reserved for them, they started to sort through a pile of bobbins of silk in a small basket.

There were still some people to come and everyone was silent and constrained as guests are before dinner when they find themselves in different moods after their various activities during the day.

As Duroy was idly looking at the walls of the room, Monsieur Walter, spying him from afar and with an obvious desire to show off his possessions, asked: 'Are you looking at my pictures?' – emphasizing *my* – 'I'll show you them.' And he fetched a lamp so that they could see all the details.

'These are the landscapes,' he said.

In the centre of the panels there hung a big canvas by Guillemet, a Normandy beach under a stormy sky. Underneath, a wood by Harpignies, then a plain in Algiers by Guillaumet, with a camel on the horizon, a tall camel with long legs, looking like some weird monument.

Monsieur Walter moved along to the next wall and in a solemn tone, like a master of ceremonies, announced: 'Major painters.' There were four canvases: 'Hospital Visit' by Gervex; a 'Woman Harvesting' by Bastien-Lepage; a 'Widow' by Bouguereau and an 'Execution' by Jean-Paul Laurens. This last work showed a priest from the Vendée being executed against the wall of his church by a firing squad of the French Revolutionary Army.

The editor's solemn face lit up with a smile as he pointed to the next panel:

'Funny painters.' First of all there was a little canvas by Jean Béraud entitled: 'The Top and the Bottom'. It depicted a pretty Parisian girl going up the stairs of a moving tram. Her head was just reaching the level of the top deck and the men sitting up there were showing every sign of satisfaction and greedy anticipation at the young face coming towards them while the men standing on the platform down below were looking at the young woman's legs with a different expression, of lust and chagrin. Monsieur Walter held the lamp at arm's length and kept repeating, with a lecherous snigger: 'Funny, eh? Funny, eh?'

Then he lit up 'The Rescue' by Lambert. In the centre of a table that was being cleared away, a perplexed kitten was sitting watching with surprise a fly drowning in a glass of water. Its paw was raised in readiness to whip the fly out. But it could not make up its mind. It was hesitating. What would it do?

Then Walter pointed out a Detaille: 'The Lesson', depicting a soldier in a barracks teaching a poodle to play a drum, saying as he did so: 'That's really witty!'

Duroy laughed approvingly, to show how much he appreciated it: 'How charming, how charming, how char...'

He stopped dead, hearing Madame de Marelle's voice behind him. She had just come in.

His employer was now lighting up other canvases and explaining them.

They had reached a water-colour by Maurice Leloir: 'The Obstacle'. It showed a sedan-chair being held up because the street was blocked by a brawl between two workers, two sturdy men locked in a titanic struggle. And peering out of the window of the sedan was a delightful female countenance showing neither fear nor impatience, but looking attentively and with a certain admiration at this display of brute force.

Monsieur Walter was continuing his tour: 'I've got other paintings in the next rooms but they're by less well-known painters, who haven't yet made their reputation. These are the pick of my collection. I'm buying up young painters at

the moment, the very young ones, and keeping their paintings in reserve in my private rooms until their authors have
become famous.' And he added in a whisper: 'It's a good
time to buy pictures at the moment. Painters are starving.
They haven't a penny, not one penny.'

But Duroy had stopped looking and was listening without understanding a word. Madame de Marelle was standing behind him. What should he do? If he greeted her,
might she not turn her back on him or make some insulting
remark? If he kept away from her, what would people
think?

He said to himself: 'I'll play for time.' He was so disturbed that for a moment he even thought of pretending
that he had been taken suddenly ill in order to be able to
leave.

The conducted tour of the pictures was over. Walter put
down his lamp and went to say good evening to the late-
comer, while Duroy went back to look at the paintings all
over again, as though finding it impossible to tear himself
away.

His mind was in a whirl. What was he to do? He could
hear the voices and distinguish the conversation. Madame
Forestier called to him: 'I say, Monsieur Duroy.' He
hastened towards her. She wanted to recommend one of her
friends to him; she was giving a party and would very much
like to see it mentioned in the columns of La Vie française.

He stammered: 'Of course I can, Madame Forestier, of
course.'

Now Madame de Marelle was very close behind him. He
did not dare to turn round to move away.

Suddenly he thought that he had taken leave of his senses.
She had said loudly:

'Good evening, Bel-Ami. Have you forgotten me?'

He spun round on his heels. She was standing behind him,

smiling, with a gay, affectionate expression in her eyes. She held out her hand.

He took it, trembling, still afraid that she might be deceiving or tricking him. She added calmly:

'What have you been up to? Nobody's seen anything of you for ages.'

He stumbled over his words, still at a loss:

'I've had a great deal to do, Madame de Marelle, a great deal to do. Monsieur Walter has put me in charge of a new section which is keeping me extremely busy.'

Still looking him straight in the face, without his being able to discern anything but friendliness in her eyes, she replied: 'I know. But that's not a reason for forgetting your friends.'

They were separated by the arrival of a stout lady wearing a low-cut gown, with red arms and red cheeks, pretentiously dressed with an excessively elaborate hair style and such a heavy tread that you could feel the weight of her massive thighs as she moved.

As people seemed to be treating her with considerable deference, Duroy asked Madame Forestier:

'Who is that woman?'

'Vicomtesse de Percemur, the one who writes under the name of "Patte Blanche".'

He was so amazed that he almost burst out laughing:

'Patte Blanche? Patte Blanche? And I imagined her to be a young woman like you! So she's Patte Blanche! Oh, that's rich, that really is rich!'

A footman appeared in the doorway and announced:

'Dinner is served.'

The dinner party was full of good cheer and platitudes, one of those parties where a great deal is said to little purpose. Duroy found himself sitting between Walter's eldest daughter Rose, the ugly one, and Madame de Marelle. His proximity to the latter rather embarrassed him although she seemed quite at ease and talked in her usual witty style. At first he felt reserved and hesitant, like a musician playing out of tune. However, his self-confidence gradually returned and as their eyes were continually meeting, they looked questioningly at each other, exchanging intimate, almost sensual, glances as in the old days.

Suddenly he thought he felt something brush against his foot under the table. He gently moved his leg and pressed it against his neighbour's; she did not withdraw it. They were not talking to each other at that moment, as each of them was turned towards their other neighbour.

With his heart beating, Duroy edged his knee a little further. He felt a gentle pressure in return. Then he realized that their affair was starting again.

What did they talk about after this? Nothing very much; but their lips were trembling each time they looked at each other.

However, wanting to be agreeable to his employer's daughter, the young man addressed a word or two to her every now and again. She replied in exactly the same way as her mother, never at a loss as to what to say.

Sitting on Monsieur Walter's right, the Vicomtesse de Percemur was behaving as if she were a princess, and Duroy, who was amused by her, whispered to Madame de Marelle:

'Do you know the other one, the one who writes under the name of "Domino Rose"?'

'Yes, indeed. She's the Baronne de Livar.'

'Is she the same sort of person?'

'No. But just as funny. She's tall and lean, sixty years old, false curls, English-style teeth, ideas dating from the 1820s and dresses of the same period.'

'Where did they unearth such literary phenomena?'

'The wreckage of the aristocracy is always picked up by the nouveau-rich middle-classes.'

'No other reason?'

'None at all.'

Then a political discussion began between the director, the two deputies, Norbert de Varenne and Jacques Rival; and it lasted until dessert.

When they had returned to the drawing-room Duroy went up to Madame de Marelle again, and looking deep into her eyes, asked: 'Would you like me to take you home tonight?'

'No.'

'Why not?'

'Because Monsieur Laroche-Mathieu, who is a neighbour of mine, always drops me off every time I dine here.'

'When can I see you?'

'Come and lunch with me tomorrow.'

And they parted without saying another word.

Duroy did not stay late because he found the party dull. As he was going downstairs, he overtook Norbert de Varenne who had also just left. The old poet took him by the arm. Now that he had nothing to fear from Duroy since their activities were so basically different, he had come to adopt an attitude of grandfatherly affection towards the young man.

'Will you come part of the way home with me?' he enquired.

Duroy replied: 'I'd be honoured and delighted.'

And they set off, sauntering gently down the Boulevard Malesherbes. On such a cold evening Paris was almost deserted; it was the sort of night which seems more spacious than others, when the stars seem higher, when the icy winds seem to be bearers of tidings from realms beyond.

For the first few moments, neither of the men spoke. Then, to break the silence, Duroy said:

'That Monsieur Laroche-Mathieu seems very intelligent and well-informed.'

The old poet muttered: 'Do you think so?'

The young man, surprised, said uncertainly:

'Surely he is? What's more, he has the reputation of being one of the most able members of the Chamber.'

'That's possible. In the country of the blind, the one-eyed man is king. The point is that all those people are mediocrities because their minds are confined between two brick walls – money and politics. They're Philistines, my dear boy, and you can't talk about anything with them, nothing that interests us. At the bottom of their minds, you just find slime or rather sewage, like the Seine at Asnières. Ah, how difficult it is to find someone with an expansive mind, someone who gives you the feeling of gulping great breaths of fresh ocean air. I've known a few men like that. They're all dead.'

Norbert de Varenne was talking in a clear, subdued voice, which would have echoed through the silence of the night had he been speaking loudly. He seemed over-excited and melancholy, with the sort of melancholy which sometimes takes hold of a person and gives him the deep resonance of earth when it is frozen.

He went on:

'Anyway, what does it matter if you have more or less genius since the end is always lying in wait for you.'

He was silent. Duroy, who was in good spirits that evening, said with a smile:

'You're gloomy tonight, my dear sir.'

The poet retorted:

'I always am, dear boy, and you'll be the same in a few years' time. Life is a slope. As long as you're going up you're looking towards the top and you feel happy; but when you reach it, suddenly you can see the road going downhill and death at the end of it all. It's slow going up but quick going down. At your age, you're cheerful. You're full of so many hopes, which, incidentally, will never be fulfilled. At my age, you don't expect anything – except death.'

Duroy laughed:

'Damn it, you're sending cold shivers down my back.'

Norbert de Varenne went on:

'No, tonight you won't understand me, but later on you'll remember what I'm saying now. You see, the day comes – and for many people it comes early – when the kissing has to stop, as they say, because behind everything you look at, you can glimpse death. Oh, I know you don't even understand the word. At your age death has no meaning. At my age, it's frightening. Yes, you suddenly understand it, how or why you never quite know, and after that everything in life looks different. In my case, I've felt death in my soul for the last fifteen years, exactly as if I had an animal eating away inside me. Gradually, month by month, hour by hour, I have felt it destroying me, like a house falling into ruins. It has disfigured me so completely that I can't even recognize myself. There's nothing left of the strong, vigorous, healthy young man that I was when I was thirty. Carefully, viciously, it has slowly, so slowly, turned my dark hair into white, it's taken away my smooth skin, my muscles, my teeth, the body I used to have. It's left me with despair in my soul and my soul will soon be going the way of my flesh. Yes, the bitch, quietly, cruelly, she's pulling me to pieces, bit by bit, slowly destroying my whole being, second by second. And now everything I do is full of death. Every step brings her closer, every movement, every breath, aids and abets her hateful work. Breathing, sleeping, drinking, eating, working, dreaming, everything we do contains death. In fact living is dying! Ah, you'll realize all this! If you were just to think about it for a quarter of an hour, you'd see her. What are you hoping for? Love? After a few more kisses, you'll be impotent. And what else? Money? What's the use of money? To buy women? A fine reward that is. To eat too much, get fat and then scream with pain all night because you've got gout? And then what? Fame? What good is fame if you can't use it any more to bring you love? And then what? Death is always waiting for you at the end of it all. I can see death now so close to me that I often feel I must push it off with my hand. It covers the earth and occupies the whole of space. I see it whichever way I turn. Tiny animals run over on the road, falling leaves, a white hair in a friend's beard, anything like that terrifies me because they seem to be screaming at me: "Take a look – that's death!" It poisons everything I do, everything I see, everything I eat and drink, everything I love, moonlight, sunrise, the open sea, a lovely river and the gentle breeze of a summer evening.'

He was walking slowly, puffing a little, almost forgetting that someone was listening.

He went on: 'And nobody ever comes back, ever ... You can keep copies of statues, moulds which can reproduce the same objects; but my body, my face, my thoughts, my desires, will never return. And yet there'll be millions and millions of people with a few square inches of face, a nose, eyes, forehead, cheeks, a mouth like me and a soul, too, yet I shall never come back, nothing recognizably *me* will ever reappear amongst all those countless different creatures, indefinably different even though more or less the same. What can one fasten on to? Who's going to listen to our cries of anguish? What can we believe in? All religions are stupid with their puerile morality and the selfish, monstrously idiotic promises they hold out. The only certainty is death!'

He stopped and, taking Duroy by the lapels of his overcoat, he said slowly:

'Think of all this, young man, think of it during the days and the months and the years to come and you'll look at life differently. So try and free yourself from everything that closes you in, make a supreme effort to escape from your living body, from your interests and your thoughts, from the whole of mankind, look elsewhere and you'll realize how unimportant are the quarrels of the Romantics and the Naturalists and the debate on the budget.'

He started off walking again at a great pace:

'But you'll come to realize, too, the dreadful anguish of despair. You'll find yourself struggling wildly in the stifling grip of doubt. You'll shout for help in every direction and no one will answer. You'll hold out your arms and beg to be rescued and loved and saved; but no one will come. Why do we have to suffer like this? No doubt the truth is that we were born to live more materialistically and less spiritually; but through too much thought we've created a discrepancy between our overdeveloped intelligence and the unchanging conditions of our life. Take the average man. Unless he's actually affected by personal disaster he's quite happy and doesn't suffer from all the unhappiness of others. Animals don't feel it either.'

He stopped once more and stood in thought for a few seconds before adding, in a tone of weary resignation:

'As for myself, I'm a lost soul. I've no father, no mother, no sister, no brother, no wife, no children and no God.'

He added, after a pause:

'All I've got is poetry.'

And he raised his head skywards to look at the pale face of the full moon and declaimed:

> *'Et je cherche le mot de cet obscur problème*
> *Dans le ciel noir et vide où flotte un astre blème.'**

They were now at the Place de la Concorde; they crossed

---

* And I seek the key to this obscure enigma
  In the black empty sky where a wan star is floating.

it and followed the Quai de Bourbon. Norbert de Varenne began to speak again:

'Get married, young man, you don't know what it's like to live alone at my age. These days, loneliness fills me with an excruciating dread; loneliness in my home, beside the fire, in the evening. I seem to be all alone on earth, horribly alone but surrounded by vague dangers, strange, terrible things; and the wall between me and my unknown next-door neighbour makes him seem as distant from me as the stars which I can see through my window. I feel a sort of fever, an agonizing, terrifying fever and the silent walls of my room fill me with horror. The silence of a room in which you're living all alone is terribly profound and sad. It's a silence that envelops not only your body but your soul and when you hear the furniture creak, it makes your heart jump because in the dismal silence all around, you don't expect to hear any sound.'

He paused for a moment and then went on:

'Ah, when you're old, how wonderful it would be to have children.'

They were now half way down the Rue de Bourgogne. The poet stopped in front of a tall house, rang the bell, shook Duroy by the hand and said:

'Forget all this old man's ramblings, my boy, and live like a young man. Good night!'

And he vanished into the gloom of the corridor.

Duroy went on his way, depressed. It seemed to him as if he had just been shown a hole full of dead men's bones into which he would inevitably fall one day. He muttered to himself: 'My God, it can't be very cheerful in his place. I shouldn't like to sit in the stalls and watch the thoughts that go through his head, damned if I would.'

But when he found himself forced to stop for a moment while a woman got out of her cab to go into her house, he greedily sniffed the fragrant scent of verbena and lilies which she left in the air as she passed. He felt a sudden quiver of joy and expectation and his whole body thrilled as he remembered that he would be seeing Madame de Marelle tomorrow.

Everything was on his side; life was welcoming him with open arms. How wonderful to realize all your hopes!

He went to sleep in a rapture of joy and rose early to take a walk in the Bois de Boulogne before going on to his assignation.

The wind had changed overnight and the weather was as warm and sunny as in April. All the regular frequenters of the Bois had made their appearance that morning, unable to resist the clear, gentle sky.

Duroy walked slowly, drinking in the fresh air which tasted as delicious as fresh bread. He went past the Arc de Triomphe and started walking along the main avenue, in the opposite direction to the riders. He watched them as they trotted or galloped, men and women, the rich ones of the world, and now he found himself barely envying them. He knew almost all of them by name, the state of their finances and their secret lives, since his duties had made him a sort of *Who's Who* for all the celebrities of Paris – and for their scandals.

Women were riding by, slim in their dark, close-fitting habits, with that indefinable hint of arrogance and un-approachability of many women on horseback. To amuse himself, Duroy recited to himself a sort of litany of the names, titles and quality of the lovers they had had or were said to have had. Sometimes, in fact, instead of saying:

'Baron de Tanquelet
Prince de la Tour-Enguerrand'
he murmured: 'Lesbos:
Louise Michot, from the Vaudeville

Rose Marquetin, from the Opéra.'

He found this a highly amusing game, as though enjoying uncovering man's fundamental and eternal baseness underneath his apparent strictness and as if this discovery excited him and gave him consolation.

Then he said out loud: 'Bunch of hypocrites!' and started looking out for the riders with particularly shady reputations.

He saw quite a number who were suspected of cheating at cards or who in any case used gambling clubs as their major source of income, certainly a dubious one.

There were others, with famous names, who lived entirely on their wives' private incomes, as everyone well knew; others who lived similarly on their mistresses', as everyone suspected. Many had paid their debts (an honourable action) without anybody's ever discovering where they had found the money (a much less honourable secret). He saw financiers whose immense wealth was based on robbery but who were welcome everywhere, in the noblest houses, and also men so respected that ordinary people raised their hats to them as they passed but whose scandalous speculation in state-controlled enterprises was perfectly familiar to all those who knew the shady things that take place behind the scenes.

All of them were haughty, with a sneer on their lips, an insolent look in their eyes, men with side-whiskers and men with moustaches.

Duroy was laughing to himself as he repeated:

'What a set, the whole filthy bunch of crooks!'

But then a smart, low, open carriage came by drawn at a brisk trot by two slim greys with flowing manes and tails, driven by a small blonde young woman, a well-known high-class tart, with two grooms sitting behind her. Duroy stopped and felt like waving and applauding this woman whose success had been won on her back and who was boldly flaunting her luxury by taking her drive at the same time as these aristocratic hypocrites. He had, perhaps, the dim feeling that they had something in common, a temperamental bond; that they were of the same breed and spirit, and that his success would be achieved by methods equally bold.

He returned more slowly, glowing with satisfaction, and he arrived at his former mistress's door slightly before the time.

She welcomed him by offering him her lips as though they had never quarrelled and for a few moments she even forgot how careful she always was to make sure that their caresses did not go beyond certain bounds. Then, depositing a kiss on the tip of his curly moustache, she said:

'You can't imagine what a boring thing has happened, darling. I was hoping for a wonderful honeymoon and now I'm going to have my husband on my hands for six weeks. He's taking his holiday. But I can't go six weeks without seeing you, especially after our little tiff, and this is what I've arranged. You must come to dinner on Monday, I've already mentioned you to him. I'll introduce you.'

Duroy hesitated, a trifle uncertain because he had never yet come face to face with his mistress's husband. He was afraid that he might somehow betray himself by being embarrassed, by a look or in some other way. He said hesitantly:

'No, I'd prefer not to meet your husband.'

Extremely surprised, she stood and looked at him with wide, innocent eyes before returning to the attack:

'But why not? What a strange idea! That sort of thing happens every day. I really wouldn't have imagined that you'd be so silly.'

Her remark touched him to the quick.

'All right, then, I'll come to dinner on Monday.'

'So that it looks quite normal, I'll invite the Forestiers. All the same, I don't enjoy having people to dinner at my place.'

Before Monday, Duroy hardly gave a thought to the meeting; but now, going up Madame de Marelle's stairs, he felt really uncomfortable. Not that he felt any compunction at shaking her husband by the hand, drinking his wine and eating his bread, but he was still afraid of something, without knowing exactly what.

He was shown into the drawing-room and he waited, as always. Then the door opened and in came a tall, serious-looking man with a white beard, wearing a decoration, every inch the gentleman, who came towards him, saying with exquisite politeness:

'I am delighted to meet you, sir. My wife has often spoken to me about you.'

Duroy went towards him, trying to appear full of cordiality, and he shook his host's hand with exaggerated vigour. Then he sat down and could find nothing to say.

Monsieur de Marelle put a piece of wood on the fire and enquired:

'Have you been in journalism very long?'

Duroy replied:

'Only a few months.'

'Indeed. You have made great strides.'

'Yes, fairly great.' And he started saying the first thing that came into his head without paying much attention to what he was talking about, uttering the usual commonplaces used by people who are not acquainted. He was regaining his confidence now and beginning to find the situation very amusing. He was watching Monsieur de Marelle's serious, respectable face with a great temptation to laugh and he thought: 'I'm going to bed with your wife, you silly old man.' And he was filled by a secret, vicious satisfaction, the glee of the successful, unsuspected thief, the delicious joy of the swindler. He suddenly felt that he would like to become this man's friend, win his trust, persuade him to unbare his secrets.

Suddenly Madame de Marelle came in, cast her smiling and inscrutable gaze over the two of them and then went over to Duroy, who was afraid to kiss her hand as usual, because of her husband.

She was cheerful and at her ease, like a woman able to handle any situation, for her inherent lack of scruples or inhibitions enabled her to take such a meeting between the two men completely in her stride. Laurine appeared and, intimidated by her father's presence, went up to Georges more circumspectly than usual to offer her forehead to kiss. Her mother said to her: 'So you're not going to call him Bel-Ami today, I see.' And the child blushed as if it had been highly indiscreet to reveal something which ought not to be said, a private, slightly guilty secret.

When the Forestiers arrived, everyone was appalled at Charles's appearance. In a week he had become dreadfully emaciated and pale and he coughed incessantly. Indeed he said that, on doctor's orders, they were leaving for Cannes the following Thursday.

They left early and Duroy said, shaking his head:

'I'm afraid he's in a very bad way. I can't see him making old bones.'

Madame de Marelle said placidly: 'Oh, he's a goner! My goodness, how lucky he was to find the wife he did!'

'Does she help him a lot?' Duroy enquired.

'In fact, she does everything. She knows everything that's happening and she knows everybody, without seeming to meet anybody. She gets what she wants how she wants, and when she wants. Oh, she's a crafty, clever woman and as scheming as they come. She's a perfect treasure for any man who wants to get on.'

Georges said:

'No doubt she won't be long before marrying again.'

Madame de Marelle replied:

'Yes, I shouldn't be surprised if she even had someone in mind ... a deputy ... unless ... unless he doesn't want to ... because ... because ... there might perhaps be grave moral ... obstacles. Anyway, there we are. I don't know.'

Showing signs of impatience, Monsieur de Marelle gently grumbled:

'You're always hinting at all sorts of suspicions that I don't like. Let's not ever meddle in other people's business. Our own conscience is enough to guide our actions. That's a rule everyone ought to follow.'

Duroy was in a state of some agitation when he left, his mind full of half-formed calculations.

The following day he called on the Forestiers and found them finishing their packing. Charles was lying on a settee, making much of his difficulty in breathing, and saying all the time: 'I ought to have left a month ago', and then made a series of recommendations about the work at the newspaper, although everything had been arranged and agreed with Monsieur Walter.

When Georges left he gave his friend a vigorous handshake:

'Well, old man, see you soon.' But as Madame Forestier was seeing him out, he said quickly: 'You haven't forgotten our pact? We're friends and allies, remember? So if you need me for anything, don't hesitate. A telegram or a letter and I'll do whatever you say.'

She said quietly: 'Thank you, I won't forget.' And her eyes said 'Thank you', too, with a deeper, gentler gratitude.

As Duroy was going downstairs he met Monsieur de

Vaudrec slowly coming up, the man whom he had already seen once before at her house. The Count seemed sad – perhaps because she was going away?

Anxious to appear a man of the world, the journalist greeted him with alacrity.

The other man responded courteously, albeit with a certain haughtiness.

The Forestiers left on Thursday evening.

CHAPTER 7

CHARLES'S absence increased Duroy's importance as an editor on *La Vie française*. He signed one or two leading articles as well as his own column, because the proprietor was anxious that each sub-editor should assume responsibility for his own work. He became involved in a number of controversies which he wittily turned to his advantage and his constant dealings with politicians were steadily preparing him to become, in his turn, a skilful and perspicacious political sub-editor.

There was only one cloud on the horizon. It was caused by an irreverent little newspaper called *La Plume* which constantly attacked him, or rather which attacked, through him, the chief editor of the gossip and news column of *La Vie française*, the column which the anonymous editor of the paper called Monsieur Walter's 'surprise' column. Every day there were insidious little jabs, ironical comments and insinuations of all sorts.

One day Jacques Rival said to him:

'You're a patient fellow.'

The other man replied, uncertainly:

'What can I do? There's never been any direct attack.'

Then one afternoon, as he came into the editorial office, Boisrenard handed him a copy of *La Plume*.

'Here you are, there's another unpleasant piece about you.'

'Oh? What for?'

'Something quite unimportant, the arrest of someone called Madame Aubert by a member of the vice squad.'

Georges took the paper and, under the title 'Duroy must have his little joke', read the following paragraph:

The illustrious reporter of *La Vie française* informs us today that Madame Aubert, news of whose arrest by the loathsome vice squad had been published by us, exists only in our imagination. In fact, the woman in question lives at 18 Rue de l'Écureuil, Montmartre. We can, of course, understand only too well the interest(s) the henchmen of the Walter Bank may have in supporting those of the police who are prepared to tolerate their deals. As for the reporter concerned, he would be better employed in letting us have some of that sensational good news which is his speciality: reports of deaths that have to be denied next day, reports of battles that never took place, reports of solemn words spoken by monarchs who never opened their mouths, in fact all those reports which go to swell Walter's profits or even one of those indiscreet little notices about parties given by women anxious to hit the headlines or about the outstanding qualities of certain products – reports which are all of great help to some of our colleagues.

Duroy was more taken aback than irritated, realizing only that the article was being extremely disagreeable towards him.

Boisrenard went on:

'Who gave you that news item?'

Duroy pondered a second, unable to remember. Then, suddenly, it came back to him:

'Oh yes, it was Saint-Potin.' Then he read the paragraph again and the colour rose angrily to his cheeks at the accusation of venality.

He exclaimed: 'What, are they saying that I'm paid to ...'

Boisrenard interrupted him:

'They are indeed. It's annoying for you. The boss is very sensitive on that score. It could happen so often in a news and gossip column.'

At this very moment, Saint-Potin himself came in. Duroy dashed to meet him:

'Have you seen the note in *La Plume*?'

'Yes, and I've just come from Madame Aubert's. She does exist but she was never arrested. There's no truth at all in the rumour.'

Duroy hurried off to see his director whom he found rather chilly, with a suspicious look in his eye. He listened to Duroy's account and then said: 'Go and see the woman yourself and then contradict *La Plume*'s article in such a way that they won't dare to write any more of that sort of thing about you. I'm talking about the bit at the end. It's very tiresome for the paper, for me and for you. Like Caesar's wife, a journalist must be above suspicion.'

Duroy took a cab, with Saint-Potin to show him the way, and shouted to the driver:

'18 Rue de l'Écureuil, Montmartre.'

It was an immense block and they had to climb up to the sixth floor. An old woman in a loose woollen jacket opened the door: 'What do you want now?' she asked when she saw Saint-Potin.

He replied:

'This gentleman is an inspector of police and would like to hear your story.'

So she let them in, saying as she did so:

'There've been two gentlemen since you for a paper, I don't know which one it was.' Then she turned to Duroy: 'So you'd like to know about it, sir?'

'Yes. Were you arrested by a member of the vice squad?'

She flung her arms in the air.

'Never, guv . . . , never. This is how it happened. I've got a butcher who sells good meat but he's not so good at weighing. I'd often noticed it and not said nothing but when I asked for two pounds of chops because I've got my daughter and son-in-law coming, I see him putting on odd bits of bone, bones from chops that aren't part of my chops.

I could have made a stew out of it I know but when I ask for chops I don't want other people's bones. So I says no and then he calls me an old stingy and I says he's an old cheat. Anyway, to cut a long story short, it comes to we're having a row and more than a hundred people watching us through the shop window all laughing like mad. And so a policeman comes along and says we should go to the police station to settle it. So we went and they said to go away and forget it. So since then, I've been going to another butcher's and I don't even go by his shop so's to avoid trouble.'

She stopped. Duroy asked:

'So that's all?'

'That's the whole truth, sir,' and after offering him a glass of blackcurrant cordial which he refused, the old woman insisted that the report ought to mention how bad the butcher was at weighing.

When he got back to the newspaper, Duroy wrote his reply:

An anonymous pen-pusher from *La Plume* has used it to try to pick a quarrel with me on the subject of an old woman who, he claims, was arrested by a member of the vice squad. This I deny. I have personally seen Madame Aubert, who is at least sixty years old, and she told me in detail about her quarrel with a butcher over a question of weighing some chops, which ended in their having to settle the matter at the police station.

That's the whole truth.

As for the other insinuations of the author of the article in *La Plume*, they are beneath contempt. In any case, no one bothers to answer such things when they are unsigned.

Georges Duroy.

Monsieur Walter and Jacques Rival, who had just come in, considered the note adequate and it was decided to put it in that very evening, at the end of the news items.

Duroy went home somewhat uneasy and worried. What would the other man say in reply? Who was he? Why had he launched such a violent attack? In view of the rough and ready ways of journalists, such a matter, trifling in itself, might lead to trouble, big trouble. He slept badly.

On re-reading his note the following day he found it more aggressive in print. He might, he thought, have toned down certain expressions.

He felt wrought up all day and once again slept badly that night. He rose at dawn to obtain the copy of *La Plume* that would contain the answer to his own reply.

The weather had turned cold again and it was freezing hard. The gutters in the streets were like two strips of ice, freezing as they flowed.

The papers had not yet arrived and Duroy was reminded of the day of his first article, 'Memories of an African Cavalryman'. His feet and hands were growing numb and beginning to hurt, particularly the tips of his fingers; and he started jogging round the glass kiosk where, through the little window, you could see the paper seller's red nose and cheeks wrapped in a woollen hood, as she crouched over her little stove.

Finally the long-awaited newspaper boy arrived and passed his bundle through the opening in the window. The woman handed an open copy of *La Plume* to Duroy. He glanced quickly over it to find his name and at first could see nothing. He started breathing more freely and then he saw an item inserted between two dashes:

Our Monsieur Duroy of *La Vie française* has contradicted us and in giving us the lie, he is lying himself. He does, however, admit that a Madame Aubert exists and that a policeman took her to the police-station. All that is needed, therefore, is to add four words: 'from the vice squad', after the word 'policeman' and there we have it.

But some journalists have a conscience to match their ability. My signature is: Louis Langremont.

Georges' heart started pounding violently and he went back home to dress without quite knowing what he was doing. So he had been insulted and in such a way that any hesitation was impossible. Why? For no reason at all. All because an old woman had quarrelled with her butcher.

He quickly pulled on some clothes and went to see Monsieur Walter, although it was barely eight o'clock.

Monsieur Walter was already up and reading *La Plume*.

'Well,' he said with a serious expression when he saw Duroy, 'you can't draw back now.'

The young man said nothing. His director continued:

'Go and see Rival straight away. He'll take care of your interests.'

Duroy stammered a few vague words and went off to see the columnist who was still asleep. He jumped out of bed when he heard the bell and after reading the article: 'By Jove there's only one thing to do. What about the other second?'

'I really don't know.'

'Boisrenard? What do you think?'

'Yes, Boisrenard.'

'Do you fence?'

'Not at all.'

'The devil! What about pistols?'

'I can shoot a bit.'

'Good. You must practise while I see to everything. Wait for me a minute.'

He went into his dressing-room and soon came out again washed, shaved and spruce.

'Come along,' he said.

He lived on the ground floor of a small town house and he took Duroy down into the cellar, an enormous one which had been fitted out as a room for fencing and shooting, with all the window-openings on the street side bricked up.

Lighting a row of gas jets which led into the far end of a second cellar where there stood an iron figure painted red and blue, he put down on the table a pair of modern breech-loading pistols and started to snap out words of command as if it was an actual duel:

'Ready?

'Fire!'

Duroy, completely bemused, obeyed, raising his arm, aiming, pressing the trigger and, as he often hit the dummy in the middle, because when he was very young he had frequently used an old horse-pistol of his father's to kill birds in the backyard, Jacques Rival said, with satisfaction: 'Good – very good – very good indeed – you'll do, you'll do.'

Then he left him:

'Go on shooting like that till lunch-time. Here's some ammunition, don't be afraid of using it. I'll come and pick you up for lunch and tell you what's happened.'

And he went out.

Left to himself, Duroy fired a few more rounds and then sat down and started thinking.

How stupid it all was, really! What did it prove? Was a rogue any less a rogue after he'd fought a duel? What did an honest man who'd been insulted gain by risking his life against a blackguard? And as his thoughts wandered gloomily on, he remembered what Norbert de Varenne had been saying about the dullness of men's minds, their banal ideas and interests and their vapid morality.

And he said out loud:

'My God, how right he was!'

Then he realized that he was thirsty and, hearing the sound of dripping water behind him, he saw a shower-bath

157

and went over to have a drink from the nozzle. Then he returned to his thoughts. It was gloomy in the cellar, as gloomy as the grave. The distant roar of the traffic seemed like the rumble of a far-off passing thunderstorm. What could the time be? In the cellar, the hours were passing as slowly as in a prison where there is nothing to indicate or differentiate them except the gaoler bringing the food. He waited a long, long time.

Then suddenly he heard footsteps and voices and Jacques Rival reappeared, accompanied by Boisrenard. As soon as he saw Duroy, he said: 'It's all fixed up!'

The latter thought that the affair had been settled by some letter of apology. His heart gave a leap and he stammered:

'Oh, thank you!'

The other went on:

'That Langremont is a very straightforward sort of chap, he's accepted all our conditions. Twenty-five paces, one shot on the word of command, raising the arm. You get a much better aim than when you're lowering it. Look, Boisrenard, see what I was telling you.'

And taking the pistols he started to shoot, showing how much easier it was to keep a straight line while raising the arm.

Then he said:

'Now let's go and have lunch, it's past twelve o'clock.'

And they went to a near-by restaurant. Duroy said very little. He ate in order not to appear frightened and then went with Boisrenard to spend the day at the paper, where he worked mechanically, his mind elsewhere. People were admiring his pluck. Jacques Rival came in to see him in the course of the afternoon and it was agreed that his seconds should come and pick him up in a landau at seven o'clock the following morning to take him to the Bois du Vésinet where the encounter was to take place.

All this had happened unexpectedly, without his having any part in it, without saying a word, without being asked his opinion, without either accepting or refusing and all with such speed that he was bewildered and startled without understanding very much what it was all about.

He came home at about nine o'clock after going to dinner with Boisrenard, who had devotedly kept him company all day.

As soon as he was on his own, he paced rapidly up and down the room for a few minutes, too confused to think. He was obsessed by one idea only: 'you have a duel tomorrow'; but his only reaction was a vague, if strong, emotion. He had been in the army, he had fired on Arabs, although without any real danger to himself, rather in the way you shoot a wild boar when you are out hunting.

All in all, he had done what was expected of him. He had shown himself the sort of person who can behave properly. People would talk about him and approve his conduct, they would congratulate him. Then speaking out loud, as one does in moments of great stress, he said:

'What a bastard the fellow is!'

He sat down and pondered. Lying on his little table where he had dropped it was one of his opponent's visiting cards which Rival had given him, so that he would remember his address. He looked at it again, as he had done a score of times in the course of the day: *Louis Langremont, 179 Rue Montmartre*. Nothing else.

He peered at all the letters printed together on the card. They seemed mysterious, full of disturbing meanings. 'Louis Langremont.' Who was the man? How old was he? How tall? What did he look like? Wasn't it revolting that a stranger, someone completely unknown, could suddenly disturb your life, without any reason, heedlessly, just because an old woman had quarrelled with her butcher?

Once again, he said out loud: 'The bastard!'

He sat motionless, pondering, his eyes still staring at the card. Anger against the piece of paste-board welled up inside him, a vicious anger mingled with a strange disquiet. God, how stupid the whole thing was! He picked up a pair of nail scissors lying there and stuck the point through the middle of the name as if he were stabbing someone with a dagger.

So he was going to fight a duel, and, what's more, a duel with pistols. Why hadn't he chosen swords? He would have got off with a scratch on his arm or hand, whereas with a pistol you could never tell.

He said: 'Come on, buck up.'

The sound of his voice made him start and he looked around him. He was beginning to feel very much on edge. He drank a glass of water and went to bed.

As soon as he was in bed, he blew out the light and closed his eyes.

He felt very warm between the sheets, even though his room was very cold. But sleep would not come. He twisted and turned, lay on his back for five minutes and then on his left side before rolling over on to his right.

He still felt thirsty. He fetched himself a drink and all of a sudden a worrying thought struck him: 'Shall I be scared?'

Why was his heart pounding so wildly at every familiar sound in his room? When his cuckoo-clock was about to strike, the squeak of its spring made him jump and he had to open his mouth to gulp in air for a few seconds to relieve the weight on his chest.

He started to philosophize on the possibility of being frightened.

No, of course, he wouldn't be frightened because he had taken the decision to see the thing through, because he was firmly resolved to fight, to show no sign of trepidation. But so deeply disturbed did he feel that he wondered to himself: 'Can one be frightened in spite of oneself?' And he was overcome by doubt and worry and dread. If some irresistible power, stronger than his own will, were to take over, what would happen? Yes, indeed, what might happen?

Of course, he would go and face his opponent because he wanted to do so. But suppose he was trembling? Suppose he fainted? And he thought of his position, of his reputation, his future.

And he suddenly felt a strange need to get up and look at himself in the mirror. He lit his candle. When he saw the reflection of his face in the glass, he barely recognized himself; it was as if he were seeing himself for the first time. His eyes seemed as big as saucers; and he was pale, yes, he certainly was pale, very pale indeed.

Suddenly, like a bullet, the thought struck him: 'Perhaps tomorrow at this time, I'll be dead.' And his heart began to pound again, furiously.

He went back to his divan and he distinctly saw himself lying on his back between the very sheets he had just left. He had the sunken face of the dead, the white hands which are now forever still.

And then he felt a sudden fear of his bed and to avoid seeing it, he opened the window to look out.

An icy blast tore at his flesh from head to foot and he recoiled, gasping.

He thought he would light a fire. He fanned it gently, without turning round. His hands were shaking nervously as they touched each object. His mind was wandering; his thoughts were whirling disjointedly round and round his aching head, panic-stricken; he felt as bemused as if he had been drinking.

And all the time he kept wondering: 'What shall I do? What will happen to me?'

He began to walk round his room again, repeating to himself mechanically all the time: 'I must show grit, I must show lots of grit.'

Then he said: 'I must write to my parents in case of an accident.'

He sat down again, took a sheet of notepaper and wrote: 'Dear Mummy and Daddy...'

Then he thought that it was too familiar a way to begin a letter in such tragic circumstances. He tore the letter up and started again: 'Dear Father, dear Mother, I'm going to fight a duel at dawn this morning and as something may happen...'

He did not have the heart to continue and sprang up hastily from his chair.

Now, like a dead weight, his mind was filled with the words and the thought 'I am going to fight a duel'. It was impossible to avoid doing so. Then what was happening to him? He wanted to fight; his mind was made up, he was quite determined to fight; and despite every effort of his will, it seemed to him that he might not even have the strength to go to the scene of the encounter.

Every so often his teeth started chattering and he wondered:

'Has my opponent already fought a duel? Does he practise shooting? Has he a reputation? Is he a really good shot?' He had never heard of him. And yet if the man were not a remarkably good shot, he would hardly have agreed to such a dangerous weapon without any hesitation or discussion.

Then Duroy pictured the scene to himself, his own attitude and the behaviour of his opponent. He endeavoured to imagine the smallest details of the fight and suddenly found himself looking into the little deep dark aperture of the barrel which was about to discharge a bullet.

All at once he was seized by black despair. He was shaking like a leaf and shudders ran through his whole body. He clenched his teeth in order not to scream out loud and he felt a wild urge to roll on the floor, to tear something to pieces, to bite into something. But then he spied a glass on his mantelpiece and he remembered that he had almost a full litre bottle of spirits in his wardrobe; he had kept up the army habit of taking a quick swig on an empty stomach every morning.

He grasped the bottle and drank out of it in long, greedy gulps. He did not put it down until forced to do so by lack of breath. It was now two thirds full.

A fiery glow quickly warmed his stomach and spread to every limb, calming and benumbing his mind.

He said to himself: 'I've found the solution.' And as his skin was now all aglow, he opened the window again.

Day was dawning; everything was still and icy-cold. Up above, the stars seemed to be dying as the sky grew brighter and in the deep canyon of the railway-line the green, red and white signals were growing paler.

The first engines were coming out of their sheds and going off whistling in search of the early trains. In the distance there were others uttering repeated shrill cries, their dawn chorus, like cocks in the country.

Duroy thought: 'Perhaps it's the last time I shall see all this.' But as he felt on the point of pitying himself again, he reacted violently: 'Come on, you mustn't think of anything until the moment you face your opponent, that's the only way to show you've got pluck.'

And he started to dress. For a second, as he was shaving, he felt his boldness evaporating at the thought that it was perhaps the last time he would see his face.

He took another swig of spirits and finished dressing.

The next hour was a trying one. He kept walking up and

down, endeavouring to stay calm. When he heard a knock on his door, he nearly fell flat on his back with shock. It was his seconds.

'So soon!'

They were wrapped in fur coats. Rival shook hands with his principal and said:

'It's as cold as Siberia outside.' Then he asked: 'Everything all right?'

'Yes, perfectly, thanks.'

'Not nervous?'

'Not a bit.'

'Splendid, you'll do. Have you had anything to eat and drink?'

'Yes, I don't want anything.'

In honour of the occasion, Boisrenard was sporting a foreign decoration, a green and yellow ribbon that Duroy had not seen him wearing before.

They went downstairs. Another man was waiting in the landau. Rival said: 'Dr Le Brument.' Duroy shook hands, mumbled: 'Thank you', and then tried to sit down on the front seat where he felt something hard which made him jump up again like a jack-in-the-box. It was the pistol-case.

Rival kept saying: 'No! The principal and the doctor in the back seat' and finally Duroy understood what he was being told and slumped down beside the doctor.

The two seconds climbed in and the driver drove off. He knew where to go.

But the pistol-case was in everyone's way and Duroy in particular would have preferred not to have it in sight. They tried to put it behind them on the seat but it dug into their backs; then they stood it on end between Rival and Boisrenard but it kept falling over. Finally, they slipped it under their feet.

Conversation flagged, although the doctor was telling various anecdotes. Only Rival answered. Duroy would have liked to show his presence of mind but he was afraid of losing the thread of his ideas and revealing how confused he was; and he was tortured by the fear that he might begin to tremble.

Soon the carriage was out in the country. It was about nine o'clock and one of those bitter winter mornings when everything in nature is glittering, as hard and brittle as glass. The trees covered in hoar-frost seem to have been sweating drops of ice; the ground echoes beneath your feet; the slightest noise travels great distances in the dry air; the blue sky shines like a mirror and the sun moves in cold splendour through space, casting its chilly rays over a frozen world.

Rival was telling Duroy:

'I got the pistols from Gastine Renette. He loaded them himself. The case is sealed. You'll draw lots, incidentally, to decide whether we use these or your opponent's.'

Duroy answered mechanically:

'Thank you.'

Then Rival started giving him meticulous instructions because he was anxious that his principal should not do anything wrong. He repeated each point several times: 'When they ask: "Are you ready, gentlemen?" you must reply loudly: "Yes!"

'When they give the order: "Fire!" you must quickly raise your arm and fire before they've counted up to three.'

And Duroy repeated to himself mentally: 'When they give the order fire, I must raise my arm – when they give the order fire, I must raise my arm.'

He was learning it like a child learning his lessons, mumbling it under his breath over and over again to fix it firmly in his mind. 'When they give the order fire, I must raise my arm.'

The landau drove into a wood, turned right down an avenue and then right again. Rival suddenly opened the window and shouted to the driver: 'Over there, down that little lane.' And the carriage turned into a rutted track between two copses where the dead leaves were stirring, limned with frost.

Duroy was still muttering to himself:

'When they give the order fire, I must raise my arm.' And the thought suddenly came to him that an accident to the carriage would settle everything. Oh, if only it could overturn, what luck that would be! Suppose he broke his leg!

But he caught sight of another carriage standing at the end of a clearing and four men stamping to warm their feet; and he had to open his mouth wide because he found it hard to breathe.

The seconds got out first, followed by the doctor and the principal. Rival had picked up the pistol-case and went off with Boisrenard to meet two of the strangers who were coming towards them. Duroy saw them greet each other ceremoniously and then walk together through the clearing, looking on the ground and up into the trees as if they were searching for something that had fallen or blown away. Then they measured paces and with great difficulty managed to thrust two walking-sticks into the frozen ground. Then they formed a group and went through the motions of tossing a coin, like children playing.

Dr Le Brument asked Duroy:

'Do you feel all right? Is there anything you need?'

'No, nothing, thank you.'

It seemed to him that he was mad or asleep or dreaming, that he was undergoing some strange supernatural experience.

Was he frightened? Possibly. But he did not know. Everything around him seemed unfamiliar.

Jacques Rival came back and whispered to him in a pleased tone:

'Everything is ready. We won the toss for the pistols.'

That was something which left Duroy completely indifferent.

They removed his greatcoat. He submitted passively. They felt his jacket pockets to make sure he had no papers or wallet that might protect him.

He was repeating to himself, like a prayer:

'When they give the order to fire, I must raise my arm.'

They led him up to one of the walking-sticks stuck in the ground and handed him his pistol. Then he saw a man standing facing him and very close, a little bald man with a pot-belly and spectacles. It was his opponent.

He could see him very clearly but he was thinking only of one thing: 'When they give the order to fire, I shall raise my arm and shoot.' In the great hush surrounding him, he heard a voice ring out as though coming from a great distance. It said:

'Are you ready, gentlemen?'

Georges said, loudly:

'Yes.'

Then the same voice gave the order:

'Fire!'

He listened to nothing else, he noticed nothing else, he realized nothing else, he merely felt that he was raising his arm and pressing the trigger with all his might.

And he heard nothing.

But straight away he saw a puff of smoke at the end of his pistol-barrel; and as the man facing him was still standing there, also in the same posture, he noticed another little cloud of smoke floating away over his opponent's head.

They had both fired. It was all over.

His seconds and the doctor were touching him, feeling him, undoing his clothes, enquiring anxiously:

'Have you been hit?' He replied without thinking. 'No, I don't think so.'

Langremont was also completely unharmed and Jacques Rival muttered with annoyance:

'It's always the same with these damned pistols, either you miss, or you get killed. What a lousy weapon!'

Duroy had not stirred, paralysed by surprise and joy. It was all over. They had to take the pistol away from him as he was still clutching it in his hand. It now seemed to him as if he would have been ready to take on the whole universe. It was all over. What bliss! He suddenly felt brave enough to challenge anyone in the world.

The seconds conferred together for a few minutes to arrange a meeting later that day to draw up the official report of the duel and then they climbed back into the carriage and the driver, who was sitting up front laughing, cracked his whip and drove off.

They all four lunched on the boulevard, chatting about the event. Duroy was giving his impressions:

'It had no effect on me at all, absolutely none. I imagine you saw that, anyway.'

Rival replied:

'Yes, you behaved well.'

When the official report had been drawn up, it was handed to Duroy for insertion at the end of the news items. He was surprised to see that he had exchanged two shots with M. Louis Langremont and somewhat anxiously he enquired of Jacques Rival:

'But we only fired one shot?'

The other smiled:

'Yes, one shot . . . one shot each, that makes two shots.'

Accepting the explanation, Duroy raised no further objections. Old Walter gave him a hug:

'Well done, well done, you've defended the honour of *La Vie française*. Well done!'

That evening Duroy made an appearance at the main newspaper offices and the main cafés on the boulevard. On two occasions he met his opponent who was doing the same rounds.

They did not acknowledge each other. If one of them had been wounded, they would have shaken hands. They each firmly claimed, moreover, that they heard the other's bullet whistle past their ears.

Next day at about eleven o'clock in the morning Duroy received an express letter: 'My goodness, how scared I was! Do come to the Rue de Constantinople this afternoon so that I can give you a big kiss, my love. How brave you are. I adore you, Clo.'

When he arrived at the rendezvous, she flung herself into his arms, covering him with kisses.

'Oh my darling, if you only knew how I felt when I read the paper this morning. Oh, do tell me about it. Tell me everything. I want to know.'

He had to tell her every minute detail. She asked:

'What a dreadful night you must have had before the duel.'

'No I didn't. I slept like a log.'

'I wouldn't have been able to sleep a wink. And tell me what happened at the actual duel.'

He gave a dramatic account:

'When we were standing face to face, twenty paces apart, only four times the length of this room, after asking whether we were ready, Jacques gave the order: Fire! I raised my arm immediately in a straight line but I made the mistake of trying to aim at his head. And my pistol had a very heavy trigger and I'm used to a light one so that the extra pressure lifted my aim. All the same, I don't think I can have been far away. He's a good shot too, the old rogue. His shot whistled right past my temple. I could feel the wind.'

She was sitting on his lap and holding him in her arms, as

if wanting to share the danger with him. She said in a trembling voice:

'Oh my poor darling, my poor darling ...'

Then when he had finished his account, she said:

'You know I can't do without you now! I must see you, but with my husband in Paris it's not very convenient. Often I'd be able to have an hour in the morning and I could come and give you a hug before you get up but I don't want to set foot in your horrible house again. What can we do?'

He had a sudden inspiration and asked:

'How much do you pay here?'

'A hundred francs a month.'

'All right, I'll take over the flat for myself and come and live here all the time. Mine's not good enough for my new position.'

She thought for a moment or two and then replied:

'No, I don't want that.'

He was surprised:

'Why not?'

'Because.'

'That's not a reason. This apartment suits me very well. Here I am, here I'll stop.'

He started to laugh:

'Anyway, it's in my name.'

But she still refused:

'No, I don't want to ...'

'But why not?'

Then she said, in a tender whisper:

'Because you'll bring other women here and I don't want that.'

He said indignantly:

'But I'd never do a thing like that. I promise.'

'No, you would still bring them all the same.'

'I swear I wouldn't.'

'Honestly?'

'Honestly and truly. Word of honour. This is our home, just for us alone.'

Impulsively she hugged him.

'All right, then, I agree, darling. But you know if you once deceive me, just once, it'll be all over between us, for ever.'

He repeated his solemn word of honour and it was agreed that he should move in that very day so that she could see him whenever she was in the vicinity.

Then she said:

'In any case, come to dinner on Sunday. My husband thinks you're charming.'

He felt flattered:

'Oh, really?'

'Yes, he approves of you very much. And listen, weren't you telling me that you were brought up in a big country house?'

'Yes, why?'

'So you must know something about plants?'

'Yes.'

'Well, talk to him about gardening and crops, he's awfully interested in that.'

'All right. I'll remember to do that.'

The duel had made her more affectionate than ever; she could hardly stop kissing him before she finally left.

And as he went off to the paper, Duroy thought: 'What a funny creature she is. What a flighty little thing. Can anyone really know what she wants and likes? And what a strange couple! What joker can ever have arranged to pair off that old man and that scatterbrain? Whatever induced that inspector to marry that student? A complete mystery. Who knows, perhaps it was love?'

And he concluded: 'Anyway, she's a jolly nice mistress. I'd be idiotic to let her go.'

His duel had made Duroy one of the leading collaborators of *La Vie française*; but as he had extraordinary difficulty in finding new ideas, he made it his speciality to rail against the lowering of moral standards, the general weakening of character, the decline of patriotism and the anaemia that was sapping the French sense of honour. (He had discovered the word 'anaemia' and was very proud of it.)

And whenever Madame de Marelle, in her usual naïve, mocking, bantering manner that goes by the name of Parisian wit, poked fun at his tirades and punctured them with an epigram, he would answer with a smile: 'Ah well, it's building up my reputation for later on.'

He had now moved into the Rue de Constantinople, a removal involving one trunk, one brush and one razor. Two or three times a week, Clotilde would arrive before he had got up, quickly slip out of her clothes and snuggle up against him in bed, still shivering from the cold outside.

On the other hand, Duroy now used to go to dinner with both of them every Thursday and paid court to the husband by talking about agriculture; and, as he himself liked things connected with the land, they sometimes became so engrossed in their discussion that they completely forgot their woman dozing on the settee.

Laurine used to doze off, too, sometimes on her father's lap and sometimes on Bel-Ami's.

And when the journalist had left, Monsieur de Marelle never failed to remark in the emphatic way which he used to speak of even the most trivial matter: 'He really is a most pleasant young man. He has a very cultivated mind.'

February was drawing to an end. You could begin to smell the violets in the streets in the morning when you passed by the flower-sellers' carts.

There was not a cloud in Duroy's sky.

Then one night when he came home, he found a letter pushed under his door. It bore the Cannes postmark. He opened it and read:

Cannes, Villa Jolie.

Dear friend, You did say, didn't you, that I could rely on you in any way? Well, I want to ask you a sad favour and that is to come and help me, so that I'm not alone during Charles' last few days in this world. He may not even survive the week, although he's still able to move about. But the doctor has given me warning.

I don't feel strong enough or brave enough to watch his final suffering day and night and I'm terrified at the thought of the last few moments that are so close. You are the only person I can ask because my husband has no family left. You were his friend, he helped you to find work on the paper. Please do come. I've no one else to turn to.

Your devoted friend,
Madeleine Forestier.

Georges was seized with a strange feeling of exhilaration and elation, as if a broad panorama had suddenly opened in front of him and he murmured: 'Of course I must go. Poor Charles. How strange life is, really.'

When he told the director about Madeleine's letter the latter grunted and gave him permission to go, at the same time pointing out that he must not stay away long:

'You're indispensable here.'

Georges Duroy left for Cannes next day by the seven o'clock express, after sending a telegram warning the Marelles, and he arrived the following day at about four o'clock in the afternoon.

A porter told him where to find the Villa Jolie, which was

half-way up the hill in the pine-wood dotted with white villas, which runs all the way from Le Cannet to Golfe Juan.

It was a small, low, Italian-style house, situated on the road that wound its way up through the trees, with superb views at every turn.

The door was opened by a servant, who exclaimed:

'Oh sir, madam was so anxious for you to come.'

Duroy asked:

'How's your master?'

'Oh sir, not at all well. He hasn't long to live.'

The drawing-room into which Duroy was shown was hung with pink chintz covered with a blue design. The tall, wide window looked out onto the town and the sea.

Duroy murmured: 'Well I'm damned. It's as elegant as a house in the country. Where the deuce do they get all that money from?'

He heard the rustle of a dress and turned round.

Madame Forestier held out both hands:

'How kind you are, how kind of you to come!' And impulsively she kissed him. Then they looked at each other.

She was a trifle paler, a trifle thinner but still as fresh as a rose and now that she looked more fragile, she seemed, perhaps, even prettier. She said quietly:

'It's terrible, you see he knows he's dying and he's tyrannizing me dreadfully. I've told him you're here. But where's your trunk?'

Duroy replied:

'I left it at the station because I didn't know which hotel you'd recommend for me to be near you.'

She hesitated and then said:

'You must stay here, in the villa. In any case, I've got your room ready. He may die any minute and if that happens during the night, I'd be all alone. I'll send for your luggage.'

He bowed:

'If that's what you'd like.'

'Now let's go up.'

He followed her. She opened a door on the first floor and there, sitting beside a window in an armchair, wrapped in blankets, Duroy saw a sort of corpse looking at him, livid in the glow of the setting sun. He barely recognized him but he realized that it must be his friend.

The room smelt of fever, ether, infusions and tar-water, that unspeakable oppressive atmosphere of a room occupied by a consumptive.

Slowly and painfully Forestier lifted his hand:

'So there you are,' he said. 'You've come to see me die. That's kind of you.'

Duroy forced a laugh: 'See you die! That wouldn't be a very nice thing to see and I certainly wouldn't choose that reason for coming to Cannes. I've come to say hallo and have a short holiday.'

The other mumbled: 'Sit down', and he let his head sink back on to his chest, like a person obsessed by despairing thoughts.

His breath was coming in short, quick gasps and he sometimes gave a little moan as though to remind them how ill he was.

Seeing that he was not talking, his wife went over to the window and nodded with her head towards the view outside: 'Look at that. Isn't it lovely!'

Below them, dotted with villas, the hill sloped down to the town which lay in a semicircle round the bay, stretching in one direction as far as the jetty dominated by the historic citadel with the old church tower on top and on the left to the promontory at the end of the Croisette, opposite the Îles de Lérins. The islands looked like two green spots set in a blue, blue sea. From this height, they seemed like two broad, flat, floating leaves.

And in the far distance, on the other side of the bay, beyond the jetty and the church tower, beneath a brilliant sky, the horizon was barred by the charming outline of a curious range of bluish mountains whose rounded, hooked or jagged peaks ended in a high pyramid which plunged steeply down into the sea.

Madame Forestier pointed: 'That's the Estérel.'

The light behind the dark mountain tops was red and gold, a blood-red light, too strong to face directly.

In spite of himself, Duroy was affected by this majestic spectacle of the dying day.

Unable to find a more vivid phrase to express his admiration, he murmured:

'Yes, it's gorgeous.'

Forestier raised his head and said to his wife:

'Let me have more air.'

She replied:

'Be careful, it's getting late, the sun's going down. You'll catch cold again and you know that that's not good for you in your present state of health.'

He waved his right hand at her in a feeble, frantic gesture as if he were trying to punch her, and with his fleshless lips and cheeks contorted by anger and a deathly expression on his bony, emaciated face, he muttered angrily:

'I'm stifling, I tell you. What does it matter to you whether I kick the bucket a day or two earlier or later now that I'm done for?'

She flung the window wide open.

The air that came in took them by surprise, for it was gentle and caressing. Soft, warm and calm, it was a spring breeze already fragrant with the scent of the shrubs and the heady perfume of the flowers which grow along the coast. You could distinguish the strong flavour of resin and the bitter smell of the eucalyptus.

Forestier drew it into his lungs in short, feverish gasps.

176

He clawed at the arms of his chair and said in a low, wheezing, infuriated voice:

'Shut the window. It's bad for me. I'd sooner peg out in a cellar.'

So his wife slowly closed the window and, resting her forehead against the pane of glass, she looked out into the distance.

Ill-at-ease, Duroy would have liked to have said something to cheer the sick man up but he could think of nothing to comfort him.

He said, uncertainly:

'So you haven't felt any better since you've been here?'

The other shrugged his shoulders impatiently and despondently: 'You can see for yourself.' And his head dropped on his chest again.

Duroy went on:

'My goodness, it's so pleasant here compared to Paris. It's still mid-winter there. It's snowing and hailing and raining and so dark that you have to light the lamps at three o'clock in the afternoon.'

Forestier asked:

'Anything new at the paper?'

'No, nothing new. They've taken on young Lacrin from *Voltaire* to replace you, but he lacks experience. It's time you came back.'

The sick man said brokenly:

'Me? I'm going to be writing my articles six feet under the ground.'

His obsession kept recurring like the tolling of a bell, whatever the subject, in his every thought, his every sentence.

Silence fell, a long, deep, painful silence. Slowly, the bright rays of the setting sun faded; the mountains were growing dark against the deepening red of the sky. The shades of nightfall, still glowing like a dying brazier, crept into the room tingeing the furniture, the walls, the curtains, the corners, with inky purple shades. The mirror over the mantelpiece, in which you could see the reflection of the horizon, looked like a pool of blood.

Madame Forestier was still standing, motionless, with her back to the room, her forehead pressed against the window-pane.

Forestier started talking, in a breathless, broken voice that was heartbreaking to listen to:

'How many more sunsets shall I be able to watch? Eight, ten, fifteen, twenty? Perhaps thirty, at the most. You've got time, you have. But for me it's all over ... And after me, everything will go on exactly as if I were there ...'

He was silent for a few minutes and then went on:

'Everything I look at reminds me that I shall never see it again in a few days' time ... It's horrible ... I shan't ever see anything again ... nothing that exists ... the smallest object's you can take into your hands ... glasses ... plates ... the beds on which you rest ... carriages. It's wonderful to go for a drive in a carriage in the evening. How I loved doing all that.'

The fingers of both his hands were twitching convulsively, as if he were playing the piano on the two arms of his chair. And his silence was even more distressing than his words, because you felt that his head was full of dreadful thoughts.

And Duroy suddenly remembered what Norbert de Varenne had said to him some weeks earlier: 'I can see death now so close to me that I often feel I must push it off with my hand. I see it whichever way I turn. Tiny animals run over on the road, falling leaves, a white hair in a friend's beard, anything like that terrifies me because they seem to be screaming: Take a look – that's death!'

At that time he had not understood but now, seeing

Forestier, he did understand. And a strange, savage anguish gripped him as though he felt the hideous presence of death right there beside him, within his reach, on the chair where this man was sitting gasping. He felt an urge to stand up and leave, make his escape and go back to Paris straightaway. If only he'd known, he would never have come!

The shades of night had by now spread throughout the room as though in premature mourning for the dying man. Only the window could now be seen with the motionless figure of the young woman silhouetted against its square patch of light.

Forestier asked petulantly:

'Well, isn't anyone going to bring a light today? That's a fine way to look after a sick man!'

The shadowy figure at the window disappeared and the sound of an electric bell echoed through the house.

In a few minutes, a servant came in and placed a lamp on the mantelpiece. Madame Forestier asked her husband:

'Do you want to go to bed or will you come down to dinner?'

He muttered:

'I'll come down.'

And they sat, all three, for almost an hour waiting for dinner, motionless, merely exchanging a word here and there, any word, however pointless or trite, as though it was secretly dangerous to let the stillness continue for too long, to allow the air of this death-haunted room to congeal into silence.

Finally dinner was announced. For Duroy it seemed interminable. Not a word was uttered as they ate without a sound and then crumbled their bread between their fingertips. And when the servant moved about the room serving the meal, his footsteps were inaudible because he was wearing slippers since the sound of his shoes was too irritating

179

for Charles. The only noise to disturb the quiet of the room was the loud, regular, mechanical tick of the wooden clock.

As soon as the meal was over, Duroy excused himself on the grounds of tiredness and went up to his room where he leaned out of his window and watched the full moon in the centre of the sky like an enormous lamp-globe lighting up the white walls of the villa with its cool, gentle light and spreading a dim shimmer over the surface of the sea like glittering fish scales. He was racking his brain to find a reason for leaving as quickly as possible, thinking up all sorts of subterfuges, telegrams he might arrange to be sent or being recalled by Monsieur Walter.

But when he awoke next morning his firm decision to escape seemed more difficult to realize. Madame Forestier would hardly be taken in by his stratagems and his pusillanimity would lose him all the credit he had gained by his display of devotion. He said: 'Well, it's a bore but it can't be helped; life sometimes has unpleasant moments that have to be put up with and anyway, perhaps it won't be long.'

The sky was blue, that bright southern blue that fills you with joy, and Duroy walked down to the sea, thinking that it would be soon enough to see Forestier later in the day.

When he returned for lunch, the servant said: 'The master has already asked for you two or three times, sir. Could you please go up and see him?'

He went upstairs. Forestier seemed to be asleep in an armchair. His wife was stretched out on a sofa, reading.

The sick man looked up. Duroy asked:

'Well, how are things? You seem to be in good form this morning.'

The other answered:

'Yes, I'm better. I'm feeling stronger. Have a quick lunch with Madeleine because we're going for a drive.'

As soon as they were alone, his wife said to Duroy:

'You see, today he thinks everything is going to be all right. He's been making plans all morning. After lunch we're going to Golfe Juan to buy some pottery for our flat in Paris. He's determined to go out but I'm terribly scared that something may happen. He won't be able to stand the jolting on the road.'

When the carriage arrived, Forestier came downstairs one step at a time, supported by the servant. But as soon as he saw the landau, he asked for it to be opened completely.

His wife protested:

'You'll catch cold. It's ridiculous.'

He refused to listen:

'No, I'm much better. I can feel it.'

First of all they followed the shady lanes, with gardens on either side the whole length of the way down, something which makes Cannes into a sort of English park, and then they reached the Antibes road and went along the sea-shore.

Forestier was describing the district. First of all he pointed out the villa owned by the Comte de Paris and mentioned several others. He was cheerful, with the forced, artificial, sickly cheerfulness of someone soon to die. He was pointing at things with his finger because he was not strong enough to raise his arm.

'Look, there's the Île Sainte-Marguerite and the castle which Bazaine escaped from. They pulled a fast one on us there.'

Then he started talking of the regiment; he spoke of the officers, and that reminded them of their experiences. But suddenly, as the road turned, the whole of Golfe Juan was revealed with its white village set in the middle and the Cap d'Antibes at the far end.

And spluttering with childish joy he suddenly exclaimed:

'Oh, there's a naval squadron, you're going to see the fleet!'

And indeed, in the middle of the vast bay you could see half a dozen large vessels looking like rocks covered in branches. They were enormous, strange, deformed objects with excrescences and towers and rams plunging into the water as if trying to take root in the sea.

They seemed so heavy, so firmly attached to the bottom that it was difficult to imagine that they could ever move and go elsewhere. One tall, round, floating battery, shaped like an observatory, looked like the sort of lighthouse they build on rocks.

Near by a big three-master was making its way out to sea, all white and gay under its full spread of sail. It was pretty and graceful compared with those sea monsters, those ugly iron monsters crouching on the water.

Forestier was trying to identify them:

'That's *Le Colbert*, *Le Suffren*, *L'Amiral-Duperré*, *Le Redoutable*, *La Dévastation* ...' and then correcting himself: 'No, I'm wrong, that's *La Dévastation*.'

They had reached a sort of large detached house with a notice saying 'Golfe Juan Art Pottery' and the carriage drove round the lawn and stopped in front of the door.

Forestier wanted to buy two vases to put on his bookshelves. As he could hardly get out of the carriage, they brought out the various types one after the other. He took a long time to choose, consulting his wife and Duroy:

'You know, it's to go on the piece of furniture at the end of my study. I can watch it all the time when I'm sitting in my armchair. I want something classical in shape, something Greek in feeling.'

He examined various samples, asked to see others, went back to the earlier ones and finally made his choice. When he had paid for them, he insisted on their being delivered immediately.

'I'm going back to Paris in a few days' time,' he said.

They made their way home but as they were going round the bay, a sudden gust of cold air hit them at the bottom of a little valley and the sick man began to cough.

At first it was hardly anything, a slight attack; but then it grew worse and turned into a continuous spasm and then into a sort of gasp, a rattle in the throat.

Now he was fighting for breath and every time he tried to breathe, he was seized by a deep, hacking cough that came from the depths of his lungs. It was impossible to check or even relieve it. He had to be carried from the landau to his room and Duroy, who was holding his legs, felt his feet jerk at each convulsive movement of his lungs.

Not even the warmth of his bed succeeded in stopping the dreadful spasm which went on until midnight. Finally they succeeded in controlling it by the use of drugs. And the sick man lay bolt upright on his bed, open-eyed, until daybreak.

His first words were to ask for the barber, because he insisted on being shaved every morning. He got out of bed for this to be done but had to go back again immediately afterwards and he began to breathe in such short, harsh, laborious gasps that Madame Forestier, horrified, asked Duroy, who had just gone to bed, to run and fetch the doctor.

He came back almost immediately with Doctor Gavaut who prescribed a potion and issued some instructions; but as the journalist was showing him out and asking him his opinion, he said:

'It's the beginning of the end. He'll be dead by tomorrow morning. Warn his poor young wife and send for a priest. There's nothing more I can do. But I'll be available should you want me.'

Duroy asked to see Madame Forestier:

'He's dying. The doctor suggested sending for a priest. What would you like to do?'

She hesitated for a long while and then, after careful deliberation, she said slowly:

'Yes, that's the best thing ... in many ways ... I'll go and prepare the ground and tell him that the priest would like to see him ... Or tell him something or other. And would you mind going to fetch a priest and see if you can get one of the right sort? We want someone who won't make too much fuss. Try and find someone who only wants him to confess and won't worry us about anything else.'

Duroy brought back an obliging old cleric who was prepared to accept the situation. As soon as he had gone into the room where Forestier was dying, Madame Forestier came out and sat down with Duroy in the next room.

'He's terribly upset,' she said. 'When I mentioned a priest, his face took on an expression of dread as if ... as if he had felt ... felt ... a breath of wind ... you know ... He realized that it was all over, in fact, that it was a matter of hours ...'

She was very pale. She went on:

'I shall never forget the expression on his face. He must certainly have seen death at that moment. He actually saw it ...'

They could hear the priest who was speaking rather loudly because he was slightly deaf. He was saying:

'No, of course, things aren't as bad as all that. You're ill but your life's not in danger. And the proof is that I've come as a friend and neighbour.'

They could not hear Forestier's reply. The old man went on:

'No, I won't give you communion. We'll talk about that when you're well. On the other hand, if you want to take advantage of my visit to confess, there's nothing that would please me more. I'm a minister of God and I take every opportunity of ministering to my flock.'

A long silence followed. Forestier must have been talking in his gasping, toneless voice.

Then all at once, the priest spoke in quite a different tone, like a priest officiating at the altar:

'God's mercy is infinite. Say the Confiteor, my child. You may perhaps have forgotten it, let me help you. Repeat after me: *Confiteor Deo omnipotenti* ... *Beatae Mariae semper virgini* ...'

He stopped from time to time to allow the dying man to catch up. Then he said:

'Now confess ...'

The young woman and Duroy were sitting stock still, in the grip of a strange, uneasy emotion, anxious and expectant.

The sick man had muttered something. The priest repeated:

'You have connived at sinful acts ... what sort of sinful acts, my son?'

The young woman stood up and said simply:

'Let's go down into the garden for a while. We mustn't eavesdrop on his secrets.'

They went and sat down on a bench in front of the door, underneath a rosebush in bloom, behind a basket of carnations whose rich, sweet scent hung in the pure air.

After a few minutes' silence, Duroy asked:

'Will it be long before you return to Paris?'

She replied:

'Oh no, I'll come back as soon as everything is settled.'

'In ten days, or so?'

'Yes, at most.'

He went on:

'So he has no relatives?'

'None, except some cousins. His father and mother died when he was quite small.'

They were both watching a butterfly feeding from the carnations, going from one to the other with a rapid fluttering of its wings which still continued, more slowly, when it had settled on the flower. And they remained silent for a long while.

The servant came to tell them that the priest had finished. They both went upstairs again.

Forestier seemed to be even thinner than he was the day before.

The priest was holding his hand.

'Goodbye, my son, I'll come again tomorrow morning.' He left.

As soon as he had gone, the dying man, gasping for breath, tried to lift his two hands towards his wife and said, brokenly:

'Save me ... save me ... my darling ... I don't want to die ... I don't want to die ... Oh save me, both of you ... Tell me what to do ... go and fetch the doctor ... I'll take anything you like ... I don't want ... I don't want ...'

He was crying. Big tears were streaming down his sunken cheeks; and his emaciated lips puckered at the corners like those of a forlorn little child.

And then his hands fell back onto the bed and he began to make a slow repeated clawing movement, as if trying to pick something up from the sheets.

His wife also started crying as she faltered:

'No, it's nothing at all. It's just a passing attack, you'll be better tomorrow, you tired yourself out yesterday with that drive ...'

Forestier's breath was coming faster than the panting of a dog which has been running, so fast that it was impossible to count and so feebly that you could barely hear it.

He kept repeating:

'I don't want to die! ... Oh God, oh God ... oh God ... what's going to happen to me? I shall never see anything any more ... nothing ... ever again ... oh God!'

He was looking in front of him and seeing something hidden from the others, something hideous which was reflected in his dreadful, staring eyes. His two hands kept repeating their horrible, tiring movement.

All at once they saw a sudden shudder run through his whole frame and he stammered:

'The cemetery ... me ... oh God!'

And he said no more but lay there motionless, gasping and haggard.

Time went by; the clock of a near-by convent struck twelve. Duroy left the room to have something to eat. He came back an hour later. Madame Forestier refused to eat anything. The sick man had not moved. He was still drawing his thin fingers over the sheet as if trying to pull it up towards his face.

His wife was sitting in an armchair at the end of the bed. Duroy sat down in another one beside her and they waited in silence.

The doctor had sent someone in to sit up with the sick man; she was dozing by the window.

Duroy himself was beginning to doze off when he had the feeling that something was happening. He opened his eyes just in time to see Forestier's eyes close like two lights being extinguished. The dying man gave a little gulp. Two thin trickles of blood appeared at each corner of his mouth and ran down onto his nightshirt. The gruesome motion of his hands over the sheets stopped. He was dead.

His wife realized what had happened and with a strangled cry sank to her knees, sobbing against the sheet. Surprised and bewildered, Georges mechanically crossed himself. The night-nurse, who had woken up, went over to the bed: 'That's it,' she said. And Duroy, regaining his composure, murmured, with a sigh of relief: 'It didn't take as long as I thought.'

Once they had recovered from their first surprise and the first tears had been shed, there were all the complicated arrangements connected with death. Duroy was kept on the go all day.

When he returned to the villa he was famished. Madame Forestier ate little. Then they both went to the dead man's room to keep vigil over the body.

Two candles were burning on the bedside table beside a plate containing a little water in which lay a branch of mimosa, since they had felt that the traditional palm was inappropriate.

The two of them sat beside the bed of the dead man. They were silent, wrapt in thought as they watched him.

But Georges, disturbed by the shadows surrounding the corpse, did not take his eyes off him; and his mind as well as his gaze were drawn towards this emaciated face and dwelt there, fascinated, as the flickering light made his features seem even more sunken. So that was his friend Charles Forestier, who had been talking to him only yesterday! What a strange and fearful thing it was, this complete end to a human being. Ah, now he remembered Norbert de Varenne's words as he spoke of being haunted by the fear of death: 'No being ever returns.' Millions and hundreds of millions of creatures would be born, more or less identical, with eyes, a nose, a mouth, a skull with a mind inside it, yet the man lying in that bed would never return.

Like everyone else, for the space of a few years he had lived, eaten, laughed and hoped. And now everything was over for him for ever. What is life? A few days and then nothing more. You're born, you grow up, you're happy, you wait and then you die. Goodbye! Whether you're a man or a woman, you'll never come back on earth. And yet everyone bears within himself the feverish, hopeless wish to be eternal, each person is a sort of universe within the universe and yet each person is soon completely annihilated on the dunghill where lie the seeds of new life to come. Plants, animals, men, stars, worlds, everything takes on life and then dies and is transformed. And no creature ever comes back, whether it be a man, an insect or a planet!

Duroy was gripped by an immense, bewildered, overwhelming terror, the terror of this ineluctable, limitless void which unceasingly destroys each short, miserable life. He could feel the threat already weighing him down. He was thinking of flies, which live a few hours, of animals which live a few days, of men who live a few years, of planets which live a few centuries. What difference was there then between them? A few extra dawns, that was all.

He turned his gaze away so that he would no longer see the corpse.

Madame Forestier was sitting with her head bowed, also apparently wrapt in painful thoughts. Her fair hair against her sad face made such a pretty sight that the young man felt a gentle feeling of something like hope stir within himself. Why be so miserable when he still had so many years of life ahead?

And he let his eyes rest on her. She did not notice him, lost as she was in her own meditation. He said to himself: 'Yes, that's the only thing worth living for. Love. Holding a woman you love in your arms! That's the limit of human happiness.'

How lucky the dead man had been to meet such a charming and intelligent helpmate! How had they met? How had she come to accept marriage to this poor, very ordinary young man? How had she finally succeeded in making something of him?

Then he thought of all the secrets hidden in people's lives. He remembered the rumours about the Comte de Vaudrec who had provided her with a dowry and married her off, some people said.

What was she going to do now? Whom would she marry? A deputy, as Madame de Marelle had been saying, or some lively young man with a future, a superior sort of Forestier? Had she any plans or projects, any settled ideas? How he would have liked to know! But why this concern as to what she would be doing? He asked himself the question and realized that it sprang from one of those confused and secret motives that you hide from yourself and only discover when you start searching deep down inside yourself.

Yes, why not try and win her for himself? How strong he would be with her at his side, how strong and how formidable! With her he would be able to go far and fast, with no risk of failure.

And why shouldn't he succeed? He could sense that she liked him, that she felt more than just sympathy for him, that it was the sort of affection that springs up between two people whose natures are similar and which is dependent as much on mutual attraction as on an unspoken feeling of conspiracy. She knew that he was intelligent, determined and relentless; she could rely on him.

Hadn't she sent for him in this moment of need? And why had she done so? Might it not be because she had in some way chosen him, a kind of admission that it was he whom she wanted? If she had thought of him at the very moment when she was about to be widowed, perhaps it was because she was thinking of him as the man who might be her new companion and ally?

And he was seized by a sudden urge to know the truth, to question her and discover what her intentions were. He would have to leave the day after tomorrow because he could not continue to stay in the house alone with the young widow. Therefore he must be quick and, before returning to Paris, discreetly worm out of her what her plans were and not let her come back and perhaps listen to someone else's endearments and commit herself irrevocably.

Deep silence reigned in the room; the only sound was the steady metallic tick of the pendulum of the clock on the mantelpiece.

He said quietly:

'You must be very tired.'

She replied:

'Yes, but above all I feel at the end of my tether.'

The sound of their voices surprised them as they echoed strangely in the sinister atmosphere of the room. And they suddenly looked at the dead man's face as though they expected to see it move and hear it address them, as it had been doing a few hours earlier.

Duroy went on:

'It's such a great shock for you and such a complete change in your life, a complete upset of your feelings and your whole existence.'

She gave a long sigh without replying.

He continued:

'It's so sad for a young woman to find herself in the situation in which you're going to be.'

He stopped. She said nothing. He said hesitantly:

'In any case, you know the pact we've made. You can ask me to do whatever you like. I'm yours to command.'

She held out her hand to him with the gently melancholy look that moves a man to the depths of his being.

'Thank you, you're kind, you're so kind. If I dared and could do something for you, I would say the same thing: "You can rely on me."'

He had taken the hand she had offered him and was

holding it tightly, with a fervid desire to kiss it. Finally, he decided to do so and he slowly lifted it to his lips and pressed its delicate, warm, quivering, fragrant flesh against them.

Then, when he felt that his friendly gesture was beginning to be too insistent, he let her tiny hand fall gently back on to her lap. She said gravely:

'Yes, I shall be very lonely but I shall try to be brave.'

He could not find a way to lead her to understand that he in turn would be glad, very glad, to take her as his wife. Obviously, he could not tell her in so many words, at this time and place, beside this dead body; yet it seemed to him that he might be able to find one of those complicated, ambiguous, and appropriate phrases whose words hide their meaning and express everything you wish by leaving things deliberately unsaid.

But he was embarrassed by this corpse lying rigid beside them. He felt it was coming between them. Moreover, for some little time he had imagined that he could detect a suspicious odour in the stuffy room, a fetid breath coming from rotting lungs, the first reek of carrion that meets the nostrils of the relatives watching over poor dead creatures as they lie on their beds, a horrible smell which will soon be filling every corner of their coffins.

He asked:

'Do you think we might open the window a little? The air seems tainted.'

She replied:

'Yes, of course. I'd just noticed it myself.'

He went to the window and opened it. Cool and scented, the night air entered, making the candle-flames flicker beside the bed. As on the other night, the white walls of the villas and the broad shimmering expanse of the sea were bathed in the calm, full light of the moon. Duroy filled his lungs and felt suddenly excited by hope and as it were elated by a quiver of approaching happiness.

He turned round:

'Do come and take a breath of fresh air. It's a wonderful night.'

She came quietly over and leant on the window-sill beside him.

Then, gently, he murmured:

'I want you to listen to what I'm going to say and try to understand me. Above all, don't be angry if I talk about such things at a moment like this but I shall be leaving the day after tomorrow and when you come back to Paris it may perhaps be too late … So here goes … As you know, I'm only a poor devil with no money at all who's still making his way. But I've got determination, I think some intelligence and I've made a start, a good start. With a successful man, you know what you're getting; with someone just beginning you never know where he'll finish up. That may be a bad thing or it may be a good thing. Anyway, I told you one day in your home that my dearest dream would have been to marry a wife like you. And I want to say that again now. Don't try to answer me. Let me go on. I'm not making you a proposal. That would be an odious thing to do at this time and place. I'm only anxious that you shouldn't fail to know that a word from you can make me a happy man, that you can make me either your friend, your brother if you like, or else even your husband, as you will, that my heart and my whole body are all yours. I don't want you to answer me now, I don't want to talk about it any more, here. When we meet again in Paris, you'll let me know what you've decided. Until then, not a word, you agree?'

He had spoken without looking at her, as if he were scattering the words in the darkness in front of him. And she seemed not to have heard him as she, too, stood motionless

193

staring vaguely ahead at the vast landscape under the pale light of the moon.

For many minutes they remained side by side, elbow to elbow, thinking in silence.

Then she murmured:

'It's a little cold,' and turning round, went back to the bed. He followed her.

As he came near, he recognized that Forestier really was beginning to smell and he moved his chair away because he would have been unable to stand the stench for long.

He said:

'We must put him in his coffin this morning.'

She answered:

'Yes, it's all arranged. The carpenter's coming at about eight o'clock.'

And when Duroy sighed: 'Poor old man', she too gave a long, melancholy sigh of resignation.

They were beginning to look at him less often now, already becoming used to the thought of his death and starting to accept that he had gone for ever, whereas but a short while ago they had been revolted and resentful at the idea, thinking of their own mortality.

No more was said but they remained awake to watch over the dead man as custom demanded.

Towards midnight, however, Duroy was the first to doze off. When he awoke he saw that Madame Forestier was dozing too and, settling himself more comfortably, he closed his eyes again, grunting: 'It's better sleeping between sheets, heavens above.'

A sudden noise made him start. It was the night-nurse coming in. It was broad daylight. Madeleine was sitting opposite him in her armchair and seemed as surprised as he was. She was a trifle pale but as pretty as ever, fresh and pleasing despite having sat up all night.

Then Duroy looked at the corpse and gave a start, exclaiming: 'Oh look at his beard!' In the space of a few hours, the beard had grown on his rotting flesh as much as it would have grown in a few days on a living man. And they were filled with shocked amazement at these signs of life continuing on a dead body, like some monstrous miracle, a threat of resurrection from another world, the sort of weird, frightening thing that bewilders and baffles our intelligence.

They both went to lie down until eleven o'clock. Then they put Charles into his coffin and at once they felt relieved and at peace. They lunched opposite each other, eager to talk of more comforting and cheerful things, to return to life since they had finished with death.

Through the wide open window the gentle warmth of spring wafted in the scent of the basket of carnations blooming in front of the doorway.

Madame Forestier suggested a walk round the garden and they sauntered round the little lawn enjoying the scent of pine and eucalyptus borne on the warm air.

And suddenly she began to talk, without looking at him, just as he had done in the room upstairs last night. She spoke slowly, in a quiet serious tone:

'Georges, I've been thinking ... already ... about the suggestion you made to me and I don't want you to leave without giving you some sort of reply. Not that I'm going to say either yes or no. We'll wait and see, we'll get to know each other better. You must give it a lot of thought as well. Don't allow yourself to be carried away too easily. But if I'm mentioning it to you before poor Charles is even in his grave, it's because, after what you said, it's important for you to know exactly what sort of person I am so that you don't continue to think of me in the way you spoke about last night unless you have the right sort of character to understand me and bear with me.

'You must understand what I'm saying. For me, marriage

is not a shackle but an association. I insist on being free, completely free to act as I think fit, go where I please, see whom I choose, whenever I wish. I could never accept any authority or jealousy or questioning of my conduct. Of course, I should undertake never to compromise the name of the man whom I married or expose him to odium or ridicule. But the man would also have to undertake to look on me as an equal, an ally and not as an inferior or an obedient, submissive spouse. I know these ideas of mine aren't everybody's but I'm not going to change them. So there we are.

'Let me add this. Don't answer me now, it would be pointless and inappropriate. We'll be meeting again and perhaps talking about all this later on.

'Now, why not go for a walk? I shall go back to him. I'll see you this evening.'

Slowly and deliberately he kissed her hand and went away without uttering a word.

That evening they met only for dinner. Then they went upstairs to their rooms, for they were both completely worn out.

Next day Charles Forestier was buried with a minimum of ceremony in the cemetery at Cannes. And Georges Duroy decided to catch the Paris express which went through Cannes at one-thirty.

Madame Forestier came to the station to see him off. They strolled gently up and down the platform waiting for the train, exchanging commonplaces.

The train came in. It had only five carriages – a real express train.

The journalist found a seat and then climbed down onto the platform to chat for a few seconds more with her, suddenly seized by a feeling of melancholy, sadness and deep regret at having to leave her, as if he was going to lose her for ever.

An official shouted: 'Passengers for Marseilles, Lyons and Paris, take your seats please!' Duroy got in and leant out of the window to exchange a few last words. The engine whistled and slowly the train moved off.

Leaning out of the carriage, the young man watched the young widow standing motionless on the platform, following him with her eyes. And suddenly, just as she was going out of sight, he raised both hands to his lips and blew her a kiss.

She hesitated and then more faintly and more discreetly returned his gesture.

BEL-AMI

PART II

GEORGES DUROY had settled back into his habits. He was installed in his little flat on the Rue de Constantinople and was living an orderly existence, like a man preparing for a new life. His liaison with Madame de Marelle was even taking on a sort of conjugal flavour as if he was practising for the coming event; and his mistress often expressed surprise at the ordered calm of their relationship, saying laughingly: 'You're even more of a stay-at-home than my husband. It was hardly worth changing.'

Madame Forestier was still in Cannes. Georges had received a letter from her telling him she would not be back until the middle of April but without making any reference to their parting words. He was waiting. He was now firmly resolved to use every possible means to marry her if she seemed to be hesitating. But he had confidence in his luck and in the powers of attraction which he felt himself to possess – vague and irresistible powers that no woman could resist.

He received a note telling him that the hour was about to strike:

I'm back. Do come and see me.
                                        Madeleine Forestier.

That was all. He received it by the morning post. At three o'clock in the afternoon of that same day, he called on her. She held out her two hands, smiling in her usual charming, friendly way; and for a few seconds they looked deep into each other's eyes.

Then she murmured:

'How kind it was of you to come down to help me in such dreadful circumstances.'

He replied:

'I would have done anything you told me to do.'

They sat down. She enquired about all the news, the Walters, his colleagues, the paper. She often thought about the paper, she said.

'I miss it a great deal, very much indeed. I had become a sort of journalist in spirit. There's nothing I can do about it, I just like that profession.'

Then she stopped. He felt that her smile, the tone of her voice, even her words were a sort of invitation and although he had promised himself not to rush things, he said hesitantly:

'Well then . . . why . . . why not start again . . . in that profession . . . under . . . under the name of Duroy?'

She suddenly became serious again and laying her hand on his arm, she said quietly:

'Don't let's talk about that yet.'

But he had guessed that she was saying yes and falling on his knees he began to kiss her hands passionately as he repeated brokenly:

'Thank you, thank you. Oh how I do love you!'

She stood up. He followed suit and he saw that she was very pale. Then he realized that she liked him and had perhaps liked him for a long time; and, as they were standing face to face, he clasped her tightly to him and solemnly planted a long and tender kiss on her forehead.

She slipped out of his grasp as he held her against his chest and said in a serious voice:

'Listen, Georges, I still haven't made up my mind about anything. Yet I might say yes. But you must promise to keep it a complete secret until I say so.'

He gave his word and left, his heart full of rejoicing.

From then on he showed great discretion in calling on her, nor did he try to persuade her to be more precise since all the time she kept speaking about the future, saying 'later on', making plans that included both of them in a way that was a better and more subtle reply than any formal acceptance.

Duroy was working hard, spending little and trying to save so that he would not be completely without money at the time of his marriage. He was becoming as mean as he had hitherto been extravagant.

Summer went by, and autumn too, without anyone suspecting anything for they saw little of each other and then always in as natural a way as possible.

One evening, Madeleine said to him, looking him straight in the eye:

'You haven't told Madame de Marelle about our plans yet?'

'No, not yet. As I promised to keep them secret I haven't breathed a word to a living soul.'

'Well, it's time to let her know. I'll look after the Walters. You'll do it this week, won't you?'

He blushed:

'Yes, I'll do it tomorrow.'

She gently averted her gaze as though not to notice his confusion and went on:

'If you like we can get married at the beginning of May. That would be the right sort of time.'

'I'm happy to fall in with anything you suggest.'

'May 10th, which is a Saturday, would be very nice for me because it's my birthday.'

'May 10th be it.'

'Your parents live near Rouen, don't they? At least, that's what you said.'

'Yes, close to Rouen, at Canteleu.'

'What do they do?'

'They . . . they have a small private income.'

'Ah! I'd very much like to meet them.'

He hesitated, at a loss to know what to say:

'But . . . the fact is . . . they are . . .'

Boldly he took the plunge:

'My dear Madeleine, they're peasants, inn-keepers who bled themselves white so that I could continue my studies. I'm not ashamed of them but they're so . . . simple . . . and . . . countrified that they might perhaps embarrass you.'

She gave a charming frank smile, with an expression full of kindness and friendliness:

'No. I shall like them very much. We'll go and see them. I insist. We'll talk about it later. My parents were humble too . . . but they're no longer alive. I've nobody in the world . . .' and she held out her hand to him as she added 'except you.'

He was touched and stirred with a feeling of respect that he had never yet felt for any woman.

'I've been thinking about something,' she said, 'but it's rather difficult to explain.'

He asked:

'What is it?'

'Well, Georges, I'm like every woman, I've got my . . . my weaknesses, my failings, I'm fond of things that glitter, that have a fine sound. I should have loved to have an aristocratic name. Couldn't you possibly use the opportunity, when we get married, of making your name sound a little more . . . noble?' Now it was her turn to blush, as if she were suggesting something dishonest.

He answered simply:

'I've thought about it very often, but it doesn't seem to me an easy thing to do.'

'Why not?'

He laughed:

'Because I'm afraid of appearing ridiculous.'

She shrugged:

'But that's not true, not true at all. Everyone does it and nobody laughs at them. Split your name into two: "Du Roy". It sounds very nice.'

But with the air of someone who knows all about the matter, he immediately replied:

'No, that won't do. That's too simple, too common, too well known. What I had thought of doing was to take the name of my village, first of all as a pseudonym, then gradually add it to mine and even, later on, cut my name in two as you were suggesting.'

She asked:

'Your village is Canteleu?'

'Yes.'

But she was hesitating:

'No. I don't like the ending. Let's see if we couldn't change the ending a bit . . . Canteleu.'

She had picked up a pen from the table and was scribbling words down to see how they looked. Suddenly she exclaimed.

'Here you are, here you are, this is it.'

And she handed him a piece of paper on which she had written: 'Madame Duroy de Cantel.'

He pondered for a few seconds and then said solemnly:

'Yes, that's very good.'

She was delighted and repeated:

'Duroy de Cantel, Duroy de Cantel, Madame Duroy de Cantel. It's splendid, it really is!'

And she added confidently:

'And you'll see how easy it will be to get everybody to accept it. But you must take the opportunity now. Afterwards it will be too late. From tomorrow you must sign your feature articles D. de Cantel and your news column simply Duroy. That's happening all the time in the press and no one will be surprised to see you take a pseudonym. When we get married, we can change it a little more by telling our friends that you had given up your 'du' as being too ostentatious, in view of your position or even without saying anything at all. What's your father's name?'

'Alexandre.'

She muttered to herself two or three times: 'Alexandre, Alexandre', to see how it sounded and then she wrote on a blank sheet of paper:

'Monsieur and Madame Alexandre du Roy de Cantel have the honour to announce the marriage of their son Monsieur Georges du Roy de Cantel with Madame Madeleine Forestier.'

She held it some distance away, delighted at the effect, and said firmly:

'A little organization and you can manage to do everything you want.'

When he was in the street, now that he was quite determined to call himself du Roy in future, and even du Roy de Cantel, he had the feeling that he had suddenly become a much more important person. He walked more jauntily and held his head higher, with a bolder twirl on his moustache, as an aristocrat should. He felt elated, with the urge to inform the passers-by:

'My name is du Roy de Cantel.'

But scarcely had he reached home than the thought of Madame de Marelle began to worry him and he wrote to her straightaway suggesting a meeting for the following day.

'It'll be tricky going,' he thought to himself. 'There's going to be a big row.'

Then he brushed it aside in his usual carefree manner which enabled him to ignore the unpleasant things in life and he started to write a humorous article on the new taxes required to balance the budget.

He suggested 100 francs a year for people having a handle to their name – de so-and-so – and a scale ranging from 500 to 1,000 francs for titles, from Baron up to Prince.

He signed it: D. de Cantel.

Next morning he received an express letter from his mistress telling him that she would come round at one o'clock.

He was rather restless as he waited for her to come but determined not to beat about the bush, tell her everything from the start and then, once the first shock was over, to argue rationally with her to convince her that he could not remain a bachelor indefinitely and since Monsieur de Marelle obstinately refused to die, he had had to think of someone else to make his wife.

But all the same he felt nervous. When he heard the bell ring, his heart started pounding.

She flung herself into his arms: 'Hallo, Bel-Ami', then realizing that his welcome was rather cool, she looked at him and asked:

'What's the matter?'

'Sit down,' he said. 'We've got to have a serious talk together.'

She sat down without taking off her hat, merely lifting her veil up over her forehead and waited for him to speak.

He had lowered his eyes; he was preparing his introduction. He began to speak in a slow voice:

'Clotilde dear, I'm very upset, very unhappy and very embarrassed at what I've got to confess. I love you very much, I really do love you from the bottom of my heart and the thought of hurting you makes me even more unhappy than what I have to tell you.'

She went pale and felt herself starting to tremble. She said falteringly:

'What is it? Tell me quickly!'

In a sad but firm voice, with the feigned look of dejection that people assume when they have glad bad tidings to announce, he said:

'I'm getting married.'

She gave a sigh as if she were going to faint, a painful sigh that came from the depths of her lungs, and then she began to gasp, unable to speak for lack of breath.

Seeing that she was not saying anything, he went on:

'You can't imagine what I've suffered in reaching this decision. But I've no status and no money. I'm all alone, quite lost in Paris. I needed someone by me who would above all be able to advise me, to comfort me and support me. I wanted an associate, an ally and I've found one.'

He stopped, hoping that she would reply and expecting an outburst of rage or violence and insults.

She had placed her hand over her heart as though to calm its pounding and she was still gasping painfully for breath, her breasts heaving, her head jerking to and fro.

He took her hand which was resting on the arm of the chair; but she swiftly pulled it away. Then as if sunk in a sort of stupor, she muttered:

'Oh God!'

He knelt down in front of her, though not daring to touch her and, more upset by her silence than he would have been had she flown into a rage, he stammered:

'Clo, my darling Clo, you must understand my situation, really understand what sort of person I am. Oh, how happy I should have been if only I'd been able to marry you. But you're married. What could I do? Just think, please, just think! I must achieve some sort of status in society and I can't do that as long as I haven't a proper home. If you only knew ... There are days when I could have killed your husband!'

He was speaking in his soft, velvety, engaging voice which caressed the ear like soft music.

He saw two big tears form in her staring eyes and run down her cheeks while two more started forming at the edge of her eyelids.

He said gently:

'Oh don't cry, Clo, don't cry, please don't. You're breaking my heart.'

Then she made an effort, a great effort, to try to be proud and dignified; and in the quavering tones of a woman on the point of bursting into sobs she enquired:

'Who is it?'

He hesitated a second and then realizing that he had to speak the truth:

'Madeleine Forestier.'

Her whole body shuddered and then she sat silent, so deeply immersed in her thoughts that she seemed to have forgotten that he was still kneeling there.

And two transparent drops kept forming in her eyes, falling and forming again.

She stood up. Duroy sensed that she was going to leave without saying a word, either of reproach or forgiveness, and he felt offended and humiliated to the depths of his being. He tried to stop her, seizing her through her dress with both arms and feeling her round thighs stiffen under the material as she struggled to free herself.

He said pleadingly:

'Please, please, Clotilde, I can't bear you to leave like this.'

And then she looked down at him, with the tearful, despairing look, so charming and so sad, of a deeply suffering woman and said, in a broken voice:

'I've ... I've ... nothing to say ... there's ... nothing I

can do ... You're ... you're right ... you've, you've ... chosen exactly the woman you needed ...'

And, stepping backwards, she freed herself and left, while he made no further attempt to detain her.

When she had gone, he stood up, as bewildered as if he had received a knock on the head; then, accepting the situation, he muttered: 'Well, for better or worse, that's that. And no fuss. It's probably better like that.' And he felt as if an enormous weight had been suddenly lifted from his mind; he felt free, all set for his new life and he began to shadow-box against the wall, throwing punches in wild intoxication at his success and his strength, as if he were taking on Fate itself.

When Madame Forestier asked him: 'Have you told Madame de Marelle?' he replied calmly: 'Of course ...'

Her clear eyes were probing him.

'And she wasn't upset?'

'Not a bit. On the contrary, she thought it was an excellent idea.'

The news soon became known. Some people expressed surprise, others claimed to have foreseen it and yet others gave a smile to hint that they had expected it.

The young man, who now signed his feature articles D. de Cantel, his news and gossip column Duroy and his occasional political articles du Roy, spent half his days at his fiancée's flat. She treated him with a sisterly affection which was nonetheless full of sincere, if hidden, tenderness, a sort of desire which she concealed as a weakness. She had decided that the wedding would be celebrated very quietly with only the witnesses present and that they would leave the very same evening for Rouen. Next day they would go to see her husband's old parents and stay with them for a few days.

Duroy had endeavoured to dissuade her from this idea without success and had finally acquiesced.

So on 10 May, they were married in the town hall, since, not having invited any guests, they thought that it would be pointless to have any religious ceremony. The newly-weds then returned home to pick up their luggage and made their way to the Gare St-Lazare where they took the six o'clock train for Normandy.

They had hardly exchanged more than a dozen words before they found themselves alone together in the compartment. As soon as they realized that they were moving, they looked at each other and started to laugh in order to conceal a certain embarrassment which they were anxious not to show.

The train went slowly through the long station of Batignolles and then crossed the desolate plain which lies between the fortifications and the Seine.

Now and then Duroy and his wife exchanged a few meaningless words and then looked out of the window again.

As they crossed the bridge at Asnières, their spirits rose when they saw the river covered with boats, anglers and rowers. The slanting rays of the powerful May sun were shining on the boats, and the river, so calm as to seem quite motionless, without the slightest current or eddy, lay like a compact mass bathed in the heat and the glow of the dying day. In the middle of the river a sailing-boat with two large triangular sails to bow and starboard, hoisted so as to catch the slightest puff of air, looked like an immense bird poised for flight.

Duroy murmured:

'I adore the outskirts of Paris. My memories of eating delicious fried fish straight out of the river are amongst the happiest in my life.'

She replied:

'And the rowing-boats! How wonderful it is, gliding over the water at sunset.'

Then once again they fell silent, as though reluctant to continue to reveal the secrets of their past lives, and they sat without saying anything, perhaps already enjoying the poetry of nostalgia.

Duroy, who was sitting opposite his wife, took her hand and slowly kissed it.

'When we come back,' he said, 'we'll go and have dinner at Chatou sometimes.'

She murmured:

'We'll have so many things to do', in a voice which seemed to mean: 'we shall have to put business before pleasure.'

He was still holding her hand, wondering uneasily how he might go further to a more intimate caress. He would not have been so perplexed had he been dealing with an ignorant girl, but the lively intelligence and shrewdness which he could sense in Madeleine made him feel embarrassed. He was afraid of appearing silly, either too shy or too bold, too slow or too impatient.

He kept giving her hand a gentle squeeze but received no response in return. He said:

'It seems very funny to me that you're my wife.'

She seemed surprised:

'Why?'

'I don't know. It just seems funny. I feel like kissing you and I'm surprised that I have the right to do so.'

She gently offered him her cheek which he kissed as if she had been his sister.

He went on:

'The first time I saw you, you remember, at the dinner when Forestier invited me, I thought: "My goodness, if only I could find a wife like that." And now it's a fact. I've got her.'

She murmured:

'That's nice.' And she looked straight at him, slyly, with her usual smile in her eyes.

He was thinking to himself: 'I'm too cold. I'm stupid. I ought to be getting a move on.' And he said:

'Tell me how you got to know Forestier.'

She replied, in a provocatively mischievous tone:

'Are we going to Rouen to talk about him?'

He blushed: 'I'm stupid. I find you very intimidating.'

She was delighted: 'Me? You can't possibly. What's the cause of that?'

He had sat down beside her, very close. She exclaimed:

'Oh! A stag!'

The train was going through the forest of Saint-Germain, and she had seen a startled roe-buck leap right across a path.

Duroy leant over her while she was looking out of the open window and deposited a long, loving kiss on the hairs in the nape of her neck.

She remained still for a few moments; then, lifting her head:

'You're tickling me. Stop it.'

But he stayed there, gently brushing his curly moustache against her white flesh in a long, insistent movement.

She shook herself:

'Do stop it.'

He had caught hold of her behind her head with his right hand and was turning it towards him. Then he pounced on her mouth like a hawk on its prey.

She was struggling and pushing him away, trying to free her head. She finally managed to do so and repeated:

'Now do stop it.'

He paid no attention, hugging her to him and covering her with greedy, trembling kisses, trying to push her over on to the cushions of the seat.

She jerked herself free and jumped to her feet.

'Oh, come on, Georges, do stop. We aren't children, you know, we can surely wait until we get to Rouen?'

He stayed in his seat very red in the face, his ardour quenched by her cool, sensible words. Then, when he had regained some of his composure:

'All right, I'll wait,' he said in a cheerful voice. 'But I shall be incapable of saying another dozen words before we get there. And please note that we are only at Poissy.'

'I'll do the talking,' she said.

She sat down again gently beside him.

And she talked in detail of what they would do once they were back in Paris. They would keep on the flat that she had been living in with her first husband; and Duroy was also taking over Forestier's duties and salary at *La Vie française*.

Before the marriage she had, moreover, drawn up all the details of the financial settlement as competently as any businessman.

Each of the parties retained the right to their separate properties and every conceivable eventuality had been provided for: death, divorce, birth of one or several children. Georges was providing 4,000 francs, he said (but 1,500 of them had been borrowed). The remainder came from the moneys he had saved up in the course of the year in anticipation of his marriage. The wife was providing 40,000 francs which, she said, she had been left by Forestier.

She came back to the subject of her first husband, quoting him as an example:

'He was a very thrifty young man, very steady and very hard-working. It wouldn't have taken him very long to make his fortune.'

Duroy was no longer listening; his mind was running on quite different matters.

Every now and again she stopped to pursue a private train of thought and then went on:

'Three or four years from now, you may very well be

214

earning 30 or 40,000 francs a year. That's what Charles would have been doing had he lived.'

Georges, who was beginning to find the lecture rather long-winded, remarked:

'I didn't think we were going to Rouen to talk about him.'

She gave him a little pat on his cheek:

'That's true. I'm sorry.'

She laughed.

He was pretending to hold his hands in his lap like a very good little schoolboy.

'You look silly like that,' she said.

He retorted:

'That's the part I've been given, as you reminded me a little while back, and I'm going to stick to it.'

'Why?'

'Because you're taking over the running of the house and even of me. Of course, as a widow, that's your concern.'

She was astounded.

'What exactly do you mean by that?'

'That you have the knowledge that will dispel my ignorance and an experience of marriage which will enlighten my bachelor's innocence, so there!'

She exclaimed:

'That's too much!'

He replied:

'But that's how it is. I don't know anything about women, I don't, so there! and you know all about men, you do, because you're a widow, so there! and you're going to educate me ... tonight, so there! and you can even start straight away, so there!'

She exclaimed, highly amused:

'Goodness me, if you're relying on me for that! ...'

Like a schoolboy reciting his homework, he gabbled:

'Yes I am, so there! I am relying on you. I'm even relying

on you to give me a sound grounding ... in twenty lessons ... ten for the elementary stuff ... reading and grammar ... and ten for the higher flights ... I don't know anything, I don't, so there!'

She exclaimed, thoroughly enjoying the joke:

'You're a fool, boy.'

He went on:

'Well, since you've started to speak to me so familiarly, I shall follow your example and tell you, my love, that I adore you more and more every second, and that I think Rouen is a long way off.'

Now he had adopted the voice and manner of an actor playing a part, pulling an amusing face in a way which the young woman found highly entertaining, accustomed as she was to the affectation and buffoonery of rich literary bohemians.

She was looking at him out of the corner of her eye, thinking how charming he was, and feeling an urge to pluck the fruit from the tree while at the same time remembering the advice that it is wiser to wait for dinner-time and eat it when it is ripe.

So blushing a little at the thoughts that were running through her head, she said:

'My dear pupil, trust my experience, my wide experience. Kisses in railway carriages are no good. They go sour.'

Then she blushed even more and said in low voice:

'Don't count your chickens before they're hatched.'

He was sniggering, excited by all the implications slipping out of her pretty lips, and he made the sign of the cross, mumbling under his breath as if he were praying and then said:

'I've just put myself under the protection of Saint Anthony, the patron saint of temptation. Now, I'm a man of ice!'

Night was falling gently, swathing the broad expanse of country to their right in translucent shadow, like a mourning veil. The train was following the Seine, and the young couple started to watch the red gleams stained with fire and purple cast by the departing sun and reflected in the river unwinding like a broad band of polished metal alongside the railway-line. Gradually their glow died down, becoming first grey, then dark and sad. And the countryside sank into gloom with that sinister, deathly shudder that passes over the earth each day as twilight falls.

Through the open window the sadness of evening permeated the whole mood of the young couple and they fell silent. Their previous cheerfulness had all evaporated as they moved closer together to watch the death throes of this beautiful clear May day.

At Mantes, the little oil-lamp was lit and its yellow light flickered over the grey upholstery.

Duroy put his arm round his wife's waist and hugged her. The ardour of his earlier desire was giving way to tenderness, a gentle tenderness, a passive desire to be fondled and comforted like a child.

He whispered very quietly:

'I'm going to love you very much, Mado dear,' and rested his cheek on her warm breasts.

The soft tone of his voice excited the young woman and sent a sudden quiver through her whole body. She leant towards him and offered him her lips.

It was a long silent kiss, long and penetrating, and then they sprang up locked in a sudden wild embrace, and after a brief, breathless tussle, copulated, roughly and clumsily. Then, tired and both somewhat disappointed, they remained lying, still tenderly, in each other's arms until the whistle of the train announced an approaching station.

Smoothing the untidy wisps of hair on her temples, she said:

'That was very stupid. We're behaving like children.'

But he was frantically kissing her hands, his lips darting from one to the other, and he replied:

'My little Mado, I adore you.'

Until they reached Rouen they sat almost motionless, cheek to cheek, looking out into the night through the window, where occasionally they could see the lights of passing houses, immersed in their dreams, happy to feel each other so close and with the growing expectation of a more intimate, unhindered, embrace.

They put up at an hotel overlooking the quayside and they went to bed after a light supper, a very light one. Next morning they were awakened by the maid shortly after eight o'clock.

When they had drunk the cup of tea on their bedside table, Duroy looked at his wife and in a sudden burst of joy, like a happy man who has just found a treasure, he seized her in his arms and stammered:

'My little Mado, I feel I love you so much ... so much ... so much ...'

She was smiling her confident, satisfied smile and as she returned his kisses she said softly:

'Me too ... perhaps.'

But he was still uneasy about the visit to his parents. He had already frequently warned his wife; he had prepared her and lectured her. He thought it was a good idea to remind her.

'You know, they're peasants, real country peasants, not comic opera ones.'

She was laughing.

'But I know that, you've told me often enough. Come on, get up and let me get up too.'

He sprang out of bed and as he put on his socks:

'We shall be very uncomfortable there, very uncomfortable. There's only an old bed with a straw mattress in my room. They've never heard of spring-mattresses at Canteleu.'

She seemed delighted:

'All the better. It'll be lovely to sleep badly ... next to ... next to you ... and to be woken up by cocks crowing.'

She had slipped on her wrap, a loose white flannel wrap that Duroy recognized at once. He found the sight of it unpleasant. Why? His wife possessed a good dozen of these morning coats, as he well knew. She could hardly destroy her whole wardrobe and buy a completely new one. All the same, he would have preferred her bedroom-wear, her nightwear, the clothes she wore when making love, to be different from those she had worn with her other husband. He felt that something of Forestier must have rubbed off on the warm, fleecy material.

And he walked towards the window lighting a cigarette. The sight of the harbour, the wide river full of slender-masted ships and stocky steamers which derricks were unloading noisily onto the wharves stirred him, although he had long been familiar with it. He exclaimed:

'My goodness, it's lovely!'

Madeleine ran to the window and placing both hands on her husband's shoulder and leaning against him in a relaxed gesture, she stood looking out full of delighted excitement:

'Oh, how pretty it is! How pretty it is! I didn't know there were as many boats as that.'

An hour later, they set off, because they were going to lunch with the old people whom they had warned in advance some days before. The rusty open cab rattled along, first of all following a long, rather ugly boulevard, then across meadows through which a river was flowing and then they began to climb up the side of the hill.

Madeleine was tired and had dozed off, caressed by the bright rays of the sun which warmed her deliciously as she snuggled down in the old carriage, as though lying in a tepid bath full of light and country air.

Her husband woke her up:

'Look,' he said.

They had just stopped two thirds of the way up, at a spot well-known for its view and visited by every tourist.

They looked down on the immensely broad long valley through which the glassy river flowed from one end to the other in sweeping curves. It could be seen coming from the distance, dotted with numerous islands and swinging round as it entered Rouen. Then on its right bank, slightly hazy in the morning mist, there appeared Rouen itself, its roofs gleaming in the sun and its hundreds of spires, slender, pointed or squat, frail and elaborate, like giant pieces of jewellery, its towers, square or round, crowned with armorial bearings, its belfries, its bell-towers, the whole host of Gothic church-tops dominated by the sharp-pointed spire of the cathedral, that sort of strange bronze needle, enormous, ugly and odd, the tallest in the world.

Opposite, on the other side of the river, rose the slim, round chimneys, swelling towards the top, of the factories of the vast suburb of Saint Sever.

They were more numerous than their brothers, the spires, and their long brick columns stretched far out into the countryside, puffing their coal-black fumes into the blue sky. And the tallest of them all, as tall as the Cheops pyramid, the second highest amongst the man-made pinnacles, almost as high as its proud companion the cathedral spire, was the 'Thunderbolt'; as it pumped out its flames, it seemed to be the queen of the laborious horde of smoky factories, just as its neighbour was the queen of the pointed throng of ecclesiastical monuments.

Further on, beyond the industrial town, lay a fir forest and after passing between the two towns, the Seine continued on its way, skirting a long undulating hill, wooded on top, with its white chalk peeping out in places like bare bones, and then it disappeared on the horizon in another long, sweeping curve. Ships could be seen moving up and down the river, towed by tugs no bigger than a fly, belching dense clouds of smoke. Islands stretched out in line all along its surface, either end to end or else with big gaps between, like uneven beads on a rosary of greenery.

The driver was waiting for his passengers' raptures to subside. He knew from experience how long the admiration of every type of tourist would last.

But when they drove off again, Duroy suddenly caught sight of two old people walking along a few hundred yards away and he jumped out of the carriage, shouting: 'There they are! I can recognize them.'

They were two peasants, a man and a woman, shuffling along, swaying from side to side, sometimes catching each other's shoulder. The man was short and squat, red-faced, with a slight paunch, still vigorous despite his age; his wife was tall and gaunt, bent and sad, the typical country drudge, who has worked ever since childhood and never had time to laugh, while the husband would be cracking jokes and drinking with his customers.

Madeleine had also got out of the carriage and she saw these two poor creatures coming towards them with a pang of sadness that she had never anticipated. They did not recognize this fine gentleman as their son and they would never have guessed that the pretty lady in her light dress was their daughter-in-law.

They were walking fast and without talking, on their way

to meet their son, not looking at these two city folk who were being followed by a carriage.

They were going past without stopping. Georges laughingly hailed them:

'Good morning to you, old Duroy.'

They both stopped in their tracks, first of all amazed and then completely dumbfounded. The old woman recovered first. Still not moving, she stammered:

'That be you, son?'

The young man retorted:

'Of course it's me, old dear,' and walking up to her he gave her a big kiss on each cheek, the sort of kiss a son gives his mother. Then he rubbed the side of his head against his father's, as the latter took off his cap, a real Rouen cap, in black silk and very tall, like the ones worn by cattle merchants.

Then Georges said: 'This is my wife.' And the two country people looked at Madeleine. They looked at her as people look at a freak, rather uneasily and a trifle scared, with a sort of satisfied approval on the part of the father and with jealousy and hostility from the mother.

The old man, who was a cheerful soul and well-primed with sweet cider and spirits, took his courage in both hands and with a glint in the corner of his eye, said:

'I cun give 'ee a kiss, I s'pose.'

His son replied: 'Of course you can, Dad,' and the embarrassed Madeleine offered her cheeks for the smacking kisses of the old peasant who then wiped his lips with the back of his hand.

When it came to the old woman, she gave Madeleine an unfriendly peck; this was certainly not the daughter-in-law she had dreamt of, a fresh-faced farmer's wife as ruddy as an apple and as round as a brood-mare. This young madam looked like a tart, with her furbelows and her musk. For the old woman, every scent was musk.

Then they set off walking again behind the cab which was carrying the young couple's trunk.

The old man took his son's arm to hold him back as he enquired with curiosity:

'Well, how's business?'

'Going very well indeed.'

'Well that's a good thing, now. Tell oi, 'as your wife got money?'

'Forty thousand francs.'

The old man gave a low appreciative whistle and he was so impressed by the amount that all he could mutter was 'Well, oi be blowed.' Then he added with force: 'Dammee lad, she's a fine wench.' He, at least, had taken a fancy to her. And he was said to have had an eye for a pretty woman, in the old days.

Madeleine and her mother-in-law were walking side by side without saying a word. The two men caught up with them.

They were coming up to the village. It was a tiny village lining the main road and consisting of ten houses on each side, cottages and ramshackle farm-houses, the former made of brick with slate roofs, the latter of clay and thatched. 'A la Belle Vue', old Duroy's café, was a shack consisting of a ground floor and a loft, situated at the beginning of the village, on the left-hand side. A pine branch over the door, in the old style, showed that people with a thirst could quench it there.

Two tables placed together and covered with two napkins had been laid in the main room of the inn. A neighbour who had come in to help with serving the meal made a deep bob when she saw such a fine lady and then, recognizing Georges, she exclaimed: 'Glory be, is that you, Georges boy?'

He answered gaily:

'Yes, it's me, dear old Brulin!'

And he kissed her too, just as he had kissed his father and mother.

Then he turned to his wife and said:

'Come and see our room and take your hat off.'

They went through a door on the right into a cold, tiled room, all white, with white-washed walls and cotton curtains round the bed. The only decoration in this clean, depressing room was a crucifix with a holy-water basin and two coloured plates depicting Paul and Virginie under a blue palm tree and Napoleon I on a white horse.

As soon as they were alone, he kissed Madeleine: 'Hallo, Mado. It's nice to see the old people again. When you're in Paris, you don't think about them and yet it's good to see them.'

But his father was banging on the partition and shouting:

'Come on, come on, dinner's ready.'

And they had to go and sit down.

It was an interminable, peasant-style meal with all sorts of unsuitable dishes one after the other, chitterlings following the roast lamb and an omelette after the chitterlings. Flushed with cider and a few glasses of wine, old Duroy trotted out all his best jokes, the ones he kept for major celebrations, coarse bawdy stories about things that, according to him, had happened to his friends. Georges recognized them all but still laughed, intoxicated by his return to his native hearth, his deep love of home and by all his past as everything flooded back, the places which he knew from childhood, sensations and memories, all the things from the past that he was seeing once more – little things such as a knife-mark on a door or a rickety chair reminding him of some tiny happening, the earthy smells, the scent of resin and trees wafting in from the near-by forest, all the odours of house, gutter and midden.

Old Madame Duroy said nothing. She was still sombre and unbending, eyeing her daughter-in-law with hatred in her heart, the hatred of an old working woman, an old peasant with her fingers gnarled and her limbs deformed by toil, towards this city woman whom she looked on with repulsion as a woman damned to eternal flames, an impure creature fit only for sloth and sinfulness. She kept getting up all the time to bring in the dishes and fill up the glasses with the tart yellow liquid from the jug or the reddish, sweet, sparkling cider in bottles whose corks were popping like fizzy lemonade.

Madeleine was eating hardly anything and saying very little, looking sad, gloomy and resigned, although she still wore her normal fixed smile on her face. She was disappointed and terribly upset. Yet why? She had wanted to come. She knew quite well that she was going to be amongst country folk, extremely modest country folk. What had she imagined them to be like since she was normally so little prone to let her imagination roam?

Did she really know herself? Don't women always want something different from the truth? Had she poeticized them from a distance? No, but she had imagined them as more literary, perhaps, more noble and affectionate, more decorative. Yet she did not want them to be distinguished as they were made out to be in novels. What was it, then, that shocked her in so many small, hidden ways, in the whole crudeness of their behaviour, just because they were country bumpkins by nature, in everything they said and did, even in their cheerful good humour?

She remembered her own mother, of whom she never spoke to anyone, a schoolmistress who had been brought up in Saint-Denis, had been seduced and deserted, and had died in destitution and despair when Madeleine was twelve years old. A stranger had seen to the little girl's education. Her father, possibly? Who was he? She never knew exactly although she had vague suspicions.

The lunch was dragging on and on. Now customers were coming in, shaking hands with old Duroy, exclaiming when they saw his son and giving a saucy wink as they cast a furtive look at his young wife, as if to say: 'Well I never! She's not bad at all, Georges' wife.'

Others, rather less familiar, sat down at the wooden tables and shouted: 'A litre of cider! A large beer! Two brandies! A raspail!' And then they started to play dominoes, making a great clatter with the oblong pieces of black and white bone.

Old Madame Duroy was coming and going the whole time, serving the customers with her woebegone look, taking the money, wiping the tables with the corner of her blue apron.

The room was filling with smoke from the clay pipes and cheap cigars. Madeleine began to cough and asked: 'Can we go out? I can't stand it.'

They had not yet finished the meal. Old Duroy was not pleased. So she got up and went to sit on a chair outside the door, on the road, waiting for her father-in-law and husband to finish their coffee and liqueurs.

Georges soon came out.

'How about going down to the Seine?' he said.

She was delighted:

'Oh yes. Do let's.'

They went down the hill, hired a boat at Croisset and spent the rest of the afternoon beside an island under the willows, both sleepy in the gentle warmth of spring, lulled by the rippling river.

Then they went up to Canteleu as night was falling.

Madeleine found the meal that evening, eaten by candle-light, even more trying than lunch. Old Duroy, still half tipsy, had nothing to say. The mother still had her sour look.

226

The wretched light cast strange shadows on the grey wall, giving heads enormous noses and exaggerating gestures. Sometimes when someone turned sideways to the yellow flickering light you could see a giant hand lifting what seemed to be a garden fork to a mouth that looked like some sort of monster's.

As soon as supper was over, Madeleine dragged her husband out of doors so as not to remain any longer in the gloomy room which still had its acrid smell of old pipe-smoke and spilt drink.

Once they were outside:

'You're bored already,' he said.

She tried to protest but he stopped her:

'No. I could see it quite plainly. If you like, we'll leave tomorrow.'

She said in a low voice:

'Yes, I would like to.'

They walked gently on. It was a balmy night and the deep, soft shadows seemed full of tiny noises, of rustlings and puffs of air. They had come to a narrow avenue of very tall trees between two dense black thickets.

She asked:

'Where are we?'

He replied:

'In the forest.'

'Is it a big one?'

'Very big, one of the largest in France.'

The avenue was full of the stagnant odour of earth, trees and moss, the cool, ancient scent of any dense wood, consisting of sappy buds and dead mouldering grass in the thickets. Lifting her head Madeleine could glimpse the stars in between the tree-tops and although there was no breeze stirring the branches, she could vaguely feel this sea of foliage fluttering all around her.

A strange shudder ran through her, penetrating to the depths of her being; her heart was gripped by an obscure feeling of distress. Why? She could not understand it. But she felt as if she were lost, drowning, surrounded by hidden dangers, deserted by everyone, all alone, alone in the world, beneath this living archway that was quivering over her head.

She whispered:

'I'm a bit frightened. I'd like to go back.'

'All right, let's go back.'

'And we'll leave for Paris tomorrow?'

'Yes, tomorrow.'

'Tomorrow morning?'

'Tomorrow morning if you like.'

They went back. The old couple were already in bed. She slept badly, continually awakened by the unfamiliar country sounds, the hooting of owls, the grunting of a pig shut up in its sty next to the wall and a cock which kept crowing from midnight onwards.

She was up and ready to leave as soon as the first streaks of dawn appeared.

When Georges announced to his parents that he was going back to Paris, they were both taken aback, and then they understood who was the cause of this sudden departure.

His father merely asked:

'We'll be seeing 'ee again soon?'

'Of course you will. Sometime this summer.'

'That'll be nice.'

The old woman grunted:

'I hope 'ee don't regret what 'ee've dun.'

He made them a present of 200 francs to appease them; and at about ten o'clock, on the arrival of the cab which a lad from the village had gone to fetch, the young couple kissed the old parents and left.

As they were going down the hill, Duroy began to laugh:

'There you are,' he said. 'I warned you. I ought not to have introduced you to Monsieur and Madame du Roy de Cantel senior.'

She began to laugh too and replied:

'I'm delighted now. They're splendid people whom I'm beginning to like very much. I'll send them little treats from Paris.'

Then she murmured:

'Du Roy de Cantel ... You'll see that nobody will be surprised by our wedding notices. We'll tell everyone that we spent a week on your parents' estate.'

And moving closer towards him, she brushed his moustache with her lips: 'Hallo, Geo.'

He answered: 'Hallo, Mado', and slipped his arm round her waist.

In the distance, at the end of the valley, they could see the broad river stretching out like a silver ribbon under the morning sun and all the factory chimneys pouring out their clouds of coal-smoke into the sky and the pointed spires dominating the old town.

THE Du Roys had been back in Paris two days and he had resumed his former duties until such time as he would leave the news section and take over Forestier's functions to devote himself entirely to politics.

That evening he was going back to his predecessor's flat for dinner in great good humour, thinking with keen anticipation that he would soon be kissing his wife, whose physical charms and barely perceptible domination were exerting a lively influence on him. As he passed by a florist's at the bottom of the Rue Notre-Dame-de-Lorette, he had the thought of taking Madeleine some flowers and he bought a large bunch of roses just about to bloom, a cluster of scented buds.

On each landing of his new staircase, he looked complacently at himself in the mirror which always reminded him of the first time he had come to the house.

He rang the bell because he had forgotten his key and the same servant whom he had kept on, following his wife's advice, came to open the door.

Georges asked:

'Is the mistress back?'

'Yes sir.'

But as he went through the dining-room he was greatly surprised to see the table laid for three and as the curtain over the drawing-room door was pulled to one side, he saw Madeleine arranging a bunch of roses identical to his in a vase on the mantelshelf. He felt upset and annoyed as though someone had stolen his kind thought from him and all the pleasure which he had promised himself from it.

'So you've invited someone,' he said as he came in.

Without turning round, she continued to arrange the flowers as she replied:

'Yes and no. It's my old friend the Comte de Vaudrec who always used to dine here every Monday and who's coming as he always did.'

Georges murmured: 'Oh, I see.'

He was standing behind her, his bunch of flowers in his hand, feeling as if he would like to hide them or throw them away. However, he said:

'I've bought you some roses.'

She spun round, all smiles, exclaiming:

'Oh, how sweet of you to have thought of that!'

And she held out her arms and her lips to him in such genuine pleasure that he felt consoled.

She took the flowers, smelt them, and like a delighted child popped them into an empty vase standing beside the other one. Then she looked at the effect and said:

'What a lucky woman I am! Now the whole of my mantel-piece is decorated.'

She added almost immediately, in a confident tone of voice:

'You know Vaudrec is a charmer, you'll make friends with him straightaway.'

A ring at the door announced that the count had arrived. He came in with an air of assurance, very much at his ease and obviously feeling at home. After gallantly kissing the young woman's fingers, he turned towards her husband and gave him a hearty handshake, saying:

'Things going well, my dear Du Roy?'

His manner was no longer stiff and haughty but affable, showing quite plainly that the situation had changed. Taken by surprise, the journalist tried to make himself similarly agreeable and respond to these advances. After five minutes, you might have thought that the two men had been bosom friends for the last ten years.

Then Madeleine, who was beaming, said to them:

'I'm going to leave you two together. I must take a peep at my cooking.' And as she went out, both men followed her with their eyes.

When she came back, she found them talking theatre and discussing a new play on which their opinions were so similar that a rapidly awakening friendship could be seen in their eyes as they realized how identical were their ideas.

It was a charming dinner, friendly and cordial; the count felt so much at home with this delightful new couple that he stayed very late.

As soon as he had gone, Madeleine said to her husband:

'Isn't he wonderful? He's a completely different person when you get to know him. He's a really good friend, trustworthy, devoted and loyal. Oh, but for him ...'

She did not finish her sentence and Georges replied:

'Yes, I find him very pleasant. I think we shall get on very well together.'

But she immediately went on:

'But you didn't know, we've got work to do this evening before going to bed. I didn't have time to mention it to you before dinner because Vaudrec arrived straight away. I heard some news about Morocco. The Deputy Laroche-Mathieu, the next minister, told me about it. We must make a big article out of it, a really sensational one. I've got facts and figures. We'll set to work at once. Look, you bring the lamp.'

He picked it up and they went into the study.

There were the same rows of books in the shelves, on which there now stood the three vases bought by Forestier in Golfe Juan, the day before his last attack. Under the table, the dead man's footmuff was awaiting Du Roy's own feet and after he had sat down, he took up the ivory penholder whose end had been slightly chewed by the other man's teeth.

Madeleine leant against the mantelpiece and, lighting a cigarette, told Du Roy her news; and then gave her ideas on the subject and the plan of the article which she had in mind.

He listened attentively, jotting down notes as he did so and when she had finished, he raised objections, went back over the question, looked at it in broader terms and in his turn sketched out not a plan for an article but a plan of campaign against the present minister. This attack would be the beginning. His wife had stopped smoking as she became interested and realized the full scope and importance of Georges' ideas.

From time to time she muttered: 'Yes ... yes ... very good ... excellent ... that's wonderful ...'

And when he had his say as well, she said: 'Let's start writing.'

But it was always difficult for him to start and he had trouble in finding words. So she came quietly up to him, leant over his shoulder and began to whisper suggestions to him as to how to phrase it.

Now and again she would hesitate and ask him:

'Is that really what you want to say?'

And he would reply:

'Yes, absolutely.'

She launched an attack on the leader of the government in the most cutting terms, with a woman's spitefulness, combining unflattering remarks about his face with similar comments on his politics, in an amusing way which made you laugh but at the same time struck you by their accurate observation.

Sometimes Du Roy would add a line or two to bring out the implications of the attack and extend its scope. He had a gift, too, for the insidious double meaning, acquired as news editor to give a sharp edge to his news, and if he felt that something which Madeleine was putting forward as a fact was uncertain or compromising he would artfully insinuate it and impress it on the reader's mind more vividly than if he had actually stated it in so many words.

When their article was finished, Georges declaimed it out loud, like a speech. They both agreed that it was excellent and they gave each other a smile of surprised delight as if they had just discovered each other. They looked deep into each other's eyes, moved by admiration and tenderness and they kissed impulsively, with a warmth which communicated itself from their minds to their bodies.

Du Roy picked up the lamp: 'And now, bye-byes,' he said, with a glint in his eye.

She answered: 'Go first, oh master, since you are lighting the way.'

He went ahead and she followed him into their bedroom, tickling his neck with her finger between his collar and his hair in order to make him go faster, because he loathed being touched there.

The article appeared over the signature of Georges du Roy de Cantel and excited much comment. It made a great stir in the Chamber of Deputies. Old Walter congratulated its author and put him in charge of the political section of *La Vie française*. The news section was given back to Bois-renard.

The paper now launched a skilful and violent campaign against the minister in charge of foreign affairs. The attack was always clever and well-informed, sometimes ironical, sometimes serious, occasionally amusing and occasionally vicious; and it hit the mark with a consistency and an accuracy which amazed everybody. The other newspapers were always quoting *La Vie française*, lifting whole passages from it, and the men in power tried to discover if it might not be possible to gag this unknown and implacable enemy by the offer of a post as *préfet*.

Du Roy's name was becoming well known amongst the political groups. He could feel how his influence was increasing by the added warmth of the handshakes he received and the alacrity with which men raised their hats to him. Furthermore, he was filled with amazement and admiration by his wife's ingenuity, her skill in obtaining information and the wide range of her acquaintance.

Whenever he came home, he would find in her drawing-room a senator, a deputy, a high official, a general, who all treated her with familiarity and respect, like an old friend. Where had she got to know all those people? Through her social connections, she would reply. But how had she been able to gain their confidence and affection? He could never understand it.

'She'd make a damned good diplomat,' he thought to himself.

Often she would come in late for meals, breathless, red in the face and excited and even before taking off her veil she would say:

'I've got a treat today. Can you imagine, the Minister of Justice has just appointed two judges who've been sitting on the joint commissions. We're going to haul him over the coals in a way he won't forget.'

And so the Minister was hauled over the coals and next day they did it again and the following day they did it a third time. The Deputy Laroche-Mathieu who dined at Rue Fontaine every Tuesday, following on the Comte de Vaudrec, who started the week, could not contain his joy as he vigorously congratulated husband and wife. He kept on saying: 'Heavens above, what a campaign! Surely we must succeed after all that?'

In fact, he was hoping to land the Foreign Affairs portfolio for himself; he had had his eye on it for a long time.

He was one of those many-faced politicians without any strong beliefs, with no great resources, no backbone and no real knowledge of anything, a country lawyer with provincial good looks, craftily walking the tight-rope between any extremist parties, a kind of republican Jesuit, a sort of dubious liberal mushroom such as flourish in their hundreds on the popular dunghill of universal suffrage.

His parish-pump diplomacy had given him the reputation of being an able man amongst his colleagues, all those futile misfits who are elected deputies. He was neat enough, polite enough, familiar enough and pleasant enough to succeed. He was successful in his social contacts, in the mixed, murky and undiscriminating society of the ruling class of the time.

Everyone went about saying: 'Laroche is going to be a Minister', and he, too, was more convinced than anyone that Laroche would become a Minister.

He was one of the principal shareholders in old Walter's paper and was associated with him as a colleague in many of his business operations.

Du Roy was confidently supporting him, with vague hopes of later benefits. He was, in fact, merely continuing the work already begun by Forestier, who had been promised the Legion of Honour once their efforts had been crowned by success. Now it would be Madeleine's new husband whose button-hole would be decorated, that was all. There was no real difference, in fact.

People felt so strongly that there was no real difference that Du Roy's colleagues had thought up a gag that was beginning to annoy him.

They had taken to calling him Forestier.

As soon as he arrived at the paper, someone would call out 'I say, Forestier.'

He pretended not to hear and would look for his letters in

his pigeon-hole. The voice called out again, more loudly: 'Hey, Forestier.' There were sniggers.

As Du Roy was making his way towards the director's office, the man who had called out stopped him:

'Sorry, I wanted to speak to you. It's silly, I always confuse you with poor old Charles. It's because your articles are so damned similar to his. Everybody's always making that mistake.'

Du Roy made no reply but he was inwardly furious; and he was beginning to feel dumb anger towards the dead man.

When people expressed surprise at the blatant similarities in phrasing and inspiration between the articles of the new political editor and those of his predecessor, old Walter himself had said:

'Yes, it's like Forestier but it's more solid, terser, more vigorous.'

On another occasion, happening to open the cupboard containing the cups-and-balls, Du Roy had found those belonging to his predecessor with a piece of black crepe round their handles while his own, the one he used when he was being instructed by Saint-Potin, had been decorated with a pink ribbon. They had all been arranged on the same shelf in order of size; and there was a written notice, such as you find in museums, which read: 'Former collection of Forestier and Co., now under the new management of his successor, Forestier-Du Roy, patent S.G.D.G.,* guaranteed never to wear out and useful in all circumstances, even when travelling.'

He closed the cupboard calmly, saying as he did so, in a voice loud enough for everyone to hear: 'There are always envious idiots everywhere.'

But his pride and vanity were offended, the pride and vanity of the author quick to take offence, producing that

* *sans garantie du gouvernement*, without government guarantee.

irritability and touchiness that is ever present, whether in a reporter or a poet of genius.

The word *Forestier* grated on his ear, he was scared of hearing it and could feel himself blushing whenever he did.

He felt that the name was jeering at him, in fact more than jeering, almost insulting him. It seemed to be proclaiming: 'Your wife does your job for you, just as she did for her first husband. Without her help you'd be nobody.'

He was perfectly willing to admit that Forestier would have been nobody without Madeleine but as for him, Good Lord, no!

Nor did his obsession end when he went home. The whole house now reminded him of the dead man, all the furniture, all the knick-knacks, everything he touched. At first he hardly thought about it; but his colleagues' practical jokes had produced a sort of trauma that was now exacerbated by a host of hitherto imperceptible trifles.

He could not pick up any object without immediately seeing Charles handling it. Everything he saw and touched had been used by Charles, they were things that he had bought and loved and possessed. And Georges even began to feel irritated at the thought of the previous relationship between his friend and his wife.

Sometimes he was surprised at this emotional reaction which he could not understand and he would ask himself: 'What on earth can be the cause of it? I'm not jealous of Madeleine's friends. I never bother what she does. She comes and goes as she thinks fit and yet the thought of that bastard Charles makes me furious!'

And he remarked to himself: 'Basically, he was a hopeless idiot. I expect that's what irritates me. I'm annoyed because Madeleine was capable of marrying such a silly ass.'

And he kept on saying to himself all the time: 'How can a woman like her ever have fallen for a moron like that?'

And every day his grievance was fed by a thousand and one tiny insignificant details that were like so many pin-pricks constantly reminding him of the other man, by something said by Madeleine or the servant or the chamber-maid.

One evening Du Roy, who had a sweet tooth, asked: 'Why don't we ever have any puddings? You never serve any.'

The young woman answered brightly:

'Yes, that's quite true, I never think of it. It's because Charles loathed them . . .'

He interrupted her, unable to control his impatience:

'Oh, for heaven's sake, Charles is beginning to get on my nerves. It's always Charles, Charles, Charles . . . Charles liked this, Charles liked that. Now that Charles has kicked the bucket, let's leave him alone.'

Madeleine was looking at her husband in amazement, unable to understand what had caused him to flare up in this way. Then, as she was shrewd, she sensed what was happening in his mind, his jealousy towards the dead man slowly gnawing away at him as he was reminded of him at every turn.

She may have thought it childish but she was flattered and made no reply.

He was angry with himself for not having been able to hide his irritation. Yet that same evening after dinner, as they were doing an article for the following day's paper, he caught his foot in the foot muff. Being unable to turn it round he kicked it away and enquired with a laugh:

'Did Charles always have cold feet, then?'

She replied, also with a laugh:

'Oh, he had a dread of catching cold. He had a weak chest.'

Du Roy said ferociously: 'Yes, he proved that, didn't he?' Then added gallantly: 'Fortunately for me.' And he kissed his wife's hand.

But as they were going to bed, still obsessed by the same thought, he asked once again:

'Did Charles wear cotton night caps to protect his ears from draughts?'

She entered into the joke and replied:

'No, a handkerchief tied in a bow on his forehead.'

Georges shrugged his shoulders contemptuously and said, in a condescending voice:

'What a nit!'

From this time onwards, Charles became a continual topic of conversation for him. He would talk about him at the slightest opportunity, always calling him: 'poor old Charles' with an infinitely pitying look.

And when he came back from the office where he had heard himself addressed as Forestier two or three times, he would take his revenge by pouring scorn on the dead man even in his grave. He used to recall his faults, his absurd ways, his pettiness, taking pleasure in retailing all the details, emphasizing them and magnifying them as though he feared Charles' rivalry and wanted to destroy his influence on his wife's affections.

He kept saying:

'I say, Mado, do you remember the time that drip Forestier wanted to prove to us that fat men were better lovers than thin ones?'

Then he tried to find out lots of intimate, private details about the dead man that the embarrassed young woman refused to tell him. But he obstinately persisted:

'Come on, do tell me. He must have been very funny when he was doing it?'

She murmured under her breath:

'Oh, do leave him alone.'

He went on:

'No, do tell me! He must have been really clumsy in bed, the silly idiot!'

And his concluding words were always:

'What a nasty piece of work.'

One evening towards the end of June, as he was smoking a cigarette at the window, he found it so hot that he felt like going for a drive.

He asked:

'Mado, my dear, would you like to come with me to the Bois?'

'Yes, certainly.'

They took an open cab, which drove along the Champs Élysées and then up the Avenue du Bois de Boulogne. It was a completely windless night, one of those sweltering evenings when the air in Paris is like an oven. Scores of loving couples were driving along under the trees in a whole army of cabs following one behind the other, end to end.

Georges and Madeleine enjoyed watching all these couples in each other's arms going by in the carriages, the women in light dresses, the men in black. An endless procession of lovers was flowing down towards the Bois under the torrid, starlit night. The only sound was the rumble of wheels. On and on they came, two creatures stretched out on the cushions of every cab, silently clasping each other, lost in the mirage of their desire and trembling in anticipation of a more intimate embrace. The warm evening seemed full of kisses. There was a feeling of tenderness and of animal desire floating out into the air, making it sultry and even more stifling. The intoxication of all these couples obsessed by the same thoughts and the same ardent desires cast an aura of feverish excitement all around. All these carriages with their cargo of love, over which you could sense the fluttering of caresses, were wafting a sort of subtle, sensual and disturbing aroma as they passed.

241

Georges and Madeleine felt seized, too, by this contagious tenderness. They took each other's hands without speaking, somewhat oppressed by the heaviness of the atmosphere and by the emotion that was gripping them both.

When they came to the turn where the avenue follows the fortifications, they kissed and she stammered, rather embarrassed:

'We're being as childish as we were on the way to Rouen.'

The main current of carriages had split up as it reached the clumps of trees. In the road round the lakes which the young couple were taking, the cabs were now somewhat further apart but the thick shadows of the trees, the air freshened by the leaves and the moisture from the little rivulets that could be heard flowing underneath the branches, a sort of coolness from the spacious star-spangled night, gave a more pervasive charm to the kisses of the couples in the carriages and made the darkness surrounding them even more mysterious.

Georges murmured: 'Oh my dear little Mado' as he clasped her tightly in his arms. She said:

'Do you remember the forest near your home and how sinister it was? I felt that it was full of horrid beasts and that it went on and on without end. Whereas here it's charming. There's a gentle breeze and I know that Sèvres is on the other side of the Bois.'

He replied:

'Oh, in my forest there was nothing but stags and foxes, roebuck and wild boar and a forester's house here and there.'

The word 'forester', so similar to the dead man's name, surprised him as he heard it coming from his lips just as if someone had suddenly shouted it from the depths of a thicket and all at once he fell silent, seized once again by his strange, uncomfortable obsession, the nagging jealous irritation that he found impossible to forget and which for some time now had been poisoning his existence.

After a pause he asked:

'Did you sometimes come here like this in the evening with Charles?'

She replied:

'Yes, frequently.'

And suddenly he felt an urge to go back home, an hysterical urge that struck him to the heart. But the memory of Forestier had forced itself into his mind, obsessing him and refusing to go away. He could do nothing but think about him and talk about him.

He asked in a disagreeable tone of voice:

'I say, Mado?'

'Yes darling?'

'Did you cuckold poor old Charles?'

She replied quietly but scornfully:

'You're making yourself ridiculous by the way you keep harping on that subject.'

But he persisted:

'Look, Mado dear, be honest and admit it. You did cuckold him, didn't you? Confess that you cuckolded him.'

She said nothing, as shocked as every woman is at hearing that word.

He went on doggedly:

'My God, if anyone looked like one it really was him. My God yes. That's why I'd like to know if Forestier was a cuckold. Eh? What a real sucker he looked, didn't he?'

He sensed that she was smiling, perhaps as she recollected something and he insisted:

'Go on, do tell me. What does it matter? On the contrary, it would be very funny to admit that you deceived him, to confess it to me.'

Indeed, he was quivering with hope, longing to hear that Charles, the hateful Charles, the dead man whom he loathed

and abominated, had suffered this ludicrous fate. And yet ...
and yet another more secret emotion was spurring him on.

He repeated:

'Mado, Mado darling, please, please, tell me. It would have
served him right. You'd have been jolly silly not to have done
it to him. Come on, Mado, own up.'

She was now being seized by little fits of giggles, no doubt
because she was finding his insistence amusing.

He had put his lips right against his wife's ear:

'Come on, come on ... Own up.'

She jerked herself away and said suddenly:

'You really are stupid. How can anyone answer that sort of
question?'

She said this in such a peculiar tone that a cold shiver ran
through her husband's whole frame and he was left completely disconcerted and dazed, gasping as if shaken by a
sudden shock.

The cab was now driving along the lake, into which the
sky seemed to have scattered its stars. Two swans could be
dimly seen gliding very slowly over the water, barely visible
in the darkness.

Georges shouted to the cabby:

'Let's turn round.' And the carriage went back, against
the line of the other cabs which were moving at walking
pace, their big lamps shining like eyes in the gloom of the
Bois.

What a strange tone of voice she had used! Du Roy
asked himself: 'Was that an admission?' and now that he
felt almost certain that she had deceived her first husband,
he was filled with a wild rage. He felt like beating her,
strangling her, tearing her hair out.

If only she had said: 'But darling, if I had been going to
deceive him, it would have been with you.' How he would
have kissed and hugged and adored her!

He sat quite still, with his arms crossed, looking up at the sky, too agitated as yet to be able to think clearly. All he could do was to feel his rancour stirring and his wrath rising, the rancour and the wrath that is lurking in the heart of every male when he comes up against the whims of a woman's desires. For the first time he felt the distress and bewilderment of a suspicious husband! He was jealous in fact, jealous towards the dead man, jealous on behalf of Forestier, jealous in a strangely tormenting way which involved a sudden hatred of Madeleine. Since she had deceived her other husband, how could he trust her himself?

Then gradually he became calmer and, to fortify himself against his misfortune, he thought: 'All women are whores. One must use them and not give them anything of oneself.'

Words of scorn and bitter disgust welled up in his heart. But he did not utter them. He kept saying to himself: 'The world belongs to the strong. I must be strong. I must rise above everything.'

The carriage was moving faster. They went past the fortifications once again. Du Roy was looking ahead, watching a reddish glow in the sky, like the gleam of an enormous forge, and he could hear an immense, confused, continuous roar, full of countless different noises, a dull roar from far and near, the huge, vague, living throb of Paris panting like an exhausted colossus on this summer evening.

Georges was thinking: 'I'd be very silly to take it to heart. Everyone for himself. Fortune favours the brave. Everything boils down to selfishness. And selfishness to achieve power and wealth is much better than selfishness for women and love.'

The Arc de Triomphe was looming up at the entrance to the city, standing like a two-legged monster, a sort of shapeless giant preparing, it seemed, to march off down the broad avenue in front of it.

Georges and Madeleine were now in the procession of

carriages bearing homewards, to their longed-for bed, the eternal couple silent in each other's arms. It seemed as though the whole of mankind was gliding along beside them, intoxicated with joy, pleasure and happiness.

The young woman had undoubtedly sensed something of her husband's thoughts and she asked in her usual gentle voice:

'What are you thinking about, Georges? You haven't uttered a word this last half-hour.'

He grinned:

'I was thinking of all those stupid idiots kissing, and saying to myself that there really are other things to do in life.'

She murmured:

'Yes . . . but it's nice sometimes.'

'It's nice . . . it's nice . . . when there's nothing better!'

And he pursued his thoughts to himself, stripping life of its poetry in a sort of vicious fury: 'I'd be very stupid to restrain myself or do without anything I want, to bother or worry or fret as I have been doing recently.' The thought of Forestier passed through his mind without causing him the slightest irritation. He felt as if they had become reconciled, that they were becoming friends again. He had the urge to shout: 'Hallo, old man.'

Madeleine was embarrassed by his silence. She said:

'Shall we have an ice-cream at Tortoni's before we go home?'

He looked at her out of the corner of his eye. Her delicate blonde profile was lit up by the glare of a festoon of gas flares announcing a *café-chantant*.

He thought: 'She's pretty. Well, so much the better. Tit for tat, my friend. But if I'm ever caught tormenting myself on your account, old girl, then I must have my head examined.' Then he answered: 'Of course, darling.' And so that she might not guess anything he kissed her.

246

To Madeleine, his lips seemed as cold as ice. But he was smiling his normal smile as he offered his hand to help her out of the cab in front of the steps of the café.

CHAPTER 3

WHEN he came into the office next day, he went to see Boisrenard.

'I want to ask you a favour, my dear Boisrenard,' he said. 'People have recently been finding it funny to address me as Forestier. I'm beginning to find it rather silly. I wonder if you would mind quietly informing my friends and colleagues that I intend to slap the face of the first person who takes that liberty in future?

'It's up to them to decide whether the joke is worth landing themselves with a duel. I'm approaching you because I know that you're a calm sort of man who can prevent things from going too far and having unfortunate consequences and also because you acted as my second in my other affair.'

Boisrenard agreed to pass on the message.

Du Roy went out on various errands and returned an hour later. Nobody called him Forestier.

When he came home, he heard women's voices in the drawing-room. He asked: 'Who's there?'

The servant replied: 'Madame Walter and Madame de Marelle.'

His heart gave a little leap, then he said to himself: 'Well, let's see', and opened the door.

Clotilde was sitting by the fireplace under a ray of light coming from the window. It seemed to Georges that she turned slightly pale when she saw him. After saying good evening to Madame Walter and her daughters, who were sitting each side of their mother, like two sentries, he turned towards his former mistress. She held out her hand, he took it and squeezed it deliberately as if to say: 'I still love you.' She responded to his pressure.

He said:

'We haven't met for ages. I do hope you've been keeping well?'

She replied, completely at her ease:

'Yes indeed, and how about you, Bel-Ami?'

Then turning to Madeleine, she added:

'You don't mind if I still call him Bel-Ami?'

'Of course, my dear, you can do anything you like.'

The words seemed to have a tinge of hidden irony.

Madame Walter was talking about a fête that Jacques Rival was going to organize in his large bachelor flat, a big fencing display, to which Paris high society was to be invited. She was saying:

'It will be most interesting. But I'm sorry, there'll be nobody to take us, because my husband has to be away at the time.'

Du Roy immediately volunteered. She accepted: 'My daughters and I will be most grateful.'

He was looking at the younger of the two and thinking: 'She's not bad at all, young Suzanne, not bad at all.' She looked like a fragile blonde doll, too small, but slender, with a slim waist, nice hips and bosom, a face like a delicate miniature painting, with lustrous grey-blue eyes which seemed to have been coloured by some meticulous, fanciful enamelpainter. Her flesh was too pale, too smooth, too glossy, too polished, lacking texture or colour, her hair was all tousled and frizzy, a skilfully arranged mass of curls, as fluffy and charming as that of a real pretty, luxury doll such as you see carried around by little girls far smaller than their toy.

The elder sister Rose was ugly, as flat as a pancake and insignificant, the sort of girl you never look at, speak to or talk about.

Her mother stood up and turned towards Georges:

'So I'm relying on you for next Thursday at two o'clock.'

He replied:

'I shall be there, Madame Walter.'

As soon as she had left, Madame de Marelle also stood up:
'Goodbye, Bel-Ami.'

And then she squeezed his hand very hard and long; he was stirred by this silent admission and felt a sudden renewal of his love for this happy-go-lucky bohemian woman, of modest origin no doubt, but who perhaps really loved him.

'I'll go and see her tomorrow,' he thought.

As soon as he was alone with his wife, Madeleine looked him mischievously in the face and said with a chuckle:

'Do you realize that Madame Walter has fallen for you?'

He could not believe his ears.

'You're joking.'

'No, I promise you, she was talking to me about you in the most glowing terms. It's so strange for her! She would like to find two husbands like you for her daughters ... Fortunately, with her, that sort of thing is unimportant.'

He did not understand her meaning.

'How do you mean, unimportant?'

She replied in the confident tone of a woman certain of her judgement:

'Oh, Madame Walter is one of those women about whom there's never been the slightest breath of suspicion, never, I promise you. She's irreproachable in all respects. As for her husband, you know him as well as I do. But she's quite different. What is more, she's had to put up with quite a lot because she's married a Jew, but she's remained faithful to him. She's an honest woman.'

Du Roy was surprised:

'I thought she was a Jewess, too.'

'She? Not in the least. She's the lady patroness of all the charities of the Madeleine. She was even married in church. I don't know if Walter went through a form of baptism or whether the Church shut its eyes.'

Georges murmured:

'Oh! So she's taken a fancy to me?'

'Positively and absolutely. If you weren't already tied else-where, I'd have advised you to ask for the hand of ... of Suzanne, don't you think, rather than Rose?'

Twirling his moustache, he replied:

'Well, the mother isn't decrepit yet.'

Madeleine said impatiently:

'Well, Georges, as far as I'm concerned you can have the mother. But I'm not worried. A woman is not likely to start that sort of game at her age. You need to start earlier.'

Georges was thinking to himself: 'Suppose it was true that I really could have married Suzanne?'

Then he shrugged: 'No, it's mad. Would her father ever have accepted me?'

Nevertheless, he promised himself in future to watch more closely the way Madame Walter behaved towards him, al-though without any thought that he might ever be able to take advantage of it.

The whole evening he was haunted by memories of his affair with Clotilde, memories both affectionate and sensual. He recalled her funny ways, her niceness, their adventurous excursions. He kept saying to himself: 'She really is a very nice woman. Yes, I'll go and see her tomorrow.'

So next day after lunch, he went to the Rue de Verneuil. The same maid opened the door and in the familiar way servants have in modest households, she asked:

'Are you keeping well, sir?'

He answered:

'Yes, thank you, my girl.'

And he went into the drawing-room where someone was playing clumsy scales on the piano. It was Laurine. He thought she would fling her arms round his neck. But she stood up solemnly, said a very polite 'Good afternoon', just like a grown-up, and went out of the room looking very dignified.

She looked so much like a deeply offended woman that he was surprised. Her mother came in. He took her hands and kissed them.

'I've been thinking of you so much,' he said.

'Me too,' she replied.

They sat down. They were smiling at each other, looking into each other's eyes, longing to kiss each other's lips.

'Clo dear, I love you.'

'And so do I.'

'So ... so ... you don't bear me too much of a grudge?'

'Yes and no. It made me feel unhappy and then I understood your reason and I said: "Ah well, he'll be back sooner or later." '

'I didn't dare come back. I wondered what sort of a welcome I might get. I didn't dare but I wanted to so much. By the way, what's up with Laurine? She barely said "Good afternoon" and went off looking furious.'

'I don't know. But she doesn't want to hear anything about you since your marriage. I do believe she's jealous.'

'No, really!'

'Yes, really, Georges. She never calls you Bel-Ami now but Monsieur Forestier.'

Du Roy flushed and then, going up to the young woman, said:

'Darling, give me a kiss.'

She raised her mouth towards his.

'Where can we meet each other?' he asked.

'In the Rue de Constantinople!'

'Oh! Is it still free?'

'No, I kept it on.'

'You kept it on!'

'Yes, I thought you'd come back there.'

He suddenly felt bursting with pride and joy. This woman really loved him, loved him deeply and faithfully.

He murmured: 'I adore you.' Then he asked: 'How's your husband?'

'Oh, very well. He's just spent a month here. He left the day before yesterday.'

Du Roy could not help laughing:

'What good timing!'

She replied ingenuously:

'Yes, it is, isn't it?'

'But he's no trouble even when he's here. You know that.'

'Yes, that's true. In any case, he's a charming man.'

'And how about you?' she said. 'How do you like your new life?'

'So so. My wife is just a good friend, an associate.'

'Nothing more?'

'Nothing more. As for affection ...'

'I understand. But she's nice.'

'Yes, but she doesn't excite me.'

He came closer to Clotilde and said softly:

'When can we see each other?'

'Well ... tomorrow ... if you like?'

'Yes. Tomorrow. Two o'clock.'

'Two o'clock.'

He stood up to go and then said, hesitantly, a trifle embarrassed:

'You know, I'll take over the flat in the Rue de Constantinople myself. I'd like to. It wouldn't be right for you to go on paying for it.'

And Du Roy went away a very contented man.

As he went by a photographer's window, he saw a portrait of a tall woman with large eyes who reminded him of Madame Walter: 'All the same,' he said to himself, 'she can't be so bad either. How is it that I'd never noticed her before?

I'll look forward to seeing how she treats me on Thursday.'

He was rubbing his hands together gleefully as he walked along, full of the private pleasure of achieving everything he wanted, the glee of the skilful egoist for whom everything is turning out well and the subtle mixture of flattered vanity and satisfied sensuality that comes from a woman's love.

When Thursday came, he said to Madeleine:

'Aren't you coming to Rival's show?'

'Oh no, that sort of thing doesn't interest me much. I'll go to the Chamber of Deputies.'

And so he went to pick up Madame Walter in an open landau, because the weather was superb.

When he saw her, he was quite surprised to see how young and beautiful she looked. She was wearing a dress of light-coloured material with quite a low neck-line which gave a hint of the curve of her plump bosom through the creamy lace. Never had she seemed so fresh and appetizing. He found her really desirable. She had such a calm, ladylike look and a certain quiet, motherly manner which made her the object of few amorous glances. Furthermore, her normal conversation was conventional, ordinary and unexciting, for her ideas were sensible, methodical and orderly, free from any excess.

Her daughter Suzanne was dressed all in pink and looked like a newly varnished painting by Watteau, while her elder sister seemed to be the governess in charge of this pretty little doll.

In front of Rival's door there was a whole line of carriages. Du Roy offered his arm to Madame Walter and they went in.

The fête was being held in aid of the orphans of the six-teenth Paris arrondissement, under the patronage of all the wives of the senators and deputies who were connected with *La Vie française*.

Madame Walter had promised to attend with her daughters but had refused to be lady patroness since she allowed her name to be used only for religious charities, not because she was particularly devout but because she thought that being married to a Jew entailed a certain strictness in her religious attitude; and the fête organized by Rival had a sort of republican flavour that could be interpreted as anti-clerical.

For the last three weeks, the newspapers of all political hues had been announcing:

Our distinguished colleague Jacques Rival has had the ingenious and generous idea of organizing a grand fencing display in the attractive fencing-hall attached to his bachelor flat, in aid of the orphans of the sixteenth arrondissement.

Invitations are being sent out by Mesdames Laloigne, Remontel and Rissolin, the wives of the senators of that name, and by Mesdames Laroche-Mathieu, Percerol and Firmin, the wives of the well-known deputies. A single collection will be made during the interval and the sum thus raised will be handed over immediately to the mayor of the sixteenth arrondissement or his representative.

It was a superb piece of self-advertisement for Rival.

The journalist stood welcoming the guests at the entrance to his flat, where a cold buffet had been laid (chargeable to the profits of the collection).

Then he smilingly indicated the little stairway leading down to the cellar where he had set up his fencing-hall and shooting-gallery, and he was saying: 'Downstairs, ladies, downstairs. The display will take place in the basement ...'

He hurried to greet the wife of his employer; then, shaking Du Roy's hand, he said:

'Good afternoon, Bel-Ami.'

The latter was surprised:

'Who told you that? ...'

Rival interrupted him:

'Madame Walter here, who thinks that it is a very nice nickname.'

Madame Walter blushed:

'Yes, I must confess that if I knew you better, I should do the same as little Laurine and call you Bel-Ami, too. It suits you very well.'

Du Roy was laughing:

'But please do, Madame Walter.'

She had lowered her eyes:

'No. We don't know each other well enough.'

He murmured:

'May I hope that we shall become better acquainted?'

'We must see,' she replied.

He stood on one side at the entrance to the narrow stairs, lit by a gas jet; and the sudden transition from the light of day to this yellow glimmer was rather gloomy. There was a smell of cellar coming up the spiral staircase, a damp warm smell of walls that had been wiped dry for the occasion as well as gusts of frankincense, which reminded one of church services, and feminine scents of Lubin, verbena, lily and violet.

This dark hole was humming with voices and buzzing with the excited activity of many people.

The whole cellar was festooned with gas jets and Chinese lanterns hidden in foliage and concealing the stone walls covered in saltpetre. You could see nothing but greenery. The ceiling was decorated with ferns and the floor covered in leaves and flowers. The effect was considered charming and delightfully imaginative. In the smaller cellar at the end they had erected a platform for the fencers, with two rows of chairs on it for the judges.

And in the whole cellar there was room for nearly 200 people on the seats arranged in rows of ten, to left and right. They had invited 400.

In front of the platform young men in fencing kit, slim, long-armed and long-legged, with turned-up moustaches, were already posing for the spectators, puffing out their chests. People were telling each other their names and pointing out the professionals and the amateurs, all the best swordsmen of Paris. Around them stood young and old men, in town dress, chatting; they had a sort of family likeness with the fencers in their uniform. They were also keen to be seen, recognized and identified: they were also notable swordsmen in mufti, fencing experts.

Almost all the seats were occupied by women who were creating a great rustling of dresses and a great buzz of voices. They were fanning themselves as if they were at the theatre because this leafy cavern was already swelteringly hot. Occasionally a wag shouted: 'Barley-water! Lemonade! Beer!'

Madame Walter and her daughters took the places reserved for them in the front row. After showing them to their seats, Du Roy was about to leave them, saying:

'I shall have to go, the men can't take up the sitting space.'

But Madame Walter replied hesitantly:

'I was rather hoping that you might stay all the same. You can identify the fencers for me. Look, if you stood there at the corner of this bench you wouldn't be in anyone's way.'

She was looking at him with her large, soft eyes. She insisted:

'Come now, do stay with us ... Monsieur ... Monsieur Bel-Ami. We need you ...'

He replied:

'I'll do all you suggest with pleasure, Madame Walter.'

All round them people were repeating:

'It's great fun, this cellar, it's very nice.'

The vaulted room was all too familiar to Georges. He remembered the morning he had spent here, the day before his duel, all alone, facing a little piece of white cardboard which looked back at him like an enormous, frightening eye from the end of the other cellar.

Jacques Rival's voice was heard from the staircase: 'We're going to begin, ladies.'

And six men wearing very tight-fitting coats which showed off their chests climbed onto the platform and sat down on the chairs reserved for the judges.

People were whispering their names: General de Raynaldi, the chairman, a little man with a big moustache; the painter Josephin Roudet, tall and bald with a long beard; Mattheo de Ujar, Simon Ramoncel and Pierre de Carvin, three young bloods, and Gaspard Merleron, a fencing master.

Two notice-boards were hung up on each side of the cellar. The one on the right read: M. Crèvecoeur, and the one on the left: M. Plumeau.

They were two fencing-masters, two good fencing-masters, if not of the first rank. They appeared, both spare, with a soldierly bearing and rather stiff in their movements. After making the appropriate salute like two robots, they began to fight, looking in their canvas and white leather uniforms like two soldier clowns fighting for a joke.

Every so often, you heard '*Touché!*' And the six judges nodded their heads in a knowing way. All that the public could see were two live puppets who were jumping about sticking out their arms; they did not understand at all what was happening; but they were pleased. Nevertheless, these two figures seemed rather graceless and vaguely ridiculous. They reminded one of the wooden wrestlers that are sold on the boulevards on New Year's Day.

The next to appear were Messrs Planton and Carapin, a civilian fencing master and a military one. M. Planton was very small and M. Carapin very fat. You would have thought that the first thrust might have punctured this balloon like an inflated elephant. People were laughing. M. Planton was jumping about like a monkey on a stick. The only thing that M. Carapin was moving was his arm, since the rest of his body was anchored to the ground by his bulk. Every five minutes he lunged forward so heavily and with such exertion that he seemed to be taking the most energetic decision of his life. Afterwards he experienced a good deal of trouble in straightening up.

The experts stated that his style was compact and firm. The trusting public approved.

Then came the turn of Messrs Porion and Lapalme, a professional and an amateur who indulged in violent gymnastics, hurling themselves on each other furiously, forcing the judges to take flight, carrying their chairs with them, rushing from one end of the platform to the other, retreating and advancing with an energy that was quite comical. This fencing match at the double called forth the puckish comment from some unknown young scallywag: 'Take it easy, you're paid by the hour.' The audience 'shushed', offended by such a tasteless remark. The experts' judgement was that the fencers had shown great vigour with occasional lapses into irrelevance.

The first part of the show was concluded with a fine exhibition match between Jacques Rival and the famous Belgian master Lebègue. Rival was greatly to the liking of the ladies. He really was a handsome young man, well built, lithe, agile and more graceful than any of the previous fencers. In the way he took guard and lunged there was a certain attractive, worldly elegance which contrasted with the vigorous but common style of his opponent. 'You can tell he's a gentleman,' people were saying.

He won the decider and received his due applause.

But for the last few minutes the spectators had been uneasily aware of a peculiar noise from the floor above. There was a great stamping to the accompaniment of rowdy laughter. No doubt the 200 guests who had been unable to find room in the cellar were finding their own way of passing the time. Some fifty or so men were jammed in the tiny spiral staircase. Down below, the cellar was becoming frightfully hot. People were shouting: 'Air!' 'Drink!' The same wag was still yelling in a shrill voice that dominated the buzz of conversation: 'Barley-water! Lemonade! Beer!'

Rival appeared, very red in the face and still in his fencing kit. 'I'll have some drinks sent down,' he said and hurried to the staircase. But all communication with the ground-floor had been blocked. It would have been as simple to make a hole in the ceiling as to make one's way through the wall of humanity piled up on the steps.

Rival was shouting: 'Send some ices down for the ladies!'

The cry was taken up by fifty voices: 'Ices!' Finally a tray appeared. It was full of empty glasses, as people had helped themselves to the refreshments on the way.

Someone shouted in a loud voice: 'We're stifling down here. Let's get on with it and then we can go.'

Someone else cried: 'The collection!' And all the spectators, gasping for breath, but still good-humoured, took up the refrain: 'The collection ... The collection ...'

So six ladies began to go round between the seats and you could hear the tinkle of money falling into the bags.

Du Roy was pointing out all the celebrities to Madame Walter. There were society people, journalists from the big papers, the well-established papers who looked down on *La Vie française* with a certain reserve born of experience. They had seen so many of these politico–financial newspapers, the product of some shady scheme, come to grief as the result of the fall of a minister. Also to be seen were painters and sculptors, who are generally interested in sport, a poet

Academician who was on show, two musicians and a large number of foreign noblemen, after whose name Du Roy added the syllable Wop, in imitation, so he said, of the English who put Esq. on their visiting-cards.

Someone hailed him: 'Good afternoon, my dear boy!' It was the Comte de Vaudrec. Du Roy excused himself for a moment to go and shake hands with him.

When he came back, he said: 'Vaudrec is a charmer. What breeding the man has!'

Madame Walter made no reply. She was a trifle tired and her chest was heaving with every breath she took, a fact that was attracting Du Roy's eye. And now and again his eyes crossed those of his employer's wife and he saw that her gaze was disturbed, hesitant and furtive. And he said to himself: 'Well, well, well. Have I got her on the run, too?'

The collectors went by. Their bags were full of gold and silver coins. And then a fresh notice was hung up on the platform announcing: 'Grrreat surprise.' The judges climbed back into their seats. Everyone waited.

Two women appeared in fencing kit and carrying foils, dressed in black tights, a very short skirt coming half-way down their thighs and a fencing-jacket so bulging in front that they were forced to hold their chins in the air. They were young and pretty. Both smiled as they bowed to the audience. They were greeted by a long burst of applause.

They took guard amidst a buzz of gallant comment and whispered jokes.

A permanent smirk appeared on the faces of the judges as they approved each thrust with a quiet 'Bravo'.

The spectators were greatly enjoying the bout, as they shouted to the two swordswomen who were exciting the men and arousing in the women the Parisian's natural fondness for mildly bawdy entertainment, for a certain elegant vulgarity, for the pretty-pretty and the meretricious, such as café singers and operetta arias.

Each time one of the fencers lunged, a thrill of pleasure ran through the audience. Mouths were gaping and eyes were almost popping out of heads at the sight of the one who had her back to the room – an extremely well-nourished back; nor was it the movement of her wrist which attracted most attention.

They received frantic applause.

A sabre bout followed next but nobody watched it because everyone's attention was distracted by what was happening upstairs. For several minutes there had been a loud noise of furniture being moved and dragged over the floor as if it was being taken out of the flat. Then suddenly the sound of a piano was heard through the ceiling and you could distinctly hear the rhythmic thud of feet. The people upstairs had organized a dance as a compensation for not being able to see the show.

There was a great roar of laughter from the audience downstairs and then, as the ladies began to want to dance, they stopped paying attention to what was happening on the platform and started talking out loud.

This idea of a dance organized by the late-comers was good fun; they certainly weren't getting bored. It would have been nice to be up there.

But another pair of fencers were saluting each other and they took guard with such authority that every eye turned to watch their movements.

They lunged and recovered with such lithe grace, with such economy of energy, such relaxed strength, such sober gestures, such restraint, such refinement of skill that the ignorant public was surprised and fascinated.

Their calmness, their alertness, their controlled flexibility, the rapidity of their movements, so studied as to appear slow, drew the attention of the crowd and held it by the sheer power of their perfection. The audience felt that it was seeing something beautiful and rare, that two great artists in their profession were giving of their best, all the ingenuity, cunning, technical knowledge and physical skill that two great masters had at their command.

Nobody was talking now as all eyes were focused on them. Then, when they shook hands after the final touch, there was a burst of loud cheering. People were stamping and shouting. Everyone knew their names: Sergent and Ravignac.

Aroused by this contest, people were becoming cantankerous. Men were looking at their neighbours as if wanting to pick a quarrel: a smile would have been sufficient provocation. Men who had never held a foil in their lives were waving their walking sticks and making little lunges and parries.

Slowly the crowd was making its way up the little stairway. Great was the indignation when it was discovered that the dancers had raided the buffet and then left, declaring that it was a swindle to put 200 people to inconvenience and then not to give them anything to see.

There was not a cake left, not a drop of champagne, cordial or beer, not a sweet, not a fruit, absolutely nothing whatsoever. They had stripped the lot and made a complete clean sweep of everything.

The details were elicited from the servants who told them the whole sad story while trying hard not to laugh. The ladies had behaved even more wildly than the men, they claimed, and had eaten and drunk enough to make them ill. They sounded like the survivors of an invasion after a town had been looted and sacked.

So there was nothing to do but to leave. Some of the men were regretting the twenty francs they had put in the collection and were indignant that the ones upstairs had had such a splendid spread without paying a penny.

The lady patronesses had collected more than 3,000 francs. When the expenses had been paid, there remained 220 francs for the orphans of the sixth arrondissement.

Du Roy escorted the Walters and waited for his landau. While taking them home, he sat facing his boss's wife and once again he met her furtive, caressing glance which seemed perturbed. He thought: 'Damn it, I think she's biting', and he smiled as he realized that he really did have luck with women, because since he had taken up with Madame de Marelle again, she seemed to be wildly in love with him.

He went home walking on air.

Madeleine was waiting for him in the drawing-room.

'I've some news,' she said. 'The Moroccan plot is thickening. France might well send an expedition there a few months from now. In any case, it's going to be used to overthrow the government and Laroche will seize the opportunity to take over Foreign Affairs.'

To tease his wife, Du Roy pretended not to believe her. Surely they wouldn't be so mad as to do the same stupid thing as they'd done in Tunis?

She shrugged her shoulders impatiently. 'I'm telling you, I'm telling you. You don't seem to understand that there's a lot of money involved for them. Nowadays in politics, you don't need to ask: "Who's the woman?" but "What's the money in it?"'

He murmured: 'No, really', with a supercilious air to irritate her.

She was irritated:

'My God, you're as naïve as Forestier.'

She was trying to offend him and expected him to be angry.

264

But he smiled and replied:

'As that old cuckold?'

She was taken by surprise and murmured:

'Oh Georges!'

He looked at her derisively:

'Well? Didn't you admit the other evening that Forestier was a cuckold?'

And he added pityingly: 'Poor devil.'

Madeleine turned her back on him without deigning to reply; and then, after a long pause, she went on:

'We shall have guests on Tuesday. Madame Laroche-Mathieu is coming to dinner with the Vicomtesse de Perce-mur. Can you invite Rival and Norbert de Varenne? I'll go and see Madame Walter and Clotilde tomorrow. We may perhaps have Madame Rissolin as well.'

For some time now, using her husband's political influence, she had been establishing connections to bring the wives of the senators and deputies in need of support from *La Vie française* into her orbit, willy nilly.

Du Roy replied:

'Very well. I'll look after Rival and Norbert.'

He was pleased with himself and he was rubbing his hands at having discovered a good gag to annoy his wife and satisfy the hidden grudge and vague, bitter jealousy that he had felt since their drive in the Bois. He would never mention Forestier without calling him a cuckold. He could feel that this would end by making Madeleine furious. And in the course of the evening he managed to find a dozen opportunities of speaking in a bantering tone of that cuckold Forestier.

He no longer bore him a grudge: he was avenging him.

His wife pretended not to hear and sat looking at him smiling and unconcerned.

Next day as she was going to deliver her invitation to

Madame Walter, he decided to anticipate her and see his employer's wife alone to discover if she really did have a tender spot for him. The thought amused and flattered him. And after all ... why not? ... if it was possible.

He was at the Boulevard Malesherbes by two o'clock and was shown into the drawing-room. He waited.

Madame Walter came in, looking pleased, with an eager, outstretched hand.

'What kind chance brings you here?'

'No kind chance but just my desire to see you. I don't know why but something impelled me to come. I've nothing to tell you. I just came and here I am. I hope you'll forgive me for calling so early and speaking so frankly.'

He said all this in a jesting, ingratiating tone, with a smile on his lips but an underlying seriousness in his voice.

She was surprised and, blushing slightly, stammered:

'Really ... I don't quite understand ... I'm surprised ...'

He went on:

'It's a declaration *spiritoso* so as not to scare you.'

They had sat down side by side. She took the matter in fun:

'So it's a ... serious declaration?'

'Indeed it is! I've wanted to make it for a long time, a very long time even. And then I didn't dare. People say you are so strict and severe ...'

She had recovered her composure. She replied:

'Why did you choose today?'

'I don't know.' He dropped his voice: 'Or rather, it's because, ever since yesterday, I haven't been able to think of anything but you.'

Her face became suddenly pale and she faltered:

'Oh, come now, enough of all this childishness. Let's talk about other things.'

But he had fallen on his knees, so suddenly that she was

frightened. She tried to stand up but he put his two arms round her waist and forced her to remain seated. Passionately he repeated:

'Yes, it's true that I've been in love with you for such a long time. Don't say anything. There's nothing I can do about it. I'm mad ... I love you ... Oh, if you only knew how much I love you.'

She was gasping and breathing heavily, trying to speak but unable to utter a word. She had seized his hair in both hands to prevent him from bringing his mouth against hers, as she felt he wanted to, and was pushing his face backwards. She was turning her head frantically to and fro as she shut her eyes to avoid looking at him.

He was fondling her through her dress, feeling her as he ran his hands over her body and she was almost fainting under the violence of his fierce caresses. Suddenly he rose to his feet and tried to clasp her in his arms but this second of freedom enabled her to wrench herself free and she escaped, dodging from chair to chair.

He thought that it was ridiculous to pursue her and so fell into a chair, covering his face in his hands and pretending to sob convulsively.

Then he sprang up, shouted: 'Goodbye, goodbye', and ran from the room.

He calmly picked up his stick in the hall and went out into the street saying to himself:

'Well I'll be damned if that's not in the bag.' And he called at the post office to arrange to meet Clotilde next day.

When he came home at the usual time, he said to his wife:

'Well, have you got everyone for your dinner-party?'

She replied:

'Yes. There's only Madame Walter who's not quite sure whether she'll be free. She's uncertain; she talked about a

267

previous engagement or her duty or something or other. In fact, she seemed very strange. It doesn't matter, I hope she'll be able to come all the same.'

He shrugged his shoulders:

'Oh, of course she'll come.'

But he was by no means certain and he was a trifle uneasy up to the day of the dinner.

That morning, Madeleine received a short note from Madame Walter. 'After considerable trouble I've managed to be free for this evening. But my husband will not be able to come.'

Du Roy thought: 'A jolly good job I didn't try again. She's recovered. Mind out!'

All the same he waited for her to arrive with a certain disquiet. When she appeared she was looking very calm, rather cool, and a trifle haughty. He was all humility, discretion and meekness.

Madame Laroche-Mathieu and Madame Rissolin came with their husbands. The Vicomtesse de Percemur talked about high society. Madame de Marelle looked delightful dressed in a strange and whimsical black and yellow Spanish outfit that fitted her charming waist, bust and plump arms like a glove and made her little birdlike head look quite energetic.

Du Roy had put Madame Walter on his right and throughout dinner he talked only about serious matters, with exaggerated respect. Now and again he looked at Clotilde. 'She really is prettier and fresher,' he thought to himself. Then his eyes wandered towards his wife whom he also found quite attractive, despite his persistent and vicious feeling of secret anger towards her.

But Madame Walter excited him not only because of the difficulty of seducing her but also because of the charm of novelty that is always attractive to a man.

She was anxious to leave early.

'I'll take you home,' he said.

She refused. He insisted.

'Why don't you want me to? You're hurting my feelings very much. Don't make me think that you haven't forgiven me. You can see how calm I am.'

She replied:

'You can't leave your guests like that.'

He smiled:

'Goodness me, I'll only be away for twenty minutes. They won't even notice it. If you refuse, you'll offend me to the bottom of my heart.'

She said softly:

'Very well, then, I agree.'

But as soon as they were in the carriage, he took hold of her hand and covered it with passionate kisses:

'I love you, I love you. Do let me tell you that. I shan't touch you. I only want to keep on telling you I love you.'

She stammered distractedly:

'Oh ... after all that you promised me ... It's wrong ... It's wrong ...'

He seemed to make a great effort to restrain himself and went on in a calmer voice:

'There, now you see that I'm controlling myself ... And yet ... But let me just say this one thing ... I love you ... and then tell you again every day ... yes, let me come and see you every day so that I can spend just five minutes kneeling in front of you and say those three words while I look at your adorable face.'

She had let him take her hand and, breathing heavily, she replied:

'No, I can't, I don't want to. Think of what people would say, think of the servants, think of my daughters. No, no, it's not possible ...'

He went on:

'I can't go on without seeing you. I must see you if only for a minute every day, at your home or somewhere else, I must touch your hand, I must breathe the air where your dress has passed, I must look at the lovely line of your figure, at your beautiful big eyes that are driving me mad.'

She was quivering as she listened to this well-worn rhapsody of love. She stammered:

'No ... no ... it's impossible. Stop talking like that.'

He was whispering softly into her ear, realizing that this woman, simple as she was, would have to be conquered little by little, that she must be brought to the point of agreeing to meet him, first of all where she wanted and afterwards where he wanted.

'Listen, you must ... I shall see you ... I'll wait in front of your door ... like a beggar ... If you don't come down, I'll come up for you ... but I shall see you ... I shall ... tomorrow.'

She kept repeating: 'No, no, you mustn't come. I won't see you. Think of my daughters.'

'Then tell me where I can meet you ... in the street ... anywhere ... at any time you like ... as long as I can see you ... I'll just greet you and say: "I love you" ... and then I'll go away.'

She hesitated, completely at a loss. And as the carriage was approaching the door of her house, she whispered, very quickly:

'Very well, I'll go into the church of La Trinité tomorrow at half-past three.'

Then she got out and called to her coachman:

'Drive Monsieur Du Roy home.'

As he came in, his wife asked him:

'Where have you been?'

In a low voice he replied:

'I went to the post office to send an urgent cable.'

Madame de Marelle came up:

'You're taking me home, Bel-Ami, aren't you? You know I only came out all this way to dinner on that condition, don't you?'

Then turning to Madeleine:

'You're not jealous?'

Madame Du Roy answered slowly:

'No, not very.'

The guests were leaving. Madame Laroche-Mathieu looked like a little provincial domestic servant. She was the daughter of a solicitor married to Laroche at a time when he was still only a very ordinary lawyer. Madame Rissolin, who was old and pretentious, gave the impression of being a former midwife whose education had been completed in public libraries. The Vicomtesse de Percemur looked down on both of them. Her 'white paw'* recoiled from contact with such vulgar hands.

As she was going out of the outer door, Clotilde, all wrapped in lace, said to Madeleine:

'Your dinner was absolutely perfect. You're soon going to become the leading political hostess in Paris.'

As soon as she was alone with Georges she hugged him:

'Oh my darling Bel-Ami, I love you more and more every day.'

Their cab was rocking like a ship at sea.

'It's not half as nice as in our room,' she said.

'No indeed,' he replied, but his mind was on Madame Walter.

* Her pen-name was *Patte Blanche*.

CHAPTER 4

UNDER the blazing July sun, the square of La Trinité was almost deserted. The city was sweltering in sultry heat and the scorched air seemed to be pouring down from above in dense, heavy waves of fire that seared the lungs.

The fountain in front of the church was flowing lackadaisically, with a tired and flabby look, and the water in the basin, covered with leaves and odd bits of paper, seemed thick and greenish, with a few touches of blue.

A dog had jumped over the stone rim and was splashing about in this murky fluid. A few people sitting on the benches of the little round garden in front of the porch were watching the animal enviously.

Du Roy pulled out his watch. It was only three o'clock. He was half an hour early.

He laughed as he thought of his rendezvous. 'Churches are useful for her in all sorts of ways,' he thought. 'They console her for having married a Jew, they provide her with an attitude of protest in the world of politics, respectability in society and a secret place for her assignments. How nice to be able to use religion as an *en-tout-cas*. If it's fine, you've got a walking-stick; if the sun's shining, a sunshade; if it's raining, an umbrella and if you stay at home, you leave it in the hall. And there are hundreds of women like that who are quite indifferent to God but don't like to hear anyone speaking ill of Him and if the need arises use Him as a go-between. If you suggested going into a block of flats they'd think it scandalous yet they think it perfectly proper to pursue love's young dream at the foot of an altar.'

He walked slowly along in front of the fountain; then he looked at the time again on the church clock, which was two minutes faster than his watch. It showed five past three.

He thought that it would be even pleasanter inside so he went in.

Inside it was as cool as a cellar. He filled his lungs gratefully and then went round the nave to reconnoitre.

He heard someone else walking, stopping, and then starting again somewhere in the vast church, matching his own steps which echoed under the high vaulted roof. He felt curious to see who this other stroller was. He looked round to find him. It turned out to be a bald fat man, who was walking about with his nose in the air and his hat held behind his back.

Here and there he could see an old woman praying on her knees, her face buried in her hands. All around there was a feeling of solitude, of complete isolation and restfulness. The light falling through the stained glass windows was soft to the eyes.

Du Roy felt the atmosphere in the church was 'damned agreeable'.

He went back towards the door and again looked at his watch. It was still only three-fifteen. He sat down at the end of the main aisle, sorry not to be able to light a cigarette. He could still hear the fat man walking slowly about near the choir at the end of the church.

Someone came in. Georges looked quickly round. It was a working-class woman in a woollen skirt, a poor woman who fell on her knees at the nearest chair and remained still with her hands clasped, looking heavenwards, lost in prayer.

Du Roy watched her with interest, wondering what sadness or suffering or despair it was that had overcome this humble creature. She was obviously completely distressed. Perhaps there was a husband who was beating her pitilessly, or else a dying child.

He muttered under his breath: 'Poor wretches. There

273

are some people who really do suffer.' And he felt a sudden anger against the cruelty of nature. Then he thought that these poor people at least thought that someone was concerned about them in heaven and that their names appeared on God's book of accounts marked with their debits and credits. 'In heaven'? Where was that?

And Du Roy, inspired by the silence of the church to indulge in vast conjectures about the world, summed it all up in one lapidary phrase: 'How stupid it all is.'

The sound of a dress made him start. It was Madame Walter.

He stood up and hurried towards her. She did not offer him her hand and said in a low voice:

'I've only a few moments. I must go home. Kneel down beside me so that we shan't be noticed.'

She walked towards the nave, looking for a suitably concealed corner, like a woman who knew the place well. She was wearing a thick veil over her face and she was stepping so softly that she could barely be heard.

When she had reached the choir, she turned round and in the peculiar whisper which people always use in churches she said:

'The aisles are better. We're too obvious here.'

She made a little bob as she bent her head reverently towards the high altar and turned to the right towards the entrance; then finally making up her mind, she took a prayer-stool and knelt down.

Georges took the one beside her and as soon as they were both kneeling in an attitude of prayer, he said:

'Thank you, thank you. I adore you. I should like to be able to say it always, to tell you how I began to love you, how you swept me off my feet the first time I saw you ... Will you let me pour out my heart to you one day and put all my feelings into words?'

274

She was listening to him in an attitude of deep meditation, as though hearing nothing; and she answered between her fingers:

'I'm mad to let you talk to me like this, mad to have come here, mad to be doing what I'm doing, mad to allow you to think that this ... this ... this escapade can lead to anything. You must forget it and never mention it to me again.'

She waited. He was trying to find some reply, to say something passionate to convince her but not being able to translate his words into action, he felt powerless.

He went on:

'I expect nothing ... I don't hope for anything. I love you. Whatever you do, I shall say it again and again, so strongly and sincerely that you will finally have to understand. I want my tenderness to flow out towards you and seep into your heart word by word, hour by hour, day by day, until you finally become imbued in it, like a liquid falling, drop by drop, to soften and soothe you, and eventually force you to say to me: "I love you, too."'

He could feel her shoulder quivering next to his. Her breast was heaving as, very quickly, she stammered the words:

'I love you, too.'

He started, as if he had received a sharp blow on the head, and he sighed:

'Oh merciful heaven ...'

She went on in a panting voice:

'Should I be telling you this? I feel guilty and contemptible ... I ... the mother of two daughters ... but I can't ... I can't. I should never have believed ... I should never have thought ... I can't help it ... I can't help it ... Listen ... listen to me ... I've never loved anyone ... but you ... I swear it ... And I've loved you for a whole year ... in secret ... in the secret of my heart ... Oh, I've suffered, you know ... and struggled ... and I can't go on, I love you ...'

She was crying into her hands and her whole body was trembling with the violence of her emotion.

Georges said softly:

'Give me your hand so that I can touch it and press it ...'

She slowly took her hand away from her face. He saw that her cheeks were all wet and that a tear-drop was ready to fall from the end of her lashes.

He took her hand and squeezed it:

'Oh, how I should like to drink your tears.'

In a low broken voice, almost moaning, she exclaimed:

'Don't take advantage of me ... I don't know what I'm doing!'

He could scarcely avoid smiling. How could he have taken advantage of her in such a place? He placed the hand he was holding on his heart, asking: 'Can you feel how fast it's beating?' He had run out of passionate expressions.

But in the last few moments, the regular step of the solitary walker could be heard approaching. He had been round the back of the altars and now, for the second time at least, he was coming down the right-hand side-aisle. When Madame Walter heard him close to the pillar which was hiding her, she dragged her hand away from Georges and once again covered her face.

And they remained motionless as if they were both addressing fervent prayers to God. The fat man passed close by with an unconcerned glance towards them and moved off towards the far end of the church, still holding his hat behind his back.

But Du Roy was anxious to arrange a meeting-place somewhere else than in La Trinité. He whispered:

'Where can I see you tomorrow?'

She made no reply. She seemed lifeless, as if turned into a living statue of prayer.

He went on:

'Tomorrow, would you like me to meet you in the Parc Monceau?'

She turned towards him, revealing a face livid and convulsed in an agony of suffering and in a broken voice she panted:

'Leave me ... leave me ... now ... go away ... go away ... just for five minutes; it hurts too much when you're beside me .. I want to pray ... and I can't ... go away ... let me pray ... by myself ... five minutes ... I can't ... let me implore God to forgive me ... to save me ... leave me ... for five minutes ...'

Her face was so distraught and full of suffering that he stood up without a word and then, after a moment's hesitation, asked:

'Shall I come back in a minute?'

She nodded as if to say yes, in a few minutes. He walked up towards the choir.

She tried to pray, to make a superhuman effort to invoke God, to appeal to Him and, trembling and distracted, she called out to heaven: 'Pity!'

She frantically closed her eyes in order not to see the man who had just left her. She drove him from her thoughts, she struggled against him, but instead of the celestial vision for which she was hoping in her deep distress, she could still see the young man's curly moustache.

For a whole year she had been struggling every day and every night against this growing obsession, against this image haunting her dreams and her body for many a long, sleepless night. She felt caught like a rat in a trap, bound hand and foot and thrown to the tender mercies of this male who had subdued and conquered her by nothing more substantial than the hair on his lip and the colour of his eyes.

And now, in this church, close to God, she felt even weaker, more deserted and more lost than in her home. She could not pray, she could only think of him. She was even suffering already because he had gone away. Yet she was struggling like a desperate creature, trying to defend herself, crying for help from the depths of her soul. She would rather have died than be unfaithful in this way, she who had never faltered in her duty. Her lips were wildly beseeching God; but her ears were listening to Georges' footsteps dying away beneath the distant vaulting of the church.

She realized that it was all over, that it was pointless to struggle. Yet she did not want to give in; and she was gripped by the sort of hysterical feeling that makes women drop, screaming, trembling and writhing on to the floor. She was shaking in every limb and feared that she was going to fall over and be found squirming and shrieking amongst the chairs.

Someone was walking quickly towards her. She turned her head. It was a priest. She stood up and rushed towards him holding out her clasped hands and stammering: 'Oh, save me, save me!'

He stopped short in surprise:

'What do you want?'

'I want you to save me. Take pity on me. If you don't come to my aid, I'm a lost woman.'

He was watching her, wondering if she was perhaps mad. He repeated:

'What can I do for you?'

He was a young man, tall, somewhat plump, with a flabby dark jowl, although close-shaven, the typical handsome curate of a rich city parish, accustomed to confessing the sins of wealthy women.

'Let me confess to you,' she said, 'and then advise me, give me help, tell me what I must do!'

He replied:

'I hear confession every Saturday from three till six.'

She had caught hold of his arm and was gripping him tightly:

'No, no, no. Now. At once. You must. He's here, in this church, waiting for me.'

The priest asked: 'Who's waiting for you?'

'A man who is going to ruin me ... who is going to get me into his power, unless you can save me. I can't run away from him any more. I'm too weak ... too weak ... so weak ... so weak!'

She fell at his knees sobbing:

'Oh, have pity on me, Father. Save me, for God's sake, save me!'

She was clutching his black robe so that he could not free himself and he was looking uneasily around in case some devout or spiteful eye might see this woman kneeling at his feet.

Realizing at last that he would not be able to escape, he said:

'Do stand up, I happen to have the key of the confessional on me.' And fumbling in his pocket, he pulled out a key-ring and went quickly towards one of the little wooden huts, a sort of dustbin for the soul into which believers tip their sins.

He went in through the centre door and closed it behind him. Madame Walter flung herself into the little compartment at the side, and with a passionate burst of hope, said in a fervent, faltering voice:

'Bless me, Father, for I have sinned.'

*

Walking round the back of the choir, Du Roy went down the left-hand aisle. Halfway down he met the big bald man still pursuing his steady progress and he asked himself:

'What on earth can that fellow be doing in here?'

The man himself had slowed down and was looking at Georges, obviously wanting to speak to him. When he was close enough, he greeted him very politely:

'Excuse me for disturbing you, sir, but could you tell me the date when this church was built?'

Du Roy replied:

'I'm afraid I don't really know much about it. I think about twenty or twenty-five years ago. In any case, it's the first time I've ever been in here.'

'Me too. I'd never seen it.'

Then as his interest began to increase, Georges said:

'You seem to be visiting it very thoroughly. You're studying it in detail?'

The other replied resignedly:

'I'm not visiting it, I'm just waiting for my wife who arranged to meet me here and who's extremely late.'

He waited for a few seconds and then said:

'It's jolly hot outside.'

Du Roy was looking at him, thinking that he was rather a nice chap and suddenly the thought came to him that he looked like Forestier.

'Do you live in the country?' he enquired.

'Yes. I come from Rennes. And you, sir, have you come here to visit the church?'

'No. I'm waiting for a woman.'

And the journalist went on his way, smiling.

As he neared the main doorway, he saw the poor old woman still on her knees, praying. He thought: 'Good God, she doesn't give up easily.' He no longer felt any emotion or pity for her.

He went on and began slowly to walk up the right-hand aisle to find Madame Walter. As he came up, he looked towards the spot where he had left her and was surprised to see that she was no longer there. He imagined that he was looking at the wrong pillar and went to the end before coming back. So she had left! He was surprised and angry. Then the thought came to him that she might be looking for him and he went round the church again. Having failed to see her he came back and sat down on the chair which she had occupied, hoping that she would come and find him. He waited.

After a while, his attention was aroused by a vague murmur of voices. He had seen nobody in this part of the church. Where was the whispering coming from? He stood up to see and caught sight of the doors of the confessionals in the near-by side-chapel. From one of them there protruded the bottom of a woman's dress. He went closer to see who it was and recognized her. She was confessing! ...

He felt a violent urge to take her by the shoulders and drag her out of the box. Then he thought: 'Ah well! It's the priest's turn today, it'll be mine tomorrow.' And he calmly sat down opposite the shutters of the confessional, biding his time, with a sly grin at the turn the adventure was taking.

He waited a long time. Finally Madame Walter stood up, turned round, saw him and came towards him. She looked cold and severe.

'Monsieur Du Roy,' she said, 'I must ask you not to come with me, not to follow me and never to come to my house again alone. You will not be allowed in. Goodbye!'

And she stalked off with a dignified air.

He let her go since he held the principle of never trying to force events. Then, as the priest, somewhat confused, came out of his little room in his turn, he marched straight up to him and sticking his head right into his face, he looked him hard in the eyes and grunted:

'If you weren't wearing a skirt, what a punch on your ugly mug you'd be getting.'

Then he swung on his heels and left the church whistling under his breath.

The fat man, tired of waiting, was standing in the porch, his hat on his head and his hands behind his back, looking round the vast square and the streets running into it.

As Du Roy went by, they greeted each other. Since the journalist had nothing else to do, he went down to *La Vie française*. As soon as he went in, he realized from the bustle amongst the messengers that something unusual was happening and he went straight into the director's room.

Old Walter was standing there in great excitement jerkily dictating an article, breaking off between paragraphs to allot particular assignments to the reporters surrounding him, making suggestions to Boisrenard and opening letters.

As soon as he saw Du Roy, he gave a shout of joy:

'Ah, what luck, here's Bel-Ami!'

He stopped short, a trifle embarrassed, and then apologized:

'I'm sorry for calling you that, I'm all upset by what's happening. And I hear my wife and daughters all calling you Bel-Ami, morning, noon and night and so I've ended by catching the habit myself. I hope you don't mind?'

Georges laughed.

'Not at all. I don't mind that nickname in the least.'

Old Walter went on:

'Splendid, then I'll christen you Bel-Ami like everyone else. Well, here it is, big things are happening. The government has fallen on a motion which they lost by 102 votes to 310. The Parliamentary recess has been postponed to an unspecified date and it's July 28th already. Spain is getting annoyed over Morocco, which is what has overthrown Durand de l'Aine and his acolytes. We're in the soup up to our necks. Marrot has been asked to form a new government. He's taken on General Boutin as War Minister and our friend Laroche-Mathieu as Foreign Secretary. He's keeping the Home Office for himself as well as the Premiership. We shall become a semi-official newspaper. I'm writing the leading article at the moment, just a statement of principles and saying what work the government has to undertake.'

The old boy gave a smile as he went on:

'The work that they are proposing to undertake, of course. But I need something interesting on the Moroccan question, something topical, something striking, a sensational feature article, something like that, eh? Can you work something out?'

Du Roy thought for a second and then said:

'I know what you want. I can let you have a study on the political situation in all our African colonies, with Tunisia on the left, Algeria in the middle and Morocco on the right, the story of the peoples who inhabit this vast area and an account of a trip along the Moroccan frontier as far as the big Figuig oasis, where no European has ever set foot and which is the cause of the present conflict. Will that do?'

Old Walter exclaimed:

'Wonderful! And what's the title?'

' "From Tunis to Tangier".'

'Splendid.'

And Du Roy went off to rummage amongst the back numbers of *La Vie française* to find his first article: 'Memories of an African Cavalryman' which, with a new title, some touching-up and a few changes, would exactly fit the bill, because it dealt with colonial policy, the population of Algeria and a trip into the province of Oran.

In three quarters of an hour, the whole thing had been gone over, patched up and adapted, with a spice of topicality and praise for the new Cabinet.

The director read the article and declared:

'It's perfect ... absolutely perfect. You're an invaluable man. Congratulations!'

And Du Roy went home to dinner delighted with his day, despite his setback at La Trinité, because he sensed that he was going to win.

His wife was waiting for him, frantically excited. As soon as she saw him, she exclaimed:

'You know that Laroche is Foreign Secretary?'

'Yes, in fact I've just written an article on Algeria for that purpose.'

'What was that?'

'You know, the first one we wrote together: "Memories of an African Cavalryman", revised and edited for the occasion.'

She smiled:

'Oh yes, that will do perfectly.'

Then after a few moments' thought:

'That reminds me of the continuation that you were supposed to be doing and which you ... didn't get round to. We could do something about it now. That will give us a nice topical series.'

He sat down to his soup and said:

'Splendid. There's no obstacle now that cuckold Forestier is dead.'

In a hurt voice she said curtly:

'That joke is worse than uncalled for and I must ask you to stop using it. You've been doing it for far too long.'

Just as he was about to make a sarcastic rejoinder, he was handed an express letter, unsigned, containing just one sentence: 'I lost my head. Forgive me and meet me tomorrow at four o'clock in the Parc Monceau.'

He understood at once and filled with a sudden joy, he slipped the piece of blue paper into his pocket and said to his wife:

'I won't do it any more, darling. It's stupid, I agree.'

284

And he started to eat.

During dinner he kept repeating the words to himself: 'I lost my head. Forgive me and meet me tomorrow at four o'clock in the Parc Monceau.' So she was surrendering. Those words meant: 'I give in, I'm all yours, wherever and whenever you like.'

He began to laugh. Madeleine enquired:

'What's the matter?'

'Nothing much really. I was thinking of a priest I met earlier today who had rather a funny face.'

Next day, Du Roy arrived exactly at the appointed time. Every bench in the park was occupied by Parisians prostrated by the heat and unconcerned nannies who seemed to be lost in dreams while the children tumbled about on the sandy paths.

He found Madame Walter in the little classical ruin which has a spring flowing through it. She was walking unhappily and uneasily round the narrow circle of little pillars.

As soon as he had greeted her, she said:

'What a lot of people there are in this garden.'

He jumped at the opportunity.

'Yes, aren't there. Do you want to go somewhere else?'

'Where can we go?'

'Anywhere, in a cab for example. If you let down the blind on your side you'll be well hidden.'

'Yes, I'd prefer that, I'm terrified here.'

'All right, meet me in five minutes at the gate on the outer boulevard. I'll bring a cab.'

And he hurried off. As soon as they had rejoined each other and she had carefully let down the blind on her side, she enquired:

'Where did you tell the driver to go?'

Georges replied:

'Don't worry yourself about that, he knows what to do.'

He had given the address of his flat in the Rue de Constantinople.

She went on:

'You can't imagine how much you're hurting me, how tormented and tortured I feel. I was harsh yesterday in the church but I was trying to get away from you at all costs. I'm so frightened at being alone with you. Have you forgiven me?'

He was clasping her hands:

'Yes, of course. What wouldn't I forgive you for, seeing how much I love you?'

She looked at him beseechingly:

'Listen, you must promise to respect me ... not to ... not to ... otherwise I couldn't go on seeing you.'

At first, he made no reply; beneath his moustache, she saw on his lips the subtle smile that women found so disturbing. In the end he said softly:

'I'm yours to command.'

Then she began to tell him how she had come to realize that she loved him when she heard that he was going to marry Madeleine Forestier. She mentioned the details, the little personal details of dates and other matters.

Suddenly she stopped talking. The cab had come to a halt. Du Roy opened the door.

'Where are we?' she asked.

He answered:

'Let's get out and go in here. We'll be less disturbed.'

'But where are we?'

'At my flat. It's one I had before I was married that I've rented again for a few days ... so that we might have a little place where we could meet.'

She had seized hold of the cushions of the cab, terrified at the thought of being alone with him, and she stammered:

'No, no ... I don't want to! I don't want to.'

He said in a firm voice:

'I swear to respect you. Come along. You can see that we're being looked at, that people will start gathering round. Hurry up, hurry up ... do come out.'

And he repeated:

'I swear to respect you.'

The owner of a bar was standing in his doorway watching them curiously. Panic-stricken, she dashed into the house.

She was about to go upstairs. He held her back by her arm.

'It's here, on the ground floor.'

And he pushed her into his flat.

As soon as he had closed the door, he pounced on her like a wolf. She twisted and struggled, stammering:

'Oh Heavens! Oh Heavens!'

He was eagerly kissing her neck, her eyes, her lips and she was unable to escape from his furious caresses; and while she was repulsing him and avoiding his lips, in spite of herself she returned his kisses.

Then all at once she gave up the struggle and, defeated and unresisting, she let him undress her. Skilfully and swiftly, like a ladies' maid, he removed all her garments, one by one.

She had seized her bodice from his hands in order to hide her face in it and she stood, all white, amidst the pile of clothes around her feet.

He left her boots on and lifted her in his arms onto the bed. Then, in a broken voice, she whispered: 'I swear ... I swear ... that I have never had a lover', just as a girl might have said: 'I swear I'm a virgin.'

And he was thinking to himself: 'Now that's something that doesn't worry me in the slightest.'

287

SUMMER had turned into autumn. The Du Roys had spent the whole summer in Paris, energetically supporting the new government in the columns of *La Vie française* during the short parliamentary recess.

Although it was only early October, the two Houses were going into session because the Moroccan question was becoming threatening.

Nobody really believed that there would be an expedition against Tangier, although on the last day of the previous session a right-wing deputy, Comte Lambert Sarrazin, had made a witty speech, acclaimed even by the centre, in which, like a former famous Viceroy of India, he had wagered his moustache against the Premier's whiskers that the new Cabinet would be unable to prevent itself from imitating the outgoing one and send an army to Tangier, to match the one sent to Tunis, through sheer love of symmetry, like putting two vases on a mantelshelf. He added: 'Africa is indeed a fireplace for France, gentlemen, a fireplace in which we burn our best wood, a fireplace with a tremendous draught which we kindle with banknotes.

'You have offered yourselves the artistic treat of decorating the left corner with a Tunisian souvenir, an expensive one, and you will find Monsieur Marrot wanting to imitate his predecessor and adorn the right-hand corner with one from Morocco.'

This speech, which created a great stir, had provided Du Roy with a theme for ten articles on the colony of Algeria, in fact for the whole series that had been stopped at the time he was just starting on the paper. He had vigorously supported the idea of a military expedition, despite being convinced that it would not occur. He had struck a patriotic note and bombarded Spain with the whole battery of scornful arguments which we employ against those nations whose interests are opposed to our own.

La Vie française had acquired great importance from its close relationship with the government. It provided political news even before the long-established papers and outlined the general intentions of its friends, the Ministers; and all the Parisian and provincial newspapers used it as their source of information. It was quoted and feared and beginning to be respected. It was no longer suspect as the organ of a group of political speculators but acknowledged as the mouthpiece of the Cabinet. Laroche-Mathieu was its leading light and his spokesman was Du Roy. Old Walter, a deputy who never opened his mouth in the Chamber, and a wily editor who was past master in the art of staying in the background, was rumoured to be secretly negotiating a big deal in Moroccan copper mines.

Madeleine's salon had become an influential centre where a number of members of the Cabinet used to meet every week. The Prime Minister himself had twice dined in her home; and the wives of politicians who had formerly been reluctant to cross her threshold now prided themselves on being her friends and visited her more often than she visited them.

The Foreign Secretary almost ranked as head of the house. He would come in at all hours of the day, bringing reports, news and information which he used to dictate either to the husband or to his wife as if they were his secretaries.

When the Minister had gone and Du Roy was left alone with his wife, his pent-up indignation at the behaviour of this mediocre upstart would overflow and he used to make insidious suggestions in a threatening tone of voice.

But she would scornfully shrug her shoulders and say: 'Do like he does. Become a Minister and then you can do what you like. Until then I should keep quiet.'

He would curl his moustache with a sidelong glance at his wife and say:

'People don't know my capabilities; perhaps one day they'll learn.'

She replied sagely:

'Time will show.'

On the morning when Parliament reopened, Madeleine, still in bed, offered her husband all sorts of advice as he was dressing to go to lunch at Laroche-Mathieu's house to receive his instructions, before the sitting opened, with regard to the political article that would appear the following day in *La Vie française*, an article that was to be a sort of semi-official statement of the government's real intentions.

She was saying:

'Above all, don't forget to ask him if General Belloncle is being sent to Oran, as rumour has it. That would be extremely significant.'

Georges said irritably:

'I know as well as you do what I've got to do. Do leave me alone, you're always harping on the same string.'

She retorted calmly:

'My dear Georges, you always forget half the things I want you to ask the Minister.'

He grunted:

'I'm getting rather bored with your Minister. He's a nitwit.'

She said quietly:

'He's no more my Minister than he is yours. He's more useful to you than to me.'

He half turned towards her with a sneer:

'I beg your pardon, he's not trying to make up to me.'

She replied slowly:

'Nor to me either, by the way. But we owe all our success to him.'

He was silent for a second or two and then said:

'If I had to choose amongst your admirers, I'd really prefer that old buffer Vaudrec. What's become of him, incidentally? I haven't seen him for a week.'

She replied placidly:

'He's not very well, he wrote and told me he's even confined to bed with an attack of gout. You ought to call round to ask how he is. You know he's very fond of you and he would appreciate it.'

Georges said:

'Of course, I'll go round later on today.'

He had now finished dressing and, with his hat on his head, was looking round to see if he had forgotten anything. Having drawn a blank, he went over to the bed and kissed his wife on her forehead:

'See you later, darling. I shan't be back before seven at the earliest.'

And off he went. Monsieur Laroche-Mathieu was waiting for him because he was lunching at ten o'clock that day, as there was a cabinet meeting at noon, before the reopening of Parliament.

As soon as they were seated at table, alone with the Minister's private secretary, since Madame Laroche-Mathieu had not wished to change her lunch hour, Du Roy talked about his article, explaining its general trend as he consulted the notes which he had scribbled on visiting cards; then, when he had finished:

'Do you think there is anything you'd like to change, Minister?'

'Very little, my dear Du Roy. You've been perhaps a trifle too positive, with regard to Morocco. Talk about the expedition as if it is going to take place while giving the impression that it's not and that you don't believe in it for a single minute. Make sure that the public can read between the lines that we are not going to embark on this sort of venture.'

'Excellent, I understand and I'll make my meaning quite plain. My wife asked me to enquire from you whether General Belloncle is going to be sent to Oran. After what you've said, I assume not.'

The Foreign Secretary said:

'No, he's not.'

Then they started chatting about the session that was about to begin. Laroche-Mathieu began to speechify, trying out the effect that he was going to use on his colleagues in a few hours' time. He was waving his right hand about, sometimes lifting his fork, sometimes his knife, sometimes a mouthful of bread, and, staring into space, he addressed an invisible Parliament, a good-looking well-groomed young man rolling his juicy eloquence round his mouth. He had a very tiny twirly moustache whose points stuck up like two scorpions' tails and his hair plastered with brilliantine and parted in the middle of the forehead, coiled over his ears like some provincial fop's. He was rather plump and a trifle bloated despite his youth; his paunch bulged under his waistcoat. The private secretary was calmly eating and drinking, no doubt accustomed to such waves of verbosity, but Du Roy, consumed with jealousy at his success, was thinking to himself: 'Go on, you silly buffer! What morons these politicians are!'

And he compared his own value with the wordy self-importance of the Minister and said to himself: 'My goodness, if I only had a clear 100,000 francs so that I could put up for Parliament in good old Rouen and outsmart my wonderful clumsy, wily Normans, what a splendid politician I'd be compared with these miserable shortsighted rogues.'

Monsieur Laroche-Mathieu talked until the coffee came and then, seeing that it was getting late, he rang to order his carriage and held out his hand to Du Roy:

'So everything's in order, my dear Du Roy?'

'Absolutely, Minister, rely on me.'

And Georges went quietly off to the paper to begin his article, since he had nothing to do until four o'clock. At four he was going to meet Madame de Marelle at the Rue de Constantinople: he saw her regularly twice a week, on Mondays and Fridays.

But when he reached the office he was handed a sealed express letter from Madame Walter, which read:

It's absolutely essential that I see you today. It's very, very important. Meet me at the Rue de Constantinople at two o'clock. It can be to your great advantage. Eternally yours, Virginie.

He swore: 'Christ Almighty, what a limpet the woman is.' And he was put into such a bad temper that he went out immediately, too irritated to work.

For the last six weeks he had been trying to break with her without succeeding in quenching her desperate love for him.

After her seduction she had suffered a dreadful attack of remorse and for the next three meetings had bitterly reproached and abused her lover. Bored by these scenes and having already had more than enough of this middle-aged woman with her taste for drama, he had merely avoided her, hoping that this might bring the affair to an end. But she had then clung frantically on to him, hurling herself into her love for him as you might throw yourself into a river with a stone round your neck. Being weak or considerate or easygoing, he had let himself be won over again, and she had grasped him in a frantic stranglehold of passion and continued to plague him with her tiresome affection.

She kept wanting to see him every day, sent him telegrams all the time to arrange brief meetings at street corners, in a shop or a public garden.

Then she would tell him again and again, always in the same phrases, how much she adored and idolized him and then would go away asserting 'how wonderful it had been to see him'.

She had turned out to be completely different from what he had imagined; she tried to attract him by girlish charm, and had adopted a childish way of loving quite ridiculous for her age. Since she had hitherto been a completely honest woman, a virgin at heart, and as impervious to feeling as she was ignorant of sensuality, this prim woman, whose staid forties were like a wan autumn after a cold summer, had all at once been thrust into a sort of faded spring, full of tiny, sickly flowers and frost-bitten buds, a strange blossoming of adolescent love, a late-flowering love both passionate and naïve, full of unexpected raptures, girlish squeals, embarrassing billing and cooing and outdated airs and graces that had never even been young. She wrote him ten letters in one day, wild and silly letters, in a ridiculous weird poetic language, with Oriental embellishments, full of names of birds and animals.

As soon as they were alone, she would kiss him with all the clumsy affection of a podgy little girl pouting her lips with almost comical effect and prancing about so that her large heavy breasts bobbed up and down under her dress. What disgusted him most was to hear her say 'My sweetie pie', 'My little Georgy-Porgy', 'My pet', 'My lovey-dovey', 'My precious' or 'My cherub' and see her feign childish modesty each time she felt like making love, with frightened

294

little gestures which she thought were charming, simpering like a depraved little schoolgirl.

She would ask: 'Whose lips are these?'

And if he failed to reply at once: 'They're mine', she would keep on until he became livid with annoyance.

It seemed to him that she should have realized that love needs extreme tact, skill, caution and care and that as a mother and woman of the world, once she had given herself to him she should do so with seriousness, a sort of restraint in her effusions, a certain sobriety, possibly with tears in her eyes but with Dido's tears rather than Juliet's.

She kept saying to him all the time:

'Oh how I love you, my little darling! Do you love me as much, my billikins?'

Now he could never hear her say 'my little darling' or 'my billikins' without wanting to call her 'my old girl'.

She would say to him: 'It was mad of me to give in to you, but I don't regret it. Love is so wonderful.'

On her lips all this seemed highly irritating to Georges. She would murmur: 'Love is so wonderful' just like an ingénue in a play.

Furthermore she exasperated him by the clumsiness of her love-making. Now that the kisses of this handsome young man had aroused her sensuality and set her blood on fire, she showed such clumsy passion, and such laboured care when they made love that Du Roy was reminded of an old man trying to learn how to read and he felt like laughing.

And when she should have held him in her arms in a vice-like grip and looked passionately into his eyes with the searching, terrible gaze that you find in certain magnificent, ageing women in the throes of the last love affair of their lives, when she should have bitten him with silent, quivering passion and crushed him beneath her warm massive flesh, tired but insatiable, she would wriggle about like a little girl, simpering in her effort to be charming:

'Me love 'ou, darling. Lovey dovey. Give little girlie a nice big hug.'

At such times he felt a wild urge to swear, pick up his hat and go off slamming the door behind him.

At the beginning they had met frequently at the Rue de Constantinople but Du Roy was terrified that Madame de Marelle might put in an unexpected appearance and he was now using every possible pretext to avoid meeting there.

As a result he had been obliged to go almost every day to her house, sometimes for lunch, sometimes for dinner. She would squeeze his hand under the table and hold up her lips for a kiss behind doors. However, his main diversion was playing with Suzanne, whose funny ways amused him. Her doll-like appearance concealed an alert, lively and mischievous mind, which was always ready to perform, like a Punch and Judy show. She poked fun at everything and everybody, caustically and always to the point. Georges stimulated her and brought out the devil in her; they got on splendidly together.

She kept calling out to him all the time:

'Listen, Bel-Ami. Come here, Bel-Ami.'

He would immediately leave her mama and hurry over to the young girl who whispered some mischievous remark into his ear and then they would both have a good laugh together.

However, Madame Walter's love became so nauseating to him that he reached the stage of being unable to bear it any longer; seeing or hearing her or even thinking of her made him too angry. So he stopped calling on her, answering her letters or listening to her pleas.

She finally realized that he no longer loved her and suffered agonies of grief. But she refused to accept the situation. She spied on him, followed him, waited for him in a cab behind drawn blinds, at the entrance to the newspaper office, outside the door of his house, even in streets through which she hoped he would be passing.

He felt an urge to abuse her, to insult her, to hit her, to tell her bluntly: 'For God's sake, I'm fed up, you're boring me.' But he never went to these extreme lengths because of *La Vie française*; and he tried to make her understand that the affair must come to an end by his chilly manner, his lack of kindness, albeit still tempered with some consideration, and occasionally even by the rough edge of his tongue.

Above all, she would insist on finding ways and means to lure him to the Rue de Constantinople and he lived in constant dread that the two women might meet face to face on the doorstep.

On the other hand his affection for Madame de Marelle had grown stronger during the summer. He called her his 'little urchin' and was very fond of her indeed. Their two natures had similar twists; they were both born adventurers and vagabonds, the sort of society vagabonds who, although they do not realize it, are very similar to real gypsy nomads.

They had spent an enchanting summer together, like two students out on a spree, slipping away to have lunch or dinner at Argenteuil, Bougival, Maisons or Poissy, spending hours in boats gathering flowers from the banks. She adored fried fish fresh from the river, rabbit fricassée and fish stew, the shaded terraces of riverside taverns and the calls of the oarsmen. He loved setting out with her on a bright, fine day on the top deck of a suburban train to go joking and laughing at nothing in particular through the ugly Paris countryside with its hideous middle-class villas sprouting on all sides.

And when he was obliged to come back to dine with Madame Walter he hated his persistent old mistress when he thought of the young one whom he had just left, who had taken the edge off his desire and culled his passion in the grass by the water's edge.

He thought that he had at last more or less succeeded in ridding himself of Virginie after telling her bluntly, indeed almost harshly, that he intended to break with her; and now he had received the telegram at the office telling him to meet her at two o'clock at the Rue de Constantinople.

He read it again as he was walking along: 'It's absolutely essential that I see you today. It's very, very important. Meet me at the Rue de Constantinople at two o'clock. It can be to your great advantage. Eternally yours, Virginie.'

He thought to himself: 'What does the old trout want now? I bet she's got nothing to say to me. She'll just tell me she adores me again. But I'd better see. She talks of something very important, and something that can be to my advantage, and it may be true. And Clotilde's coming at four o'clock. I'll have to get rid of the first one by three o'clock at the latest. My God, as long as they don't meet. These damned women!'

And he reflected that in fact the only woman who never bothered him was his wife. She lived her own life and she seemed to love him very much, at the times set aside for love, because she would not allow anything to interfere with the unchanging order of her normal occupations.

He walked slowly towards his rendezvous, working himself up into a rage against his employer's wife:

'My God, I'll give it to her if she hasn't anything to say. The air will be blue. The first thing I'll tell her is that I shall never set foot in her house again.'

With these sentiments, he went into his flat to wait for Madame Walter.

She arrived almost at once and as soon as she saw him, she exclaimed:

'Ah, you got my telegram. What luck!'

He had an ugly look on his face:

'Yes, indeed, I got it at the office just as I was off to the Chamber of Deputies. What do you want now?'

She had lifted her veil so that she might kiss him and she went up to him with the timid, cringing look of a dog used to being beaten:

'How cruel you are to me ... You're so hard on me ... What have I done to you? You can't imagine how miserable you make me!'

He grunted: 'You're not going to start again, I hope?'

She was standing very close to him waiting for a smile or a movement on his part to throw herself into his arms.

She said in a low voice:

'You ought not to have seduced me and treat me like this, you ought to have left me as I was, a happy and faithful wife. Do you remember what you said to me in the church and how you forced me to come to this flat? And look how you speak to me now! Look what sort of a welcome you give me. Oh God, oh God, how you make me suffer!'

He stamped his foot and said violently:

'Oh, for God's sake. That's enough of that. As soon as I see you it's the same old story. You'd really think that you were twelve years old when I had you and didn't know anything about the facts of life. No, my dear, let's get things straight, you weren't under the age of consent. You gave yourself to me as a consenting adult. Thank you very much, I'm very, very grateful to you, but I'm not obliged to be tied to your apron strings for the rest of my life. You've got a husband and I've got a wife. We're neither of us free. We fancied each other and that's that. Now it's over.'

She said:

'Oh, you're so unspeakably harsh and rough! No, I wasn't a young girl but I had never, never been unfaithful ...'

He cut her short:

'I know that, you've already told me so a dozen times. But you'd had two children, so I didn't deprive you of your virginity.'

She recoiled:

'Oh, Georges, that's not fair . . .'

And she put her two hands on her chest and began to gasp, as she choked back her sobs.

When he saw tears in her eyes, he picked up his hat from the mantelpiece:

'Oh, so you're going to cry. In that case, goodbye. Is that the performance you invited me to attend?'

She stepped in front of him to prevent him from leaving and hastily pulling a handkerchief out of her pocket, she hurriedly wiped her eyes. Making an effort to speak firmly, she said in an anguished and quavering voice:

'No, I came to . . . to tell you some news . . . some political news to help you . . . to earn 50,000 francs . . . or even more . . . if you like.'

Suddenly mollified, he asked:

'How's that? What do you mean?'

'Yesterday evening I overheard by chance a few remarks exchanged by my husband and Laroche. As a matter of fact, they weren't particularly trying to hide it from me. But my husband was advising the Minister not to let you in on the secret because you would divulge everything.'

Du Roy had put his hat down again on a chair. He was all ears:

'So what's going to happen?'

'They're going to take Morocco!'

'Come now. I've just lunched with Laroche who more or less dictated the government's intentions to me.'

'No, my darling, they've been pulling wool over your eyes because they're afraid their scheme might become known.'

'Sit down,' said Georges.

And he sat down himself in an armchair. She drew up a little footstool and squatted down on it between his legs. She went on in a wheedling voice:

'As I'm always thinking of you, I listen carefully to all the whispering that goes on around me.'

And she quietly began to explain how she had guessed some time ago that they were plotting something without his knowledge and that although they were using him, they were anxious to avoid his cooperation.

She said:

'You know, love makes you cunning.'

And then at last, yesterday, she had realized what was happening. It was a very big and secret operation they were planning. She was smiling now, pleased at being so clever; she became excited, like the financier's wife she was, accustomed to Stock Exchange wheeling and dealing, the movements of shares, bulls and bears, when in the space of two hours speculators can ruin thousands of small savers and small investors who have put their savings in stocks guaranteed by men whose names are honoured and respected, politicians or bankers.

She was saying:

'Oh, they've done something very clever. Very clever. It was in fact my husband who was conducting the whole deal and he knows what he's doing. It really is a wonderful operation.'

He was becoming impatient at all these preliminaries.

'Come on, out with it.'

'Well, it's like this. An expedition against Tangier had been agreed upon between the two of them the day Laroche became Foreign Secretary and gradually they've been buying up the whole of the Moroccan loan which had dropped to sixty-four or sixty-five francs. They did their buying very

301

cleverly, using suspect brokers, shady dealers who wouldn't arouse any suspicion. They even succeeded in fooling the Rothschilds who were surprised at seeing such a steady demand for Moroccan stock. Their reply was to mention the names of all the dealers involved, all unreliable and on their beam ends. That calmed the big banks' suspicions. And so now we're going to send an expedition and as soon as we've succeeded, the French government will guarantee the Moroccan debt. Our friends will have made about fifty or sixty million francs. You see how it works? You can see too why they're afraid of everybody, afraid of the slightest indiscretion.'

She had laid her head against the young man's waistcoat and resting her arms on his legs, she was pressing and cuddling up against him, sensing that she was interesting him now and ready to do anything or risk anything in the hope of a caress or a smile.

He asked:

'Are you absolutely sure?'

She replied confidently:

'Oh, absolutely.'

He said:

'It really is very clever. As for that louse Laroche, I'll get even with him for this. The blackguard! He'd better look out ... he'd better look out ... I'll have his ministerial blood for this!'

Then he began to think. He said more quietly:

'But we ought to take advantage of it.'

'You can still buy some of the loan,' she said. 'It's only at seventy-two.'

He went on:

'Yes, but I haven't any spare cash at the moment.'

She looked up at him with pleading eyes:

'I thought of that, my cherub, and if you were really very

kind and nice and loved me just a little, you'd let me lend you some.'

He replied abruptly, almost sharply:

'No, that's out of the question.'

She murmured imploringly:

'Listen, there's something you can do without borrowing money. I was wanting to buy 10,000 francs' worth of the loan as a little extra for myself. Well, I'll buy 20,000 francs' worth. You can take a half share. As you realize, I shan't be paying my husband anything. So that there'll be nothing to pay out for the moment. If it comes off, you'll make 70,000 francs. If it doesn't come off, you'll be owing me 10,000 francs that you can reimburse as and when you like.'

He repeated:

'No, I'm not very keen on that sort of scheme.'

So she argued with him to convince him, proving that in fact he was pledging himself for 10,000 francs, that as a result he was incurring a risk and that she was not advancing him any money because all the payments were being made by the Walter Bank.

She also pointed out that it was he who had been running the whole campaign in *La Vie française* which had made the deal possible and that he would be very naïve not to take advantage of it.

He was still hesitant. She added:

'But just think that it's really Walter who's advancing you these 10,000 francs and that you have done things for him that are worth more than that.'

'All right, then, I accept,' he said. 'I'll go half shares with you. But if we lose, I'll repay you 10,000 francs.'

She was so pleased that she stood up and taking his head in her hands, she started to kiss him greedily.

At first he did not resist but as she became bolder and

started to hug him and devour him with kisses the thought came to him that as Clotilde was due shortly, if he were to weaken now, he would waste time and expend on this older woman energy which would be better reserved for the younger one.

So he gently pushed her away.

'Come now, be sensible,' he said.

She looked at him with a grieved expression:

'Oh Georges, you won't even let me kiss you any more.'

He replied:

'No, not today. I've got a bit of a headache and it's hurting me.'

So she meekly sat down again between his legs. She enquired:

'Will you come and dine with us tomorrow evening? You know how it would please me.'

He hesitated but hardly dared to refuse:

'Yes, of course.'

'Thank you, my darling.'

She was slowly rubbing her head to and fro against the young man's chest, gently stroking him, and one of her long black hairs caught in his waistcoat.

She noticed it and a wild notion suddenly came into her head, one of those superstitious ideas which are often a woman's only form of reason. Very gently she started to wind the hair round a button. Then she fastened another one to the next button and another one on the button above. To each of his buttons she attached one hair.

In a minute, when he stood up, he would pull them out. He would hurt her, how wonderful that would be! And without knowing it he would take away something of hers, a little lock of hair, a thing for which he had never asked. It was a link by which she would be binding him to her, a secret, invisible link, a talisman that she was leaving with him. Without intending to, he would be thinking of her, dreaming about her and loving her a little more next day.

Suddenly he said:

'I shall have to go because I'm expected in the Chamber for the end of the session. I can't miss today.'

She gave a sigh:

'So soon?' And then resignedly, added:

'All right, my darling, but you'll come and dine tomorrow?'

And she pulled herself abruptly away. She felt a short, sharp pain on her head as if her skin had been pricked with needles. Her heart was pounding; she was happy to have suffered a little because of him.

'Goodbye,' she said.

With a compassionate smile, he took her into his arms and coldly kissed her on the eyes.

But she was distracted by this contact with him and whispered: 'So soon', once again. And beseechingly her eyes looked towards the bedroom whose door was open.

He eased her away from him and said in a brisk tone:

'I must be off, I shall be late.'

Then she put up her lips, which he barely touched, and giving her her sunshade that she had forgotten, he said again:

'Come on, come on, let's get on, it's after three.'

She went ahead, saying again:

'Seven o'clock tomorrow.'

He replied:

'Tomorrow at seven.'

They parted. She went off to the right while he turned to the left.

Du Roy walked up as far as the outer boulevard. Then he started to go slowly down the Boulevard Malesherbes. As he passed a confectioner's he noticed some marrons glacés in a glass bowl and he thought: 'I'll get a pound of those for Clotilde.' He bought a bag of the candied fruits of which she was passionately fond. By four o'clock he was back in the flat waiting for his young mistress.

She arrived a trifle late because her husband had come back for a week. She asked:

'Can you come to dinner tomorrow? He'd be delighted to see you.'

'No, I'm dining with the boss. We've got a whole lot of political and financial schemes on hand at the moment.'

She had taken off her hat; she was now taking off her bodice which was too tight.

He pointed to the bag on the mantelpiece:

'I've bought you some marrons glacés.'

She clapped her hands:

'Oh lovely! You're an angel!'

She picked them up, tasted one and declared:

'They're delicious. I've a feeling I'm not going to leave a single one.'

And with a playful and voluptuous look, she added:

'So you're flattering all my vices.'

She was steadily devouring the chestnuts and kept glancing into the bottom of the bag to see if there were still some left.

She said:

'I say, you sit down in the armchair. I'll snuggle down between your legs to nibble my sweets. I'll be very comfortable.'

He smiled, sat down, and opened his legs for her to place herself as Madame Walter had done earlier.

She lifted her head to speak to him and said with her mouth full:

'I didn't tell you darling, I had a dream about you, I dreamt that we were both going on a long trip together on a camel. It had two humps and we were each sitting astride a hump, crossing the desert. We'd packed some sandwiches and brought a bottle of wine and we were having a picnic on our humps. But I was annoyed because we couldn't do anything else because we were too far apart and so I wanted to get down.'

He replied:

'I want to get down too.'

He was laughing at her story, encouraging her to go on prattling away with her childish, tender, foolish nonsense in the way lovers do. Such childish remarks captivated him in Madame de Marelle whereas he would have been exasperated had Madame Walter been saying them.

Clotilde also called him: 'My darling, my cherub, my sweetie-pie', and he found such expressions affectionate and gentle. When spoken by the other woman earlier on, they had irritated and nauseated him. For loving words, which are always the same, take their flavour from the lips by which they are uttered.

But at the same time as he was being amused by her antics, he was thinking of the 70,000 francs that he was going to earn and suddenly he gave her two little taps on the top of her head to cut short her flow of words:

'Listen sweetie, there's something I want you to pass on to your husband. Will you tell him from me to buy 10,000 francs' worth of the Moroccan loan tomorrow? It's at seventy-two now and I promise him he'll have made a profit of 60,000 to 80,000 francs before three months are out. He's to keep it absolutely dark. Tell him from me that they've decided to launch an expedition against Tangier and that the French government will be underwriting the Moroccan debt. But don't let the cat out of the bag to anyone else. I'm entrusting you with a State secret.'

She was listening to him carefully. She said quietly:

'Thank you, darling. I'll pass the news on to my husband this very evening. You can rely on him, he won't say a word. He's very trustworthy. There's no danger.'

But she had now eaten up all the chestnuts. She screwed the bag up and flung it into the fireplace. Then she said: 'Let's go to bed.' And without standing up she started to unbutton Georges' waistcoat.

Suddenly she stopped and holding up a long hair between her two fingers, she said with a laugh: 'Look what I've found in your buttonhole. You've brought one of Madeleine's hairs away with you. That's what I call a faithful husband.'

Then, becoming serious, she placed the imperceptible thread which she had found on her hand and examining it closely, muttered:

'It's not one of Madeleine's, it's brown.'

He smiled:

'It's probably one of the housemaid's.'

But she was inspecting the waistcoat with the care of a detective and she picked off another hair twisted round the next button; then she noticed a third one and going pale and trembling a little, she exclaimed:

'Oh, you've been to bed with a woman who's put hairs on all your buttons.'

He looked surprised and stammered:

'Of course I haven't ... You must be mad ...'

Suddenly he remembered and realized what had happened; and although rather flustered at first, he hastened to deny it, with a grin on his face, not displeased that she suspected him of having success with women.

She was still searching for, and finding, hairs which she rapidly unwound and flung down onto the carpet.

Her woman's crafty instinct told her what had happened and, furious with anger, on the point of tears, she stammered:

'She's a woman who loves you . . . and she wanted you to take something of hers away with you . . . Oh you're so crooked . . .'

And then she gave a nervous, high-pitched cry of pleasure: 'Oh! Oh! She's an old woman . . . Look, here's a white hair . . . So you're going with old women now . . . Do you get paid for it? Tell me, do they pay you for it? So you've descended to old women now . . . Then you don't need me any more . . . you can stick to her.'

She stood up and rushed over to put on her bodice which was lying on a chair.

He was trying shamefacedly to hold her back as he stammered:

'No, Clo, no . . . you're silly . . . I don't know what it is . . . listen . . . stop . . . look here . . . stop . . .'

She kept repeating:

'You can stick to your old woman . . . stick to her . . . have a ring made with her hairs . . . her white hairs . . . You've got enough of them to do that . . .'

She had hurriedly flung on her clothes, her hat and her veil and as he tried to catch hold of her, she gave him a resounding slap across the face. While he was standing there bewildered, she opened the door and slipped out.

As soon as she was gone, he was seized with a furious rage against that old hag Madame Walter. My God, he was going to teach her a lesson and no mistake.

His cheek was all red and he sponged it in water. Then he left too, thinking how he could get his revenge. There would be no forgiveness this time, damn it!

He went down to the boulevard and as he was strolling along, he stopped in front of a jeweller's to look at a chronometer which he had had his eye on for some time and which was priced at 1,800 francs.

Suddenly, with a little thrill of joy, he thought: 'If I get my 70,000 francs, I'll be able to afford it.' And he began to dream of all the things he could do with those 70,000 francs.

First of all, he would be elected a deputy. And then he would buy his chronometer and then he would play the Stock Exchange ... and then ... and then ...

He did not want to go back to the newspaper because he wanted to talk with Madeleine before seeing Walter and writing his article; so he set off on his way home.

He had just reached the Rue Drouot when he stopped short; he had forgotten to enquire after the Comte de Vaudrec, who lived in the Chaussée d'Antin. So he strolled idly back, still dreaming blissfully of nice things, of wonderful things, of the wealth that was within his grasp, as well as of that bastard Laroche and that old bitch the boss's wife. In any case, he was not worried at all by Clotilde's anger because he knew very well that she forgave easily.

He asked the concierge of the house where the Comte de Vaudrec lived:

'How is Monsieur de Vaudrec? I heard that he hasn't been very well these last few days.'

The porter replied:

'The count is very ill, sir. They're afraid that he won't last the night. The gout has affected his heart.'

Du Roy was so taken aback that he did not know what to do. So Vaudrec was dying! A turmoil of disturbing thoughts which he did not even dare to admit to himself flitted through his mind.

He stammered:

'Thank you ... I'll come back,' without realizing what he was saying.

Then he leapt into a cab and drove home.

His wife was in. He rushed breathlessly to her room to tell her the news at once.

'Have you heard? Vaudrec is dying!'

She was sitting reading a letter. She looked up and repeated three times:

'Eh? What's that ... ? what's that? ... what's that ... ?'

'I'm telling you that Vaudrec is dying from an attack of gout that has affected his heart.' Then he added: 'What do you intend to do?'

She had jumped up, deathly pale, her cheeks twitching nervously, and then hiding her face in her hands she began to cry in a heart-rending fashion, stricken by grief and shaken by sobs.

Then suddenly she took hold of herself and wiped her eyes:

'I'll ... I'll go and see him ... don't worry about me ... I don't know what time I'll be back ... don't wait up for me ...'

He replied:

'All right. Off you go.'

She clasped his hand and left so quickly that she forgot her gloves.

Georges dined alone and began to write his article. He wrote it exactly on the lines indicated by the Minister, letting his readers think that the Moroccan expedition would not take place. Then he took it to the paper, chatted for a few moments with the director and left cheerfully smoking, without knowing why he was so cheerful.

His wife had not yet returned. He went to bed and slept.

At about midnight Madeleine came back. Waking with a start, Georges sat up in bed.

He enquired:

'Well?'

Never before had he seen her looking so pale and upset. She said very quietly:

'He's dead.'

'Ah! And ... did he say anything to you?'

'No. He was unconscious before I arrived.'

Georges was thinking. There were questions on his lips that he did not dare to utter.

'Come to bed,' he said.

She quickly undressed and slipped into bed beside him. He went on:

'Were there any relatives at the bedside?'

'Only a nephew.'

'Oh! Did he see the nephew often?'

'Never. They hadn't met for ten years.'

'Had he any other relatives?'

'No ... I don't think so.'

'So ... it'll be the nephew who'll inherit?'

'I don't know.'

'Vaudrec was very rich, wasn't he?'

'Yes, very rich.'

'Do you know roughly how much he had?'

'No, not exactly. Perhaps a million or two.'

Georges said no more. She blew out the candle. And they lay side by side in the dark, in silence, both awake and thinking.

He no longer felt sleepy. He was beginning to think that the 70,000 francs that Madame Walter had promised him were rather small beer. Suddenly he had the impression that Madeleine was crying. He asked to make sure:

'Are you asleep?'

'No.'

Her voice was quivering with tears. He went on:

'I forgot to tell you earlier that that Minister of yours has been having us on.'

'How?'

He told her at length and in great detail about the scheme hatched by Laroche and Walter.

When he had finished, she asked:

'How do you know all that?'

He replied:

'You won't mind if I don't tell you that, I hope. You have sources of information that I don't probe into and I have mine that I want to keep to myself. In any case, I can promise you that it's completely accurate.'

She murmured:

'Yes, it's possible. I suspected they were doing something without letting us know.'

But Georges could not get to sleep and he moved gently towards his wife and kissed her on the ear. She brusquely pushed him away:

'Please leave me alone. I'm not in the mood for that sort of romp now.'

He turned over resignedly towards the wall, shut his eyes and finally managed to fall asleep.

CHAPTER 6

THE church was draped in black and the sight of a large coat-of-arms surmounted by a coronet over the porch told the passers-by that a nobleman was making his last journey.

The service had just come to an end and the Comte de Vaudrec's nephew was shaking hands and exchanging greetings with the mourners as they filed slowly past the coffin.

After leaving the church, Georges Du Roy and his wife started to walk back to their flat. Both were silent, deep in thought. Finally, as though thinking out loud, Georges said:

'It really is most surprising.'

'What is, Georges?' his wife enquired.

'That Vaudrec shouldn't have left us anything.'

A sudden flush spread upwards from her neck to her face as though someone had quickly thrown a pink veil over her white flesh.

'Why should he leave us anything? He had no reason to do so.'

Then, after a few moments' pause, she went on:

'He may have left a will with his solicitor. We shouldn't have been told anything yet.'

He thought for a moment and then murmured:

'Yes, that's probable, because after all he was our best friend, for both of us. He used to dine with us twice a week and come and see us whenever he wanted to. He felt at home with us, completely at home. He loved you like a father and he had no family, no children, no brothers or sisters, nobody but a nephew and a distant one at that. Yes, there must be a will. I wouldn't want much, just something to remember him by, something to prove that he had given us a thought, that he was fond of us and recognized the affection we felt for him. He did owe us some token of friendship.'

With a pensive, unconcerned air, she said:

'Yes, it's possible that there is a will, in fact.'

When they reached home the servant handed Madeleine a letter which she opened and then held out to her husband.

Maître Lamaneur,
Notary,
17, Rue des Vosges,
Paris.

Dear Madam,

May I request you to be so good as to call at my office, between two and four o'clock on Tuesday, Wednesday or Thursday, for a matter which concerns you?

Yours faithfully,
Lamaneur.

This time Georges' face went red:

'That must be it. It's queer that he should ask you to call on him and not me, when I'm the legal head of the household.'

She did not answer at once and then, after a brief moment of reflection, she said:

'Shall we go and see this afternoon?'

'Yes, let's do that.'

They went immediately after lunch.

When they arrived at Maître Lamaneur's, the head clerk rose with obvious alacrity and ushered them into the solicitor's office.

Lamaneur was a rotund little man, completely round all over. His head looked like a ball nailed onto another ball resting on two tiny legs so short that they looked almost like balls, too.

He greeted them, offered them a seat and then, turning to Madeleine, said:

'I asked you to come and see me, Madame Du Roy, in order to inform you with regard to the will of the late Comte de Vaudrec, which affects you.'

Georges could not prevent himself from muttering:

'I suspected as much.'

The solicitor went on:

'Let me read the will to you. It is very short.'

He took a piece of paper out of a file lying on his desk and read:

I, the undersigned Paul Émile-Cyprien-Gontran, Comte de Vaudrec, being sound in mind and body, hereby declare my last will and testament.

Since in the midst of life we are in death, in preparation for this eventuality, I am taking the precaution of drawing up my will which will be left in the keeping of Maître Lamaneur.

Since I have no direct heirs, I bequeath all my worldly goods, consisting of approximately six hundred thousand francs in stocks and shares and five hundred thousand francs in real estate, to Madame Claire-Madeleine Du Roy, without any condition or encumbrance. I ask her to accept this gift from a dead friend as proof of his deep, affectionate and respectful devotion.

The solicitor added:

'That is the whole will. This document is dated last August and it replaces a will in similar terms made two years ago in favour of Madame Claire-Madeleine Forestier. I have this first will which would prove, in case the will is disputed by the family, that the Count did not change his intentions.'

Madeleine had gone very pale and was looking down at her feet. Georges was nervously twirling the end of his moustache. The solicitor waited a moment and then went on:

'It goes without saying, Monsieur Du Roy, that your wife cannot accept this legacy without your consent.'

Du Roy stood up and said sharply:

'I shall need time to think it over.'

The solicitor nodded with a smile and said in a friendly tone:

'I can understand your qualms, Monsieur Du Roy, and your hesitation. I ought to add that Monsieur de Vaudrec's nephew, when he heard of his uncle's last intentions this very morning, stated that he was ready to accept them on condition that he receives a consideration of 100,000 francs. In my opinion the will is irrefutable but a law suit would cause a stir that you might perhaps prefer to avoid. The world often passes uncharitable judgements. In any case, could you let me have your decision on the matter before next Saturday?'

Georges nodded: 'I shall do so.' Then he bowed stiffly and, letting his wife, who had not uttered a word, pass in front of him he left the room with a haughty demeanour that wiped the smile from the solicitor's face.

As soon as they reached home, Du Roy closed the door sharply and flung his hat onto the bed:

'So you were Vaudrec's mistress?'

Madeleine, who was taking off her veil, turned round with a start:

'Me? Oh Georges!'

'Yes, you. You don't leave your whole fortune to a woman unless . . .'

She had started trembling so much that she was unable to take out the pins holding her veil.

She thought for a moment and then stammered agitatedly:

'But Georges . . . look . . . you're mad . . . you're . . . you're . . . Didn't you yourself, earlier on . . . weren't you hoping . . . that he'd leave you something?'

Georges was standing close beside her, observing all her emotions, like a judge trying to detect the slightest weakness in a prisoner. Emphasizing every word, he said:

'Yes . . . he should have left me something . . . to me, your husband . . . me, his friend . . . do you understand that? But not to you . . . you, his friend . . . you, my wife. The distinction is most important, in fact essential, from the point of view of the proprieties . . . and of public opinion.'

Now it was Madeleine who was staring at him strangely, straight in the eye, probing as though to discover the unknown quality of his being, which can never be fathomed but merely glimpsed for a few split seconds, in moments of inattention or surrender or carelessness, like a door left ajar on the inner workings of the mind. And she said slowly and carefully:

'But it seems to me that if . . . that people would have found it at least as strange if he had made a bequest as large as that to you.'

He asked sharply:

'Why?'

She said:

'Because . . .'

She hesitated and then went on:

'Because you're my husband . . . and you haven't known him really very long . . . because I've been his friend for a very long time . . . because his first will, made when Charles was still alive, left everything to me.'

Georges was striding up and down. He said firmly:

'You can't accept it.'

She replied unconcernedly:

'All right. In that case, it's not worth waiting until Saturday. We can inform Maître Lamaneur immediately.'

He stopped in front of her and once again they stood eyeball to eye-ball, each endeavouring to pierce the impenetrable secrets of the other's heart, to probe each other's thoughts to the quick. Without speaking, they interrogated each other in a passionate attempt to lay bare what was in their two minds: a tussle between a couple who, although they live side by side, never really know each other, who suspect each other, sniff round and spy on each other without ever fathoming the murky depths of their two souls.

And suddenly, thrusting his face into hers, he said in a low voice:

'Go on, admit that you were Vaudrec's mistress.'

She shrugged her shoulders:

'You're stupid. Vaudrec was very fond of me, very fond, but nothing more . . . ever.'

He stamped his foot:

'You're lying. It's not possible.'

She replied calmly:

'Yet that's how it was.'

He started walking up and down again and then, stopping once more:

'Then tell me how it is that he left all his money to you.'

Coolly and casually she explained:

'It's quite simple. As you said earlier, we were his only friends or rather I was, because he knew me when I was a child. My mother was companion to some relatives of his. He used always to be coming here and as he had no natural heirs he thought of me. It's not impossible that he felt a little love for me. But what woman hasn't ever been loved like that? And why shouldn't his secret, hidden affection for me have led him to put down my name when he decided to draw up his will? He used to bring me flowers every

Monday. You weren't surprised at that at all, were you, and yet he didn't give you any: and now he's left me his money for the same reason and because he had nobody else to offer it to. On the contrary, it would have been extremely strange if he had left it to you. Why should he? What were you to him?'

She spoke so naturally and calmly that Georges hesitated.

He went on:

'All the same, in the circumstances, we can't accept this bequest. It would create an extremely unfortunate impression. Everybody would believe that it was the case, everybody would gossip and people would laugh at me. As it is, my colleagues are only too ready to envy me and attack me. I've got to be more careful than anyone of my honour and reputation. It's impossible for me to agree to allow my wife to accept a legacy of that sort from a man who is already rumoured to have been her lover. Forestier might perhaps have tolerated such a situation but I won't.'

She murmured gently:

'All right then, let's not accept, we'll be a million francs worse off, that's all.'

He was still walking up and down and he began to think out loud, speaking so that his wife could hear without actually addressing her.

'Well, yes, a million ... it can't be helped. When he made his will, he didn't realize how thoughtless he was being, how careless of the proprieties. He didn't see what a false and ridiculous position he would be putting me into. Life is a question of tact. He should have left half to me and everything would have been all right.'

He sat down, crossed his legs and began to twirl the ends of his moustache as he did when he was bored, anxious or had a problem to solve.

Madeleine took up a piece of tapestry on which she used

to work now and again and said, as she selected her threads of wool :

'Well, there's nothing more for me to say. It's up to you to think what to do.'

He said nothing for a long time and then, hesitatingly :

'The world will never understand that Vaudrec made you his sole legatee and that I agreed to it. Accepting all that money like that would be an admission ... on your part that you had had a scandalous affair with him and on my part a shameful acceptance of such a situation ... Do you realize how people would interpret our acceptance? We must find a way round, some clever method of wrapping it up so that it doesn't show. For example, we could let it be known that he shared his money between us by giving half to the husband and half to the wife.'

She enquired :

'How could that be done, seeing that the will is quite explicit?'

He replied :

'Oh, that's very simple. You can leave me half the legacy by a donation *inter vivos*. We've got no children, so it's quite possible. In that way we'd stop the scandalmongering.'

She retorted rather impatiently :

'I can't see how that would stop the scandalmongering either because the document is there with Vaudrec's signature on it.'

He replied angrily :

'Do we need to advertise it and pin it up on the wall? You really are stupid. We'll say that the Comte de Vaudrec left his money to us in equal shares ... That's all ... In any case you can't accept this legacy without my permission. I'll let you have it on condition that you agree to share so that I shan't become a laughing-stock.'

Once again she gave him a piercing glance :

'As you like. I'm willing.'

Then he stood up and started walking up and down again. He seemed to be hesitating again and now he was avoiding his wife's penetrating gaze. He said:

'No, definitely not ... perhaps it would be better to give it up altogether ... it's more dignified ... more honest ... more honourable ... And yet, like that, nobody could imagine anything, anything at all. Even the most fastidious people would have nothing to cavil at.'

He stopped in front of Madeleine:

'Well darling, if you like, I'll go back and consult Maître Lamaneur by myself and explain the matter to him. I'll tell him I have qualms and I'll add that we fixed on the idea of sharing for the sake of propriety and so that people wouldn't gossip. Once I agree to accept half the legacy, it's quite obvious that no one will have the right to find it strange. It's as if I'm saying: "My wife accepts because I, her husband, am accepting as the only person competent to judge what she may do without compromising herself." Otherwise, it would have caused a scandal.'

Madeleine merely said gently:

'Do what you like.'

Now his words were beginning to flow freely:

'Yes, it's all as clear as daylight, with this arrangement of splitting the legacy in two. We shall be inheriting the money from a friend who didn't wish to make any distinction or difference between the two of us, who was anxious not to appear to be saying: "I like one or the other of them better after my death, just as I did during my lifetime." Of course, he preferred the wife but by leaving his money to the two of them he wanted to make it quite plain that his preference was purely platonic. And you can be sure that if he had thought of it, that's what he would have done. He didn't think, he didn't foresee the consequences of what he'd done. As you rightly said a moment ago, it was you he offered flowers to every week and it's you he wanted to give his last thought to without realizing . . .'

She cut him short with a note of irritation in her voice:

'Yes, we've agreed. I can understand, there's no need to keep on explaining. Go and see the solicitor at once.'

He blushed and stammered:

'You're right, I'll be off.'

He picked up his hat and then, just as he was going out:

'I'll try and settle the business with the nephew for fifty thou, shall I?'

She replied witheringly:

'No, give him the hundred thousand which he's asking for. And you can take them out of my share if you like.'

Suddenly abashed he mumbled:

'No, I shan't do that, we'll go halves. If we each give up 50,000 francs, there's still a clear million.'

Then he added:

'See you shortly, my little Madou.'

And he went off to the solicitor to explain the scheme, which he attributed to his wife.

Next day they signed a gift *inter vivos* whereby Madeleine gave 500,000 francs to her husband.

Then, after leaving the solicitor's office, as it was a nice day, Georges suggested strolling down to the boulevards. He was amiable, attentive, full of consideration and affection. He kept laughing cheerfully at everything, while she was pensive and a trifle stern.

It was quite a chilly autumn day. Everyone seemed in a hurry and was striding along quickly. Du Roy took his wife to the shop where he had so often looked at the timepiece on which he had set his heart.

'Would you like me to give you a piece of jewellery?' he asked.

Without enthusiasm she replied quietly:

'If you feel like it.'

They went in. He enquired:

'Which do you prefer, a necklace, a bracelet or earrings?'

But the sight of all the glittering trinkets of gold and precious stones made her pretence of indifference evaporate and her eyes sparkled as she eagerly looked round at the showcases full of jewellery.

Suddenly, something caught her fancy:

'That's a very pretty bracelet.' It was in the form of a strangely shaped chain in which each link was set with a different stone.

Georges asked:

'How much is that bracelet?'

The jeweller answered:

'Three thousand francs, sir.'

'I'll take it if you'll let me have it for two thousand five.'

The man hesitated, and then answered:

'I'm afraid that's impossible, sir.'

Du Roy continued:

'Look, you can throw in that watch for 1,500, that'll make 4,000 and I'll pay cash. Is that a deal? If you don't want to, I'll have to go elsewhere.'

The puzzled jeweller finally agreed.

'Very well, sir.'

The journalist gave his address and then added:

'Have my monogram G.R.C. engraved on the watch, under a baronial coronet.'

Surprised, Madeleine started to smile. And when they left the shop she took him almost tenderly by the arm. He's crafty and forceful, she thought to herself. Now that he had his private income, it was only reasonable to have a title to go with it.

The jeweller was saying as he showed him out:

'You may rely on me, my lord. I'll have it ready on Thursday.'

They passed by the Vaudeville. There was a new play on.

'If you like,' he said, 'we'll go to the theatre this evening, let's try and get a box.'

There was a box free and they booked it. He added:

'How about dining out?'

'Oh yes, I'd like that.'

He was as happy as a king and was trying to think of something else to do.

'Suppose we went to see if Madame de Marelle can spend the evening with us? I heard that her husband's in Paris. I'd be very happy to have a word with him.'

They went to see. Georges was rather dreading his first meeting with his mistress and was not sorry that his wife would be there to avoid any awkwardness.

But Clotilde seemed to have forgotten the whole matter and even prevailed on her husband to accept the invitation.

They had a lively dinner-party and spent a charming evening together.

Georges and Madeleine did not arrive home until very late. The gas had been turned off and in order to light up the staircase, Du Roy had to keep striking matches.

As they reached the first-floor landing, the match flared up as it was struck and lit up their two faces in the mirror against the gloom of the staircase.

They seemed like ghosts, all ready to disappear into the night. Du Roy raised his hand to illuminate their reflection in the mirror and said, with a triumphant laugh:

'Look at these millionaires on their way.'

MOROCCO had been conquered by the French two months ago. Now that she possessed Tangier, France held the whole of the North African littoral as far as the Regency of Tripoli; and she had guaranteed the debts of her newly annexed territory.

Two Ministers were said to have made some 20,000,000 francs in the process and Laroche-Mathieu's name was quoted almost openly.

As for Walter, the whole of Paris knew that he had brought off a double event by adding some thirty to forty millions to his fortune through the loan and some eight to ten millions through copper and iron mines as well as vast tracts of land bought for a song before the occupation and sold immediately afterwards to companies interested in colonial exploitation.

In the space of a few days he had achieved world-wide power and become one of those omnipotent businessmen more powerful than kings before whom people bow their head and speak in deferential tones and who arouse every feeling of envy, cowardice and baseness hidden in the heart of man.

No longer was he 'that Jew Walter', the proprietor of a shady bank and the owner of a dubious newspaper, a deputy suspected of all sorts of dishonest transactions. He was Monsieur Walter, the wealthy Israelite.

He had every intention of proving it.

Knowing the financial straits of the Prince of Carlsbourg, the owner of one of the finest private houses in the Rue du Faubourg-Saint-Honoré, he offered to buy it from him within twenty-four hours with all the furniture, exactly as it stood. His figure was 3,000,000 francs. The prince, tempted by the amount, accepted.

Walter moved into his new residence the very next day.

Then he hit upon another idea, an idea that could only have been conceived by someone determined to take Paris by storm, an idea worthy of a Bonaparte.

At that time, the whole town was thronging to look at a large picture by the Hungarian painter Karl Marcovitch, representing Christ walking on the waters, on show at the gallery of the art fancier Jacques Lenoble.

The art critics were describing it enthusiastically as the most amazing masterpiece of the century.

Walter bought it for half a million francs and removed it to his own house, thereby putting a stop to the curiosity which had been aroused amongst the public and compelling the whole of Paris to talk about him, either in envy, blame or praise.

Then he announced in the papers that he would invite every well-known member of Parisian society to come to his house one evening in order to view this masterpiece by the outstanding foreign painter so that no one would be able to say that he had impounded a work of art.

He would hold open house. Anyone who wished could come. All that was needed was to show the letter of introduction at the door.

This letter read: 'Monsieur and Madame Walter request the honour of your company at home, on 30 December from 9 o'clock until midnight to see Karl Marcovitch's painting "Jesus walking on the waters", illuminated by electricity.'

Then followed a postscript: 'After midnight there will be dancing.' This was written in very small letters.

So those who wanted could stay on and from them the Walters would recruit their future acquaintances.

The others could look at the picture, the house and its owners with the insolent or nonchalant curiosity of those who belong to high society and then could make their way home at their own convenience, just as they had come. And old Walter knew very well that they would come back later on, just as they had done with others of his race who had become wealthy like himself.

The first thing was for all these penniless aristocrats whose names figure regularly in every newspaper to cross the threshold of his house and this they would do in order to discover what sort of man this was who had earned 50,000,000 francs in six weeks; they would do so also in order to see and reckon up who else was there; and finally they would do so because, although being a son of Abraham himself, he had had the good taste and cleverness to invite them to admire a Christian painting in his own home.

He seemed to be saying to them: 'There you are, I've paid 500,000 francs for Marcovitch's religious masterpiece, "Jesus walking on the waters". And this masterpiece is going to stay in my house for ever for me, Walter the Jew, to look at.'

In the world of high society, the society composed of duchesses and members of the Jockey Club, a good deal of discussion had been aroused by this invitation which, when all was said and done, did not commit anyone to anything. You would visit the house just as you went to look at watercolours at Monsieur Petit's. The Walters had acquired a masterpiece; they were holding open house for one evening so that everybody might be able to admire it. What could be better?

Every morning for the last fortnight *La Vie française* had been fanning public interest by featuring the entertainment that was being offered on 30 December.

Du Roy could hardly contain his rage at Walter's brilliant coup.

He had considered himself to be rich after extorting the half a million francs from his wife and now he felt himself a veritable pauper when he compared his paltry sum with the millions which he had seen showering down all around him without being able to pick up any of it for himself.

His envy and rage grew stronger every day. He felt a grudge against everybody, against the Walters, whom he had stopped visiting, against his wife, who had been misled by Laroche when he had advised her not to buy any of the Moroccan loan and, above all, he bore a grudge against the Minister who had tricked him, exploited him and was still dining at his table twice a week. Georges acted as his secretary, his agent and his mouthpiece and whenever he was taking down what Laroche dictated, he felt a wild urge to strangle this coxcomb puffed up with his own success. As Minister, Laroche took care not to crow too loudly and in the interests of retaining his portfolio he made no parade of his exorbitant wealth. But Du Roy could smell all the money of this upstart lawyer in the increased arrogance and insolence of his speech and manner, in his greater outspokenness and his utter self-confidence.

Laroche had now taken over Du Roy's home, usurping the place formerly occupied by the Comte de Vaudrec, as well as his visiting times, and he used to treat the servants as if he was a second master of the house.

Georges accepted all this with barely suppressed irritation, like a dog which would like to bite and dare not. But he was often harsh and savage with Madeleine who would shrug her shoulders and treat him like a clumsy child. Furthermore, she was surprised by his persistent ill-humour and kept saying:

'I can't understand you. You're always complaining. Yet you've got a superb position.'

He would turn his back on her without saying a word.

At first, he had stated that he would not accept his boss's

invitation and never set foot in the dirty Yid's house again.

For the last two months, Madame Walter had been writing to him every day begging him to come, to suggest some place where they might meet so that, as she said, she could hand over the 70,000 francs which she had earned for him.

He had not replied and flung her desperate letters into the fire. Not that he had given up the idea of taking his share of the profits but he wanted to wound her, to treat her with contempt and trample her underfoot. She had too much money! He wanted to show that he had pride.

On the very day the picture was due to be exhibited, when Madeleine pointed out that he was very wrong not to want to go, he retorted:

'For heaven's sake leave me alone. I'm staying at home.'

Then after dinner, he suddenly stated:

'I suppose we'd better go and do our duty. Hurry up and get ready.'

She had been expecting him to act like this.

'I'll be ready in a quarter of an hour,' she said.

He kept grumbling while he was dressing and was still venting his bad temper in the cab.

The court of honour of Carlsbourg House was lit by four electric globes, one at each corner, looking like four little blue-tinted moons. A magnificent carpet covered the steps leading up to the front terrace and on each step a footman in livery was standing stock-still, like a statue.

Du Roy muttered:

'There's swank for you.'

He shrugged his shoulders, eaten up by jealousy.

His wife said:

'Don't talk so much about it and do the same yourself.'

They went in and handed their heavy outer garments to the footmen who came towards them.

There were a number of women there, with their hus-

bands, also removing their furs. There were murmurs of:
'How lovely! How really lovely!'

The vast entrance hall was draped with tapestries representing the love of Mars and Venus.

Two branches of a monumental staircase rose up on each
side of the hall to meet on the floor above. The soft gleam of
the superb wrought-iron balustrade, gilded in old gold, was
discreetly reflected in the red marble steps.

At the entrance to the reception rooms two little girls
in cap and bells, one dressed in pink, the other in blue, were
presenting bunches of flowers to the ladies. Everyone
thought this a charming touch.

The reception rooms were already packed.

Most of the women were not in evening dress so that it
could be seen that they had come here just as they might
have come to any private exhibition. Those who were intending to stay for the dancing were wearing low-cut sleeve-
less dresses.

Surrounded by friends, Madame Walter was greeting her
guests in the second drawing-room. Many of them did not
know her and were walking around without paying any attention to the owners of the house, as though they were in
a museum.

When she caught sight of Du Roy, she went deathly pale
and made a movement as if to go and speak to him. Then
she checked herself and waited for him to come to her. He
greeted her somewhat stiffly whilst his wife was effusive,
affectionate and congratulatory. Then Georges left Madeleine with his employer's wife and lost himself in the crowd
in order to listen to the spiteful things which people must
surely be saying.

There were five drawing-rooms leading one to the other,
each of them draped in rich fabrics, Italian embroideries or
Oriental carpets of varying styles and shades while the walls

were adorned with paintings by old masters. People were pausing above all to admire a small Louis XVI room, a sort of boudoir completely padded in silk with pink bunches of flowers on a pale blue background. The low gilt-wood furniture covered in a material similar to that on the walls was outstandingly elegant.

Georges recognized a number of celebrities, the Duchess of Terracina, General Prince d'Andremont, the entirely lovely Marchioness des Dunes and all those men and women who are regularly seen at first nights.

Someone tugged at his arm and he heard a young, happy voice whisper in his ear:

'Ah, there you are at last, you naughty Bel-Ami. Why haven't we seen anything of you recently?'

It was Suzanne Walter peering at him with her delicate, lustrous eyes from under her mass of fluffy blonde hair.

He was delighted to see her and, taking her warmly by the hand, he said apologetically:

'I haven't been able to. I've had so much to do these last two months that I haven't been out at all.'

She went on, speaking more seriously:

'It's naughty of you, very naughty indeed. Mummy and I are very, very fond of you and you've made us quite miserable. As for me, I can't do without you. When you're not there, I'm bored to tears. You see I'm speaking quite frankly so that you won't have the right to vanish again like that any more. Give me your arm, I'm going to show you "Jesus walking on the waters" myself. It's at the very end, behind the conservatory. Papa put it there so that people would have to come all the way through. It's amazing, he's just like a peacock showing off this house.'

They made their way slowly through the crowd. People turned round to look at this handsome young man and this delightful little doll.

A well-known painter's voice was heard to say:

'Well, what a pretty couple that is. How absolutely charming.'

Georges was thinking:

'If I'd been really clever, this is the girl I should have married. It was possible, too. Why didn't I think of it? Why did I let myself marry that other woman? I must have been mad! One's always too impulsive, one never stops to think enough!'

And envy, bitter envy seeped drop by drop into his heart, like a poison corroding all his pleasures and making his life seem hateful.

Suzanne was saying:

'Oh, do come often, Bel-Ami, we'll be able to do all sorts of extravagant things now that Daddy is rich. We'll do the wildest things.'

Following his train of thought, he replied:

'Oh, you'll get married now. You'll marry some slightly ruined handsome prince and we'll hardly ever meet any more.'

She exclaimed candidly:

'Oh no, I won't, not yet, I want someone I like, whom I like very much, whom I like completely. I'm rich enough for two.'

He gave a superior, ironical smile and began to list the names of the people who were going by, people of noble blood who had sold their rusty titles to bankers' daughters like herself but who now, whether they led their lives close to or far from their wives, were free, shameless, famous and respected.

At the end, he added:

'I don't give you six months before you're caught by that sort of bait. You'll be a marchioness or a duchess or a princess and you'll look down on me from a great height, Miss Walter!'

She protested indignantly, tapping him on the arm with

her fan and assuring him that she would never marry except for love.

He gave a wry smile:

'We'll see, we'll see. You're too wealthy.'

She said:

'But you've had a legacy, too.'

He replied pityingly:

'Yes, what about it? A measly 20,000 francs a year. It's not a great sum with things as they are.'

'But your wife inherited, too.'

'Yes. A million between the two of us. Forty thousand a year. We can't even afford a carriage with that.'

They had reached the end drawing-room and were standing in front of the conservatory, a large winter garden full of tall tropical trees towering over clumps of rare flowers. As you went into the gloom of all this greenery, where the light filtered like a silvery shower, your nose was assailed by the warm, fresh smell of damp earth and heavily scented air. It was a strange feeling, gentle, unwholesome and captivating, artificial, soft and enervating. Underfoot, carpets almost moss-like in texture led through two thick banks of shrubs. Suddenly, on his left beneath a broad canopy of palm-trees, Du Roy glimpsed a vast ornamental basin in white marble, big enough to swim in and with four large Delft pottery figures of swans along its edge spouting water through their half-open beaks.

The bottom of the pond was sprinkled with gold dust and some enormous goldfish were moving about in it like weird Chinese monsters with their protruding eyes and their scales edged with blue, mandarins of the deep which, as they swam to and fro over this golden floor, reminded one of the strange embroideries of that distant land.

Du Roy halted in his tracks, his pulse quickening. 'Now that's real luxury,' he said to himself. 'That's the sort of house to live in. Others have managed it, so why shouldn't I?' He started imagining how to set about it, failed to think of any way immediately and was vexed at being so powerless.

His companion had become thoughtful and silent. He looked at her sideways and thought once again: 'All that was needed was to marry this little living marionette.'

But Suzanne suddenly seemed to arouse herself:

'Look out,' she said, and pushing Georges through a group that was blocking their way, she made him turn sharply to the right.

Amidst a group of strange plants whose leaves were like open hands with slim fingers waving in the air, there could be seen a man standing motionless on the sea.

The effect was remarkable. The sides of the picture were hidden by the moving greenery so that the painting looked like some black hole opening onto a fantastic and wonderful background.

You had to look closely to understand what was happening. The frame cut across the middle of the boat containing the apostles, dimly lit by the slanting rays of a lamp which one of them, sitting on the thwarts, was pointing directly at Jesus as He approached.

Christ was coming towards them over a hollow in the waves which were flattening out in quiet submission and gently lapping His feet as they pressed down on them. Darkness surrounded the Son of God. Only the stars were sparkling in the sky. In the dull glow of the lantern carried by the apostle who was pointing towards our Lord, the faces of the others seemed convulsed in amazement.

It was plainly a powerful and unusual work by the hand of a master, the kind of work which troubles the spirit and gives food for thought for many years.

The people looking at it were first of all struck dumb

335

and then went pensively away, leaving any discussion of the quality of the picture until later.

After looking at it for some time, Du Roy uttered this comment:

'Nice to be able to treat yourself to little knick-knacks like that.'

But as people were jostling him from behind to come and look at the painting, he moved off, still holding Suzanne's hand under his arm, squeezing it a little.

She enquired:

'How about a glass of champagne? Let's go over to the buffet. Daddy will be there.'

And they went slowly back through the reception rooms where a steadily increasing throng, the sort of elegant crowd you meet at any large public celebration, was surging to and fro, making itself at home.

Georges suddenly thought he heard someone say: 'That's Laroche and Madame Du Roy.' The words impinged dimly on his ears like distant sounds carried on the wind. Where were they coming from?

He looked all round him and then caught sight of his wife walking past arm in arm with the Minister. They were engaged in a very private conversation, lowering their voices and smiling as they looked into each other's eyes.

He received the impression that people were whispering as they watched them and he felt a stupid, violent urge to hurl himself on the two of them and batter them with his fists.

She was making him ridiculous. He thought of Forestier. Perhaps people were saying: 'That cuckold Du Roy'. Who was she after all? An ambitious little upstart, quite clever but with no great resources, really. People came to his house because they were afraid of him and because they could feel that he was a force to be reckoned with but they probably showed scant respect when talking about this petty journalist couple. He would never go very far with this woman who would always give his house a bad name, who would continually compromise herself and whose whole manner revealed her intriguing nature. She was going to be a chain round his neck now. If only he had guessed, if only he had understood the situation! He would have played a more forceful game for rather higher stakes! What a splendid coup he might have achieved with little Suzanne as the prize! How could he have been so blind as not to realize it?

They had reached the dining-room, an immense room with marble columns and walls hung with antique Gobelin tapestries.

As soon as he caught sight of his editor, Walter bustled up to him and took hold of both his hands. He was beside himself with joy:

'Have you looked at all there is to see? Suzanne, have you shown him everything? What a lot of people, aren't there? Did you see the Prince de Guerche? He was having a glass of punch here a moment ago.'

Then he dashed off to speak to Senator Rissolin who was trailing his bewildered wife along with him, all decked out like a fair stall.

Suzanne was greeted by a tall, slim, slightly bald young man with blond whiskers and an unmistakable air of good breeding. Georges caught his name: the Marquis de Cazolles, and he suddenly felt jealous. How long had she known him? Presumably since her father's sudden access of wealth. Du Roy sensed that here was a suitor.

Someone took him by the arm. It was Norbert de Varenne. The aged poet with his greasy hair and well-worn suit looked tired and apathetic.

'That's what they call having a good time,' he said. 'Later on there'll be dancing and then everyone will go to bed and all the little girls will be happy. Have some champagne, it's quite decent.'

He had a glass filled and raising it to Du Roy, who had done the same:

'I drink to the victory of the mind over the millions.'

Then he added mildly:

'Not that they worry me very much when they belong to other people. I don't begrudge them their money but I protest on principle.'

Georges was not listening to him. He was looking for Suzanne who had just disappeared with the Marquis de Cazolles; so he quickly gave Norbert the slip and set out in pursuit of her.

His way was blocked by the throng of people looking for a drink. When he had eventually made his way through them, he came face to face with the Marelles.

He had continued to see Clotilde but he had not met her husband for some considerable time. The latter grasped both his hands:

'My dear Du Roy, I'm so grateful to you for the tip you gave me through Clotilde. I made almost a hundred thousand francs from the Moroccan loan. It's all thanks to you. One can really say that you're a precious friend.'

Men were turning round to look at such an elegant, pretty brunette. Du Roy replied:

'In exchange for the favour, my dear Marelle, I'm going to steal your wife or rather offer her my arm. Wives and husbands must always be kept apart.'

M. de Marelle bowed:

'Quite right. If I miss you we'll meet here in an hour's time.'

'Agreed.'

And the young couple plunged into the crowd, followed by the husband. Clotilde was saying:

'What lucky dogs those Walters are. What a wonderful thing it is to be good at business.'

Georges replied:

'So what? If a man's strong enough he'll get to the top, somehow or other.'

She went on:

'And the two girls will be getting twenty or thirty millions apiece. Not to mention the fact that Suzanne is pretty to boot.'

He made no reply. Hearing his own thoughts expressed by someone else irritated him.

She had not yet seen 'Jesus walking on the waters'. He suggested that they go and see it. They amused themselves by making malicious remarks about the people present and poking fun at those whose faces were unfamiliar. Saint-Potin went by, wearing a large number of decorations on his lapel and this greatly amused them. A former ambassador following him was less lavishly decorated.

Du Roy said:

'What a set!'

Boisrenard came up to shake hands with him. He was also wearing the green and yellow ribbon which he had sported on the day of the duel.

Vicomtesse de Percemur, bedizened and enormous, was chatting with a duke in the little Louis XVI boudoir.

Georges said in an undertone:

'A lovers' meeting.'

But as they went through the conservatory, he saw his wife sitting close beside Laroche-Mathieu. The pair of them were almost hidden behind a clump of plants. They seemed to be saying: 'We've made an assignation here, a public assignation. We don't give a damn for public opinion.'

Madame de Marelle acknowledged that Karl Marcovitch's

'Jesus' was a very surprising work; and they retraced their footsteps. They had lost sight of her husband.

He asked:

'Is Laurine still annoyed with me?'

'Yes, as much as ever. She says she doesn't want to meet you and goes off whenever we talk about you.'

He made no reply. The little girl's hostility made him unhappy and he found himself unable to forget it.

Suzanne caught them as they were coming through a doorway and exclaimed:

'Ah, there you are. Well, Bel-Ami, you're going to be lonely. I'm carrying our beautiful Clotilde off to show her my bedroom.'

And the two women hurried off, slipping through the crowd with the sinuous, snaky movement that women have when they are surrounded by people.

Almost immediately he heard a voice whispering:

'Georges!' It was Madame Walter. She went on in a very low voice: 'Oh, how can you be so unkind and cruel! You're making me so miserable for no reason at all. I arranged for Suzanne to take your companion away so that I could have a word with you. You must listen to me, you must ... let me talk to you this evening ... or else ... or else ... you don't know what I shall do. Go into the conservatory. You'll find a door on the left leading to the garden. Go down the path facing you. At the very end, there's an arbour. Wait for me there in ten minutes' time. If you won't, I swear I'll cause a scene, here and now!'

He replied arrogantly:

'Very well. I'll be where you say in ten minutes' time.'

They parted. But he was nearly late because of Jacques Rival who took him by the arm and insisted on telling him all sorts of things in a very excited manner. No doubt he had spent some time at the bar. At last Du Roy handed him on

340

to Monsieur de Marelle, who had finally appeared from somewhere or other, and managed to slip away. He then had to take care not to be seen by his wife and Laroche. He was able to do so because they seemed engaged in very animated conversation and he made his way to the garden.

The cold air hit him like an ice-cold bath. He thought: 'My God, I'm going to catch a chill', and he put his handkerchief round his neck as a sort of muffler. Then he picked his way slowly down the path, finding it rather difficult to see after the bright lights of the drawing-room.

To left and right he could distinguish leafless shrubs whose slender branches were waving to and fro. Their boughs were bathed in a dim glimmer that was filtering through the windows of the house. He caught sight of something white in front of him in the middle of the path and then he heard the trembling voice of Madame Walter, bare-armed and wearing a low-cut dress, saying falteringly:

'Oh, there you are. Are you trying to kill me?'

He replied calmly:

'Now please, no histrionics, eh? Otherwise I'm off.'

She had clasped him round his neck and with her lips close to his, she said:

'But tell me what I've done wrong? You're behaving like a blackguard. What have I done?'

He tried to push her away:

'You wound your hair round all my buttons last time I saw you and that nearly broke up my marriage.'

She was taken aback and then she shook her head:

'No, your wife wouldn't care in the least. One of your mistresses must have made a scene.'

'I haven't got any mistresses.'

'Don't say that! But why haven't you even been to see me? Why won't you dine at our house, even if it's only one day a week? Oh, the agonies I've been suffering. I love you so much that I can't think of anything else. I can't look at anything without seeing you. I daren't say anything for fear of mentioning your name! You can't understand that. I feel as if I'm caught in a trap or tied up in a bag. I just don't know what to do. I keep thinking of you all the time and I can't even breathe without feeling a dreadful pain here, in my chest and in my heart. I'm so weak that I can't even walk. I just sit on a chair all day, like a dumb animal, thinking of you.'

He was looking at her in astonishment. She was no longer the large, skittish schoolgirl that she had been before but a frantic, desperate woman, capable of anything.

However, a plan was dimly taking shape in his head. He replied:

'My dear woman, love doesn't last for ever. Easy come, easy go. But when it goes on as it did between us, it's like having a millstone round your neck. I've had enough. That's the truth. All the same, if you're prepared to be reasonable and invite me and treat me just as a friend, I'll come to your house as I used to. Do you feel able to do that?'

She put both her bare arms on Du Roy's coat and whispered:

'I can do anything if it means that I can see you.'

'All right then, it's a bargain,' he said. 'We're good friends and nothing else.'

She faltered:

'All right.' Then she held up her lips towards his. 'Just one more kiss. The last one.'

He gently held her off.

'No. We must keep to our agreement.'

She turned her head aside, wiping away two tears, and then pulling a bundle of papers tied in pink ribbon from the bodice of her dress, she held it out to Du Roy: 'Here you are. It's your share of the profits in the Moroccan business.

I was so pleased that I was able to do that for you. Here you are, do take it . . .'

He began by refusing:

'No, I'm not going to accept that money.'

But this was too much for her: ·

'You can't do that to me now. It's yours, all yours. If you don't take it, I'll just toss it down the drain. Georges, you won't do that to me, will you?'

He took the bundle and slipped it into his pocket.

'We must go in,' he said. 'You'll be catching pneumonia.'

She murmured:

'I wish I would! If only I could die.'

She took one of his hands, kissed it passionately, wildly, despairingly and ran back into the house.

He followed her quietly, thinking to himself. Then he went into the conservatory holding his head in the air, with a smile on his lips.

His wife and Laroche were no longer to be seen. The crowd was diminishing. It was becoming plain that people would not be staying on to dance. He caught sight of Suzanne holding her sister's arm. They both came up to ask him to dance the first quadrille with the Comte de Latour-Yvelin.

He expressed surprise:

'Now, which one is that?'

Suzanne replied mischievously:

'He's a new friend of my sister's.'

Rose blushed and mumbled:

'You're naughty, Suzette, he's no more a friend of mine than he is of yours.'

Her sister smiled:

'If you say so.'

Rose was annoyed and, turning her back on them, she walked away.

Du Roy took the other girl's elbow familiarly as she was standing beside him and said in his soft caressing voice:

'Tell me, my dear Suzanne, do you think of me as a real friend?'

'Of course I do, Bel-Ami.'

'You trust me?'

'Completely.'

'Do you remember what I was saying to you earlier on?'

'What about?'

'About your marriage or rather about the man you'll marry.'

'Yes.'

'Well, will you make me a promise?'

'Yes, what is it?'

'It's to consult me every time anyone asks to marry you and not to accept anyone without asking my opinion.'

'Yes, all right.'

'And that's a secret between us. Not one word about it to your father or mother.'

'Not a word.'

'Word of honour.'

'Word of honour.'

Rival came bustling up:

'Suzanne, your papa is asking for you, for the dancing.'

She said:

'Let's go, Bel-Ami.'

But he declined, having decided to leave straightaway as he wanted to be alone to think. Too many new ideas were beginning to pass through his mind and so he set out in search of his wife. After a while he caught sight of her drinking chocolate at the buffet with two men he did not know. She introduced him to the two but did not introduce them to him.

After a few moments, he asked:

344

'Shall we leave?'

'Whenever you like.'

She took his arm and they made their way back through the reception rooms which were now rapidly emptying.

She enquired:

'Where's Madame Walter? I'd like to say goodnight to her.'

'There's no point. She would try and make us stay for the dancing and I've had enough for one evening.'

'True enough, you're right.'

Throughout their journey home, they remained silent. But as soon as they had gone to their room, even before she had taken her veil off, Madeleine said to him with a smile:

'You'll never guess. I've got a surprise for you.'

'What is it?' he grunted, bad-temperedly.

'Guess.'

'I can't be bothered.'

'Well, tomorrow is the first of January.'

'Yes.'

'It's the day for New Year's gifts.'

'Yes.'

'Well, here's yours. It was given me by Laroche earlier this evening.'

She handed him a tiny black box that looked like a small jewel-case.

He opened it with a bored expression and saw that it was the Cross of the Legion of Honour.

He went a trifle pale and then he smiled and said:

'I'd sooner have had ten million. This didn't cost him much.'

She had expected him to be overjoyed and felt irritated by his cold reaction.

'You really are incredible. Nothing pleases you now.'

He replied calmly:

'That man is merely paying off his debt. And he still owes me a lot more.'

She was astounded to hear his tone of voice and said:

'All the same, it's wonderful at your age.'

He retorted:

'Everything's relative. Today I could get more.'

He had taken the case and put it down open on the mantel-shelf. For a second or two he looked at the shining star-shaped cross lying inside it. Then he closed it with a shrug and got into bed.

On 1 January the *Journal Officiel* did, in fact, announce that the political journalist Monsieur Prosper-Georges Du Roy had been made Chevalier of the Legion of Honour for outstanding services. His name was written in two words, and this pleased Georges more than the decoration itself.

An hour after reading the public announcement of the award he received a note from Madame Walter begging him to come to dinner that evening, with his wife, to celebrate the occasion. He hesitated for a few minutes and then, throwing the letter, which was couched in ambiguous terms, into the fire, he said to Madeleine:

'We're going to dine at the Walters' this evening.'

She was surprised:

'Goodness me, I thought you were never going to set foot in their place again.'

He merely replied mildly:

'I've changed my mind.'

When they arrived Virginie Walter was sitting by herself in the little Louis XVI boudoir which she used for her private parties. She was dressed in black and had powdered her hair, which made her look charming. From a distance, she seemed to be an old lady, from close up, a young one and when one looked even more closely she was both fascinating and alluring.

'Are you in mourning?' Madeleine enquired.

She replied sadly:

'Yes and no. I'm not in mourning for any of my family. But I've reached the age when you have bid farewell to life. So I've put on mourning to show that I'm starting today. From now on, my heart will be in mourning.'

Du Roy thought to himself:

'I wonder how long that New Year's resolution will last?'

Dinner was rather dreary. Only Suzanne never stopped chattering. Rose seemed preoccupied. Du Roy received many congratulations.

Later, they wandered, chatting desultorily, through the drawing-rooms and the conservatory. As Du Roy was bringing up the rear with Madame Walter, she held him back by his arm.

'Let me talk to you,' she said in a low voice. 'I'll never say anything to you again about anything, ever. But do come and see me, Georges. You can see I'm trying to put our love on a different footing. But it's impossible for me to go on living without you, absolutely impossible. You can't imagine what a torment it is. I can feel you, my eyes and my heart and my body remember you, night and day. It's as though you'd made me drink a poison that is eating me up inside. I can't go on like this, I just can't. I'm quite ready to be merely an old woman for you. I've whitened my hair for you to prove it; but do come here, now and again, just as a friend.'

She had caught hold of his hand and was squeezing and crushing it in hers, digging her nails into his flesh.

He replied calmly:

'All right. It's pointless to start talking about all that again. You can see that I came today, as soon as I got your letter.'

Walter had gone ahead with his two daughters and Made

leine was standing waiting for Du Roy beside the 'Jesus walking on the waters'.

'Just imagine,' he laughed, 'yesterday I found my wife kneeling in front of this picture as if she was in a chapel. She was saying her prayers there. It was so funny.'

Firmly but in a voice vibrating with deep, hidden emotion, Madame Walter replied:

'That Christ is going to save my soul. He gives me strength and courage every time I look at Him.'

And stopping in front of the Son of God standing on the waters, she said softly:

'Isn't He handsome! How afraid those men are of Him and yet they love Him! Just look at His face and His eyes, see how simple He is, and at the same time how supernatural!'

Suzanne exclaimed:

'Bel-Ami, He looks like you. I'm sure He does. If you had whiskers or if He was clean-shaven, you'd both look the same. It's absolutely remarkable!'

She insisted on his standing beside the picture and everybody could see that the two faces were, in fact, very similar.

Everyone was surprised. Walter thought that it was most peculiar. Madeleine smiled and said that Jesus looked more manly.

Madame Walter stood motionless staring at her lover's face side by side with that of Christ and her own face had turned as white as her hair.

CHAPTER 8

DURING the rest of the winter the Du Roys were often at the Walters'. Georges even dined there frequently alone, as Madeleine complained of being tired and preferred to stay at home.

They had settled on Friday and on that evening Madame Walter never invited anyone else: it was reserved for Bel-Ami and him alone. After dinner they played cards, they fed the tropical fish and spent a cosy family evening together. On a number of occasions Madame Walter had suddenly clasped the young man round the body behind a doorway or a clump of bushes in the conservatory, in some dark corner and hugged him to her chest with all her might, furtively exclaiming: 'I love you! ... I love you! ... I can't help it, I'm in love with you!' But he had always pushed her coldly away and replied sharply: 'If you do that sort of thing again, I shall stop coming.'

Suddenly, towards the end of March, there was a rumour that the two sisters were going to be married. Rose was supposed to be marrying the Comte de Latour-Yvelin and Suzanne the Marquis de Cazolles. The two had become friends of the family and enjoyed all the special favours and privileges that such a status implies.

Georges and Suzanne had become like brother and sister. In their free and easy way, they would chatter for hours together, poking fun at everybody and seeming to enjoy each other's company a great deal.

They had never mentioned the possibility of Suzanne's marriage again nor discussed the available suitors.

One morning when Walter had brought Du Roy to lunch

349

and his wife had been called away after the meal to talk to a tradesman, Georges said to Suzanne: 'Let's go and feed some crumbs to the goldfish.'

They each took a big piece of bread from the table and went off to the conservatory.

Cushions had been placed on the floor all round the marble basin so that people could kneel down and be closer to the water. The two young people each took a cushion and leaning over the edge, side by side, they began to roll little balls of bread between their fingers and throw them into the pool. As soon as the fish saw them they came swimming up with a flourish of their tails and a flick of their fins, rolling their big protruding eyes, somersaulting and diving to seize the balls of bread as they sank and then immediately coming up to the surface again for more.

Their mouths made queer shapes as they darted quickly and suddenly to and fro, looking like weird little monsters; and their glowing red stood out against the golden sand on the bottom as they shot, flamelike, through the transparent water or displayed the strip of blue round their scales as soon as they were still.

Georges and Suzanne could see their own faces upside down in the water and they were smiling at their reflections.

Suddenly he said, very softly:

'It's not very nice of you to be hiding things from me, Suzanne.'

She enquired:

'What do you mean, Bel-Ami?'

'Don't you remember what you promised me on the night of the party, exactly where we are now?'

'No, I don't think so.'

'It was to consult me every time someone asked to marry you.'

'Well?'

'Well, someone has asked.'

'Who is it?'

'You know perfectly well.'

'No, I swear I don't.'

'Yes, you do. That fatuous Marquis de Cazolles.'

'First of all, he's not fatuous.'

'That's possible, but he's stupid. And ruined by gambling as well as worn out by loose living. He really is a fine match for a pretty fresh young girl like you, and so intelligent too.'

She smiled and asked:

'What have you got against him?'

'Me? Nothing.'

'Yes, you have. He's not what you say he is.'

'Come now. He's dim and he's a schemer.'

She turned a little and stopped gazing in the water:

'Come on, out with it, what's wrong with you?'

He replied, as if reluctant to bare his heart:

'What's wrong with me ... is ... that I'm jealous of him.'

She was mildly surprised:

'You are?'

'Yes, I am!'

'Well, well. Why are you?'

'Because I'm in love with you and you know it perfectly well, you unkind girl!'

She replied in a stern voice:

'Bel-Ami, you must be mad!'

He went on:

'I know very well that I'm mad. How can a married man like me possibly be admitting such a thing to a girl like yourself? I'm worse than mad, I feel quite guilty and almost wicked. I've got nothing to hope for and when I realize that I lose my head. And then when I hear that you're going to get married, I become so furious that I feel like killing someone. You must forgive me, Suzanne.'

He stopped talking. Now that they were not being thrown any more bread, the fish were motionless, looking almost like a line of English soldiers as they watched the faces of the two people bending over the pool and no longer paying any attention to them.

Half ruefully, half jokingly, the girl said:

'What a pity you're married. But there you are. There's nothing to be done. That's the end of it.'

Abruptly, he turned round to look at her and asked her point blank:

'If I was free, would you marry me?'

She replied with complete sincerity:

'Yes, Bel-Ami, I would because I like you much better than all the others.'

He rose to his feet and stammered:

'Oh, thank you ... thank you ... Please, please don't say "Yes" to anyone yet. Wait just a little while longer. Please, I do beg of you. Will you promise?'

Slightly perturbed and not really understanding what he meant, she said quietly:

'I promise.'

Du Roy flung the big piece of bread that he was still holding into the water and without saying goodbye, rushed off like a person suddenly demented.

The fish all flung themselves eagerly on to the lump of bread which, not having been kneaded into a ball, stayed floating on the surface, and greedily tore it into shreds. They dragged it off to the far end of the pool and bustled about underneath it, this time in a busy cluster, a sort of animated, whirling flower, a flower endowed with life that had fallen head first into the water.

Surprised and uneasy, Suzanne stood up and went back very slowly into the house. The journalist had left.

He went home very calmly and as Madeleine was writing letters, he asked her:

'Are you dining with the Walters on Friday? I'm going.'
She hesitated:
'No. I'm not feeling terribly well. I'd sooner stay at home.'
He replied:
'It's up to you. Nobody's forcing you.'

Then he picked up his hat and went out again straight away.

He had had his eye on his wife for some time, keeping her under observation and following her so that he knew her slightest movement. The hour for which he was waiting had struck at last. He had not been deceived by the tone in which she had said: 'I'd sooner stay at home.'

During the next few days, he showed himself very amiable towards her. He even seemed in a good humour, which was a rare thing for him these days. She said to him:

'You're being nice again now.'

He dressed early on Friday, saying that he had to run a few errands before going on to the Walters'.

Then at six o'clock he kissed his wife and left. He picked up a cab in the square of Notre Dame de Lorette.

He said to the driver:

'Drive to number 17 Rue Fontaine and wait there until I tell you to leave. After that, drive me to the Cock Pheasant Restaurant in the Rue Lafayette.'

The horse trotted gently off and Du Roy let down the blinds of the cab. As soon as he was outside his own front door, he watched it intently. After a ten-minute wait he saw Madeleine come out and walk up towards the outer boulevard.

As soon as she was some distance off, he stuck his head out of the window and called: 'Off you go.'

The cab moved off and dropped him at the Cock Pheasant, a solid well-established restaurant in the quarter. Georges went into the main restaurant and had a leisurely meal, looking now and again at his watch. At seven-thirty, after drinking his coffee, two glasses of liqueur brandy and slowly smoking a good cigar, he left the restaurant, hailed another passing cab and was driven to a house in the Rue La Rochefoucauld.

There, without speaking to the concierge, he went straight up to the third floor and when the maid opened the door:

'Monsieur Guibert de Lorme is at home, I believe?'

'Yes, sir.'

He was shown into the drawing-room where, after waiting a few moments, he was joined by a tall military-looking man wearing a decoration and already grey haired, despite the fact that he was still young.

Du Roy wished the commissioner of police good evening and then said:

'As I anticipated, my wife is having dinner with her lover in the furnished flat in the Rue des Martyrs which they have rented.'

The commissioner bowed:

'I'm at your service, Monsieur Du Roy.'

Georges went on:

'We've got till nine o'clock, have we not? After that time you're not allowed to enter a private house in order to ascertain if adultery is being committed?'

'Not exactly, Monsieur Du Roy. In winter it's until seven p.m., and nine p.m. from 31 March onwards. Today is 5 April and so we have until nine o'clock.'

'Well, Commissioner, I have a cab downstairs. We can pick up the police officers who are coming with you and then we'll wait outside the door for a while. The later we arrive the more likely we are to catch them in the act.'

'As you wish, Monsieur Du Roy.'

The commissioner went away and returned wearing an overcoat which hid his official sash. He stood aside to

354

let Du Roy pass. But the journalist was preoccupied and stood back, repeating:

'After you, after you.'

The officer said:

'Do go ahead, Monsieur Du Roy, we're in my home.'

The latter immediately bowed and went through the doorway.

First of all they went to the police station and picked up three policemen in mufti who were waiting for them, because Georges had given notice earlier that day that the raid would take place in the evening. One of the men clambered up on to the seat beside the driver. The other two got into the cab which then drove to the Rue des Martyrs.

Du Roy was explaining:

'I've got a plan of the flat. It's on the second floor. First, there's a small hall and then beyond is the bedroom. The three rooms communicate with each other. There's no other way of escape. There's a locksmith a little further on. He's holding himself in readiness should you want to call upon him.'

By the time they had reached the house in question it was still only a quarter past eight and they waited silently for more than twenty minutes. But when they saw it was about to strike a quarter to nine, Georges said: 'Let's go.' And they went upstairs without bothering about the porter, who in any case failed to see them. One of the policemen remained in the street to keep an eye on the exit.

The four men stopped on the second floor and Du Roy first of all stuck his ear against the door and then put his eye to the keyhole. He could not hear or see anything. He rang the bell.

The commissioner said to his men:

'Remain here and be ready to come if I call you.'

They waited. After a couple of minutes, Georges tugged

at the bell several times in succession. They heard a sound at the other end of the flat and then gentle footsteps approaching. Someone was coming to see what was happening. Then the journalist rapped sharply on the wooden panel with his knuckles.

A voice, a female voice which was trying to disguise itself, asked:

'Who's that?'

The officer replied:

'Open in the name of the law.'

The voice repeated:

'Who are you?'

'I'm the commissioner of police. Open up or I shall have the door broken down.'

The voice went on:

'What do you want?'

And Du Roy said:

'It's me. There's no point in trying to escape.'

The bare feet padded away and then came back after a few seconds.

Georges said:

'If you won't open up, we'll break the door down.'

He was holding the copper door-handle and pushing gently with his shoulder. When there was no further reply, he gave such a sudden powerful thrust that the old lock of the apartment house gave way. The hinges came out of the wood and the young man nearly fell on top of Madeleine who was standing in the hall holding a candle in her hand, dressed in a shift and petticoat with her hair dishevelled and bare legs.

He exclaimed: 'That's her. We've got them!' And he rushed into the flat. The commissioner followed, removing his hat. The startled young woman brought up the rear with the light.

They went through a dining-room where the table, which was uncleared, was still covered with the remains of a meal, empty champagne bottles, an open dish of foie gras, a chicken carcass and half-eaten pieces of bread. On the sideboard there were two plates piled high with oyster shells.

The bedroom looked like a battlefield. A dress was lying over one chair and a pair of men's drawers was hanging over the arm of another. At the foot of the bed, two pairs of boots, one large and one small, were lying scattered about on their sides.

It was a typical apartment-house bedroom, with cheap and nasty furniture and the loathsome all-pervading smell of stuffy hotel rooms oozing out of the curtains, the mattresses, the walls and the chairs, the smells left by all the people who had slept or lived in this public lodging house for a day, or six months, leaving behind some of their odour, the smell of humanity which, when added to that of their predecessors, eventually produces the same indefinable, sickly, unbearable stench which you find in all such places.

On the mantelpiece stood a cake-dish, a bottle of Chartreuse and two half-empty liqueur glasses. The bronze figures on the clock were hidden under a large man's hat.

The commissioner turned sharply round and looked Madeleine in the eyes:

'You are Madame Claire-Madeleine Du Roy, the legal wife of Monsieur Prosper-Georges Du Roy, political journalist, here present?'

In a strangled voice, she replied:

'Yes.'

'What are you doing here?'

She made no reply.

The officer of the law repeated: 'What are you doing here? I find you in a place which is not your home, in a fur-

357

nished apartment in a state of undress. What brings you here?'

He waited a few moments. Then, as she still remained silent:

'Since you are not prepared to confess, madam, then I shall be obliged to ascertain for myself.'

On the bed the shape of a body could be seen hidden under a sheet.

The commissioner went over to it and said:

'Well, sir?'

The man in the bed did not stir. He looked as if he was turning his back, with his head underneath a pillow.

The commissioner touched what seemed to be his shoulder and said again: 'I would ask you, sir, not to force me to have recourse to action.'

But the covered body remained as still as a corpse.

Du Roy stepped quickly forward, took hold of the covering, pulled it back and snatching the pillow away, revealed the ashen face of Monsieur Laroche-Mathieu. He leant towards him and trembling with the urge to take him by the neck and strangle him, hissed between clenched teeth:

'At least have the courage of your filthy conduct.'

Once more the officer of the law asked:

'Who are you?'

As the lover, in desperation, still made no reply, he went on:

'I am a commissioner of police and I call upon you to give your name!'

Georges was trembling like a wild beast.

'Answer, you coward, or I'll give your name myself,' he shouted.

At that the man in the bed said in a quavering voice:

'Commissioner, you must not let this person insult me. Is this a matter for you or for him? Do I have to answer you or him?'

His mouth seemed to have completely dried up.

The officer replied:

'You have to answer me and me only. I am asking you who you are.'

The other man said nothing. Holding the sheet tightly up to his neck, he was looking all round him with bewildered eyes. His little curled-up moustache seemed completely black against the deathly pallor of his face.

The commissioner continued:

'So you won't answer? Then I shall be compelled to arrest you. In any case, you must get out of bed. I'll interrogate you when you are dressed.'

The body wriggled about under the sheet and the head mumbled:

'But I can't do that in front of you.'

The officer asked:

'Why not?'

The man stammered:

'Because ... because ... I've got nothing on.'

Du Roy gave a scornful snigger and picking up a shirt from the floor, he flung it onto his body, exclaiming:

'There you are ... now get up. As you got undressed in front of my wife, you can easily get dressed in front of me.'

Then he turned his back and went over to the fireplace.

Madeleine had completely recovered her composure and seeing that the game was up, she was ready to brazen it out. With a glint of bravado in her eye, she calmly rolled up a piece of paper and lit the ten candles of the hideous candelabra standing on the corner of the mantelpiece, as if preparing for a party. Then leaning with her back against the marble, she held out her naked foot to the dying embers of the fire, lifting as she did so the hem of her petticoat which was almost slipping off her hips, took a cigarette from its pink paper wrapping, lit it and started to smoke.

The commissioner had walked over towards her while waiting for her accomplice to get dressed.

'Do you do this sort of job often?' she enquired with studied impertinence.

'As little as I can help, madam,' he replied solemnly.

She smiled straight in his face:

'I'm glad for your sake. It's a shabby business.'

She was deliberately avoiding looking at her husband and pretending not to see him.

The man in the bed was getting dressed. He had pulled on his trousers, put on his boots and he now approached them, slipping on his waistcoat.

The police officer turned towards him:

'Now sir, will you please tell me your name.'

The other man made no reply.

The commissioner said:

'Then I shall be compelled to arrest you.'

At that, the man exclaimed suddenly:

'Don't dare lay your hands on me. I have official immunity from the law.'

Du Roy strode up to him as if he was going to knock him down and hissed in his face:

'You were caught red-handed ... red-handed. I can have you arrested if I want ... yes, I can.'

Then, in ringing tones, he said:

'This man is Laroche-Mathieu, the Minister for Foreign Affairs.'

The commissioner recoiled in amazement and stammered:

'Sir, will you tell me truthfully who you are, after all this?'

The other man finally made up his mind and said in a firm voice:

'For once, that scoundrel was not lying. I am, in fact, the Minister Laroche-Mathieu.'

And, pointing his arm towards Georges' chest, where you could see a small gleam of red, he added:

'And that blackguard there is wearing the cross of the Legion of Honour which I got for him.'

Du Roy had gone livid with rage. With a sudden jerk, he tore the little strip of red ribbon from his buttonhole and flung it into the fireplace:

'That's where a decoration belongs when it comes from the sort of bastard you are.'

They were glaring at each other face to face and jaw to jaw, beside themselves with anger, clenching their fists, a thin man with a flowing moustache and a fat one with a curled-up one.

The commissioner hastily interposed himself between them and pushed them apart with his hands:

'Gentlemen, you are forgetting yourselves. Please remember your dignity.'

They said no more and turned their backs on each other. Madeleine had not stirred and stood smoking her cigarette with a smile on her face.

The police officer went on:

'Minister, I have discovered you alone with Madame Du Roy here, you in bed and she in an almost complete state of undress. Since your various articles of clothing were scattered all over the flat, this amounts to being caught *flagrante delicto* in adultery. You cannot deny such an obvious situation. Have you anything to say in reply?'

Laroche-Mathieu muttered:

'I've nothing to say. You may do your duty.'

The commissioner turned to Madeleine:

'Do you admit, madam, that this gentleman is your lover?'

She replied jauntily:

'I don't deny it. He is my lover.'

'That is all that is required.'

He then made a number of notes concerning the state and arrangement of the rooms. As he was coming to the end, the Minister who had finished dressing and was waiting with his overcoat over his arm and his hat in his hand, enquired:

'Do you need me any more? What am I to do? May I withdraw?'

Du Roy turned towards him with an insolent smile on his face:

'Why do that? We've finished. You can go back to bed. We'll leave you both alone.'

And touching the police officer on the arm, he said:

'Let us leave, Commissioner, we've no further business here.'

A trifle surprised, the commissioner followed him out; but in the doorway, Georges stepped aside to let him pass. The other man courteously demurred. Georges insisted: 'Please go first.' The commissioner said: 'After you.' At that Georges bowed and said in a politely ironical voice: 'It's your turn, Commissioner. In a sort of way it's my home here.'

Then he quietly shut the door behind them with exaggerated discretion.

One hour later he was at the offices of *La Vie française*.

Monsieur Walter was already in because he continued to control and watch over the fortunes of his paper solicitously now that it had grown so enormously and was so useful in his increasingly ambitious financial dealings.

Walter looked up and asked:

'Oh, it's you. You seem very strange. Why didn't you come to dinner with us? Where have you been?'

Realizing that he could not fail to produce a sensation, Du Roy replied, emphasizing every word:

'I have just overthrown the Minister of Foreign Affairs.'

Walter thought he was joking.

'Overthrown ... What do you mean?'

'I'm going to change the cabinet, that's what! It's time to kick that swine out.'

The old man, quite taken aback, thought that his editor was tipsy. He said quietly:

'Come now, that doesn't make sense.'

'Oh yes it does. I've just caught Monsieur Laroche-Mathieu red-handed in adultery with my wife. The police commissioner was there to corroborate. The Minister is done for.'

Walter, completely dumbfounded, pushed his glasses right up on to his forehead and asked:

'You're not pulling my leg?'

'Not at all. I'm even going to write a news item on it.'

'But in that case, what do you want to do?'

'Overthrow that scoundrel, that ruffian, that public malefactor!'

Georges placed his hat on an armchair and added:

'Anyone who stands in my way had better beware. I'm not the forgiving type.'

Walter was still not quite certain if he understood. He murmured:

'But ... how about your wife?'

'I'll start divorce proceedings tomorrow morning. She can go back to the late lamented Forestier.'

'You intend to obtain a divorce?'

'Of course. I was a figure of fun. But I had to pretend to be stupid to catch them out. Now I've done so. I'm in control of the situation.'

Monsieur Walter could hardly believe his ears, and he was watching Du Roy with a scared look in his eyes, thinking to himself: 'My God. There's a determined character who needs careful handling.'

Georges went on:

'I'm a free man now ... I've got a bit of money. I'll put myself up as candidate in the next elections in October in my part of the world where I'm very well known. I couldn't have any sort of position or command any respect with that woman whom everybody was suspicious of. She thought I was a fool, she led me on and got her claws into me. But as soon as I saw what she was up to, I had my eye on her, the slut.'

He gave a laugh and added:

'That poor old Forestier was a cuckold without suspecting it, gentle and trusting as he was. Now I've got rid of that bitch that he passed on to me. My hands are freed. Now I can go far.'

He was sitting astride a chair and repeated, as if dreaming out loud: 'I'll go far.'

And old Walter, his spectacles still perched on his forehead, was looking at him with his naked eyes and saying to himself: 'Yes, he'll go a long way, the rogue!'

Georges stood up:

'I'll go and write that article. I'll have to do it discreetly. But you know I'm not going to show the Minister any pity. He's going overboard and nobody is going to be able to rescue him. It isn't in our paper's interest to show him any further consideration.'

The old man hesitated for a few moments and then accepted the situation:

'Go ahead,' he said, 'all the bigger fools to land themselves in the soup like that.'

CHAPTER 9

THREE months had gone by. The Du Roys' divorce had just been pronounced. His wife had taken the name of Forestier again and as the Walters were going to leave for Trouville on 15 July, it had been decided to spend a day in the country before separating.

They settled on a Thursday and by nine o'clock in the morning they were on the road in a large touring landau, a six-seater drawn by four post-horses.

They were intending to lunch at Saint-Germain, in the Henri IV lodge. Bel-Ami had asked to be the only man in the party because he could not stand either the presence or the appearance of the Marquis de Cazolles. But at the last minute it was decided to pick up the Comte de Latour-Yvelin immediately after breakfast. He had been warned the day before.

The carriage went briskly up the Champs-Elysées and through the Bois de Boulogne.

It was delightful summer weather, not too hot. The swallows were swooping across the blue sky, leaving the impression that you could still see them even after they had gone.

The three women were sitting in the back seats of the landau, the mother between her two daughters; the three men had their backs to the driver, with Walter in the middle of his two guests.

They crossed the Seine, skirted the Mont-Valérien and then, passing through Bougival, they followed the river to Le Pecq.

The Comte de Latour-Yvelin was gazing at Rose with

tender eyes; they had been engaged for a month now. He was a man of rather mature years, with long, fluffy whiskers whose ends fluttered in the slightest breeze, so that Du Roy used to say: 'He produces pretty wind effects with his beard.'

Georges, who was very pale, kept looking at Suzanne who was equally pale. Their eyes continually met and seemed to exchange a conspiratorial glance, full of understanding and secret thoughts before quickly looking away. Madame Walter was calm and happy.

They spent a long time over lunch. Before going back to Paris, Georges suggested taking a turn on the terrace.

First, they stopped to examine the view. They all stood in line along the wall and fell into raptures at the sight of the vast horizon. At the foot of a long hill, the Seine could be seen flowing towards Maisons-Laffite like an immense snake stretched out amongst the greenery. To the right, at the top of the slope, the Marly aqueduct stood out against the sky like an enormous long-legged caterpillar and below it Marly itself was hidden in a thick clump of trees.

Across the broad plain which lay in front of them they could see scattered villages. The lakes of Le Vésinet formed neat tidy patches in the scanty greenery of the tiny forest. On the left, in the far distance, they could make out the spire of Sartrouville rearing skywards.

Walter was pontificating:

'Nowhere else in the world can you find such a panorama. There's not one like it in Switzerland.'

Then they strolled gently on in order to appreciate more of the prospect before them.

Georges and Suzanne lagged behind. As soon as the others were a few steps ahead he said in a restrained, low voice:

'I adore you, Suzanne. I'm head over heels in love with you.'

She replied softly:

'Me too, Bel-Ami.'

He went on:

'If I can't marry you, I'll go away from Paris and from France, too.'

She answered:

'Try asking Papa for me. Perhaps he'll agree.'

He made an impatient gesture:

'No, for the umpteenth time I tell you it's pointless. They'll forbid me to come to the house, they'll kick me off the paper and we shan't even be able to meet any more. That's all I'm certain to achieve by approaching your father officially. They've promised the Marquis de Cazolles that you'll marry him. They're hoping that you'll eventually say yes. And so they're waiting.'

She asked:

'What must we do then?'

He hesitated and looked at her out of the corner of his eye:

'Do you love me enough to do something mad?'

She replied sturdily:

'Yes.'

'Quite mad?'

'Yes.'

'Completely mad?'

'Yes.'

'Would you be prepared to stand up to your father and mother?'

'Yes.'

'Really and truly?'

'Yes.'

'Well, there is a way and it's the only one. It must come

367

from you and not from me. They spoil you and let you say what you like so they won't be too surprised if you do something particularly outrageous. So listen. This evening when you get home, go and see your mother first, just your mother. You'll confess that you want to marry me. She'll be very shocked and very angry . . .'

Suzanne interrupted him:

'Oh, Mummy will agree.'

He replied hastily:

'No she won't. You don't know her. She'll be more annoyed and furious than your father. You'll see that she'll refuse. But you must stand firm and not give way. You'll have to keep on saying that you want to marry only me and nobody else. Will you do that?'

'Yes, I'll do it.'

'And when you've seen your mother, you must go and say the same thing to your father, very seriously and firmly.'

'Yes, yes, I see. And then what?'

'That's when it will really become serious. If you're really determined, really, really determined to be my wife, my darling little Suzanne . . . I'll elope with you.'

She jumped for joy and had difficulty in restraining herself from clapping her hands.

'Oh, what fun! You'll elope with me! When shall we elope?'

All the old ballads about midnight elopements, post-chaises, inns, all the wonderful adventures you read about in books, flashed through her mind like an enchanting dream about to come true. She repeated:

'When shall we elope?'

He replied in an undertone:

'This evening, in fact . . . tonight.'

Quivering with excitement she asked:

'And where shall we go?'

'That's my secret. But do think what you're doing. You must realize that after we've run away, the only course open to you is to become my wife. It's the only way but it's ... it's very dangerous ... for you.'

She said:

'I'm quite certain ... but where shall I meet you?'

'Can you manage to get out of your house by yourself?'

'Yes. I know how to open the little gate.'

'Well, when the porter has gone to bed about midnight, come and meet me at the Place de la Concorde. I'll be in a cab standing in front of the Admiralty offices.'

'I'll be there.'

'Promise?'

'Promise.'

He took her hand and squeezed it:

'I love you so much. You're such a dear, nice girl. So you don't want to marry Monsieur de Cazolles?'

'Indeed I don't.'

'Was your father terribly annoyed when you said no?'

'He really was. He wanted to send me into a convent.'

'You can see that it's necessary to take energetic action.'

'I'm ready.'

She was looking out over the vast horizon, her head full of the idea of eloping. She would go far, far away from this ... with him ... She was going to elope! She felt so proud at the idea! She hardly gave a thought to her reputation or to anything nasty that might happen to her. Did she even know anything about it? Did she even suspect it?

Madame Walter turned round and called out:

'But do come along, Suzanne. What are you doing with Bel-Ami?'

369

They caught up with the others. They were talking about the sea-bathing that they would soon be enjoying.

They came back via Chatou to avoid going over the same road twice.

Georges was silent. He was thinking to himself: 'Well, if little Suzanne is bold enough, I'm going to succeed, at last.' For the last three months he had been wrapping her up in an irresistible cocoon of tenderness. He was attracting her, captivating her, winning her over. He had made her love him as he was used to doing with other women. The flighty little doll had offered hardly any resistance.

First of all he had succeeded in persuading her not to accept Monsieur de Cazolles. He had just succeeded in persuading her to run away with him. There was indeed no other possibility.

He realized quite well that Madame Walter would never consent to letting him marry her daughter. She still loved him and always would, violently and uncompromisingly. He was able to restrain her by his deliberate coldness but he could feel that she was devoured by an insatiable, helpless passion. He would never succeed in making her change her mind. She would never permit him to take Suzanne.

But once he had absconded with the girl, he could bargain on equal terms with the father.

With all these thoughts running through his mind he lent only half an ear to the remarks addressed to him and made only perfunctory replies. Not until they reached Paris did he gather his wits about him.

Suzanne was also pensive: and the bells on the four horses were ringing in her head and conjuring up visions of driving along highways stretching to infinity beneath everlasting moonlight, through sombre forests; of roadside inns and the hurried changing of horses by the stablemen, because everyone had guessed that they were being pursued.

When the landau drove into the courtyard of their house, the Walters tried to persuade Georges to stay to dinner. He refused and went back home.

After a light meal, he tidied his papers as if he were going away on a long journey. He burned some compromising letters, hid a number of others and wrote to a few friends.

Every so often, he glanced at the clock, thinking: 'Exciting things must be taking place over the way.' And he had a nagging feeling of uneasiness. Suppose he failed? But what was there for him to be frightened of? He would always get by somehow! All the same, he was playing for high stakes that evening.

He left home at about 11 p.m. and walked around for a while before taking a cab and driving to the Place de la Concorde, where he waited beside the colonnade of the Admiralty offices.

Now and again he lit a match to see the time on his watch. When he saw that it was nearly midnight, his impatience grew to fever pitch. He kept continually putting his head out of the window to look.

In the distance, a clock struck twelve, then another nearer one, then two together and finally one much further away. When this last one had finished striking, he thought: 'That's that. It hasn't worked. She won't be coming.'

However, he was determined to stay until daybreak. In such matters, you have to be patient.

He heard it strike a quarter past, then half-past, then a quarter to; and all the clocks repeated the stroke of one o'clock just as they had struck midnight. He was now not so much waiting as staying on, racking his brains to guess what could have happened. Suddenly a woman's head appeared at the window and asked:

'Are you there, Bel-Ami?'

He gave a start and could scarcely breathe:

'Is that you, Suzanne?'

'Yes, it's me.'

He could barely open the door quickly enough and he kept repeating:

'Oh, it's you, it's you. Come in.'

She came in and collapsed on the seat beside him. He shouted to the driver: 'Off you go!' and the cab set off.

She was panting and speechless.

He asked:

'Well, how did it go?'

She said in a low voice, almost on the point of fainting:

'Oh, it was dreadful, especially with Mummy.'

He was trembling and anxious:

'Your mother? What did she say? Tell me about it.'

'Oh, it was awful. I went to her room and recited my little piece which I'd carefully prepared. Then she went pale and shouted: "Never! Never!" Then I cried and got annoyed and swore I'd never marry anyone but you. I thought she was going to hit me. She almost went mad. She said that they'd send me back to the convent the very next day. I'd never seen her like that, never! Then Daddy came in when he heard her saying all those stupid things. He didn't get as annoyed as Mummy but he told me that you weren't a good enough match. As they had made me angry too I shouted louder than they did. And Daddy told me to go in a dramatic voice that didn't suit him at all. That's what finally made me decide to run away with you. Here I am. Where are we going to?'

He replied:

'It's too late to catch a train so we're going to take this cab as far as Sèvres where we can spend the night. And tomorrow we'll go on to La Roche-Guyon. It's a pretty village on the bank of the Seine between Mantes and Bonnières.'

She said soberly:

'There's one thing, I haven't got any clothes or anything else. I came away with nothing at all.'

He smiled cheerfully:

'Never mind, we'll fix something up when we get there.'

The cab was rumbling along the streets. Georges took one of the girl's hands and began to kiss it slowly and respectfully. He did not know what to say to her, not being at all used to platonic expressions of love. But suddenly he thought he saw her crying.

Terrified, he asked her:

'What's the matter, my darling?'

She replied in a tearful voice:

'I'm thinking of poor Mummy who won't be able to sleep if she's discovered I'm gone.'

And poor Mummy was, in fact, unable to sleep.

As soon as Suzanne had left the room, Madame Walter stood facing her husband.

Completely at a loss, she asked him desperately:

'Heavens above! What does all this mean?'

Walter shouted furiously:

'It means that ... that intriguing scoundrel has got round her. He's got her to turn down Cazolles. He likes the size of the dowry, damn his eyes!'

And he began to pace furiously up and down the room, as he went on:

'You kept egging him on, too, you flattered him and coaxed him, you couldn't do too much for him. It was Bel-Ami here and Bel-Ami there from morning till night. Now you've got your reward.'

She said faintly, as pale as death:

'I egged him on?'

He shouted at her:

'Yes, you did! You're all besotted with him, the Marelle

373

woman, Suzanne and all the others. Do you think I didn't realize that you couldn't go two days without having him here?'

She drew herself up like a tragic actress:

'I cannot allow you to speak to me in that way. You're forgetting that, unlike you, I wasn't brought up in a shop.'

He halted in his tracks, completely flabbergasted, and then, uttering a furious: 'God Almighty!' he went out, slamming the door.

As soon as she was alone, she instinctively went to look at herself in the mirror, to see if she were changed by the impossible, monstrous events that seemed to be overtaking her. Suzanne was in love with Bel-Ami and Bel-Ami wanted to marry Suzanne! No, she must be mistaken, it couldn't be true! The girl had naturally been infatuated by such a handsome young man and hoped that she would be allowed to have him as her husband; she had acted impulsively. But what about him? He couldn't be party to it. She turned the thought over in her mind, distraught as one is when caught up in a major catastrophe. No, Bel-Ami couldn't have known anything about Suzanne's mad idea.

She pondered long over the possibility of his trickery or innocence. What a wretch he was if he had hatched the plot! And what would happen now? She foresaw all kinds of dangers and troubles.

If he did know nothing about it, everything might still turn out all right. They could take Suzanne away on a trip for six months and it would be all over. But how could she herself possibly see him afterwards? Because she was still in love with him. Her passion for him had pierced her heart like an arrow whose barbs cannot be pulled out.

It was impossible to live without him. She would be better dead.

In her agony of uncertainty, she did not know what to

think. Her head was beginning to ache; her thoughts were becoming confused and distressed and painful. She was anxiously searching and exasperated because she could not be certain. She looked at her clock; it was past one o'clock. She said to herself: 'I mustn't remain like this, I'm going out of my mind. I must know. I shall go and wake Suzanne up and question her.'

Candle in hand, she went to her daughter's room, having removed her shoes in order to make less noise. She opened the door very quietly, went in and looked at the bed. It had not been slept in. At first she failed to understand and thought that her daughter was still arguing with her father. But suddenly a dreadful suspicion crossed her mind and she hurried to her husband's room. She rushed in pale and breathless. He was in bed, still reading.

He said in a startled voice:

'What on earth? What's the matter?'

She stammered:

'Have you seen Suzanne?'

'Me? No. Why?'

'She's . . . she's . . . gone. She's not in her room.'

He sprang out on to the rug, put on his slippers and without even pausing to slip on his underpants, he dashed along to his daughter's room, his nightshirt flapping in the breeze.

As soon as he went in, he realized the truth. She had run away.

He collapsed into an armchair and put his lamp down in front of him.

His wife had meanwhile arrived.

'Well?'

He was too weak to reply. He was not even angry any more. He groaned:

'That's that, then. He's got her. That's the end of that.'

She failed to understand.

'What do you mean?'

'Well, of course, that's the end of it. He'll have to marry her now.'

She uttered an animal-like cry:

'Him? Never. You must be mad.'

He answered sadly:

'There's no point in making a fuss. He's eloped with her and so destroyed her reputation. The best thing is to let him have her. If we arrange things properly no one will know about this escapade.'

She repeated, deeply shocked:

'Never! He'll never have Suzanne. I shall never agree.'

Walter muttered dejectedly:

'But he's got her already. It's already happened. And he'll hang on to her in hiding until we give in. So in order to avoid any scandal, we shall have to give in at once.

Tortured by grief, which she dared not confess, his wife said:

'No! No! I shall never agree.'

He was beginning to lose patience:

'But there's no point in arguing. We've got to. What a crafty fellow he is! How cleverly he succeeded in pulling the wool over our eyes! He really is smart. We might have found someone with a much better social position but nobody more intelligent or with better prospects. He'll go far. He'll be a deputy and a Minister.'

Madame Walter kept repeating with savage energy:

'I shall never let him marry Suzanne. Do you understand? Never!'

He was becoming annoyed and, being a practical man, ended by defending Bel-Ami:

'Do be quiet . . . I keep on telling you that we've got to . . . It's absolutely unavoidable. And who knows? We may even not regret it in the end. With men of that quality you never know what can happen. You saw how he dispatched that silly ass Laroche-Mathieu in three articles and that he did it with dignity too, which was damned difficult when he was the husband concerned. Anyway we shall see. The fact remains that we've been caught. We can't get out of it now.'

She felt an urge to scream, throw herself on the floor, tear her hair out by the roots. Once more she exclaimed angrily:

'He won't have her ... I shan't allow it.'

Walter stood up, picked up his lamp and said:

'Ah well, you're stupid like all the rest of your sex. You can never act sensibly. You're incapable of accepting a situation. You're all stupid! And I'm telling you that he will marry her. He must.'

And he shuffled out in his slippers. He went along the broad corridor of the enormous house like some weird ghostly figure in his nightshirt and without a sound returned to his room.

Madame Walter remained behind in an unbearable agony of mind. Not that she fully understood what was happening. She was merely suffering. Then she realized that she could not remain standing there, not moving, until day came. She felt a violent need to escape, to run away and keep on running in search of help and consolation.

She tried to think to whom she could turn. Who was there? She could not think of anyone. A priest, yes, a priest. She would fall on her knees in front of him and tell him everything, confess her sin and her despair. He would understand that that scoundrel could not marry Suzanne and he would put a stop to it.

She must go to a priest and at once! But where could she find one? Where could she turn? And yet it was impossible for her to go on like this.

377

And she had a sudden vision of Christ walking serenely on the waves. She could see Him as clearly as when she had been looking at the picture. So He was calling to her and saying: 'Come unto me. Come and kneel at my feet. I shall console you and through me you shall learn what you must do.'

She took a candle, left the room and went down to the conservatory. The picture was at the far end, in a little room enclosed by a glass door so that the dampness of the soil would not harm the canvas.

It formed a kind of chapel in a strange forest of trees.

Madame Walter had never seen the winter garden except when it was lit up and on going in she was startled to find how dark it was. The atmosphere was oppressive with the overpoweringly heavy scent of the luxuriant tropical plants. And as the doors had been left shut, the air of this strange jungle enclosed beneath its glass dome made it painful to breathe and set her head swimming with a sort of intoxication that was both a pleasure and a pain, while her body was seized by a vague feeling of languorous and morbid delight.

The poor woman walked slowly and nervously on through the gloom in which, in the flickering light of her candle, the weird contorted forms of outlandish plants loomed up like people or monsters.

Suddenly, she saw Jesus. She opened the separating door and fell on her knees.

At first she poured out her soul distractedly, stammering words of love, calling on Him in desperate, fervent prayer. Then when her passionate outburst had grown calmer, she lifted her eyes towards Him and was gripped by a sudden anguish. In the weak flickering gleam of this single candle, lighting Him from below, He looked so much like Bel-Ami that it was not God but her lover who seemed to be watching her. It was his eyes and forehead, his expression, his cold, haughty look.

She stammered: 'Jesus! Jesus! Jesus!' And the word Georges rose to her lips. Suddenly the thought came to her that at that very moment Georges was perhaps possessing her daughter. He was alone with her somewhere, in some bedroom. Georges ... and Suzanne.

She kept repeating: 'Jesus! Jesus!' But she was thinking of them ... her daughter and her lover! They were alone in a bedroom ... and it was night time. She could see them so vividly that they stood between her and the picture. They were smiling at each other. They were kissing. The room was dark, the sheets had been turned back. She stood up to go nearer to them to catch hold of her daughter's hair and drag her away from his embrace. She was going to seize her by the throat and strangle her, her hateful daughter. This daughter who was giving herself to that man. She was on the point of touching her and her hands encountered the canvas. She had come up against the feet of Christ.

With a loud cry, she fell backwards. Her candle fell over and went out.

What happened next? She had long, strange, frightening dreams. In all of them Georges and Suzanne passed in front of her eyes, locked in a close embrace and Jesus Christ was blessing their horrible love.

She had the vague sensation that she was not in her own home. She would have liked to stand up and run away but was unable to do so. She had sunk into a torpor which paralysed her limbs and left only her consciousness awake, confused and tortured by dreadful, unreal fantasies, lost in unwholesome dreams, the sort of strange drugged dream that can lead to death, caused by the cloying fragrance of the weird tropical plants.

When day came Madame Walter was discovered lying

379

unconscious and almost asphyxiated in front of 'Jesus walking on the waters'. She was so ill that they feared for her life. It was not until the next day that she completely recovered her reason. Then she began to cry.

They explained Suzanne's disappearance to the servants by telling them that she had been suddenly sent away to a convent. And Monsieur Walter received a long letter from Du Roy to which he replied by granting him his daughter's hand in marriage.

Bel-Ami had posted this epistle as he was leaving Paris, having written it in advance the night before his departure. In it he stated, in respectful terms, that he had long been in love with Suzanne, that they had never concerted any plan of action but that when she had come to him of her own free will and told him that she wanted to be his wife, he had felt justified in keeping her and indeed hiding her until he had received a reply from her parents, whose legal authority was less important than the expressed wishes of his fiancée.

He asked Monsieur Walter to reply poste restante as a friend had undertaken to pass the letter on to him.

When he had obtained what he wanted, he brought Suzanne back to Paris and sent her home to her parents, at the same time refraining from putting in an appearance himself for a short while.

They had spent six days at La Roche-Guyon on the banks of the Seine.

The girl had never enjoyed herself so much before. She had acted like a make-believe shepherdess. As he was passing her off as his sister, they had spent their time together completely undisturbed, in a sort of tender, friendly, intimate yet chaste companionship. He thought it would be wise not to take advantage of her. The day after their arrival she had bought a country girl's outfit, underwear and all, and started fishing in the river with an immense straw hat adorned with wild flowers on her head. She found the countryside delightful. There was an old tower and an old castle full of wonderful tapestries.

Georges had bought a reach-me-down jacket from a local shop and took Suzanne for walks along the river or for boat trips. They kept kissing each other passionately all the time, she in all innocence while he was barely able to restrain himself. But he was strong-willed enough to do so and when he said to her: 'We're going back to Paris tomorrow, your father has agreed to our marriage,' she said naïvely: 'So soon? It was such fun being your wife!'

THE little flat in the Rue de Constantinople was still in darkness because Georges Du Roy and Clotilde de Marelle, having met in the doorway, had gone in so abruptly that he had not had time to open the blinds before she asked him:

'So you're going to marry Suzanne Walter?'

Mildly, he admitted the truth, adding:

'Didn't you know about it?'

She stood facing him, furious with rage and burst out:

'So you're marrying Suzanne Walter! It's too bad, it really is! For the last three months you've been getting round me so as to keep me in the dark. Everyone knows about it except me! I had to learn it from my husband!'

Du Roy gave a rather embarrassed grin and putting his hat down on the corner of the mantelshelf, sat down in an armchair.

She stood looking him straight in the face and said in a low, angry voice:

'You've been scheming to do this ever since you left your wife and you were kindly keeping me on as a stop-gap. What a thorough blackguard you are!'

He asked:

'Why do you say that? My wife was being unfaithful to me. I caught her out, divorced her and now I'm marrying somebody else. What could be simpler than that?'

She was quivering as she said in a low voice:

'Oh, what a cunning dangerous man you are!'

He smiled again:

'Why not? It's fools and innocents who are always being taken in.'

But she was pursuing her own train of thought:

'I should have seen through you from the start. But I couldn't really imagine that you could be such a swine.'

He put on a dignified air:

'Do you mind keeping a civil tongue in your head?'

His hypocrisy nauseated her:

'What's that you said? You expect me to handle you with kid gloves, do you? You've behaved like an utter cad ever since we've known each other and now you don't think I should call you one? You go around deceiving and exploiting everyone and everybody, you take your pleasure when and where you like and money from anyone who'll give you it and you still want me to treat you like a gentleman.'

He rose to his feet, his lips trembling:

'Keep quiet or I'll throw you out.'

These words left her almost speechless:

'Throw me out ... throw me out ... You'd throw me out, would you?'

She was choking with fury so much that words failed her, and then suddenly, as if the floodgates of her fury had finally opened, she exploded:

'Throw me out! You're forgetting that I've been paying for this flat from the very beginning. Oh, I know you've taken it over once or twice. But who was it who rented it? Me. Who was it who kept it on? Me ... And now you talk about throwing me out. For Christ's sake, shut up, you rotten waster. Do you think I don't know how you stole half of Vaudrec's legacy from Madeleine? Do you think I don't know that you made Suzanne Walter go to bed with you so as to force her to marry you ...'

He seized her by the shoulders and shook her:

'Don't you dare mention her name! I forbid it!'

She screamed:

'You went to bed with her, I know you did!'

Anything else he would have accepted but this lie was too much. The truths which she had been flinging in his face had incensed him but this slander against the young girl who was going to be his wife filled him with a savage urge to lash out.

He repeated:

'Stop that! I'm warning you. Stop it!' And he went on shaking her like someone shaking the bough of a tree to bring down the fruit.

Dishevelled and wild-eyed, with her mouth hanging open, she shrieked:

'You went to bed with her!'

He stood back and hit her so hard across the face that she went reeling and fell down against the wall. But she turned over towards him and supporting herself on her wrists, she screamed once more:

'You went to bed with her!'

He hurled himself on her and holding her down, began to hit her as hard as if she were a man.

All of a sudden she stopped shouting and started to moan as he continued to strike her. She lay quite still, her head hidden in the angle of the floor and the wall, uttering plaintive little cries.

He stopped hitting her, stood up and took a few steps across the room to regain his composure. Then he had an idea and went into the bedroom, filled the basin with cold water and dipped his head in it. After that he washed his hands and went back to see what she was doing, carefully drying his fingers as he did so.

She had not stirred. She was still lying quietly weeping on the floor.

He enquired:

'Are you going to go on snivelling much longer?'

She made no reply. So he remained standing in the middle

of the room, rather embarrassed and somewhat ashamed at the sight of this woman lying on the floor in front of him.

Then he took a sudden decision and picking up his hat from the mantelpiece he said:

'Goodnight. You can hand the key over to the porter when you're ready. I'm not going to hang about waiting for you.'

He left, shutting the door behind him, and went into the porter's lodge:

'My wife is staying. She'll be leaving shortly. Tell the owner of the flat that I want to terminate my lease from 1 October. It's 16 August, so I'm inside the period.'

And he hurried off for he had a number of urgent errands to undertake for the final purchases for his marriage.

The wedding which had been fixed for 20 October, after the opening of the new parliamentary session, was to be celebrated in the church of the Madeleine. There had been a great deal of gossip, although no one knew anything for certain. All sorts of stories were going around. The rumour was that there had been an elopement but nobody was quite sure about it.

According to the servants, Madame Walter was refusing to talk to her future son-in-law and had tried to poison herself out of spite the night the marriage had been decided upon, after taking her daughter off to a convent in the middle of the night.

She had been brought back almost at death's door. She would certainly never recover. She now looked like an old woman; her hair had gone quite grey and she had become very pious, going to Communion every Sunday.

Early in September, *La Vie française* announced that its new editor was to be Baron Du Roy de Cantel. Monsieur Walter kept the title of director.

Then, by offering handsome salaries, they attracted a

whole army of columnists and reporters, political editors and art and dramatic critics from the big newspapers, the powerful and old-established ones.

Respectable senior journalists no longer shrugged their shoulders at the mention of *La Vie française*. Its sudden rapid rise to fame had wiped out the disrepute in which serious professional writers had held it when it had first started.

The wedding of its editor was what is known as a Parisian event, for Georges Du Roy and the Walters had recently been exciting a good deal of interest. All the people whose names appeared regularly in the gossip columns of the newspapers made a point of going.

The ceremony took place on a bright autumn day.

By eight o'clock in the morning, as the whole staff of the Madeleine spread out a broad red carpet on the steps leading up to the terrace in front of the church dominating the Rue Royale, the passers-by stopped to watch and the people of Paris realized that a grand event was about to take place.

Office workers, little working girls and shop assistants stopped to look and wondered vaguely about all the money spent by the rich just to pair off.

By about ten o'clock, a few curious spectators began to gather. They stopped to watch for a few minutes, hoping that it might perhaps be starting immediately and then went off.

At eleven o'clock, squads of police arrived and immediately began to move people on, because groups of bystanders were forming all the time.

Soon the first guests appeared, the ones who wanted to be well placed in order not to miss anything. They took the end seats along the central aisle.

Others began arriving steadily, women with rustling dresses – silk dresses – and solemn-looking men, almost all of them bald, walking with great decorum, all the greater because they were in church.

The church was slowly filling up. The sun was pouring through the vast open door on to the first few rows of guests. In the rather gloomy choir, the wan yellow light of the candles covering the altar seemed humble in comparison with the bright aperture of the main doorway.

People were nodding to each other, waving and gathering in groups. The literary fraternity, less respectful than the social set, were chatting without bothering to lower their voices very much. They kept looking at the women.

Norbert de Varenne, who was looking for someone he knew, caught sight of Jacques Rival somewhere in the middle of the chairs and went over to join him.

'So there we are,' he said. 'Blessed are the crafty ... !'

Rival, who was not in the least an envious man, merely replied:

'The best of luck to him. Nothing can stop him now.' And they began to count up the people they could see.

Rival asked:

'Do you know what's become of his wife?'

The poet smiled:

'Yes and no. I've been told that she's living quietly tucked away in Montmartre. But – there's a but – for some time now I've been reading political articles in *La Plume* which are terribly like Forestier's and Du Roy's. They're written by someone called Jean Le Dol, young, good-looking, intelligent, the same sort of man as our friend Georges, and he knows Madeleine. From which I conclude that she's fond of beginners and always will be. She's got money, of course. Vaudrec and Laroche-Mathieu weren't regular visitors at her house for nothing.'

Rival said:

'Little Madeleine's really not too bad. Very bright and

very smart! She must be charming. But tell me, how is it that Du Roy is getting married in church after being divorced?'

Norbert de Varenne replied:

'He's getting married in church because the Church doesn't recognize his first marriage.'

'How's that possible?'

'Either to save money or because he didn't care, our Bel-Ami thought that a registry office wedding was good enough for Madeleine Forestier. So he did without the blessing of the Church and thus our Holy Mother Church considered him as merely living in sin. As a result, the Church regards him as a bachelor and so she can allow him to enjoy all this pomp and ceremony which is going to cost old Walter a pretty penny.'

As the throng of people increased, so did the hubbub of voices under the vaulted roof. Voices could be heard speaking almost loudly. People were pointing out famous men who were complacently posing, carefully maintaining their public image and accustomed to showing themselves at all such functions at which they considered themselves to be an indispensable attraction, the cynosure of all eyes.

Rival went on:

'Tell me, my dear Norbert, I know you often go to the old man's house, is it true that Madame Walter and Du Roy are not on speaking terms?'

'No, they never speak to each other. She didn't want to let him have her daughter. But he had a hold over the father because of some skeletons that had been discovered apparently, skeletons that had been buried in Morocco. So he threatened the old man with hair-raising revelations. Walter remembered what had happened to Laroche-Mathieu and caved in at once. But the mother, pigheaded like all women, swore that she would never speak to her son-in-law again. She looks like a statue, the statue of Revenge, and he's extremely embarrassed, although he puts a brave face on it, because his self-possession is really fantastic.'

Colleagues came up and shook hands. You could overhear scraps of political gossip. And the hum of the people massed in front of the church came in through the doorway together with the sunlight and rose up towards the vaulting above the more discreet bustle of the chosen few gathered together in the church itself.

Suddenly the beadle struck the paving three times with the shaft of his halberd. With a rustle of skirts and a scraping of chairs the whole congregation turned to look. And the bride appeared in the bright light of the porch, holding her father's arm.

She still looked like a doll, a charming little white doll with orange-blossom on her head.

For a moment or two, she remained standing in the doorway and then as she stepped into the aisle, the organ pealed out announcing in thunderous tones the arrival of the bride.

She advanced with eyes downcast but not in the least shy, filled with vague emotion, a nice, charming girl, a miniature wife-to-be. As they watched her go by, the women smiled and whispered. The men murmured under their breath: 'Exquisite. Adorable.' Monsieur Walter was walking with exaggerated dignity, slightly pale, his spectacles planted firmly on his nose.

Behind them, like the court of this dainty little queen, came four bridesmaids, all four pretty and dressed in pink. The hand-picked pageboys, all typical pages, were walking in step as though drilled by a dancing-master.

Following them came Madame Walter, holding the arm of the Marquis de Latour-Yvelin, her other son-in-law's father, who was seventy-two years old. She could hardly be described as walking but dragging herself along, almost ready to faint with every step she took. You could sense that her feet were like lead and that her heart was bursting like that of some wild beast leaping away to make its escape.

She had lost weight. Her white hair made her face look even paler and more sunken.

She was looking straight ahead in order not to see anyone, perhaps in order to listen only to the thoughts that were tormenting her.

Then Georges Du Roy appeared with an old lady whom no one knew. He was holding his head high and he, too, was staring straight ahead, hard-eyed, with a slight frown. His moustache seemed to be curling angrily on his lip. He was judged a very good-looking young man. He bore himself proudly, slim-waisted and straight-legged and he looked very smart in his morning coat, in the buttonhole of which the rosette of the Legion of Honour glowed like a spot of blood.

Then came the relatives, Rose with Senator Rissolin. She had been married six weeks ago. Vicomte de Latour-Yvelin was accompanied by the Vicomtesse de Percemur.

Then followed the strange procession of Du Roy's friends or associates whom he had introduced to his new family, people well-known in the betwixt and between world of Paris society, men who immediately become friendly with or, on occasion, the distant cousins of rich upstarts, aristocrats who have come down in the world, have lost their money or their reputation and who are sometimes married, which is even worse. There was Monsieur de Belvigne, the Marquis de Beaujolin, Comte and Comtesse de Ravenel, the Duc de Ramorano, the Prince de Kravalow, the Chevalier Valreali and then Walter's guests, the Prince de Guerche, the Duke and Duchess of Terracina, the beautiful Marquise des Dunes. In this procession, some of Madame Walter's relatives provided an image of provincial propriety.

And still through the mighty edifice the great voice of the organ, which carries men's joy and suffering to heaven, boomed and pealed in steady harmony.

The great entrance doors were closed and it was suddenly as dark as if the sun itself had been obscured.

Now Georges was kneeling in the choir beside his wife, facing the lighted altar. The newly-appointed bishop of Tangier appeared from the sacristy, with mitre and crozier, to bless their union in the name of Eternal God.

He asked the customary questions, exchanged the rings, uttered the words which bind as tight as chains and addressed a Christian homily to the young couple. He talked pompously and at great length about faithfulness. He was a big, tall man, one of those splendid prelates whose very paunch has majesty.

The sound of sobbing made a few heads turn. Madame Walter was in tears, her face buried in her hands.

She had been forced to give in. What else could she have done? But ever since the day when she had refused to embrace her daughter on her return home and had sent her from the room, since the day when she had whispered in an undertone to Du Roy when he was greeting her ceremoniously for the first time after his own return: 'You are the vilest creature I have ever met, don't speak to me again ever, because if you do I shall refuse to answer you!', she had suffered unspeakable and unremitting torment. She felt a bitter loathing towards Suzanne, a loathing compounded of exacerbated passion and excruciating jealousy, the strange, savage, unforgivable jealousy of a mother and a mistress, which seared her like a raw wound.

And now a priest was marrying her daughter and her lover, in church, in the presence of 2,000 people and herself. And she could say nothing? She could not prevent it?

She could not cry out loud: 'But he's mine, my lover! This union which you are blessing is a criminal one!'

A number of women whispered sentimentally: 'How upset her poor mother is.'

The bishop was pontificating: 'You are one of the fortunate ones of the earth, one of the wealthiest and most respected. Baron Du Roy, you whose profession is that of a writer and a teacher, whose talent raises you above other people, who leads the people, who advises them, you have a noble mission to fulfil and a splendid example to offer ...'

Du Roy was listening, ecstatic with pride. It was he who was being addressed in this way by a prelate of the Roman Church. And behind him he could sense the throng of celebrities who were present on his behalf. He felt a great power urging him on, uplifting him. He was becoming one of the lords of the earth, he, the son of two poor peasants from Canteleu.

He suddenly saw them in his mind's eye in their humble inn at the top of the hill, above the vast Rouen valley; he saw his father and mother serving drink to the local country folk. He had sent them 5,000 francs out of the Comte de Vaudrec's legacy. Now he would be sending them 50,000 and they could buy a small property. They would be satisfied and happy.

The bishop had ended his harangue. A priest dressed in a golden stole was moving towards the altar. And the organ burst out again in a paean of praise for the young couple.

First its pipes swelled in vast continuous waves of sound, so powerful and resonant that it seemed as though they might lift the roof and spread out into the blue sky. The church vibrated to their resonance and body and soul thrilled in unison. Then suddenly, the notes died down and were followed by others gliding daintily through the air, caressing the ear like a fresh, gentle breeze; it was a joyful, graceful, tiny little song, hopping and fluttering like a bird; and then suddenly this delicate music swelled out again, terrifying in its power and strength as though a grain of sand had expanded into a whole world.

Then human voices were heard, echoing out over the bowed heads of the congregation. Vauri and Landeck from the Opéra were singing. A soft fragrance of incense pervaded the church and at the altar the divine sacrifice was being celebrated. At the call of the priest, the Man–God was descending on earth to consecrate the triumph of Baron Georges Du Roy.

On his knees beside Suzanne, Bel-Ami lowered his head. For a moment he felt almost like a believer, almost religious, full of gratitude towards the deity who had shown him such favour and treated him with such respect. And without knowing exactly whom he was addressing, he thanked this deity for his success.

When the service was over, he stood up and giving his arm to his wife, he went into the sacristy. Now began the interminable procession of guests. Beside himself with joy, Georges felt like a king receiving the acclamation of his people. He kept shaking hands, mumbling meaningless words, greeting people, acknowledging congratulations: 'You're very kind.'

Suddenly he spotted Madame de Marelle and the recollection of all the kisses he had given and received from her, the memory of their caresses, of her kindness and niceness, of the sound of her voice, sent a thrill through his body and a sudden desire to go back to her again. She was pretty and elegant, with her impish, mischievous look and sparkling eyes. Georges thought to himself: 'What a wonderful mistress she is, really.'

She came up to him rather timidly, a trifle uneasy, and held out her hand. He took it in his own and held it. And as he did so, he felt the discreet pressure of her woman's fingers, a gentle squeeze, which meant: 'I forgive you and we'll begin again.' And he returned the pressure of her little hand as though to say: 'I still love you, I'm yours.'

Smiling and full of love, their eyes shone as they looked at each other. She said in her charming voice: 'I hope we may meet again soon, Monsieur Du Roy.'

He replied gaily:

'Very soon, Madame de Marelle.'

She moved on.

Others were pressing forward. The crowd was streaming past like a river until finally it began to diminish. When the last guest had left, Georges took Suzanne's arm again to go out through the church.

It was full of people, since everybody had returned to their seats to watch them leave together. He walked slowly and calmly, head high, his eyes fixed on the vast sunny bay of the door. He could feel cold thrills running all through his body, the thrills that come from great happiness. He noticed no one. He was thinking only of himself.

When he reached the doorway, he could see the assembled crowd in front, a black, bustling throng of people who had come to see him, Georges Du Roy. The people of Paris were watching him and envying him.

Then raising his eyes, in the distance beyond the Place de la Concorde he could see the Chamber of Deputies. And he felt as if he could leap in one single bound from the porch of the Madeleine to the porch of the Palais Bourbon.

Slowly he went down the steps between the two lines of spectators. But he did not see them; now his thoughts had gone back and dancing before his eyes dazzled by the glare of the sun, was the vision of Madame de Marelle in front of her mirror tidying her little kiss-curls, which always used to come out in bed.

AVAILABLE FROM PENGUIN CLASSICS

A Parisian Affair and Other Stories

These thirty-four short stories focus on
the complexity of close relationships,
and reveal two sides of human nature:
its grace and generosity, but also its
greed and hypocrisy. Piquant and varied,
Maupassant's stories lay humanity bare
with deft wit and devastating honesty.

ISBN 978-0-14-044812-2

Pierre and Jean

An intensely personal story of suspicion,
jealousy, and family love, this novel shows
the influence of such masters as Zola and
Flaubert on Maupassant's writings.

ISBN 978-0-14-044358-5

PENGUIN
CLASSICS